THE THRE

'Intriguing . . . MacBird artfully alternates among multiple plotlines, maximizing suspense. With its deep probe into the friendship between the detective and the doctor, this is a good choice for fans of Sherlock Holmes.'

—*Publishers Weekly*

'Bonnie MacBird's *The Three Locks* satisfies a hunger for more adventures of Holmes and Watson on so many levels. Not only does she perfectly capture their voices, she captures that most critical element—their humanity. Brava!'

—Leslie S. Klinger, editor, *New Annotated Sherlock Holmes*

'Bonnie MacBird's sly plot and admirable sense of pacing keeps the story twisting and turning in a way that would have kept Doyle himself turning the pages.'

—Michael Sims, author of *Arthur and Sherlock: Conan Doyle and the Creation of Holmes*

'Though stage magic features in *The Three Locks*, the real magician is author Bonnie MacBird, who once again brings humour, action, rigorous period detail, and the characters we love to her latest Holmes adventure.'

—Dennis Palumbo, author of the Daniel Rinaldi series, *Writing from the Inside Out*

'Bonnie MacBird has conjured up a captivating three-card monte of murder, mystery and magic. *The Three Locks* may be her best yet.'

—Dan Stashower, author of *Teller of Tales: The Life of Arthur Conan Doyle*

'The solutions are as intricate as anything from the pen of Conan Doyle himself and are woven together in an extraordinarily skilful web which will satisfy all those who revere the intellectual brilliance of Sherlock Holmes. Recommended.'

—*Promoting Crime*

'Bonnie MacBird is an extremely talented writer and this is an admirable addition to her long list of credits'.

—*Sherlock Holmes Journal*

'If you like your pastiches with social conscience, a dash of action, and a whole lot of heart, this is the book for you.'

—*Baker Street Babes*

'True to the Watson tradition, giving readers the feeling they are delving into an authentic Sir Arthur Conan Doyle narrative, *The Three Locks* is a treasure.'

—*Historical Novel Society*

THE THREE LOCKS

Also by Bonnie MacBird

Art in the Blood
Unquiet Spirits
The Devil's Due

The Three Locks

A SHERLOCK HOLMES ADVENTURE

BONNIE MacBIRD

COLLINS
CRIME
CLUB

COLLINS CRIME CLUB

An imprint of HarperCollins*Publishers*
1 London Bridge Street
London SE1 9GF

www.harpercollins.co.uk

HarperCollins*Publishers*
1st Floor, Watermarque Building, Ringsend Road
Dublin 4, Ireland

This paperback edition 2021
1

First published by HarperCollins*Publishers* 2021

Copyright © Bonnie MacBird 2021
All rights reserved.

Drop Cap design © Mark Mázers 2021

Bonnie MacBird asserts the moral right
to be identified as the author of this work.

A catalogue record for this book
is available from the British Library

ISBN: 978-0-00-838087-8

Set in Sabon by Palimpsest Book Production Ltd, Falkirk, Stirlingshire

Printed and Bound in the UK using 100% Renewable Electricity at CPI Group (UK) Ltd

MIX
Paper from
responsible sources
FSC
www.fsc.org
FSC™ C007454

Contents

PART EIGHT – THE UNLOCKING

For
Miranda Andrews

Prologue

When a mysterious woman going by the name of 'Lydia' offered me a cache of unpublished tales written by Dr John H. Watson some years ago, I was astonished to discover previously unknown adventures he had shared with the master detective – and his most admirable and unusual friend – Mr Sherlock Holmes.

It soon became apparent that there was a reason within each of these newly discovered tales for Watson *not* to have made them public at the time he released the others. By 'the others', of course I mean those which were brought to light by Arthur Conan Doyle. Dr Doyle's precise role in these, be it literary agent or in some way promoter, remains buried in the sands of time.

Without giving the story away in advance, I can conjecture that both Dr Watson and Sherlock Holmes may have had cause to delay release of the tale which follows – or in Holmes's case, to disapprove entirely of its publication.

I hope the reader – and Dr Watson and Mr Holmes, wherever they dwell at present, either in heaven or as motes of stardust – will forgive me for deciding to put forward this story now, one which has been locked away for more than a hundred and thirty years.

—Bonnie MacBird
London, December 2020

PART ONE

THE BOX

'By the pricking of my thumbs
Something wicked this way comes.
Open, Locks,
Whoever knocks.'
—William Shakespeare,
Macbeth

CHAPTER 1

The Box

t was late September of 1887, and an unusually hot Indian Summer. For two weeks London had suffocated with furnace-like temperatures, keeping me indoors for days. The blinding heat on Baker Street rose from the pavement in shimmering waves, the stench of refuse and horse droppings adding to the misery. Only the hordes of raucous city-dwellers, whom I knew were flocking to the seaside with their dripping ice creams and shouting children, prevented me from fleeing to Brighton or Cornwall with them.

My name is Dr John Watson, and at age thirty-five I was six years into sharing both rooms and many adventures with my friend, the remarkable consulting detective, Mr Sherlock Holmes.

But sadly, Holmes seemed to have forsaken my company

of late. I had seen little of him for three weeks. I longed for a distraction from the misery of this weather. Not only had he not invited me on his recent escapades, but he had dismissed my questions with a petulant wave of his hand.

When Holmes did not wish to reveal something, no cajoling, guesswork or sleuthing could prise it free. He likewise kept his personal history, which I always suspected to be tinged with the dramatic, locked away as securely as any treasure stored in a bank vault. But even I have a few secrets of my own.

Locks, after all, are in place for a reason – whether privacy, security . . . or safety.

It happened that a locked and deadly secret played a key role in each of the two cases – and a puzzle of my own – which presented themselves to us that fateful month. So complex were these gruesome mysteries, and so tragic the outcomes, that it took the genius, bravery and resourceful-ness of Sherlock Holmes to solve them, and a certain transparency of my own to tell of them now. My hesitation in doing so earlier will become apparent, perhaps only at the very last.

Our rooms faced east on Baker Street, and on that day I had closed the heavy curtains against the morning sun, leaving the windows behind them cracked open and myself sitting in half light, too hot even to read. Despite my claim that I had become inured to the heat during my army years in India and Afghanistan, I suffered mightily.

I contemplated asking Mrs Hudson for an iced lemonade, but the poor woman was no doubt prostrate on her bed from the heat. A paper fan lay next to me, useless in this oven. My ruminations were interrupted when the postman arrived with a small rectangular package, addressed to me and postmarked Edinburgh.

I welcomed the distraction.

The package was perhaps half the size of a shoebox, and heavy. The sender was a mystery, one 'E. Carnachan'. I unwrapped it, only to find a smaller box inside covered by another layer of brown paper wrapping, this one stained, faded and tied with string. A note had been slipped under the string.

I removed and unfolded it, my hands sticky with sweat. The handwriting was old-fashioned and feminine, shaky, perhaps with age or illness. I read:

Dr John Watson—

You do not know me, but I am Elspeth Carnachan, a name you may not recognise. Carnachan is my married name, but I was born a Watson and your father's half-sister. Your father and I parted ways while still in our youth, and I was effectively erased from the family history before you were born. It is doubtful that he ever mentioned me to you.

Your mother, bless her kindly soul, maintained contact despite your father's ill opinion of me. You can confirm my familial connections, if you so choose, by public records in Edinburgh.

I am an old woman now and consumption will soon take me. In clearing my affairs, I came upon something in my attic last week that was meant for you. It is enclosed.

When you were only eleven your mother gave it to me for safekeeping with the direction to give it to you on your twenty-first birthday. She was in perfect health when she entrusted it to me, and so I wondered why.

By a strange twist of fate, she died only two days later. Perhaps she was prescient? We shall never know.

I placed it in my attic, intending to deliver it at the designated time. But life intervened and it slipped my mind.

I will now make a shameful admission. Upon redis-covering this last month, dear nephew, I was feverish with the thought that I might have caused some disaster by my careless delay in sending it to you. To quiet my mind, I tried to open your gift, even going to the extent of having several of Edinburgh's finest locksmiths apply their skills, to no effect.

I hope you will forgive me. I think your mother would have done so. Please receive this in her spirit – she was the soul of kindness and generosity – and not with the judgemental anger so characteristic of your father.

God bless,

Elspeth Carnachan (née Watson).

A tumult of emotions coursed through me. Anger at this woman's carelessness, her imposition, and my own grief at the reopening of an old tragedy vied for captaincy with tender childhood memories.

My mother. The soul of kindness and generosity. Her unexplained death when I was but eleven was a wound that had never healed. It was a mystery that I thought would never be solved. I wiped a rivulet of sweat from my brow.

Elspeth Carnachan, an aunt I had never known, had not only forgotten her promise to my mother, but then tried to open something meant for me. No wonder my father had forsaken this careless and duplicitous creature! I flung down the letter.

I turned my attention to the package, wrapped in aged brown paper. On it, inscribed in delicate handwriting which I recognized as my mother's, I read: 'For John, upon the occasion of your twenty-first birthday. I hope you will understand. In my heart always, Mother.'

I tore off the string and paper. Inside was a worn cardboard box with a faded floral label, once containing two fancy bars of soap. I raised it to my nose. A scent from my childhood – Lily of the Valley – emanated from it. It had been my mother's favourite. I was blindsided with a sudden wave of grief, and my vision blurred. I blinked and regained my focus.

I opened the soap box and discovered within a strange silver box about the size of two decks of cards. It was ornate and complicated. Engraved on its surface in finely traced lines were Celtic dragons, and the box itself was bound up with a dozen flat metal bands of different colours: silver, gold, copper. These were braided and wrapped around it, fastened securely along the front edge in a kind of Celtic knot. The ends of these bands were tucked under the edges of a large lock of a type I had never before seen. At the keyhole of this lock were many scratches, as though a breech had been attempted numerous times.

It was a beautiful object, like something from a fairy tale. But what was within? And why had my mother left this for me?

No key was included. I tried opening it, pressing and tugging here and there in case the keyhole was a ruse. Perhaps the box was locked in some way which could be released by pressing the right spot. But the lock and the metal banding did not move.

A second wave of sadness swept over me. Many miles had passed under my feet since my mother's tragic and puzzling drowning. Suicide? Accident? But she had been a stable and formidable woman, and a good swimmer. Painful ruminations tormented me in my youth, but medical school, my war experiences and my exciting life with Holmes had eventually rendered my childhood grief a pale and distant thing. I had successfully pushed the mystery of my mother's death from my mind.

Until today.

Here, in my hands, was a word from beyond the grave. Once again, I fingered the metal bands.

'Leave it,' came a sharp voice behind me.

I turned to see that Sherlock Holmes had soundlessly entered the room. He was pale and drenched with sweat, his dark hair damp and awry.

'Put it down, I say!' he cried.

CHAPTER 2

Thwarted

'hat?' I asked. 'Why should I leave it?'

'Why are you sitting in the dark? The sun is past our windows now!' said Holmes. He peeled off his frock coat and crossed to the window, throwing aside the heavy curtains. He opened the window wider to let in a draft. 'Ah, air!' he said. 'A breeze at last!'

'Holmes? *Why* should I leave it?'

'Do you know who sent it?'

'Yes. An aunt.'

He turned to face me, unbuttoning his waistcoat.

'You don't have an aunt. As I recollect, you had no one when you returned to London after the war.'

'Well, I didn't know I had this one.'

He tossed his waistcoat onto a chair. 'Then you do *not* know the sender. It could be anyone.'

He approached me and glanced down at the silver box, undoing his tie. His face was shiny with sweat. 'Ah, it is a bonny little thing. Careful, Watson.'

'Why?'

He shrugged, moving back to the window. Throwing his tie onto the table, he unbuttoned his collar and began splashing water from a carafe onto the front of his shirt. The back was already drenched in perspiration.

'There's a letter which explains—' I began.

'You do not know the person who sent this. Instinct tells me you should leave it.'

I shook my head. 'What on earth are you worried about, Holmes?'

He ignored the question, then rolled up his shirtsleeves, pulled back the sheer lace curtains and opened the window even wider, standing now quite exposed, his shirt soaked and clinging to his bony frame.

I felt a faint breeze move languidly into the room. Holmes untucked his shirt and was now preposterously flapping its soggy front in the stifling air to cool himself.

'Holmes!'

If our sheer curtains were not in place, the elderly couple who lived straight across Baker Street had a direct view into our lodgings, and I'd caught them more than once peering over at us with birding glasses. His state of undress would surely provoke remark.

He ignored me, but of course Holmes cared as much for propriety as I did for knitting.

'Holmes! If you think for one moment that either of us

might be a target, aren't you inviting danger standing in the window like that?'

'Hmm,' said he, nevertheless stepping back and closing the curtains. 'For a moment, I thought you might be concerned about the neighbours.' He flashed a quick smile at me. 'I am sorry, dear friend. I am being perhaps too careful.' He dropped down into a chair facing me. 'By Jove, this heat! I have just put my eleventh case to rest this year. A couple masquerading as Japanese royalty who were actually importing adulterated opium into – Watson, I said put that box down!'

'Holmes, this is *my* business.'

'Come, Watson, you have no business. Oh, sorry, don't take offence. It is one of the things I most treasure about you; you are almost an entirely blank page. Which means you are then free to accompany me on my cases.'

I was nettled to hear that my availability seemed to be my greatest asset. 'What do you think is so dangerous?' I asked, waving the box at him. 'Have you set off some munitions expert recently?'

'It is unlikely to be a bomb at that size, Watson. But please put it down! Locks can be rigged, you know, and even fatal.'

'Balderdash.'

'Spring-loaded, poison-tipped darts. Blades that pierce the eye when you look inside. Oh, yes, Watson!'

I set it down, reluctantly. 'Are you receiving death threats, Holmes?'

He said nothing.

'Are you?'

He cleared his throat. 'Nothing specific. But in my line of work it is wise to take care.' Holmes sighed. 'I'm sorry, Watson. It was not my intention to leave you out of my recent cases. Some of them require – they happen so quickly – I must stay nimble-footed.'

Hot with anger, I stood. I had recently declined to join friends for an excursion to Bath, but in a fit of pique changed my mind that instant. 'In any case, let me *not* be your anchor. I'm leaving in an hour for a holiday.'

Holmes was the picture of dismay. 'For how long? Where? Why on earth?'

'I have had enough of this heat. A friend invited me to Bath. Several of us are going. Cards, a great deal of swimming, dining. Nothing that you would enjoy.'

'Bath! Cards, you say? Dear fellow, I have had to lock your chequebook away for the third time! Your gambling debts will sink you. And as for fine dining, you really might reconsider.' He said no more but eyed my middle.

That confirmed it. 'I'm off to pack. Unlock your desk and have my chequebook out, or I shall break open the damned drawer.' Normally I am a patient man, but perhaps it was the heat.

I was off within the hour, chequebook in hand and the mysterious box tucked safely in an inner pocket of my linen jacket. I would see to finding a locksmith in Bath, far away from prying eyes.

As the train steamed westward that evening, I slid open the window in my first-class carriage and felt the evening air rush in as a cooling breeze. I was relieved to be departing London, and to be honest, Sherlock Holmes.

An image of his thin face when I left, drawn and, dare I say, a bit sad, floated into my brain. Let him miss me, I thought crossly.

It was not one of my finer moments, and one I came to regret.

CHAPTER 3

You Left Me Hanging

en days later, even though lowering clouds darkened London with the promise of a summer storm, my mood was light as I returned in a cab from Paddington Station towards Baker Street. My extended holiday in Bath had been restorative. Given Holmes's disputatious and dismissive mood of late, it was a welcome break to spend time with James Montgomery, a fellow soldier whom I had known in India, and two other comrades, whose ready laughter and playful demeanours had lifted my spirits.

Despite Holmes's ill-placed concern, I had won a fair amount of money at cards. And while the best locksmith in Bath could do nothing with the mysterious box, I was sure a London expert would soon have it open. And so I had allowed myself to enjoy the baths every day and partook of wonderful cuisine: roast beef, oysters, champagne.

A dense tropical heat blanketed Baker Street. My medical colleagues who still believed in the miasmic transfer of disease were likely to be frantic at this weather.

As my cab pulled up to 221, I glanced up at our windows. The curtains were closed against the morning light, which was muted through a canopy of summer storm clouds. But the windows, too, were closed. That was odd.

Just as I descended from the carriage, the sky broke open and a torrent of rain dumped down as though some mischievous god had upended an enormous bucket on Baker Street.

'Mrs Hudson!' I exclaimed, greeting our landlady as she glided into the vestibule. But instead of her usual warm response, she took my drenched hat and coat wordlessly, her face cloudier than the sky outside.

While I may 'see but not observe', as my friend so often remarked, it would be difficult for any man to miss her distinct aura of reproach.

'Dreadful weather!' I put on my best smile. 'But it is supposed to break the heat. Good to be home. How are you, Mrs Hudson?'

'Just go on up, Doctor. It has been a challenging two weeks.'

'Ten days, Mrs Hudson!'

'Well, it seems a month. Go see to him.' She disappeared downstairs. This was hardly the welcome I had expected.

I passed the sitting-room on the first floor landing, but

the door was shut. Upstairs in my room, I set down my luggage and took out the small silver box from my mother. It gleamed in the morning light from my window, its tantalizing mystery intact. I locked the beautiful object in my drawer thinking I would find the right locksmith tomorrow.

I was not ready for what I found downstairs.

The first thing my eyes were drawn to was the floor, awash in clutter – inches deep with scattered papers, stained napkins, dirty ashtrays, pipe dottles, plates of dried food and random oddities. A box of snake-skins sat next to a carafe of something that looked like dried blood. Flies swarmed around it.

Mrs Hudson had clearly withdrawn her usual services, no doubt in one of her rare fits of pique.

And the room was as hot as a tea kettle on full boil. Yet a fire burned in the grate! Why? A gust of wind just then shot down the chimney and a spray of sparks escaped and landed on a pile of papers. One ignited, and I ran to it, just in time to toss the smouldering paper into the fireplace before it set the room afire. I drew the fire screen across it.

A near disaster! But that gust down the flue meant a breeze, so I next rushed to the windows and opened two of them against the stifling heat. The violent summer storm continued to pour down rain. But why was the room closed up like this?

And where was Holmes?

I turned to look and that is when I discovered him: hanging silently in a corner of the room. His body dangled from a rope and was suspended four feet off the floor. He was encased from the knees up in a straitjacket! One foot was bare, the other slippered. The bare foot wriggled.

He was alive, at least.

CHAPTER 4

New Skills

 stared at him for a long moment.

He frowned in concentration and began moving silently under the canvas of the restraint. It was a rather elaborate contraption, tightly bound, with leather straps and buckles, fastened with padlocks. The toes of his bare foot wriggled in concert with his efforts.

He must have seen me come in. I cleared my throat.

Nothing.

'Holmes.'

'Yes?'

'Why the fire?'

'Is that the first question you have, Watson?'

'Yes. Why the fire?'

'I was cold.'

'In this weather! Are you eating?'

'Burning papers.'

A plate of sandwiches sat untouched next to his chair. His movements under the straitjacket now involved his legs, hanging in the air, jerking from side to side.

'Who helped you into that?' I asked.

'Billy.'

The page. A predicament of Holmes's own devising, then. A minute passed. It did not look like he was making headway. A bead of sweat ran down his forehead and into his eye. He shook it away. Smiled at me.

'You won in Bath, then. A tidy sum,' he said.

'What? Oh, for heaven's sake, Holmes.'

'Tie pin. A handsome one from here. But it is not like you to purchase adornments.'

'Stop this. No one likes to be scrutinized in this way.'

'You are usually amused.'

'Never mind! What the devil are you doing there?'

'I am attempting to replicate The Great Borelli's hanging escape trick. I have almost got it, I think.'

'The Great Borelli?'

'Travelling escape artist and magician. A wonder, at least in his own mind.'

Why Holmes felt the need to emulate some itinerant performer was a mystery. He flailed about a bit, and I could see that one arm had escaped its sleeve and was snaking underneath the canvas of the straitjacket. But the other remained pinioned.

A chair which had been placed underneath him had tipped over, and his legs now dangled limply in the air. I stood up, walked over and replaced it under his feet.

'Don't help me!' he shouted. 'I kicked it over for a reason.'

'What reason?'

He did not answer but struggled a bit more. His pale face grew red with the exertion. Had this been staged for my benefit? Holmes did so enjoy an audience. But, of course, he had not known my return date from Bath, so . . . no. I moved the chair back away from him, then took a stack of papers piled on my usual armchair and dumped them on the floor. I espied today's *Times* and freed it from the clutter.

On the way to my chair, I noticed on his chemistry table a black cylinder, perhaps eighteen inches long and six inches in circumference, mounted on a brass and wood device. Connected by cables were two small poles with a strangely shaped glass tube suspended between them. It had a somewhat malevolent look to it.

'What the devil is this thing?' I asked.

'A Ruhmkorff coil,' said he. 'It's a kind of induction coil. I can make tiny bursts of lightning at my desk. No, no, don't touch! And a Geissler tube.'

I was sorry I had asked. It reminded me of the various quack devices I was constantly solicited to buy for my non-existent medical practice. It looked dangerous.

I sat and opened up the newspaper. After a few moments I glanced surreptitiously at Holmes, whose eyes were now closed in concentration. His struggles were painful to watch.

I looked about the room and debated tidying it but decided the task was beyond my reach.

As I flipped through the pages, a review of 'The Great Borelli's First London Appearance' caught my eye. The magician was appearing at Wilton's Music Hall. A lurid picture had the handsome, moustachioed Italian performer hanging from a similar contraption, but with many straps and padlocks all around, and a beautiful lady standing in attendance.

I heard a groan from across the room but ignored it.

'This Borelli fellow has received an excellent review in *The Times* today. "Spectacular! Supernatural? How does he do it?"' I read aloud. I tapped the advertisement. 'Of course, Holmes, *he is hanging upside down.*'

'That is the next phase.'

'And there is a beautiful assistant standing by. I wonder what her role is?'

'That is not his assistant. It is his wife,' said Holmes, slightly out of breath. 'And she designed the trick.'

'Lucky man,' I said.

A pause.

'This is a bit more difficult than I had imagined,' he murmured.

'Try harder,' I said and returned to my paper. Utterly mad. If I had not been there, the room might have caught on fire and all my things would have burnt up. And oh, yes, Holmes would be dead. I wondered if I could entice Mrs Hudson to bring me a lemonade.

'Watson, be a good fellow. Go over to the table and read

me what's in those pages spread open. Step three, if you would.'

'I already was a good fellow and righted the chair. You didn't like it.'

'Watson!'

I complied none too graciously. On the table were three pages, spread open, typed with a faulty typewriter in uneven lettering, in Italian, with some diagrams and an awkward English translation pencilled in. 'Step three,' I read aloud. 'The left hand unlocks the lock which control the sleeve of the right. Take pick and release, then with other arm which out the *shoolder* – "shoulder" is spelled wrong – with three fingers, find the fold where are hidden the ties—'

There was a faint metallic clatter. I looked over to see that Holmes had dropped something small onto the polished wood floor.

'I dropped my lockpick. Hand me that, would you?' said he.

'What would you do if I were not here?'

'But you *are* here. Hurry, now!'

'No.'

I was being obstreperous, but a man can take only so much. Instead of retrieving his lockpick, I pocketed it, then picked up the chair and placed it under him again. He could give up this foolish nonsense and step down from there as a sane person might. I sat back in my old easy-chair and once again took up the newspaper. Silence.

He kicked the chair away and struggled on. A few minutes later, his face had grown redder and the struggling more pronounced.

The Three Locks

'You had no idea I would be returning,' I said. 'What was your plan, anyway, Holmes? It is clear that Mrs Hudson has given up on this room, the mess you've made! And that fire!'

No acknowledgement. I went back to my paper.

I heard the sounds of more struggling, a groan, some clicks, and I put down the paper just in time to see him slip free of the jacket and drop to the floor, landing almost soundlessly like a cat.

I will admit I was astonished. 'Bravo, Holmes!' I said.

He smiled in delight, then bowed with a flourish and a groan. He rubbed his shoulder. At thirty-four, Holmes was wiry and fit, far too thin by some accounts, but remarkably athletic in spite of never, to my knowledge, taking exercise for its own sake.

'All right, how did you do that after dropping your lockpick?' I asked.

'The locks are the least of it. Preparation is all.'

He was paper-white, and his face was covered with a thin sheen of sweat.

'What do you mean, "The locks are the least of it"?' He was standing oddly, favouring one side. 'And what is the matter with you?'

'Well, some of the locks are left in place. One has to more or less dislocate one's shoulder to escape that particular straitjacket. Borelli spent two years stretching his ligaments to accommodate it. I had only ten days.'

'Oh, come Holmes! You haven't dislocated your shoulder. You would be writhing in pain. And you would need me to yank it back in place for you.'

I glanced up at him. His dark hair, usually neatly groomed, was a mess and damply stuck to his skull. He inhaled shakily, then moved to a large bookcase and slammed himself against it. There was the sound of a loud pop.

'Good God, Holmes!'

He carefully flexed his left arm. Back to normal. He smiled at me in amusement. 'It worked, didn't it?'

I threw the paper down. 'What are you thinking, Holmes? You risk serious damage, dislocating a shoulder like that! How did you do it? And more to the point, how did you stand it?'

'A touch of morphine, going in. Borelli uses it, I will wager, but he claims not. It does fog the thinking. I shall try to do without. And I've learned to pop it back myself.'

'*You have learned?* How many times have you done this?'

'This is the third.'

'Idiotic, man! Of all your bad habits, this takes the prize. What of your violin playing? Boxing? You could do yourself permanent harm! Those ligaments don't always return to their original length.'

'Light me a cigarette, would you, Watson?' Still rubbing his shoulder, he stepped out onto the landing outside the room. 'Mrs Hudson! Some ice, if you please!'

He came back in and sat before me.

'There is no ice, Mr Holmes,' came Mrs Hudson's voice. I detected a note of irritation in it.

'Send Billy,' he shouted. Then as an afterthought, 'Please!'

No reply. Manners had eroded in this terrible heat, I thought. Londoners were unaccustomed to tropical life. And Mrs Hudson's new ice box, purchased for us all by Holmes, was often empty. Ice was very expensive, and income, of late, had been scarce. I felt a twinge of guilt about my recent holiday.

'We really must clean this place up, Watson. Get back in her good graces.'

He picked up a cigarette and lit it with difficulty. I shook my head.

'Foolish, Holmes. You forget that I am a doctor. I know more of injuries than you do.'

'I am careful, Watson. One can train one's muscles, extend the ligaments over time with repetition. How else might one dance the ballet?' He waved his good arm in a dramatic arc.

'Over time, perhaps some so built can do so. But with repetition, you can also have your arm hanging uselessly out of the socket, Holmes.'

'Watson, you win the ill temperament sweepstakes today. And this, after a successful trip in which you won money, swam, ate well—'

'Stop! I am not interested in hearing this!'

'You have gained two – no, three pounds. And I see you have begun a diet, starting today. Failing, however.'

'Holmes!' He could not possibly know this. It had only been a thought that very morning.

He grinned at me. 'You have celery in your waistcoat pocket. You hate celery. One cannot buy celery on the train, therefore you have brought it with you all the way from Bath. I wager you planned to eat the celery on the train instead of—'

'Stop!'

'But a sandwich must have won you over. Salmon, no doubt. Day One of your reducing plans, and already you have failed!'

I shook the newspaper roughly and returned to my article in a fury. I glanced down surreptitiously at my waistcoat. Indeed, a piece of celery poked out. He was right about it all. In a fit of pique, I tossed the celery to the floor.

It landed next to a plate of uneaten food, a collection of seashells, a revolver, a dog's collar, and what might have been a piece of flesh-coloured rubber and was perhaps a false nose. Home.

I looked up at him. 'The salmon, Holmes?'

'I will admit that was a guess. But it is your favourite.'

'You never guess!'

'But of course I do. Watson, let us call a truce. No luck, then, with your secret box in Bath? You would be crowing over that, if so.'

I glowered at him. 'Two locksmiths failed to open it.'

The sound of the doorbell interrupted us, and Mrs Hudson appeared, announcing 'a lady who would not give her name but insists that you have some papers of hers.' She eyed the room with disdain. 'If you can find them.'

Holmes glanced about, as if having forgotten the chaos with which he'd surrounded himself. 'Give us a moment, please, Mrs Hudson. Watson, why don't we quickly tidy up?' He was on his feet, scooping up newspapers in a flash and, irritation notwithstanding, I took up a stack of papers near my chair and rose.

'Not those, Watson!' he cried, but I ignored him and threw them into the grate where the flames caught. 'They are my laboratory notes!' he cried.

Mrs Hudson shook her head and departed.

Holmes attempted to rescue the burning pages but failed. 'Holmes!' He would set us all alight some day!

We heard footsteps on the landing and he flung himself into his chair, instantly assuming a pose of casual interest.

Our client appeared on the threshold. She was a striking woman of perhaps thirty, in a long red dress and an enormous hat topped with a red plume. Her black hair was arranged in a voluminous pompadour, her high cheekbones and olive skin conveying a southern birth. A waft of Oriental perfume assailed my nostrils. She was stunning, forthright, and, despite the heat, seemed coolly impervious. She put me in mind of the bow of a mighty ship.

I rose politely but Holmes remained seated and smiled calmly at her, his hands steepled.

She paused at the doorway and waved a folded newspaper in one hand. 'Mr Holmes, I did not know you were a famous detective!' Her voice was a honeyed contralto, with the seductive lilt of an Italian accent. 'You told me you write about science. But I read of you, in this paper—'

She stepped over the threshold, took in the junkyard that was our sitting-room and laughed. 'Oh my!' she exclaimed. But when her eyes alighted on the hanging straitjacket, the laughter caught in her throat, and she made a sudden guttural sound, like a tiger.

'What! You liar!' she roared, flinging the newspaper to the floor. 'You are no scientist. No detective either. You steal our famous illusion!' She grimaced. 'I will kill you!'

'Madame Ilaria Borelli,' said Holmes cordially. 'You are early.'

CHAPTER 5

Madame Borelli

er face a mask of fury, the lady scanned the clutter, glancing past me as though I were something to be stepped over on the street.

Her eyes lit upon the papers mounded on the table. She rushed over to them, snatched them up and waved them at us, her face black with rage. Opening her reticule to receive them, she then thought better of it, and with a dramatic gesture stuffed the papers down the front of her dress.

She stared triumphantly at the two of us as though she had just thwarted a mad effort to stop her.

But neither of us had moved. Holmes remained seated. He smiled.

'Forgive me if I don't stand, Madame Borelli.'

'You beast!' she cried, facing Holmes. 'You lie to me!'

Looking around, she seized upon a life-size plaster head of Goethe and hurled it at my friend, who leaped from his chair just in time to miss being concussed by the philosopher.

Goethe bounced off the chair and landed on a small Moroccan table, upending it, and sending a teacup and some books crashing to the floor to join in the general chaos there. The bust splintered into several pieces.

Given the state of disarray, this hardly worsened the room.

'Pagan! Reprobate! Liar! Thief!' she shouted, then lunged at him. I caught her mid-stride, grasping her by both arms. She appeared dainty but was muscled like an athlete.

'Madame, please sit down,' I said. 'You are clearly distraught. Let us help you.'

'Distraught! Help me?' Her voice rose to a shout. 'This man, he misrepresents himself. Says he is a scientist. But then I read in the newspaper he is famous detective. I ask Scotland Yard, one man there say amateur only.'

I laughed.

She turned to me. 'But . . . what do you say? He is pastry chef? He is ironmonger? And who are you?'

'I am Doctor John Watson, this man's friend. Yes, he is a detective *and* a scientist. Please . . . calm down, dear lady.'

She took a deep breath and stopped struggling. I removed my hands from her arms. 'Forgive me, Madame. May I pour you a brandy?' I asked. 'Please, do sit down.'

She ignored this and turned to Holmes.

'The Great Borelli, he knows. *Dario mio*, he finds these pages missing, and *he knows*. Look!'

She undid a button at the cuff of her dress and rolled up the sleeve. A series of bruises was evident.

Holmes was instantly at her side. He gently took her arm and examined the injury. 'Oh, Madame,' he said. 'I would never have – oh, not for the world—'

'Let me have a look, would you?' I brushed him aside. 'I am a doctor.'

Mollified by the caring attention of two men, the woman seemed to calm herself into some semblance of normality as she let me examine her bruises.

'It looks like someone grasped you hard enough to leave these marks,' I said.

'I never should give you the pages, Mr Holmes,' said the lady.

She looked around her and took in the utter chaos that was our sitting-room. As she did so, a frown passed over her lovely features. Her skin was pale olive, her hair nearly black but burnished with red. She was indeed a fiery beauty.

'And you lie to me,' she said. 'You told me you are scientist. I see no science, but only big mess.'

Her eyes fell on Holmes's chemistry table.

'Ah, science, yes, over there. But that is not the escape science, that is chemistry. No, it is physics! Who are you, Mr Holmes? You lied to me!'

'By omission only, and I apologize. I shall indeed write a small monograph, Madame Borelli, but fear not, I will not reveal all,' said Holmes. 'Please do sit down.' She did not. 'Stage conjuring, and escapology in particular, has long been a topic of interest to me. Most people enjoy trickery, but it is particularly vexing that some illusions – your husband's for example, are attributed to supernatural gifts. I wish to set the record straight.'

'I forbid it! The illusion is the magic. It is part of the performance, Mr Holmes. Dario and I – we will not be happy if you choose to expose him. You promised me to write in such a way not do this. And to do this later, much later. But—' She gestured angrily to the straitjacket, still hanging from the ceiling. 'Then I see you trying to duplicate this trick. Traitor! But, of course you cannot. What you do not know is—'

She broke off, staring hard at Holmes. He seemed nonplussed, but I knew my friend well enough to recognize discomfort. She walked over to him. He stood his ground. She suddenly reached around with her right hand and punched him in the shoulder. The left shoulder. The hurting one.

He gasped. I was on her in an instant, taking her from behind with both arms. But she was not to be held back. She trod on my right instep with her sharp heel, and I cried out, releasing her.

She withdrew a tiny Derringer from her reticule, pointing it at Holmes. We both froze. She backed up so that neither of us could reach her in a single move. This was certainly a lady who could look after herself.

'You are not the first to try this. I created this trick especially for Dario. He has – how you say? – the double joints. Over time, he developed, just like a strong man develops muscles. Which he also does. But he is special: a loose man. Bends like rubber. That is not in those pages. You cannot know this unless you are very smart, and you hurt your own shoulder trying this. Ha, ha, you lying man!'

'Madame Borelli, one thing I am not is a performer.'

I stifled a laugh. He most certainly was, although perhaps not on the stage.

'I am a scientist and repeating results of something another man has devised is *exactly what scientists do.*'

'No!' she cried. 'What a *woman* has devised. *I* invent this trick! Not Dario!'

'Nevertheless, repeating the results—'

'Are you double jointed, also?' I asked Madame, straining to picture it.

'Watson, good grief! Forgive us, Madame. I can see how this might be construed.'

'No performer, you say? Then what is this?' Madame Borelli strode to my chair and scooped up something from the floor next to it.

It took a second for me to realize what it was. The false nose. A laugh escaped me. Holmes shook his head when she turned to stare at me.

'Madame, I can explain all that you see here,' said Holmes.

'Explain quickly.' She caught me shifting my weight as I stealthily attempted to draw nearer. 'Stop there, you. Or I will shoot Mr Holmes.'

Just then Mrs Hudson appeared in the doorway, brandishing a tennis racquet as a weapon. I had wondered where my racquet had gone. She stared at the three of us.

'Mr Holmes, I heard the commotion. Put that gun away, young lady, unless you plan to shoot all three of us. And sit down, all of you.' She glanced at the clutter. 'If you can find a seat.'

No one moved. Mrs Hudson was full of surprises today. She advanced into the room, tennis racquet raised.

'Sit, or I shall knock sense into all three of you!'

Madame Borelli did not seem inclined to shoot the eminently reasonable Mrs Hudson in cold blood. She wavered, then replaced the gun into her reticule and looked round for a seat. I removed a large box of what appeared to be human bones from an armchair and brushed off its dusty wool surface. Madame Borelli glanced down, gave it one more furious brush and sat.

'Tea, then, in a few minutes. Meanwhile, behave yourselves,' said Mrs Hudson. She gave our visitor her sternest look. 'This is a civilized house.'

Some minutes later, we sat facing hot tea and ginger biscuits, a veneer of respectability floating above the sea of clutter. Madame Borelli had calmed herself to some degree. The summer shower had dropped the temperature, and a tepid, damp breeze wafted into the room with salubrious effect.

'Now, Madame Borelli, you have come here on another matter, I perceive, and not merely to retrieve the pages you so kindly lent me,' said Holmes in the soothing manner, absent of any sarcasm, which he used at times to great effect.

'Yes, I come. But I am not sure you are what I need. I am not sure—'

34

'Tell me what is troubling you. You did not wish to open your reticule when you located your husband's pages. And you have been keeping it close to you for your entire visit. But as you drew your gun, I glimpsed—'

'Yes, yes. I brought something.'

My attention turned to the tapestry bag with gold fringe, on a braided golden cord which hung around the lady's neck and was fastened with a small gold clasp to the sash of her dress. Even at this moment, one hand rested protectively upon it.

She glanced down at it nervously, then looked at Holmes from under her heavy fringe of dark eyelashes.

'It is true. You said when we met that you . . . you write for science journals. But you solve crimes. Scotland Yard man says *amateur*. Are you any good at this?'

'He is very good, Madame Borelli,' I interjected. 'Mr Holmes is the world's first consulting detective. In fact, he invented the term. The police turn to him on cases they cannot solve. Some of the men are perhaps a little—'

'Jealous,' she said. 'Yes, I see this.'

Holmes smiled. 'What is troubling you?'

'Well . . . Dario. He has a temper. What you see on my arm, it is not serious, it is him clutching my arm when he is too nervous or excited.'

'What is he nervous and excited about?' asked Holmes.

'He received . . .' She opened her small bag carefully and removed from underneath the gun a small, oblong object wrapped in a handkerchief. She slowly unwrapped it. 'This.'

It was a human finger.

PART TWO

ENTANGLEMENT

'The moving Finger writes; and, having writ,
Moves on: nor all thy Piety nor Wit
Shall lure it back to cancel half a Line,
Nor all thy Tears wash out a Word of it.'
                                                    —Omar Khayyam

CHAPTER 6

Fingering the Threat

Holmes eyed the gruesome digit with interest. 'May I?'

He took up his magnifying glass from the table next to him and held out his hand.

She gave the thing to him and he examined it carefully, saying nothing.

Holmes handed me his glass. 'Take a look, Watson. Male, about fifty; workman from the callus, here, and dirt under the nail. Judging from the amount of blood on the handkerchief—'

'There *is* no blood on the handkerchief,' I said.

'Precisely. And by the look of the cut edge, severed postmortem. Tell me what you see, Doctor.'

I took up the gruesome item. The cut was neat, done

with a very sharp instrument. I could add nothing other than this to Holmes's observations and said so.

He turned to the lady. 'Do you know who sent this?'

There was a pause.

'Yes. It is complicated,' she said. 'Dario says he does not know who sent this thing. But he knows. I can see that he knows.'

Holmes stared at her sternly. 'Fine, you both know. Who sent it? And if you know who sent it, why have you come here instead of to the police?'

She paused. 'I see you are detective, a real one,' said she. 'All right. It is Santo Colangelo, another magician, who send. A great rival to Dario. But no, more than a rival. Because he lost tip of right index finger in accident. An accident for which he blames *mi Dario*. I would like you to . . . to help me fix.'

'Fix? How do you mean?'

She shrugged. 'I do not wish to harm Santo Colangelo.'

Holmes glanced at me then turned a stern eye to the lady. 'The man who threatens your husband?'

She paused and looked uncertain.

'You want to keep this private,' he said.

'Yes.'

'This Santo Colangelo, what is he, a rival in performance? In . . . ah, you are blushing. In romance, then?'

She looked down at her reticule, caressing the long, gold tassel. 'Both,' she answered finally. 'He tries to win our bookings. Not successful.'

'But whose finger is this?' I interjected.

They ignored me.

'Give me the history,' said Holmes. 'And then about the finger. Leave nothing out.' He leaned back and closed his eyes.

Madame Borelli hesitated but I nodded to her to continue.

'Santo and I, we were once engaged to be married. He was, *is*, a good magician. He was looking for a pretty woman to assist him in his act. He hired me from many girls because I do more than assist. I invent, direct, improve. He quickly saw my value.'

'How did you gain your skills, Madame?' Holmes asked.

'But the finger!' I exclaimed. 'What of this finger?'

She ignored me. 'My father and my uncle. Both magicians in Sicily. We had a library of books, all of them I read. I improved their acts. At twelve years old.'

She had clearly captured Holmes's interest. 'Yes, go on,' he urged.

'Most men do not listen to a girl. But I did not care, and I made them hear me. I went to Rome, working as assistant to famous magician, and helping him too. My reputation grew. Then I met Santo. Together we form a great act, and he does mind-reading and also the hand magic.'

'Hand magic?' asked Holmes, opening one eye. 'Do you mean close-up magic?'

'Yes. You can stand very close and look carefully, and still you cannot see how is done. I gave him many ideas, so he is very, very good. Very fast, the hands. Coins, cards, even things on fire, he hides quickly. Dangerous. I designed all this. We were good partners.'

'But *this finger* . . .' I said.

Holmes gave me a sharp glance. 'Stolen from a cadaver, most likely, Watson. A theatrical touch but not one of interest to us at this precise moment. Isn't that right, Madame Borelli?'

The lady waved her hand dismissively, then put a finger to her lips. True or not, she was not about to say.

'You were in love with Santo, working with him and helping him with his act, then you met Dario?' prompted Holmes.

The lady smiled. 'Yes. Dario and me, one year ago, we were in love, even from the first seeing. The first seconds. It was instant. It was perfect. But Santo . . . he saw, of course.'

'Yes, a mind reader,' said Holmes sardonically.

'You mean an *actual* mind reader?' I asked.

Holmes sighed. 'There are no *actual mind readers,* Watson. Dear God, what happened to you in Bath? This Colangelo is probably just observant. And for performances, there are devices. Spies who provide advance information. Codes to convey facts without others noticing. It is all rather simple.' He turned to the lady. 'In any case, Santo did not miss the attraction. Go on.'

'Dario and I, we married a month later. Two days after wedding, Santo threatened Dario. Nothing came from this, but eight months later Santo made the mistake while performing, and he lost the tip of a finger.'

Holmes leaned forward. 'How?'

'Yes, how do you lose a finger while mind-reading?' I asked. The two of them had vexed me beyond all patience.

'Another part of show: the close-up. Santo has a little guillotine. Is a device Dario sold to him. Very common trick, but I have changed it and made much more exciting. But something . . . something went wrong. It chopped off the end of Santo's finger. And this for him is a tragedy. The close-up magic relies on the quick fingers.'

'Did you examine the device after?' asked Holmes.

'No. Santo did not allow.'

'You said Dario sold him the device, which you had improved. In what way did you make this trick more exciting?' persisted Holmes.

'A real human finger come out. With real blood.'

'Ugh,' I said.

'The children love it!' said Madame.

'More fingers! And how does one manage the sheer volume required?' I asked.

'Purchased, Watson!' Holmes asked. 'As this one no doubt was!'

I wondered about the black market in body parts for stage magicians. 'Perhaps you could patronize Madame Tussaud,' I suggested.

'Many tricks are dangerous,' said the lady. 'And complicated. They require skill and courage. Especially those of the Great Borelli. *Mi Dario* is the escape-artist king. He goes chained into the ocean or a big tank of water. We set fire to a big copper pot while he is tied up inside. Or in a box which falls from great height. Tricks require great skill, great courage. Otherwise, everyone would do them.'

'Back to this finger,' Holmes said. 'This Santo Colangelo

fellow is vengeful. He believes Dario carried out this sabotage. So just now he sent you a finger. A warning, perhaps?'

'That is what I would like you to find out.'

Holmes did the calculation. 'This accident that ruined Colangelo's finger? Three months ago, then?'

'Three months, yes.'

Holmes offered a cigarette to the lady. She declined and he lit one for himself. 'You have been married only eleven months. And yet already you have fallen out of love with your new husband.'

She stood up abruptly. 'You! *You* are a real mind reader. How you know this? How you see this?'

'Oh, do sit down,' said Holmes irritably.

I stood and gestured politely. She was certainly an excitable lady. '*Please*,' I added. I poured her another tea. At least one of us had manners. 'Have a biscuit.'

She eyed the platter, took one, and sat down.

'I merely observe,' remarked Holmes. 'You are twisting your wedding ring constantly and flicking it with your finger. Dismissive. You wish to be rid of it. You wish to be rid of Dario. Those bruises are exactly what we first surmised. Your husband is rough with you. He does not appreciate you. But aside from all that, you have come here for help.'

'All right, yes. I want you to find who hurt Santo, causing him to lose a finger. It is not Dario Borelli, I am sure. If we learn the truth, Santo will no longer threaten Dario. Then . . . only then . . . I can leave Dario, happy because I know he will be safe.'

Holmes and I exchanged a glance. This was a formidable

lady who not only improved her lovers' magic acts but protected them, as a mother might look after a wayward child. Fickle, perhaps, but she could afford to be. Ilaria Borelli defined, I suppose, a bold new kind of woman. I briefly wondered what being married to such a woman, perhaps an expert in my own medical field, might be like. The thought brought a smile to my lips.

The doorbell rang for the second time that morning. Soft voices came from below. A male visitor. Madame Borelli stood again.

'I go. Will you help me, Mr Holmes? I will pay you, of course.'

'When I deliver your result, you can pay me then. I will visit this Santo Colangelo and see if I can discover the cause of his accident, although I must warn you that trail is cold. Why do you think he waited so long after his accident to send a threat?'

'He is trying to win me back. But cannot. Santo is not the bad man. But now he is angry that he cannot have me. And jealous. And Dario recently is a big success.' She took two tickets from her reticule and placed them on a table next to Holmes. 'Come tonight. See the show again.'

Holmes sat still for a moment, considering. Then, 'Tell the Great Borelli, er, your Dario, that I will come. I have a few questions for him. I will also visit Colangelo and see if I cannot get to the bottom of this.'

'Very good. Thank you. And no word to Dario that you have read these pages!' With a final glance around the room and a haughty sniff, Madame Borelli departed.

'Not your usual case, Holmes,' I said. 'Seems more a matter of the heart than the brain.'

'Hearts drive more crimes than brains do, Watson. And the conjuring element is intriguing. I always enjoy a good magic show, although most of it is glaringly obvious.'

'If you know how it's done,' I said, 'does that not remove half the fun?'

Holmes regarded me with amusement. 'Come, come, Watson. Everyone enjoys a little sleight of hand.' With a wave of his arm, his cigarette suddenly disappeared.

I did not favour him with a reaction. 'Why do I need the theatre when you are a constant source of amusement, Holmes? Alternating, like the current, with being vexatious.'

'I am sorry, Watson, it is the heat.' He winced. 'Ouch!' he said, pulling the still glowing cigarette from his sleeve. 'I need to keep practising this.'

'And, perhaps, your manners,' I remarked.

CHAPTER 7

The Deacon

efore Holmes could retort, Mrs Hudson entered and interrupted us.

'Peregrine Buttons, Deacon, Church of Our Lady of the Roses, Cambridge. Says you are expecting him, Mr Holmes?' She stepped aside, leaving us facing a young man.

Holmes clearly had forgotten this appointment. 'Ah, Deacon Buttons!' He gestured to the chair recently vacated by Ilaria Borelli.

Surely he would not take on a second case? But I had not long to worry.

This slender fellow edged past Mrs Hudson and paused at the threshold. He was garbed in black, with a cleric's collar and wide black Saturno hat. I put his age at twenty-two or so. His eager, innocent expression, wide-set blue eyes and handsome, boyish face conveyed both hope and trepidation.

He paused, realizing that his clothing was soaked and dripping onto the rug. He had apparently worn no overcoat.

'Oh, please forgive me!' He flushed, backing into the hallway, brushing the moisture from his jacket.

'Come in, young man! Never mind the rug,' said Holmes, impatiently.

The young deacon entered, removing his hat. Raindrops dotted his gold spectacles. A wild mop of fair hair, flattened on the top from the hat but curling wildly all around the sides from the dampness, gave the amusing effect of a faux tonsure with a peculiar shape. Noticing my stare, he ruffled his hair, erasing the effect, and attempted a shy smile. He had remarkably straight, white teeth.

I also observed carefully manicured hands and a small gold ring. Here was a handsome young man of the cloth who was rather aware of his appearance. Unusual, I thought.

'Mr Buttons. Your name was derived from *Bouton*? French?' said Holmes.

The young man nodded.

'I received your note early this morning.' He turned to me. 'Watson, it concerned a young lady who has gone missing in Cambridge. Come and sit down – here, Deacon, place this cloth underneath you on the chair – and begin at the beginning. I would like my colleague Dr Watson to hear your story.'

The young man sat. 'Well, Mr Holmes, as I wrote to you last night, Miss Odelia Ann Wyndham – Dillie, as she is known – is missing. This is a young lady of my acquaintance, a regular at our services, and the daughter of Richard Anderson Wyndham.'

'Yes, the famous Cambridge don, the classics professor and wayward archeologist? I inferred her relationship from the name. Is she his only child?'

'He has two daughters. She is the younger. In any case, Dillie has been missing since Monday afternoon.'

'Dillie? You are on a first-name basis?'

The young man shifted in his chair. 'Father Lamb, my superior, encourages us to consider each of our flock as family . . . children of God.'

'Hmm. Watson, the deacon's is a new Catholic church in Cambridge, recently reopened after a scandalous closure eight years ago. Go on, Deacon.'

'Er . . . yes!' said the young man. 'How do you know all this, if you do not mind the question, sir?'

'I read. In any case, Miss Wyndham was last seen on Monday, and you wrote to me the next day. That is not much time to have passed. What is your concern?'

'Well, on Tuesday after evening services, we – that is, I – run a discussion group in the church, and Dillie has always attended. But not last night. I was already worried, Mr Holmes, because we had made an informal arrangement for earlier in the day, and she did not show up as planned for that, either.'

'What kind of arrangement?'

'We were to have lunch.'

'Where?'

'At the The Bull and Rat.'

'A pub, from the name. Is it a regular habit of yours to meet single female congregants in pubs for lunch?'

The young cleric flushed to the roots of his hair. 'Father Lamb says that if we can counsel a person in need, it does not matter where or when, only that—'

'How old is the lady?'

'Eighteen, I believe.'

'You believe, or you know?'

'Eighteen and four months.'

Holmes said nothing for a long moment. Then, 'On what subject were you to counsel her?'

'She is troubled by a young man at the university. Frederick Eden-Summers. A third year, going for law.'

'Ah, some facts at last. Eden-Summers, that name is familiar. Watson, be so good as too look that up in my files. Would we be correct in consulting Debrett's as well, Deacon?'

The young man nodded once again.

I was already wading through the clutter to Holmes's alphabetized files. I retrieved the appropriate box, and Debrett's as well, wherein the details of peerage soon revealed that Frederick Eden-Summers was the oldest son of the Duke of Harbingden, and therefore set to inherit his father's estate and title. Once that matter had been determined, Holmes turned again to our young visitor.

'Now, how is Mr Eden-Summers troubling the young lady?'

'She is being pressured to accept his marriage proposal.'

'By the young man himself?'

'Apparently, and by her father as well. It is shameful! I am of the school of thought that a young lady should choose for herself. My own sister is at Girton. A very independent young lady. Our parents raised us this way.'

'Yet *you* chose a profession with many restrictions. Are your parents pleased with your choice?'

'My parents are dead, Mr Holmes. I left the university after one year, as I had no way to support myself once my father was gone. And so I entered the Church. But what has this to do with Miss Wyndham?'

'Perhaps nothing. How do you propose to help the young lady?'

'Spiritual counselling, of course.'

'Of course. What says her family about this brief disappearance?'

'Strangely, nothing. Polly, her maid, says they are not concerned.'

'You are on intimate terms with her maid?'

'Mr Holmes, sir! Polly attends our church!'

'Why, then, Deacon Buttons, if the family is unconcerned, are *you* worried?'

The young man looked down at his hat.

'Be forthcoming, Mr Buttons, or I shall send you home on the next train.' Holmes leaned back in his chair, arms crossed. His foot tapped in the air, giving away his impatience. He caught my frown and stopped the foot.

Mrs Hudson arrived with a glass of water. She set it down next to Buttons, kicked a small stack of refuse out of her way, glanced at me, and departed.

The deacon turned his hat in his hands, acutely uncomfortable. After a moment, Holmes broke the silence.

'Is Miss Wyndham aware of your affections?'

The young man looked up, startled. I had seen such a reaction so many times.

'Come now, it is patently obvious,' said Holmes.

'I . . . I have said nothing. Perhaps she has intuited. But in my position, I am unable . . . I cannot offer her, and she deserves . . .'

Holmes got up and moved to the fireplace. He rummaged among several pipes in his rack and selected one. This kind of sentiment made him uncomfortable. He turned and leaned against the mantel, lighting his pipe with a match, then tossed it into the fire, which had sunk to embers, I was relieved to note.

'I believe you mean well, Mr Buttons, but you have wasted your time. The family's response is telling. It is most likely the young lady is away shopping or visiting relatives. Or perhaps she needs time alone to think. Please return to Cambridge. But do cable me if Miss Wyndham does not return in two days, or if her family also become worried. Then, and only then, will I consider this a case of a missing person. I wish you well with Miss Wyndham. Dr Watson will see you out.'

I accompanied the young deacon to the door where I gently reiterated Holmes's offer. He nodded tearfully and departed. I returned to find my friend frowning as he shuffled papers on the table.

'Why do people bother me with these trifles? The girl is

obviously fleeing his unwanted attentions. Any fool can see that.'

'I don't know, Holmes. He is a terribly good-looking young man. He seems sincere.'

'With few prospects, as he pointed out.'

'Not every young girl is so concerned about that.'

'But priests are meant to be celibate,' he said. 'Unless I have missed something. Where are those notes?'

'Catholic clergy may marry, if they do so before ordination,' I offered.

Holmes shrugged. 'Romance is your department, Watson. But it hardly matters.' He glanced about him as if noticing for the first time the mounds of his personal clutter. 'My friend, I have let things get out of hand here. Will you help me for a couple of hours? Then off to dinner and the Great Borelli's performance as compensation?'

I hesitated. 'I will help you, Holmes, this time. But it will all go into the fire.'

'No! Some of these papers are vital. I need to find—ah, what a mess Madame has made of these!'

'No promises.' I bent down to relight the fire, and sighed. It was still too hot in the room for it. But perhaps burning his papers was the reason he had had it blazing in the first place.

As I leaned in with a match, this was confirmed for me. The charred remains of a stack of papers lay at the bottom of the grate. I made out the words at the top of one. It was a treatise on medieval locks. Was he going try opening my little box?

CHAPTER 8

A Close Escape

hat evening we sat amidst a varied crowd in the cavernous, drafty stalls at Wilton's Music Hall, located in Grace's Alley, Whitechapel. While the place lacked the cachet of a West End theatre, it was a storied venue for variety acts and attracted a wide range of London's social classes.

We did not know it at the time, but the place would be shuttered within a year and turned into a mission for feeding the poor, but at this moment it was filled with eager theatre-goers. Above our heads, with elbows resting on the overhanging balcony surrounding on three sides, was a noisy crowd of working-class men, women and children. One small boy – his mother occupied with her flashy swain seated beside her – was folding tiny pieces of paper and dropping them on the heads of the better-dressed patrons sitting beneath him in the stalls.

I had been only ten years old myself when I first saw a magic show. That one had featured dancing dogs, and I recalled the canines were infinitely more entertaining than the florid, grotesque man who had performed after them, sweating under his battered top hat and manipulating cards on a stained, felt-covered table. But that was long ago.

The Great Borelli promised to entertain at an entirely different level. A spangled red and silver curtain billowed at the back of the stage. In front were arrayed various gleaming contraptions and velvet topped tables.

Seated next to me in the stalls, Holmes drummed his long thin fingers on his knee, as impatient as the young boy above us.

At the sound of a musical flourish from a small band on the right side of the stage, the lights dimmed. Followed by a spotlight, the Borellis appeared from behind the curtain. Tall, dark-skinned, with the pointed beard and trimmed moustache of Renaissance portraits, the Great Borelli boasted an athletic physique and the light-footed movements of a sportsman in his youthful prime.

Madame Borelli was glamorous far beyond her already striking appearance at Baker Street earlier in the day. A red silk gown draped over her statuesque figure like molten lava, adorned with red and black sequins that seemed to give off sparks from the limelights at the front of the stage.

The act proceeded with a fast-paced series of magic tricks, most employing lavishly decorated pieces of equipment, including a gold filigreed coffin-like box into which Madame Borelli was locked, her head and feet sticking out of either end, promptly followed by Borelli piercing the coffin with swords. Holmes leaned in to whisper, 'Either careful choreography, and Madame is a contortionist, or trick swords which fold in on themselves.'

I nodded. 'Shhh.'

Holmes leaned in again. 'Those feet sticking out are false feet. Look, the soles are unworn!' whispered the spoilsport.

'Let me enjoy this!' I hissed back.

Borelli flung a red satin drape over the whole thing, intoned incantations, then tossed it away with bravado, revealing Madame Borelli standing intact next to the gold coffin. The audience erupted in applause.

More tricks followed, in which the magician seemed to be in flirtatious competition with his mischievous wife. The charming Ilaria threatened to upstage him at every turn, but he won the day by making a variety of objects – including a teacup apparently filled with liquid, and a small, live rabbit – appear and disappear into his hat.

'Fabric pocket at the edge of the table. See there, he drops the rabbit in while you are watching the scarf, it never goes *in* the hat,' said my companion. 'And there is no liquid—'

'Oh, Holmes,' I groaned.

A woman in front of us turned to look at us. 'Yes, go *home*, you rude man!'

Holmes chuckled, but for the next several illusions did manage to hold his tongue.

After more remarkable hat tricks, the audience exploded into enthusiastic applause. I leaned over and said, 'Now that was well done, wouldn't you say, Holmes?'

'*Mmph*. Sleight of hand. Misdirection. Pre-rigged table and hat,' came the reply. 'This is not what I came for.'

But the music started up again, and the stage lights dimmed. The table was whisked away and a large tank was rolled in, some six feet high and four feet square. A spotlight followed it in. It was filled to the brim with water, which sloshed over the edges as the thing was wheeled to the centre of the stage. Lowered from above was a large clock, with a vivid second hand slowly ticking round.

The band's music grew ominous. The top of the tank was removed and in it were embedded two iron cuffs.

'Ladies and gentlemen! In our next adventure,' the Great Borelli boomed with his Italian accent, 'holding the breath is important. First, I ask you to try. Do I have a volunteer to be submerged with these iron cuffs around your ankles and try to escape?'

The audience went silent, except for some nervous laughter. I stole another glance at Holmes. 'Not ready for this one?' I asked.

'Perhaps one day,' said Holmes.

I regretted my joke.

'How long can the average man hold his breath?' Madame tapped him on the shoulder. 'Or woman?' He looked out over the audience. 'Let us see. Will you give it a try? Upon my signal, my assistants will keep watch. Keep your eyes on the clock. Raise your hand to start. Lower it when you must take a breath. We shall see who is best among you. Ready? Deep breath in now, ready . . . go.'

There was a collective gasp from the audience and many

hands went up. Why not? I thought, and raised my hand, taking in a big breath.

As the clock ticked and we literally held our breath with one hand in the air, the Great Borelli stripped off a layer of clothing, revealing a grey woollen bathing costume underneath. After displaying his remarkable physique in a classic strongman pose, he removed his shoes and socks. He then made as if to remove his bathing costume to a collective gasp from the ladies. He stopped with a wink. The clock ticked on . . . thirty seconds, forty seconds.

Borelli next climbed up a ladder to the top of the tank and sat on a small platform. Two assistants removed the top, displayed to the audience the iron cuffs securely welded into it, then carefully locked his ankles into them, clicking them shut like handcuffs and then adding padlocks on top of these.

They fastened a thick chain around his waist, and to this, a pair of what looked like police regulation handcuffs. Once locked, the assistants gave a sharp tug, showing that the cuffs were not only secure, but tight.

Around us a series of gasps sounded out and one by one the hands went down—forty-five, fifty, sixty seconds. I made it to seventy-five, then gasped. The Great Borelli smiled. 'The longest an audience member has ever held his breath was eighty seconds. One minute and twenty seconds. Most of you can do this for less than a minute. I will now escape this tank, but it will take time. Longer than two minutes. It is extremely dangerous. A colleague of mine recently drowned attempting to duplicate this trick. Are you ready?'

The audience responded in affirmation. Holmes leaned forward in his chair. The Great Borelli, now upside down with chains connecting his handcuffs to his waist, was upended so he was hanging from his pinioned ankles.

The entire thing was winched into the air and Borelli was suspended upside down, over the tank. He took in a deep breath of air, and nodded at his assistants to lower him in.

The clock began.

Madame Borelli stepped forward. 'My husband is risking his life. In the case that something goes wrong, we do not wish for you to see him drown.' A curtain on a frame was then rolled in to block our view of the tank.

The audience gave audible disapproval. Some boos were heard.

Madame Borelli smiled. 'Oh . . . you want to see?'

'Yes! Yes!' came the louder response.

'He's unlocking the handcuffs just now,' whispered Holmes. 'Stop it.'

She nodded at an assistant and the curtain was wheeled off. Forty seconds, fifty, a minute. Borelli could be seen writhing as he seemed to struggle with the handcuffs.

'I think he's having trouble,' I whispered to Holmes. He just smiled at me.

Borelli continued to struggle. The music began to play ominously.

'I don't know. This looks like a problem,' I said.

Ninety seconds. Suddenly Borelli cast off the handcuffs. A ripple of applause. Then the illusionist contorted in the narrow tank to bend at the waist to address his ankle restraints. The clock indicated two minutes.

The audience vocalized its thrilled concern. I glanced at Holmes. He was watching closely. I turned my attention back to Borelli, who was working at the ankle cuffs. One ankle was free, the other still trapped. He paused and threw his head back in seeming despair, beating his hand against the window.

Two minutes and twenty seconds.

Madame Borelli appeared concerned.

'Holmes!' I said.

He seemed fascinated. Perhaps not as wide-eyed as those around us, but definitely interested.

Borelli once again attacked the remaining ankle cuff.

Two assistants approached Madame Borelli and appeared to confer with her in something of a dither. She shook her head.

Two minutes and forty seconds.

'That is a terribly long time to hold one's breath,' I said.

'He is practised, Watson,' said my friend.

One ankle was free. The other was not. Borelli worked at it, apparently frantic. One assistant came out with a sledgehammer. Then the second.

Three minutes. Were we going to watch a man die before us?

'Holmes?'

'He *is* having trouble with that second ankle cuff,' said Holmes.

Three minutes and ten seconds. The music stopped. Silence.

Borelli seemed to collapse and float downward, becoming caught halfway, still bent at the waist, against the side of the tank, unconscious perhaps. The assistants raised their sledge-hammers and glanced at Madame Borelli.

Her posture had changed. She was leaning forward, the picture of alarm.

'Oh no!' I said.

Suddenly Borelli gave a great twist and his second ankle came free. He folded like a jackknife, reversed position in the water, and shot to the top.

He pushed the top free! Borelli surfaced, gave a huge gasp, and then shook his head violently, sending a spray of water into the air.

The musicians played a triumphant flourish. The audience burst into applause.

The top was taken in hand by the two assistants who had scrambled up two ladders on either side. One assistant held a hand down to pull him out of the tank. Borelli waved the man away and stayed in the tank, perched on the edge and leaning on his two arms. He gave a salute to the audi-ence, who continued to applaud wildly.

The assistants looked a bit confused. I glanced at Holmes. He was staring at Borelli, his forehead creased in a frown. What had just happened?

Borelli waved to the two assistants. They clambered down the ladders, and with the help of two more stagehands wheeled the giant tank off the stage, Borelli still within. Madame Borelli came to the front of the stage. She bowed deeply.

'On behalf of the Great Borelli and myself, we thank you for coming today. *Grazie. Grazie.*' She bowed again, blew kisses as the music played, and the curtains closed.

I looked at Holmes.

'Backstage, Watson,' he said. 'I am curious about what just happened.'

CHAPTER 9

Misdirection

e pushed past a large crowd of fans and well-wishers to a guardian at the stage door who turned all away. Not to be thwarted, my friend led us to the side of the building to another entrance, a plain locked door which he handily picked with a small tool from his pocket.

In a moment we were greeted by Madame Borelli at the door to their dressing room. The Great Borelli sat on a chair by his cluttered dressing table, still wet and in his bathing costume but royal in demeanor, with a luxurious, embroidered silk robe thrown over all. One leg was elevated, his foot resting on a chair. His foot angled oddly, and I saw in an instant that the ankle was broken. It was swollen and tinged blue. He grimaced in pain as he issued sharp commands in Italian to two stagehands and his wife.

One assistant held the top bar of the tank as Madame Borelli examined the cuffs embedded in it. One was open, but the closed one held her focus. She was frowning and said something in Italian to her husband and their voices rose.

A stagehand pushed through to interrupt urgently. I made out the words '*il dottore*' and stepped forward. 'I am a doctor,' I said. 'May I assist you?'

The Great Borelli looked up and took us in. 'Who are you?' he demanded. 'And how you get in here?'

His accent was thick. The magician eyed the two of us with scorn.

'I invited them,' Madame Borelli intervened. 'This is Mr Sherlock Holmes and Dr Watson. Mr Holmes, he solves crimes. A famous detective, very good. I called him about the finger you received, about Santo Colangelo. It is especially important, Dario, now that someone else is trying to kill you.'

'Simple! Is Colangelo,' cried Borelli.

'Darling,' said Madame, 'Maybe not Santo. He has not the skills.'

'But perhaps an agent of his?' said Holmes.

'You have spoken before, you two,' said Borelli, his eyes darting between Holmes and his wife. His face grew red with rage. 'Why do you two speak without me?'

'Dario, *caro mio*,' began the lady in a soothing tone. 'I wanted his help. I read in the paper, and Scotland Yard recommended.'

Borelli stared at Holmes, considering this.

'I am a great appreciator of your skills, Mr Borelli,' said Holmes.

'A detective? Who tries to flatter me? Who meets in secret with my wife?' Borelli eyed Holmes from head to toe and snorted. 'No. For you I have no use.' He said something in Italian to his wife, who flushed.

Holmes smiled. 'I am not Madame's "type", apparently, Watson,' said he.

I did not realize my friend spoke Italian. Six years into our partnership, he continued to surprise me.

Borelli turned to me. 'But you? You are a medical doctor?'

I nodded.

'Where is your bag?'

'At home. We came to see your show,' I said. 'May I have a look at that ankle?'

'He is an army surgeon,' said Holmes. 'That is a very nice dressing gown, by the way.'

The magician paused only for a moment, then nodded. 'Look, then.'

I pulled up a chair and leaned in to examine the injury. I had barely touched him when Borelli leaned over his leg, thrusting his face towards mine. He took me by the arm, his fingers digging into my flesh. '*Ah!*' I said.

'You will be *very* careful, no?' His dark marble eyes bored into mine.

'Of course.'

'You make like new.'

'I will know after I have examined you.'

'I must perform. Important shows. Make right very fast.'

'I will do my best,' I said.

'*Grazie, grazie.*' Still leaning forward, he released my arm and patted me on the back with his other hand. He remained uncomfortably close.

'Sit back, sir, and try to relax. It will go easier for you. Is there any brandy about?' I had uncharacteristically left my own flask at home.

'No, no! I no need,' said Borelli, waving a hand dismissively.

'Sit back, please, sir!' I said.

The magician paused, took a deep breath, then finally relaxed back into the chair, giving me room. As he did, he noted Holmes examining the contraption that had held his ankles.

'Interesting,' said Holmes.

'Put that down!' ordered Borelli.

'Dario, please,' said Madame Borelli. 'I believe he can help to prove that you did not tamper with Santo's guillotine trick. We must clear this up, Dario, or who knows what Santo may do?'

Holmes set down the contraption with the ankle cuffs and wiped his hands with a nearby towel. 'The lock appears untouched. The wood around it is not scratched. If the one lock that malfunctioned was indeed tampered with and not merely broken, then the culprit is an expert.'

'Colangelo did this,' snarled the magician. Then, to me, '*Ach!* Easy there, you!'

'How and when did he allegedly do this? Surely you check your equipment?' asked Holmes.

'Always. I examined it at six p.m. tonight.'

'But the show commenced at seven-thirty. Did you not look again, just before going on? Such a mistake can be fatal,' remarked the detective.

Borelli waved a hand. He was not yet ready to let Holmes in on the case. 'But it was not fatal. I escaped! You are so smart, tell me how I do this!'

'Impressively! You twisted your ankle at an extreme angle until you could slip free by force – abrading the skin there and breaking your ankle in the process. Few could manage this.'

I looked up at the man. 'You broke your own ankle? On purpose?'

'Better than drowning, Watson,' said Holmes. 'Or perhaps worse, failing the trick.'

Madame Borelli smiled at this. The magician did not.

'Why should I trust you?' he said. His eyes swept over Holmes, taking in everything from my friend's sleek hair and closely fitted frock coat to his polished boots. 'You say admirer. But . . . *you* are dressed like magician.'

Holmes laughed.

'Like a gentleman, Dario,' corrected Madame Borelli. 'It is the fine English tailoring of Mr Holmes.' The lady gave her husband a stern look. 'You need to listen, *caro mio*.'

The man raised his eyebrows. 'Speak, woman.'

'We must discover not just Santo Colangelo's guillotine mystery, but also who tampered with your equipment tonight, Dario,' continued his wife. 'Possibly it was the same man.'

'Or woman,' I said.

'Many are jealous of my illusions, my fame,' said Borelli.

'Oh, to be sure,' I said. This man's conceit knew no bounds.

'Who guards your stage properties when you are away?' asked Holmes.

Madame Borelli gave a low growl. 'Falco Fricano. He was married to Dario's sister, before her death. He watches over things, or says he does.'

'He is a good man,' said Borelli. 'Falco!' he shouted.

'He is the wrong man for this job,' said Madame.

Borelli grunted. 'What do you know, woman?'

His dismissive manner raised my ire.

'But you know Falco, *caro mio,*' she said before turning to Holmes and me. 'Falco likes the cards and wine. He is very good for organizing the travel but not for the long, boring jobs like sitting backstage and watching all the equipment. I think he is not there all the time.' To her husband, she added, 'I tell you this before.'

A tall, handsome man with the flushed countenance of someone who indeed was a fan of the grape poked his head in the door.

'Falco!' cried Borelli.

Fricano smiled and nodded at us. 'Si, Dario?' he said.

Borelli said something in rapid Italian to the fellow, who responded with a short, conciliatory burst of words. Borelli replied with a sharp retort, then waved him away. Fricano saluted us with a smirk and disappeared.

'Falco, he admits,' said Borelli. 'Maybe he stepped away for an hour. After five p.m. Maybe after six. He is not sure.'

Madame Borelli turned back to Holmes. 'You see.'

'Was he unsure of the hour, or the length of his absence?' asked Holmes.

'He says he was gone only one hour,' she said. 'But I think it was more.'

'Whoever did this obviously came between six when you checked and seven-thirty, then,' said Holmes. 'I wonder that you put your faith in this Falco Fricano, Mr Borelli.'

'He is family. He never will cross me,' said Borelli. 'Maybe make mistake – he will not make again.'

'Do you have any theories about who might have tampered with the lock tonight?' Holmes asked. 'Anyone with a long-standing grudge, perhaps?'

'Many people are jealous of the Great Borelli,' said the magician with another wave of his hand. 'Could be one of a hundred. *Ah!* Do not poke at ankle so.'

'I am palpating to find the exact break,' I said. 'You have fractured the lateral malleolus – the area where the fibula joins the foot. Not an uncommon break for a sportsman. You will have to immobilize this for a while. It will require a splint,' I announced. Spotting a stagehand at the door, I called him over and described what I needed. As he departed, strident voices floated in from the hall. The word 'officer' was clearly in the mix.

'Ah, the police are here. Wife!' said Borelli. 'Send them away!'

Madame Borelli stepped outside and closed the door. I could hear her conferring with several male voices.

'Have you had any recent threats by post, or directly? Any

suspects from this list of a hundred who seem more likely than others?' persisted Holmes.

Borelli glanced at Holmes. 'I do not need you. Are you still here? Go, go!'

'Fine, then,' said Holmes, taking up his hat. 'Watson, I will find you in Baker Street.' I remained seated next to Borelli's afflicted ankle.

Madame Borelli returned. 'I told them we know it was an accident. They go away.' Noting Holmes was about to leave, she attached herself to his arm. 'Mr Holmes, please stay.'

'Madame, if you don't mind,' said he, attempting to disengage.

But the lady clung to his arm. She turned to her husband. 'Mr Holmes is very good, Dario. Some say he is like magic. In his profession.'

Just then the stagehand returned with some items that could serve as a splint. I chose a wooden ruler and set about breaking it in half. 'Holmes, I will need your help,' I said. I did not want to be left here with this explosive fellow. 'Hold this piece of ruler just here, while I wrap this around.' I indicated the makeshift splint and a strip of fabric. Reluctantly, Holmes complied.

'Ha, you are "like magic", she say?' Borelli challenged Holmes. 'Do you know, then, what is the secret of my success? Why I am the Great Borelli? Who next year will be playing in Prince Albert Hall?'

'Let me suggest it is not due to your diligent stage personnel,' said Holmes, 'or your immense personal charm.'

'One time only, Falco, he leave the tank. This never happen before and will never happen again! Believe me, I make sure. Now, enough. But why am I great? The secret of my success? You will never guess!'

'That is true. I never guess.'

'What, then are you a genius?'

Holmes glanced up at Borelli. I recognized that look. There would be trouble.

'You have six attributes. Three of which, of course, are quite common.'

'Only six? Ha! Name them.'

'The first is showmanship – that is, a well-written patter, delivered with a certain panache. Second, custom props: special, pre-rigged equipment, a kind of cheat.'

'This is no cheat!'

Unruffled, my friend continued. 'Pre-rigged equipment has not much to do with skill. One can purchase, for example, the floating lady illusion or—'

Borelli shot a quick angry glance at his wife. 'All my equipment is made by me!'

'Designed by your wife, I understand.' Holmes turned to me as though I'd asked for an explanation. 'Pre-rigged tricks are the kind that creative artists, such as Madame here, sell to lesser magicians, Watson. Special boxes, tables, card decks. Guillotines that *seem* to cut off fingers.'

At the mention of the guillotine, Borelli glanced again at his wife.

'Yes, I told you I consult about Santo's accident,' she said. 'I gave him *all* the details. Mr Holmes will find who sabotaged Santo's trick, and Santo will stop troubling you.' When he grimaced, she pleaded, 'Dario, listen.'

Holmes had warmed to the topic. 'The table is rather well done, Madame. Flicking the scarf, for example, as he disposes of the teacup and then the rabbit into a hidden pocket.'

The hidden pockets again! I wondered what happened afterwards and looked about the dressing room in concern, until I spotted the baby rabbit in a small cage, happily chewing some greens. Madame Borelli caught my concern.

'A very soft bag for little Peter,' offered Madame, moving to the cage to peer in at her tiny charge. She looked up at me. 'My illusions will never harm a living creature.'

'*My* illusions,' shouted Borelli.

Madame smiled at us out of sight of her husband.

I returned my attention to the ankle. Her illusions would never harm a creature . . . except, perhaps, her boorish husband. That thought gave rise to a sudden suspicion. As I tightened the bandage around Borelli's ankle, he jerked again, sending the makeshift splint awry.

'Hold still, Mr Borelli! Holmes, press down here, and do not let go.'

'I am not a nurse, Watson.'

'Try,' I said, sharply.

'You say I have six special somethings. You name two only,' said Borelli.

'The third is also common,' said Holmes. 'Misdirection. You direct the audience's attention to the wrong thing.'

'*Pah*, you read in a book. Every fool thinks they understand this. But any faker on the street can make money with a shell game.'

Holmes carried on, undaunted. 'Lock-picking is your fourth bird in hand, and here you pull ahead of your competition. I have read that regulation police handcuffs are child's play to you.'

'You think this is magic?'

'No. It is a skill acquired with a great deal of practice and research. You are a master at picking most known locks. Even a Chubb, if I am not mistaken.'

'You flatter me. But you miss the main point. Nothing can restrain me! Not just the locks. Ropes, chains, a strait-jacket. Bandages wound around me like the mummy. I will escape from anything.'

'Indeed, I have read of your exploits. You have been bound upside down. Hung off buildings. Underwater. Buried alive. However, your ankle cuffs tonight required your fifth skill.'

Borelli cried out in pain as I manipulated the broken ankle. 'Finish quickly, you, Doctor!' Then, to Holmes, 'What fifth skill?'

Holmes continued, his enthusiasm growing, 'Physical cultivation has turned you into a man of steel – but in addition, you are nearly double-jointed. An extremely rare combination.'

Borelli laughed. 'Watch!' he exclaimed. 'The mirror, Ilaria!' She picked up a large mirror and moved behind him so that we could easily see his back. Leaning forward he made the prayer sign over his heart, then circling his arms behind his back, made the identical sign *behind his back, fingertips reaching skyward.*

'My God!' I exclaimed. 'That is impossible!'

'And yet there it is,' said Holmes. 'Astonishing! May I touch your arm?'

Borelli looked up, startled at this. To my surprise he said, 'Come. Touch. Marvel.' He raised his arm as if displaying a trophy.

Holmes moved around to grasp Borelli's upper arm. He felt the man's biceps, nodding in admiration. Patted him on the back. 'Like a rock. You are indeed an unusual specimen, sir!'

Borelli shrugged, nodding. 'How long will this take to heal, Doctor?'

'You must stay off of it for a month,' said I. 'After that—'

'That is too long,' said Borelli. 'I have many shows to perform.'

Holmes remained standing next to Borelli, 'Will that splint hold, do you think, Watson?' he asked, leaning over Borelli and tapping it.

'Ah! Get away, you! And hurry, *dottore*, be finished,' the magician demanded. Then, to Holmes, 'What is number six, in the list, you are so smart?'

Holmes stepped back and crossed his arms. 'Number six is your wife. Madame Borelli is your ace in the hole.'

Borelli shot a quick, dismissive glance at his wife. 'Ilaria? She help me, of course. Some. But no.'

'I am finished here, sir.' I stood up. 'Shall we be off, Holmes?'

'You are not so smart, Mr Detective. Most people think they see my illusions, but they do not see,' said Borelli.

'Perhaps,' said Holmes. 'But I did see you pick Watson's pocket as he examined you.'

'Dario!' exclaimed his wife. 'What did you take? Show us!'

Borelli grinned at his wife and shrugged as if he had no idea what Holmes was on about.

I patted my pockets in alarm. 'My keys! Mr Borelli, that is hardly sporting of you!' I cried. 'Give me those, sir!'

'Shame, Dario, these men try to help you,' said Madame. 'Give the gentleman his keys!'

Borelli laughed, delighted at his little joke, then reached into his pocket. He stopped, surprised. He patted the other pockets in alarm. He looked up at Holmes and his eyes widened in shock.

There in Holmes's hand were my keys! Holmes handed them to me. He'd stolen them from the thief himself.

I expected an explosion, but to my surprise, the arrogant fellow laughed. 'Not too bad,' he said. Then his laugh died in his throat. 'Wait! What is that?'

Holmes was holding a hotel key in the air. 'Yours, I believe, sir?' Holmes handed Borelli his own key. The magician snatched it away.

Holmes turned to go, then paused, turning back. 'And your handkerchief, sir?' He flicked a white handkerchief from his pocket and held it in the air.

Madame Borelli took it, amused. Holmes patted his trouser pockets and pulled out a third item. 'Oh dear me!

And this Ace of Diamonds. I believe this is yours as well.'
He handed Borelli the playing card.

'Get out,' said the magician. 'All of you.'

CHAPTER 10

A Lady's Desire

e found ourselves ousted summarily and standing in the hallway, from which we had a view onto the empty stage. Madame Borelli rushed out, and taking Holmes's arm said, 'Oh, Mr Holmes, I am so sorry. I hope you will help us. Help me. Please, we will not tell Dario. You must find out who caused Santo Colangelo's accident.'

Holmes looked at her strangely.

'Colangelo's? His cut finger is your concern, rather than the culprit behind tonight's fiasco that nearly killed your husband?'

'Yes . . . er . . . mainly, yes.'

I did not follow the lady's reasoning. Nor did my friend, evidently.

'You know, then, this evening's perpetrator?' asked Holmes.

'No!'

'Explain yourself, Madame.'

Behind her, Falco Fricano and two other stagehands were clearing away the Great Borelli's props and equipment. 'Please, wait one moment,' said Madame Borelli as she strode onto the stage. She had a word with Fricano, who shrugged and began to direct the others.

Holmes had clearly overheard something. 'You are preparing another act?' said he incredulously, as the lady returned to us.

She again took hold of Holmes's arm. 'Dario will insist. Sitting down, of course. We will be very careful. But Mr Holmes . . . Santo Colangelo hates Dario, it is true, and Dario may change his mind and tell the police his suspicions. Then they will arrest Santo. Santo, he is angry enough to do this, and the police will see.'

'But your husband did not want the police!' I said.

The lady shrugged. 'He maybe want to handle himself. I fear this.'

'Your Dario is unpredictable, Madame Borelli. Of course, Mr Colangelo does have a clear motive, if your husband caused his career-changing accident.'

'Yes, but I think Santo did not do this to Dario.'

'And so?'

'I would like you to confirm.'

'To investigate your former lover with an eye to clearing him?'

'Yes, please. And also to be sure Dario did not harm Santo with the guillotine.'

'You want me to investigate both stage accidents? And if I discover the two men are waging a vendetta?'

She hesitated. Her face clouded. 'I . . . well I suppose then you must tell the police.' A reasonably believable tear appeared in one eye. She wiped it away.

'Of course, then both would go to gaol, Madame,' said Holmes. 'Which might well be convenient for you, given that your interests look to the future.'

Holmes stared at the woman in a fashion that I had seen unnerve the sternest barrister and the most violent street thug.

Madame Borelli met the challenge. 'Mr Holmes, why you look at me so?' she demanded.

'If that lock was rigged tonight, and I could not spot it, then it took a real expert to do so.'

'Yes.'

'I expect you could name more than one suspect with the skills needed to sabotage that one lock tonight.'

'I . . . I am not sure.'

'Madame, I believe you have one or even more definite ideas.'

'I do not wish to point the finger.'

The finger. A lot of fingers involved in this case!

'For example, if not Santo Colangelo, it might be your new lover?' asked Holmes.

'What? How do you know I have a—'

'It is your pattern. As I said, you are looking to the future. You are out of love with your husband. We have covered this ground. And he treats you badly. Also, you brought me his secret files. That was not a loving act. Rather a self-serving one. You perhaps wish for your own recognition eventually? And his arrogance was on clear display tonight. Is the Great Borelli's replacement in view?'

'You overstep, sir, attempting to work your magic—'

'Not magic, simple observation. Is your new lover a stage conjurer?'

'All right. You are too smart for me. Well, he is not exactly a conjuror but he has ideas for the magic. A young professor of the science. There is a future.'

'I see. The pattern again. And you will make him a star?'

She was taken aback by this. 'We have some interesting ideas, he and I. He is no performer. Yet. But very handsome, Mr Holmes. A bit young. But . . . why you look at me this way? You disapprove, I see.'

'Madame, I have no opinion on your personal life. However, you must realize that with your young professor on the horizon, this makes you a prime suspect in tonight's dramatic events?'

The lady laughed. 'Mr Holmes,' she said quietly. 'If I wanted Dario to die, you can believe me that he would be dead already, and no one would know how, why or who. Even you.'

Holmes was silent.

'Sir – *Dario mio*, I can handle. I wish him no harm. Nor Santo Colangelo. Please, Mr Holmes, clear both men of this vendetta, if indeed they are innocent, then I can leave knowing one will not destroy the other. I leave each man better than he was before we met. That is my pattern. *Do you see, sir?*'

Holmes considered this. 'Of course, there is a third possibility. The "Great Borelli" might have engineered his own mishap, tonight? Perhaps with the help of that Falco Fricano?'

'Possible.'

'If so, it went a little bit wrong?'

'Yes, went a little wrong.'

'But why would your husband do such a thing?'

'Dario maybe want attention and sympathy and to point finger at Santo Colangelo, make him go to gaol. But I do not know. You will make clear, no? All will be resolved.'

'Madame, I have already agreed to visit Santo Colangelo. You said there could be one or two other suspects. Give me those names, please.'

'Later. But first, I hire you to clear Santo. Then Dario and Santo will stop trying to harm the other.'

'This is highly unusual, Madame. No promises. Watson, shall we?'

We were shortly in a hansom cab on the way back to Baker Street. As the cab pulled away from Wilton's Music Hall, the faint, intermittent gaslights of Whitechapel washed dimly across Holmes's keen, ascetic features.

'A strange woman,' remarked my friend. 'I am not entirely convinced *she* is not the culprit tonight. What do you think, Watson?'

'I suppose it is possible.'

'But you do not think so, Doctor?'

'No. I rather like her.'

Holmes did not reply but looked out of the window. The few trees lining the streets drooped from the day's heat, their parched leaves lit faintly by the streetlamps. Even at this late hour the temperature was oppressive, and I could feel a drop of sweat making its way down my back.

Holmes closed his eyes. 'Unlikely, perhaps. I do believe her when she says that she could have dispatched her boorish husband earlier and without clues, if she so chose. She is more than capable.' He paused, then opened his eyes. 'If he did not engineer his own mishap tonight, Borelli is a fool to keep performing with this mystery hanging over him.'

'Don't you find Madame sympathetic, though, Holmes?'

He looked out of the window again. 'No. Intriguing, perhaps. But I will admit I am mildly curious about this case of warring magicians. I shall give it more consideration tomorrow. In the meantime, I hope Mrs Hudson has replenished the ice. I would appreciate something chilled after tonight's little adventure.'

'Indeed!' I said, with sudden visions of a lemonade and perhaps a splash of gin, and a long sleep following.

But it was not to be.

PART THREE

THE DOLL

'I am turned into a sort of
machine for observing facts and
grinding out conclusions.'
—Charles Darwin

CHAPTER 11

The Floating Doll

fter midnight, Holmes and I sat together near the fireplace in shirtsleeves over our last drink. The cold hearth was filled with ash from the disposal of Holmes's papers earlier in the day. The windows were wide open to catch the faintest cooling breezes. Outside, the tumult of Baker Street had settled into a calmer rhythm—the night soil men attending to those very few near us still without plumbing, the policeman making rounds, the dairy carts, a few late revellers.

Both of us had difficulty sleeping in this heat. At least the floor had been cleared, and stacks of papers in the corners were all that remained of Holmes's recent flurry. The straitjacket had been taken down, and I noted a few other touches that indicated Mrs Hudson had followed our efforts with a few of her own.

We had continued to discuss the mysterious Borellis. Holmes was unwilling to drop the subject. 'It is a bit of a hornet's nest, Watson. Madame has not been fully forthcoming. I sense an agenda.'

'A benign agenda, then,' I said. 'Madame seems to be a magician's angel.'

'By her own description, and yet fickle. The magicians are a tight but jealous community. They steal from each other regularly, and their temperaments are often volatile. When you combine the performer's ego with the mechanical ability and focus it takes to do stage conjuring, the result can be a dangerous combination.'

'A magician would make an excellent thief, I would imagine,' I added.

'Or murderer,' said Holmes.

There was the sound of loud knocking downstairs. Who might it be at this hour?

I answered, not wishing to disturb our dedicated landlady. To my great surprise it was Deacon Buttons, returned with a large canvas sack and looking much the worse for wear. His clothes were damp and wrinkled, his hair plastered to his head, his face white, eyes distended in panic. He looked as if he had been dunked in a river before running directly onto a train to London. As it turned out, that was almost exactly what had happened.

'Calm down, Deacon, and begin again,' said Holmes in a soothing tone, once the young man was seated before us, panting slightly from exertion and the heat. I handed him a whisky. The fellow took a big gulp, then choked and began coughing violently, his face going bright red.

'Watson, perhaps some soda, if you would?' said Holmes.

After a minute or two, the young man had gathered his wits enough to speak.

'Please, Mr Holmes. It is dire. Dillie . . . she is in trouble. In danger, I am sure of it. I was walking along . . . along the river tonight . . .'

'Near the Wyndhams' home, then?'

The young man flushed. 'Well, yes, actually . . .'

'Something you do regularly?'

'Mr Holmes, please! I was walking along the river. I passed the Jesus Lock and I saw something white floating in the water.'

My stomach lurched.

'Here it is!' From his canvas satchel, he pulled a bedraggled object, a lace dress, a tiny hand, a—

'A baby doll,' said Holmes. 'And—?'

'This is Dillie's doll. It was specially made to look like her. It normally sits on her bed!'

Holmes's eyebrow lifted slightly at this, and my own suspicions followed. Had this deacon been in her bedroom?

'Give it to me,' said Holmes.

But the deacon clutched it to his chest. 'The arm is missing,' he said.

'May I?' I asked calmly. 'It is late.'

Reluctantly, the young man let go of the soggy object. It was twisted, all in a tangle. The head, right arm and legs were hard, the body soft and limp. The doll's long blonde hair was wet and matted, the head askew.

I handed it to Holmes, who drew a light closer and wiggled the remaining arm. He stared at the doll, intrigued.

Holmes lifted the white lace dress and there on the cloth body was a large stain of dark, purplish blue, spread out from the centre and lighter on the edges. Holmes brought his magnifying glass to the stain. 'Something has been written here,' he said. 'Unfortunately, not in waterproof ink. Too bad. This perpetrator, whomever he might be, is lacking in finesse. Six lines of similar length, aligned on the left but not the right. A poem, perhaps. I can make out only two words on the right. One is either "word" or "Lord". The other is "page" or perhaps "rage".'

Holmes set the doll on the table while still gazing at it. It was so soggy that the dress, hanging over the edge, dripped upon the floor. I looked about for something to catch the drips. I located a crystal bowl of peaches on the mantel, removed the fruit, and placed it under the doll.

'Oh, Mr Holmes,' said Buttons. 'I fear this is a sign that there is danger to Dillie, that someone has her and—'

'What is your theory about this doll's appearance?'

'I don't know. Perhaps it is cry for help from Dillie herself.'

'And so your theory is that she was abducted with her doll and a pen? Carried to the Jesus Lock where she wrote on it, then threw this in—'

'Or from a boat, going through—'

'Would she be able to do this, but be unable to scream for help? This makes no sense, Deacon.'

The young man buried his head in his hands and sobbed. Holmes shook his head in frustration, then rose and stepped towards the fireplace where he busied himself with his pipe. He nodded to me, indicating that I could be of help.

I moved to the young man and took Holmes's chair facing him. 'Mr Buttons,' I said gently. 'Look at me.'

The young man did so.

'We both realize that you are genuinely concerned about Miss Wyndham's safety. That is not in question. But we need to be assured that yours is a complete and truthful account of how you came upon this object.'

The young man attempted to control his tears, wiping his face with his handkerchief.

'I did not place the doll in the lock. I saw it floating in there and retrieved it, just as I described. You must believe me. I ran to the Wyndham house with it first. I woke the maid. We both went to Dillie's room to confirm it was her doll.'

'But you knew it was her doll before this,' said Holmes. 'How?'

'I – well, I—'

'You have been in her room?'

'No. Yes. I . . . Well, yes. Once.'

'Under what pretext?'

'I, er, had been asked to look in on Mrs Wyndham. She was ill. Her room is upstairs—'

'And you happened to pass Dillie's room?'

'The door was open and I . . . yes, sir, I did look in.'

Holmes looked sharply at the deacon. 'Continue with recent events.'

'The maid confirmed the doll was Dillie's. She begged me

to come to you. Really, sirs, it is all true. When I left, the maid was just about to wake the household. I am sure they are all alarmed now. Perhaps they have even called the police!'

'And yet you took the evidence away and hurried to London to consult with me,' said Holmes.

'I am worried that no one there will take this seriously.'

'That contradicts what you have just said about the maid and the family, Deacon. You realize, of course, that you have given us every reason to doubt you?' Holmes asked sharply.

The young man stood up. 'I suppose this was a wasted journey, then, sir?'

I stood to accompany him to the door. He was the picture of dejection.

'I understand that you occasionally take cases *gratis*. I . . . had hoped to hire you, Mr Holmes. But I have no money of my own.'

I took him by the arm and gently propelled him into the hallway. 'It is not a matter of money, Deacon. Mr Holmes is quite busy at present. But do keep us informed, please,' said I, attempting to soften the blow. 'We shall be all ears.'

'Just a moment, Watson,' said Holmes.

Deacon Buttons and I paused on the landing to face my friend.

'Call it an instinct. Call it whatever you wish, Watson, but whatever the story is behind this doll . . . there is something chilling in the very fact of it. I have decided to investigate.'

'Oh, thank you, Mr Holmes!' cried Buttons.

'But Madame Borelli?' I said.

'In time, Watson. I believe we can quickly wrap things up in Cambridge. But I would like to satisfy my curiosity on one or two points. This missing young lady may indeed be in danger. Book us a train, would you please?'

The deacon closed his eyes in relief and offered up a prayer.

Without another word, I reached for our *Bradshaw* and attended to worldly matters. The last train to Cambridge had departed. It would have to wait until morning.

CHAPTER 12

The Wyndhams

fter a few short hours of sleep, with the deacon stretched out on our divan in the sitting-room and the windows wide open to catch any breath of air, the three of us departed for the ancient town early the next morning. The Indian summer days were still long, and the sun was up when we arrived shortly after six. After securing a driver at the station, we raced through Cambridge's dusty streets. Early morning light slanted off the strange mix of ancient and modern architecture as we headed directly for the Wyndham residence, located in a favourable riverside location at the city's northern end.

When we arrived, it was still early, but the police were in attendance at an impressive three-storey stone house, one surly looking officer placed at the door. An expensive brougham, trimmed in red, stood between the front door and a small stable off to one side.

Wyndham was evidently a wealthy and important man.

Holmes, the deacon and I alighted from our carriage and my friend took us both by the arm, directing us away from the house and towards an adjacent carriage house.

'Where are we going?' I asked.

'Shh.' Indicating we should wait for him behind this building, out of sight of the Wyndhams', Holmes left us and went around the back of the main house. I noted him examining the ground, pulling his magnifying glass from his pocket as he did so. He disappeared round the back of the house and was gone for a full five minutes. The deacon looked increasingly uncomfortable.

'What is he doing?' he asked, shifting uncomfortably from one foot to the other. 'Shouldn't we be talking to family?'

'In time, Mr Buttons,' I said. Holmes, I surmised, must have been looking for clues of anyone who might have breached the house surreptitiously to take the doll.

Presently he returned, apparently satisfied, and we proceeded to the Wyndhams' front door. The frowning sergeant regarded us coldly. The man was sallow, with thinning hair the colour of dirty laundry water, and had upon his bony face a look of permanent indigestion. He glanced at the damp sack containing the doll. 'There it is! Wait here, Buttons,' he snarled, and disappeared into the house, locking the door behind him. He brought to mind a scurrying lizard.

Holmes eyed the deacon. 'Who was that?'

'Sergeant Pickering. He's not a very kind—'

'I take it you did not ask permission of anyone in the police to remove the doll?'

Before he could answer, the reptilian Pickering returned with a senior officer of perhaps fifty. This older man, a tall, well-built and nattily attired fellow with red muttonchops greying at the temples and the eyes of a hawk, gave us one angry glance, then focused on the canvas bag. 'Give us that, Deacon Buttons!' he roared. 'How dare you remove a valuable clue to whatever has transpired? Just because you found it, it was not yours to take!'

'Inspector H-H-Hadley. Let me explain,' stammered the deacon.

Pickering grabbed the bag and opened it for his superior. Satisfied the doll was there, Hadley waved it away. 'Take that inside, Sergeant, and give it to Mrs Wyndham,' he ordered.

The unpleasant Pickering favoured us with a venomous look and departed.

Hadley took in Holmes and me with a critical glance. 'And who the devil are you two? Londoners, by the look of you.'

'This is the esteemed detective Mr Sherlock Holmes, and his associate Dr Watson,' said the deacon. 'I – I – brought the doll to London. To induce Mr Holmes to help find Miss Wyndham.'

'Sherlock Holmes, you say? The London, er, crime solver, detective, or whatever it is that you do. I seem to have read something, somewhere.' While Holmes's achievements had occasionally made the papers, at this time he was not yet widely known outside of law enforcement. Inspector Hadley stared hard at my friend as though he could read a man's worth by this look, or perhaps diminish it by his dismissive gaze.

Holmes did not flinch but smiled warmly. 'Ah, are you Inspector George Hadley, then? I have heard of you, sir! You solved the case of the stolen artefacts intended for the new Fitzwilliam Museum. A matched pair of Roman vases worth an untold fortune, if I remember correctly. A puzzle and great distress for the donor's family – but brilliantly handled.'

Hadley melted visibly at the flattery. 'Indeed, I did,' said he. 'It made the London papers, did it?'

I remembered nothing of this, but Holmes smoothly replied, 'I make it a point to keep up on excellent police-work. You, sir, are well thought of in London.' While this clearly soothed the senior officer, the disagreeable young Pickering reappeared behind him and stared at us with obvious suspicion.

'I will admit to having heard your name before,' said Hadley. 'I am friends with Jones and Lestrade up in London. All right then, come in, meet the family.' He turned and went into the house.

Holmes followed him, but the younger policeman barred me at the door. 'Wait right here, mister,' said he. 'We don't need all manner of people disturbing the Wyndhams.'

Holmes appeared over his shoulder in an instant. 'Mr

Pickering, this is Dr John Watson. He is my colleague and assists me in my work. It is both or none.'

The officious fellow paused, his lip curling in distaste. He stifled himself, however, and stepped aside. As Buttons attempted to follow, Pickering put up a hand. 'Not you. Go back to your church. The police will summon you if needed.'

Buttons hesitated.

'Go. That is an order,' said Pickering.

Professor and Mrs Wyndham awaited us in a grand but slightly shabby salon littered with papers, books, and notable for an enormous marble head, an ancient Greek goddess perhaps. She appeared to be glowering at the gathering from a stand in one corner with those ghostly, vacant eyes possessed by all old statues.

'Professor Wyndham,' said Hadley, deferentially. 'I have brought in the esteemed London detective, Mr Sherlock Holmes. And his, er . . .'

'—colleague, Dr John Watson,' said Holmes smoothly.

Professor Richard Anderson Wyndham, an enormous, muscular and handsome man of about sixty, leaned back on a red velvet sofa, relaxed as though he were passing a normal Sunday afternoon in anticipation of a good roast. En route Holmes had mentioned another fact about the fellow. Despite his esteemed academic credentials, Wyndham was known by his students as 'the Blustering Berry Bulwark' for his red-faced temper tantrums while teaching. But at this moment the don reclined languidly, his arms spread wide along the back of the sofa, appearing not the least bit worried. As he turned away from us to snap his fingers at a maid hovering in the doorway, he revealed his long white hair brushed into a plume at the back of his head like the bottom of a duck.

He slowly turned to regard us, with his head tilted backwards, managing to look down his long nose at us, even from a seated position.

'That was prescient of you, Hadley. An "esteemed" man, you say? Are you out of your depth already?' he drawled. Echoes of Eton and years in the Ivory Tower coloured his speech. He turned to my companion and eyed him slowly from head to toe. 'Sherlock Holmes? Never heard of you.'

'It is well you have not had the occasion, sir,' said Holmes, more respectfully than his usual manner with such pedants. 'My trade is a sad and difficult one.'

'He is a private detective, sir,' said Hadley, somewhat more stiffly. 'Something of a London legend,' he added.

'Consulting detective,' said Holmes, amiably.

Before the don could reply, Holmes turned smoothly to Mrs Wyndham, a wan creature of fifty or so who sat stiffly on a velvet chair nearby, holding the doll at arm's length, with tears coursing down her pale face. I noted she was wearing what appeared to be expensive lace bedclothes. A maid had rushed over to her to hand her a fresh handkerchief and to place a towel under the object, still damp from its immersion in the River Cam.

Mrs Wyndham handed the doll to the maid and dabbed at her tears.

'Madam,' said Holmes, 'if I may be so forward with you. Can you confirm that the doll is your daughter Odelia's?'

The lady looked up at Holmes. She glanced quickly at her husband, then replied, 'Yes. It is Dillie's. I had it made to resemble her.' Her voice was a mere whisper. I wondered if she was ill, and if so, with what. She was pale but did not look emaciated or jaundiced. And although she was crying, her breathing did not have the sound of the consumptive's.

'At what time was the doll discovered missing?'

Mrs Wyndham began to respond but her husband over-rode her. 'Ten-thirty last night. We were all abed!' he said in disgust.

'Is your daughter in the habit of disappearing from time to time?' asked Holmes.

Again, Mrs Wyndham started to speak but her husband cleared his throat loudly. She seemed to shrink in her chair.

'Odelia is incorrigible. Yes, she is in the habit,' Wyndham said.

'Then you are perhaps less worried than you might be, sir?' asked Holmes.

'I was not worried, particularly,' said the supercilious father. 'But in the matter of this doll, I suppose one must take note.'

'Do you know where she has gone on the other occasions, by chance?'

'I have no idea and no desire to know. I have given up on Odelia. Fortunately, it does not seem to have ruined her chances. Young men today are less interested in the past history of their brides. Ianthia, here, was as pure as the driven – well, in any case, I do not know about Odelia. If the police approve, then go about your business here, Mr Holmes. I suppose if you've bothered to make the journey, you might as well. Now, if you do not mind, Mrs Wyndham and I have business to attend to.'

His wife started and looked at him in alarm.

'Life goes on, dear one,' he said without a trace of warmth. 'The student luncheon will proceed. Get dressed, Ianthia, and see to the final preparations.' He stood up and turned to face us. 'I am hosting a luncheon with my very best young men.'

A fresh stream of tears burst forth from Mrs Wyndham, and the same maid leaned in with a second dry handkerchief. She helped Mrs Wyndham to her feet.

'Pull yourself together, Ianthia,' the professor said crisply. The maid led the feeble woman from the room. Holmes and I exchanged a glance.

'May I have a look at Miss Wyndham's rooms, please?' said Holmes.

The professor waved a dismissive hand at my friend, then called out, 'Polly!' A pale young servant with red hair and a starched cap rushed in and curtseyed nervously to us. 'Show them to Miss Odelia's room. Hadley, a moment, please,' he said to the senior policeman.

He gave Holmes a hard look. 'I don't know who is paying you, Mr Holmes, but it will not be me. Be out of here within the hour, before the students arrive,' he ordered, and departed the room.

CHAPTER 13

Polly

e were escorted upstairs by the young servant. Holmes paused in the hallway at the entrance to the missing girl's sitting-room, and beyond it, her bedroom. He glanced across the hall to what looked like a similar suite, but this one with a closed door leading into the bedroom. 'Her sister's rooms?' Holmes asked the girl.

'Yes. Miss Atalanta.'

'Older?'

'By two years. Atalanta is twenty.'

We next entered Dillie's sitting-room, and we passed through to her bedroom. It was a large, airy room, with windows on two walls, the leaves of a large plane tree next to the window providing a lacy screen through which another grove of trees was visible at some distance. Behind that, the beautiful Cam glittered in the bright morning sun. The furniture, including the canopy bed, was all in white, and the bed was made up. On it sat several dolls, with a vacancy where the drowned doll must have resided.

Holmes's magnifying glass was out, and he began his typically minute examination of the room. He started with the windows, opening each in turn and examining the sills. As I waited for him to do this, I perused the bookshelves. In addition to Greek and Roman history volumes, which I assumed had been influenced by her famous father, there were the usual Jane Austen, George Eliot and Dickens. But there were also two colourful rows of novels and poetry I did not recognize, presumably aimed at young ladies. They had titles such as *Penelope's Terrible Surprise*, *The Tragedy of Annie LaMonte* and *Faded Blossoms*.

I looked idly at Dillie's dressing table. It was impeccably neat. In fact, the entire room was.

Holmes asked the maid for a glass of water, then as soon as she was gone he went through the bookshelves like an automaton, stopping to study the colourful collection of girls' novels. He examined one or two, opened one, lingered upon it briefly, then pocketed it. From another pocket he retrieved a small notebook and silver pencil and made some notes.

He then looked under the bed, examined the carpet, and inside the closet. He was looking through the lady's shoes when the maid returned.

'Holmes,' I signalled.

He looked up and smiled at the nervous girl. 'Ah, my water. Please come in and tell us your name,' said he.

'Polly,' said the maid with a slight curtsy. She served him a glass from a silver tray. She was a fresh-faced girl of perhaps sixteen, with red hair tucked away in a neat knot under her maid's cap, freckled hands clenching the tray.

'I am Sherlock Holmes, and this is Dr Watson. You are a ladies' maid, then?'

'Yes, sir. For Miss Odelia and Miss Atalanta.'

I noticed the girl's distinct discomfort. 'You may be wondering why we are here,' I said. 'Miss Odelia's doll was found in the Jesus Lock, Polly. We are concerned for her safety, and we hope to discover something that will help us find her.'

The girl nodded.

Holmes, in his usual manner, leapt in. 'I understand that your Dillie, er, Miss Odelia, disappears on a regular basis?' said he.

'I wouldn't say "regular", sir, but yes, she has done so before.'

Holmes moved to Miss Wyndham's dressing table. 'Where is her hairbrush? Something to clean her teeth? Pomade? Powder? A number of personal items one expects to see are missing from this table, are they not?'

The maid remained silent.

Holmes scanned the room. 'There is no sign of violence here. She was not abducted; she packed to go somewhere,' said Holmes. 'That is a good sign. Might she have taken the doll with her?'

'No, sir. She never liked that doll, sir.'

Holmes looked up sharply at her. 'Then the doll was still here on Monday?'

The girl nodded.

'When did you notice it gone?'

'Er . . . Tuesday, sir.'

'When exactly?'

'Night. Nine-thirty, sir.'

'What were you doing in her room on Tuesday night?'

The girl shifted uncomfortably. 'I often checks all the rooms, sir, afore I goes to bed. To make sure no lights are left lit. Close the windows.'

'What did you do when you discovered the doll missing?'

'I felt sick. Somebody were in the room. Secret, like. I was scared.'

'Perhaps Dillie herself returned for her doll?'

'No, sir. Like I said.' A shy smile. 'It's her mother likes dolls, not Miss Odelia.'

Holmes shrugged. 'But anyone could come in. What about her sister? Or Mrs Wyndham? Why did you not first think of a family member?'

The girl hesitated. 'That window.' She pointed to the largest, adjacent to the tree.

'It was open?'

'Yes, a little.'

'But not when you tidied the room earlier?'

'No, sir.'

Holmes moved to the window, examined the lock, opened, shut it. He stood motionless for a few seconds, then turned back to the girl with that piercing stare that intimidated all who encountered it.

'Excellent, Polly. And what of yesterday? When Deacon Buttons arrived at this house with the drowned and dismembered doll. What time was that, I forget?'

Of course, Holmes forgot nothing. The girl hesitated. He did not take his eyes from her.

'Nine, or so,' said she.

'Mrs Wyndham did not hear of the doll until ten-thirty,' he said. 'Where were you in the hour and a half between Deacon Buttons arriving with it, and when her parents were informed?'

The girl froze, eyes wide.

Holmes sighed, then made an effort to soften his approach. His voice took on a gentler tone. 'You were not worried about Dillie before this, Polly?'

'N-not really, sir.'

'Young lady, I believe you know more than you are telling us. This doll is disturbing. Your mistress may now be in danger. I suggest that you know where she is hiding, and between nine, when the drowned doll showed up here with the deacon, and ten-thirty, when the Wyndhams were informed, you went to see if she was all right. And you took the doll with you so that Deacon Buttons could not alert the parents just yet. But she was not there, and you became worried. You then returned to the house and alerted her mother. Have I got that right?'

The girl was preternaturally still, like a small wild animal that wishes to be invisible.

'I take that as a yes. How is it that Deacon Buttons allowed you to run off with the doll?'

'I just did it, afore he could stop me. He found me on the way back though. He offered to escort me through the streets, so as I would not get caught again, and—'

'Caught?'

The girl looked down and blushed.

'Caught by whom?'

She hesitated. Then, 'The proctor's men.'

'Oh, yes, of course, I had forgotten,' said Holmes.

At my puzzled look, Holmes explained. 'There is a kind of private police force run by proctors from the University. In the interest of keeping "moral order", they arrest random young women seen to be consorting with students after curfew. An indiscriminate sweep, I am told. Many are shop-girls, servants, innocent working girls. They hold them without charges in private prison called the Spinning House.'

And in our modern times! I thought. What an outrage.

'That could be dangerous,' continued Holmes. 'Have you been stopped before, Polly? Perhaps on an errand for your mistress?'

Polly nodded and looked down, ashamed. ''Tweren't her fault, sir. I was stupid. I stopped to ask directions and a young man . . . he . . . he started to show me the way, and I were arrested.' The trembling increased, and a tear escaped her eye and ran down her face. She swiped it away. 'It was a close one, sir. I was let off with a warnin'.'

I wanted to know more of these 'proctor's men', but Holmes pressed on.

'That was fortunate. Yet you risked another arrest last night? Why did you go alone to your mistress?'

'Miss Odelia, she wanted Mr Buttons not to know where she was.'

'I see,' he said. 'That was brave of you. Polly, your mistress may be in a bit of trouble.'

The maid looked at her feet and refused to reply.

'Help us to help her,' Holmes whispered.

Polly stole a glance up at him. It was telling, even to my eyes.

'Hello,' came a low-pitched, female voice from the doorway.

CHAPTER 14

CHAPTER 14

Atalanta

e turned to see a tall, willowy young woman with short, curly dark hair, clothed in an expensive lacy nightgown and velvet dressing gown. Her face was translucently pale, and while nearly my height, she was slender and wiry, with something of the woodland sprite about her. Not exactly beautiful, but striking in her way. The older sister, of course. I wondered why she was still abed at this hour. Her eyes shone with either fever or something else. That and her short hair suggested she might be suffering or recovering from some illness.

She placed a hand on either side of the doorway, her voluminous, lace-trimmed sleeves flopping back, revealing finely muscled porcelain arms. She smiled at us in an overly bright manner I found unnerving.

Except for the mother, these Wyndhams were all of a kind with their studied posturing, I thought.

'Who are you?' she asked, taking in both of us.

'Atalanta Wyndham, I presume?' said Holmes, glancing up from where he was examining Odelia's shoes with an air of distraction.

'I am she.'

He shrugged and returned to his inspection of a fine silk slipper.

'Have we awakened you?' I asked.

'No,' the young woman said. 'But I write, you see, sometimes all night long. Now, about you, sirs. Are you from the police?'

Holmes, without turning, waved to me to answer her, and continued his inspection of the missing girl's shoes. Atalanta Wyndham's smile faded instantly at this rudeness.

I stepped forward. 'No, Miss Wyndham, not the police,' I said. 'This is Mr Sherlock Holmes, a consulting detective. I am his colleague, Dr John Watson. We have come up from London in the matter of your missing sister.'

'Well *that* was certainly quick.' She paused, staring at Holmes. 'Mr Sherlock Holmes, you say?' Still he did not respond. 'Mr Holmes, do they not teach you manners in London?'

Not deigning to answer, Holmes stood and returned to the dressing table. He ran his hand underneath it. With the merest glance at the older sister, he asked. 'Did you notice your sister's doll missing yesterday?'

'No.' Atalanta Wyndham's expression had turned icy. 'I

rarely come in here. It was the maid.' She turned to Polly. 'Leave us, Polly,' she said sharply. 'Shoo!'

Polly melted from the room.

'Means well, but really a rather stupid girl,' the young woman said to me. 'I can't help you. My sister is incorrigible.'

Holmes stood up from the dressing table and turned to face the sister. As his eyes took her in, he appeared to be abruptly taken by her beauty. 'Miss Wyndham, please forgive me,' he said in a curiously mollifying tone as if he had suddenly been presented a rare prize. 'I am easily distracted when on a case.' He crossed over to her and took her right hand in his and gently kissed it. As he raised it to his lips, her lacy sleeve fell back once again. All this was grossly out of character, and I wondered at his purpose.

'Miss Wyndham. Author of *Faded Blossoms*!' said Holmes.

I was startled but endeavoured to hide it. This must be the book from her shelf that he had pocketed! Atalanta Wyndham looked pleased and strangely triumphant.

'How did you hear of that, pray tell? I am published, but not widely.'

Holmes danced on. '"December Roses". A perfect sonnet of the Shakespearean type. You show great feeling.'

To my knowledge, Holmes had little use for poetry. The young woman smiled warmly at Holmes. 'Do you like poetry, Mr Holmes?'

He said nothing but smiled.

'When did you have occasion to read my work?'

'I will be honest with you, Miss Wyndham. Just now,'

said Holmes pleasantly, nodding to her sister's bookcase. He removed the book from his pocket, waved it at her and replaced it. The man could charm when he wanted to.

Atalanta Wyndham was clearly entranced, as would be any author whose work garners appreciation, even if just in the moment. She laughed. 'You thought to fool me!'

'You are too intelligent for that. Though I am new to your work, it is quite lovely, Miss Wyndham. I intend to read more. Given the observant eye of the poet, perhaps you might be able to help us, I think?'

Her eyes glanced about the room, and a shadow crossed her face. It was obvious even to me that the sisters were not friends. 'Well, I will certainly try, although I doubt it.'

'I understand your sister goes missing on a regular basis?' said Holmes.

The young woman coughed. The wheeze was familiar. 'Would you like to sit down, Miss?' I asked, noting also a drop of perspiration on her forehead. It could indicate the early stage of consumption.

She waved a dismissive hand at me and remained in the doorway, stifling a second cough. 'She does. Quite often.'

'For how long?'

The girl shrugged. 'One or two days, usually. Some of the time our parents don't even notice. I write at night, mainly. They don't notice that, either.'

'Do they care that your sister runs away?' asked Holmes.

'Our mother might. But she is too busy attending to her own needs,' said Miss Wyndham. 'A lady of constant small woes.' Her smile softened her dismissive comment.

'Ah, understood,' I said.

'And the servants?' asked Holmes.

She rolled her eyes.

'With two invalids in the house, the servants are quite occupied, I would imagine,' I said.

She flashed a look of anger, then willed it away. 'My mother is *not* an invalid. She is just a rather weak person, given to strong emotions.'

'And you, Miss Wyndham,' I said. 'That cough—'

'You overstep, Doctor,' she responded sharply. 'I am both mobile and self-sufficient. As you can easily see.'

Holmes looked at her steadily for a long moment. 'Miss Wyndham, do you have any information about your sister that might help us to find her?' he asked. 'Might there be a young gentleman she is seeing?'

'Only this. Dillie has another place she goes to. It happens often enough. She is, well, she *will do as she pleases*. Always.'

'This other place – do you know where it is?' asked Holmes.

'It is somewhere in town, close by. I know this because she once left, forgot something, came back, and left again. All within an hour. Find it, and you will find her.'

Holmes nodded at me. That fitted with the maid's timeline last night as well. 'Have you anything more for us?' he asked her.

Atalanta Wyndham shrugged.

'You don't seem worried,' said Holmes. 'Do you think that there is a threat to your sister? Her doll was found partially dismembered. Somewhat suggestive, don't you think?'

'How terribly dramatic! Well, let's see, who would dislike my sister? I would wager there is a list.' She laughed at this.

'Do give us your thoughts, Miss Wyndham.'

'You asked about a young man? There are many. She is rather carefree in bestowing her affections, with little thought to their effect.'

'We know, of course, of Mr Frederick Eden-Summers,' said Holmes.

At the mention of this name, a shadow passed across the features of this ethereal young woman. It was gone so quickly that I doubted my perception, but the quality of Atalanta Wyndham's voice changed. It became stronger, more strident. 'A sterling young man. Award-winning sportsman. And of the finest family. Dillie could not do better.'

'A match, then?' prompted Holmes.

'Hardly! My sister does not value his qualities. She treats him abominably.'

Holmes said nothing.

The girl cleared her throat and reverted to her softer voice. 'By her own admission,' she added.

'Ah, a shame. A sportsman, you say. What is his sport?'

'He is an archer. A Woodman of Arden!' she added proudly.

'Impressive! And at quite a young age!' said Holmes. I presumed this was some honorary society of archers.

'His father was a member as well.'

'I see. Does your sister partake in the sport?'

'Dillie? Ha! No. She does play at tennis a bit.' She said this with a hint of disdain. 'I don't know what Freddie sees in her!'

'Freddie?' asked Holmes.

'Mr Eden-Summers and I were childhood friends.'

'I note you are an archer yourself,' said Holmes.

Atalanta Wyndham stepped back in surprise, crossing her arms. 'My parents told you this?'

'No. I merely observe.'

'I still do not see,' she said.

I was glad that for once someone other than me 'saw but did not observe', as Holmes so frequently chided.

'Really quite simple, Miss Wyndham,' said Holmes. 'Before we entered here, I made an inspection of the yard surrounding the house. I noticed that there are several large burlap sacks at the foot of some trees, stuffed with hay. Archery targets, from the holes, and one arrow left embedded. Facing these, I now learn, is your bedroom.'

Atalanta shifted uneasily.

'The angle of that arrow indicated it was shot from above. Unless someone was aiming from the large plane tree that abuts your – and your sister's – bedroom windows, it was shot from one of these windows. That and the evidence on your person, Miss Wyndham, are strongly suggestive.'

'*Evidence on my person?*'

'You do not use an arm guard – but you really should – and have the bowman's scars on your left arm. And the calluses on the fingers of your right drawing hand. Do you

113

only do this in secret then? Shooting from your window, perhaps?'

Knowing Holmes's abilities as I did, nevertheless this train of inferences was impressive. And the notion of this young woman practising archery from her window . . . what a very odd family, I thought.

'I presume you do this at night, as I cannot imagine your parents condoning this activity,' said Holmes. 'Accidents will happen.'

Atalanta Wyndham smiled. 'I shoot at dawn. First light. Only the cook is awake, preparing breakfast – and she is on the other side of the house. My parents keep the rest of the staff working late and have moved their hours to start later in the morning.'

'How convenient. But I thought you stayed up at night to write?'

'I do both,' said she.

'And who retrieves the arrows for you?'

'The gardener.'

'And you compensate him . . . in some way?'

The slender creature drew herself up at this question. 'Sir! You imply impropriety!'

'Not at all, Miss Wyndham, nor did it occur to me. Do you pay him?'

'Yes. What has all this to do with Dillie's disappearance?'

'I do not know which facts pertain until I have them in hand. Earlier you said Dillie has several admirers. Do you know who they might be?'

'Well, at last you attend to the *real* issue,' snapped Atalanta

Wyndham with a toss of her head. 'That young deacon is infatuated with her. Hopeless fool. Buttons, what a stupid name! Then, of course, Mr Eden-Summers – if she hasn't scared him away. And there is another: a science student at St Cedd's. I did glimpse him once, in Dillie's room. His name is Leo Vitale.' She pronounced his name 'vih-tally'.

'Italian name?' said Holmes.

'I suppose. But English now. Pale, glasses. Face of a surprised baby owl. I don't know what she sees in him.'

'Here? Young Mr Vitale visited your sister here?' I blurted out. 'How is it that your parents would allow—'

Holmes held up a hand to silence me. 'Thank you very much, Miss Wyndham, you have been helpful. And have no fear, I will not give away your secret archery practice.' He turned to leave but paused at the door and turned back. 'Oh, but one other question, if you would. Has it rained here in Cambridge in the last few days?'

'No, but I wish it would. This heat is oppressive!'

So, I felt, was the Wyndham family.

We returned downstairs. Holmes asked to speak with Polly, the maid, but we were told she had been sent on an errand. He informed Professor Wyndham that evidence pointed to his daughter Dillie's planned departure, and that he did not believe an abduction had taken place.

Wyndham's response was quick, decisive, and rude. 'Deliver this observation to the police, then, and they will take it from there. If there is no abduction, we have no further need for your services.'

'Professor Wyndham, yet I believe this doll – designed to look like your daughter and found dismembered in the lock – is clearly a kind of message. It could well be a direct threat of bodily harm. I would like to find your daughter and get to the bottom of it.'

'This is a private matter now, and the family will deal with it. Return to London, Mr Holmes, and not a word of this to anyone, or I shall have legal proceedings instituted.'

'Sir,' said Holmes in his chilliest manner, 'your idle threat is uncalled for. I have no interest in bringing shame to anyone. Only to solve a crime where a crime has been committed. Not in this house, apparently.' He turned abruptly and left. I followed.

I was more than happy to depart this strange household.

A servant was sent to fetch us a carriage as we waited near the road some twenty yards from the house.

'What of this doll, Holmes? Who could have put it in the river, and why?'

'I mean to find out.'

'But Madame Borelli?'

'Yes, Watson, I have not forgotten. But the threat here may be more imminent. The severed arm. Cut, not broken. It is an ugly act, after all.'

'Indeed!'

'I am uneasy about Miss Wyndham's three suitors. When a girl of her nature plays with so many hearts . . . I fear the message is a warning. And she clearly has no guidance from her family.'

'How would this fellow have obtained the doll from the girl's room?'

Holmes nodded in the direction of the house. 'Do you see that tree? Its heaviest branch extends directly to one of the windows of Miss Odelia's sitting-room. It would be a simple matter for an agile person to climb in through the window in the cover of darkness.'

Of course, Holmes had examined that area before entering the house. 'You saw footprints at the base, I suppose?' I said.

'Yes, there is evidence of one female and two male climbers. One of the men's boots has a patch on the right sole.'

Just then the maid Polly exited a side door to the house and furtively approached us.

'Sirs?' she began, 'I can give you the address.'

'Ah,' said Holmes, 'I thought so. She is all right, then?'

'She was when I went back to check there this morning.'

'What time?'

'Early. Maybe five?'

'Before dawn. Another risk for you, young lady!'

The girl nodded, embarrassed, then gave Holmes a slip of paper which he passed to me. On it was an address, written in an extremely untutored hand.

'What is your mistress's game?' asked Holmes.

'No game, sir. She just needs to . . . escape.'

I could well imagine it.

'But I think she needs . . . She might need . . .'

'Go on, Polly.'

'Well, Miss Odelia, she—' began the girl. 'She might ought to use some help. Three fellows loves her. But I think she is . . . confused?'

I suddenly became aware of being watched. I turned back to the house to see the white face of Atalanta Wyndham staring down at us from the third floor. Polly followed my gaze, and her own face paled. Without a word, she ran back into the house. Atalanta Wyndham's fierce expression was pinned on us. She vanished from the window and pulled the curtains shut.

That maid would face some trouble, I thought. And so, to my surprise, would we.

CHAPTER 15

Bloom Where You Are Planted

hen no carriage appeared, we started out walking towards the address provided by Polly. It was only ten in the morning but already the sun beat down upon us mercilessly. Despite our linen suits and straw hats, I found myself sweating uncomfortably. Holmes seemed oblivious, fired up as he was by the intrigue of the Wyndham family.

'Breakfast, Holmes?' I enquired.

'A poet, Watson. A poet who is jealous of her sister,' he said. 'And yet . . .'

'Atalanta!' I cried. Of course! Whatever had been written on the doll was a poem, as he had noted. 'Could she be the culprit behind the dismembered doll?'

'My thought when I found her book of poems. But ultimately . . . I lean away from this theory.'

'Why?'

'The ink stains on Atalanta's hand were slight. She is fastidious. But they were of a distinct aqua blue. Not the colour of the note.'

'Perhaps she has more than one colour ink.'

'I saw only one bottle on her sitting-room desk when I glanced inside. No, Watson, I think not.' He was silent for a moment as we trudged through the sunbaked streets.

'Those footprints!' he exclaimed. 'What a tremendous amount of clambering up trees has been done in the name of love. And then the secret archer. Ha! What a family! Have you ever climbed a tree to reach a young lady, Watson?'

I had to think a moment. 'No. But I once tried to wade across a river. Ended up a mile downstream. Have you done anything so rash?'

'For a girl? No,' said Holmes. 'But neither have I practised archery from my window.'

We looked at each other and laughed.

'You shoot, then?' I asked.

'Not for some time. Wait, I think we turn left here.' We did so.

'Were you any good?'

Holmes glanced at me with a smile. 'I was invited into the Woodmen of Arden myself. I declined.'

'Who are the Woodmen of Arden?'

'An honorary society of men who practise archery with the longbow. Invitation only. One must be an accomplished archer and also have friends who are Woodmen. Something of a closed society. They do have tournaments and prizes, however.'

'Robin Hoods, then?'

'Ah, Watson, always the romantic,' said Holmes. 'Sportsmen, to be sure.'

'I think we turn right, here. Let me see the map. But you turned them down?'

Holmes smiled. 'I am no club man, Watson, you know that.'

Carrying on through the town, we discovered we were lost. A student then misdirected us, but we eventually found the place we were seeking.

The address belonged to a lodging house behind a brewery on the eastern edge of the town. A small pub fronted the building, The Cross and Anchor. We walked into the low-beamed, darkened interior, and Holmes introduced himself and asked to see the owner. As he did so, I eyed some tempting ham sandwiches on the counter. But Holmes was not to be delayed.

The Wyndham name and a half sovereign were sufficient to induce the owner, a surly elf of a man, to cooperate, and he unlocked a door to a stairway leading to several lodging rooms above.

Holmes asked whether he had seen Miss Odelia Wyndham of late.

'You won't hear that name from me,' said the man. The fellow gestured to the stairs. 'Two flights up. Room Three.'

We were up the narrow, worn stairs in a rush and then encountered the door marked 'Three'. We knocked. There was no reply. Holmes tried the knob. It was locked. He put his ear to the door and listened, shook his head.

'It appears no one is home,' he whispered.

He then withdrew a familiar small leather kit from his frock coat and opened it to reveal an array of precise metal instruments. Holmes had the door unlocked in what seemed mere seconds, and in complete silence. His timing had improved since I had witnessed a similar display in an earlier case.

We opened the door to a surprising sight. It was a large room painted in white, as Dillie's bedroom had been, with a large double bed in one corner, long blue curtains with sheer panels flapping in the breeze from an open window, and a long blue velvet sofa, on which sat a poised young woman. She was motionless, calm, and obviously expecting us.

Miss Odelia Wyndham, or Dillie, lounged in a curiously studied pose in the centre of this sofa, her arms extending along the back of it, head tilted back, replicating the arrogant yet languid bearing of her father, Richard Wyndham.

She took us in haughtily – two strange men who had unlocked the door to her private sanctuary – but said nothing. Her position and attitude struck me as odd in the extreme, given the circumstances.

'Miss Odelia Wyndham, I presume,' said Holmes, formally.

'Mr Sherlock Holmes, I presume,' said the lady. Clearly her father's daughter, she managed to be dismissive and wry at the same time. It was a peculiar effect coming from an eighteen-year-old.

She was, as the deacon had described, singularly beautiful, with mocking eyes and golden hair arranged in a knot high on her head, and curls escaping around her face in a look of disarray that was both casual and becoming. She was dressed in a striped cotton summer frock, and from the bottom of it peeked long matching bloomers. These ended in curiously large white tennis shoes of the kind I have worn on the court myself.

She was clearly one of the new, sporty breed of young ladies who bicycled and partook of racquet sports. I glanced around me, and there was indeed a tennis racquet leaning up against the wall under the window. I was certain she must own a two-wheeler parked nearby. I could well imagine Atalanta would be jealous of this glowing creature, who possessed not only beauty but, perhaps even more enviable, vibrant good health.

Holmes said nothing to her but took in the room in his comprehensive manner. I followed his gaze to an open closet door, from which hung a young man's suit of dark blue summer linen, a boater hat, and a wrinkled white shirt and navy tie. I inferred a regular visitor.

He turned to the lady. 'Miss Wyndham,' said he severely, 'since you know my name and were expecting me, you have been informed that I have been called in from London to find you. You have given your family and friends quite a fright. Was that your intention?'

She stared at him before answering, as if deciding whether or not he was worth her time.

'I can have you arrested for breaking in on a young lady who is minding her own business,' said she, pleasantly.

'You will not, however,' said Holmes, 'as you do not want the police to know of this private sanctuary. Who sent word we were coming? It certainly was efficient.'

123

'Polly. You've met her,' said she. She smiled and stood up. 'She preceded you here by minutes.' She was clearly proud of the fact. 'You are not familiar with Cambridge?'

'Not as much as I intend to be,' said he. 'Miss Wyndham, I have reason to believe that you may be in danger. A doll designed to look like you was found in the Jesus Lock last night. Mutilated, I might add.'

She threw back her head and laughed. It was a tinkling, charming laugh. 'That *is* creative!' said she. 'And so somebody called a London detective.'

Holmes and I exchanged a look.

She sized us up and came to some kind of decision. We were not prepared for what came next. Dillie Wyndham approached Holmes and stood before him, dangerously close and most improperly. She proceeded to inspect him minutely in a presumptuous and arrogant manner. A man doing such a thing would have received a sharp retort or worse. To his credit, Holmes did not move a muscle.

'You are not so terrible, up close,' she said with the hint of a friendly smile. 'Though I wouldn't have you.'

Holmes said nothing but returned her unwavering look.

She reached out and straightened his tie. It had not needed straightening. Holmes was nothing if not fastidious in his dress. The girl was outrageous, and it was clearly a cultivated act.

'You are too thin,' said she. 'You live on, I don't know, coffee and nerves, perhaps? Or worse. Your eyes are tired. There is a sadness there.'

Holmes did not reply, which frustrated her. She changed tactics.

'I do not care about this or about you!' she exclaimed. 'Be sad. Be whatever you like. You think you are much smarter than you are. Some women find you attractive. I do not.'

My friend appeared not to respond but I noticed his right hand twitch almost imperceptibly. I guessed it was from her proximity rather than her words.

I stood at the ready, but for what I could not fathom.

Without stepping back from Holmes, she looked over at me. 'And you! You have the appearance of a faithful dog, awaiting scraps to be thrown to you. But ready to defend the pack with loud barking and perhaps even a bite or two. Down, boy.'

I stifled a retort and wondered at this peculiar display.

She turned her attention back to Holmes. 'Now what are you going to do?' she said, thrusting her face inches from his.

Again, he did not move. 'This act must impress your young university gentlemen,' he replied coolly. 'Daring, I suppose, is what they think. Daring and exciting! How often do you disguise yourself in men's clothing and accompany them to parties and sporting events?'

She looked momentarily surprised, then backed off to glance over at her closet at the man's linen suit hanging there. She exhaled sharply in frustration, then jabbed a long delicate finger not so delicately at Holmes's chest more than once for emphasis as she said, '*You* don't know that. What makes *you* think that that is *mine*? I may not be so daring after all. Just extremely improper. Perhaps that costume belongs to a suitor.'

She poked him once more, hard. She was trying to provoke him, and I wondered why.

He reached up and clasped her hand, lowering it gently to her side. 'Perhaps. As I assume someone, not your father, is paying for this room. And yet those clothes are yours,' said Holmes, indicating the blue linen suit. Then, with surprising impropriety equal to the young lady's own, he reached out and placed his hand flat upon her hair at the top of her head. She recoiled, and I noticed a moment of extreme fear. But of course he would never hurt the girl. Instead, he deftly removed a long hairpin. She gasped.

He held it up before her.

'You have pinned all of your hair up under that straw hat over there and have done so recently. The dampness I remark on that linen shirt hung out to air – and on your own hair there – indicates a recent outing in the hot sun. You have not bothered to change your shoes – men's tennis shoes, I wager – since you have returned. And that pair of dark spectacles meant for the bright sun, there on your bedside table, added an effective touch to your disguise. One of the better male impersonations, I would imagine, and the trousers, being a bit worn at the hems, tell me that this was certainly not your first such adventure.'

As he spoke, her fear transformed into anger at having been so revealed, and a storm of emotions clouded her beautiful face. Clearly she had not expected his response. But then fury won out and she slapped him. Hard.

He winced only momentarily, averting his face from the stinging blow, then looked back at her, undaunted. The red imprint of her hand showed on his pale face.

Holmes smiled at this improbable creature, and I marvelled at his self-control. My friend was never fully at ease with women, and at times could be oblivious. But he was always civil and usually a gentleman, except in the face of duplicity. To have two women slap him in the space of twenty-four hours was certainly some kind of record.

I almost suppressed a laugh at the thought, but the remarkably spoiled young lady before us did not find this humorous at all. She glanced at me.

'Stop smiling. It is not funny. Get out! Both of you!' she cried.

CHAPTER 16

An Uneasy Alliance

olmes did not move. 'Or what, exactly, Miss Wyndham?' said Holmes gently. 'We have already agreed you will not call the police.'

'Do not be so sure! I . . . I will say you attacked me!' said she. 'You broke in here and attacked me! It will not go well for you.'

I stepped forward. 'Young lady, I am a witness here and will stand up for this gentleman. He is known by the London police, whom he assists on a regular basis, Miss Wyndham, and his reputation is impeccable.'

Her own reputation would clearly be compromised had she called the police, but the situation was not without risk, and Holmes and I knew it.

She was improvising, frightened, and the momentum of her anger seemed to add wind to her sails. 'The *two* of you

came in and attacked me!' She stepped away from my friend and slammed her wrist hard on the edge of the table with a cry of pain. 'You see!' She exclaimed, holding her arm out before us, her eyes shining. The blow brought up an immediate welt.

Holmes glanced at me uneasily. This young woman seemed dangerously unbalanced. He held up his hands and took a step back towards the door.

'All right, Miss Wyndham. I realize you do feel invaded,' he said, gently. 'This room is a kind of sanctuary from a life of dissatisfaction. I suppose if I were a female, and felt, well, as excluded from life as you do, I might consider not only securing an escape like this one – but also defending it with the same passion and conviction. Please calm yourself. I do not intend to force you to do anything you do not want to do, nor to give you away.'

She stared at Holmes uncertainly. This was not the response she was expecting.

'You are patronizing me.'

'Miss Wyndham, not at all,' I said. 'Mr Holmes has only your best interests at heart.'

'Why should I trust you?' she said.

'Why not? I am here to help, not point a finger,' said Holmes. 'May I suggest we all sit down and discuss the dilemma of your disappearance in a civilized manner? No one wishes you harm. In fact, just the opposite. Let us attempt to negotiate a truce.'

Holmes stepped further away from her on the pretext of setting down his hat on a table. He looked about for something on which to sit, espied a low stool tucked under that same table, drew it out and sat down. 'Do join me, Watson. Sit here.'

I noticed another stool under the table, drew it out and sat next to him. It felt extremely awkward in that strange room, seated so low to the floor, facing the standing young woman. She faltered, not expecting this. But the odd choreography had the intended effect. It allowed the girl to feel in charge.

She paused. Then, with sudden resolve, she returned to her blue velvet divan and resumed the relaxed position she had occupied when we entered the room, now peering haughtily down at us.

Holmes had successfully averted disaster.

'I would like to help you, Miss Wyndham,' my friend said, as though everything that had just transpired had not happened. 'And at the same time put the fears of those who care for you at rest. Let us come to a method together. First of all, do tell me your reasons for this subterfuge.'

'It is obvious,' said she, angrily. 'I am suffocating at home.'

'Tell me about this,' said Holmes.

She paused, but not for long. 'You have no idea of the frustration a person of my position endures. The constraints upon my life! The boundaries of propriety, of position, of womanhood, of God knows – everything. It is enough to drive one mad. Mad, truly! I cannot go to the market alone, play tennis with a boy, say this, do that, wear clothes that do not constrict my body here!' She put her hands to her waist. 'Or here!' Both hands went over her heart. 'All the rules, the whispered admonitions, yes, and even the shouted ones! I cannot bear it, cannot bear it I say, and what you see here is the culmination of years of planning. If you give me away, it will go very badly for you, sir! Of that I will make certain!'

'We have covered that ground, Miss Wyndham, and once again I assure you that is not my intent. But even if you refuse to see danger, people have been concerned for your safety. You do understand that? People who care about you. They are suffering.'

'Or claim to be,' she said and looked away.

'Your mother, for one,' said Holmes.

A small frown flashed across the beautiful young face, but if she felt any contrition, she shook it off like a dog shaking off water. 'She will recover.'

'And yet she is suffering, Miss Wyndham. And I believe your maid Polly was arrested one night, presumably on an errand for you. I understand that a girl like that can be gaoled without trial here in Cambridge, if the University so wishes. You know of the Spinning House? Ah, I see you know what I am talking about.'

Miss Wyndham was clearly uncomfortable at this.

'I'm sure Polly is careful,' she said.

'But let us turn to your reasons for needing to hide, Miss Wyndham,' said Holmes. 'Do you not see various escape routes from what you feel to be an awful confinement in the home of your father? For example, have you not considered studying at Girton, or Newnham? I understand that opportunities have opened there for women to expand their—'

'I have grown up steeped in academia. Statues. Greek plays. Pah! That is the last thing I want!'

'I see.'

'And anyway, my father forbids it.'

Holmes paused at this. 'I am sorry to hear it. But what of marriage? I understand that you are being courted, and by more than one suitor.'

His words contained no trace of sarcasm.

'Escaping from the frying pan into the fire?' she said bitterly. 'As it is, I am being steered, none too gently, towards one of them.'

'Which one do you prefer?'

'What does it matter? Being steered *at all* is objectionable,' she cried. 'Everything I do has been controlled by others. I hate my life. I hate my parents. I hate this world that tries to rein me in, that excludes me from an education, adventures, excitement, and – well, everything I want!'

Holmes was silent for a moment.

'I see. And I may understand this better than most. Like you, Miss Wyndham, I too have a secret location where I go to get away when life is oppressive.'

I had long suspected that Holmes had a bolt-hole, or even more than one in London, although I always presumed these had to do with the danger of his profession, not a need for privacy.

'Even Watson here needs to get away from time to time.' Holmes continued.

'Holmes, I—'

'Bath. Just recently. So yes, Miss Wyndham, we do understand.'

She stared at us, trying to make up her mind to accept this or not. 'You men have far more freedom.'

'I will admit that this is so. Miss Wyndham, why do you think your maid shared your location with me?' Holmes asked.

'I have been wondering that,' said the girl, 'and I shall take Polly to task for it.'

'She did so because she knew I could help you. I believe you are in danger.'

'Well, I don't, Mr Holmes. That doll, it's just a bid for attention. Stop trying to scare me! It will not work. I do not wish to be helped. I only wish to live my life as I please, and I am prepared to do whatever it takes for freedom. And if that includes smearing your reputation – both of you – I will not hesitate!'

'You are playing a dangerous game, Miss Wyndham. I am not a vengeful or easily insulted person. You may fear no harm or repercussions from me. If I am not successful with my mission here, I shall simply go back to London and leave you all to sort out your difficulties. But not every man is so fitted.'

'What do you mean, a dangerous game?'

'You are fomenting drama with your disappearances. Perhaps *you* wrote a message on your doll, tore off its arm, and then threw it into the Jesus Lock. A "bid for attention", as you just said.'

'What a stupid notion. You are a stupid man.'

Holmes said nothing.

'I did no such thing,' said she. 'I suppose someone wanted everyone to worry about me. That would *not* be me, Mr Holmes. I would prefer that everyone forget about me and leave me to pursue my own happiness.'

'Do you often find yourself in the vicinity of the Jesus Lock?'

'Well, of course. Our house is nearby. I need to get out for air. Anyone would.'

'And the footbridge there, do you cross it on a regular basis? Meet up with anyone there repeatedly?'

'Yes. And, no. This is not your business.' She looked away, and I noted, finally, a touch of unease.

'The mutilated doll found in the lock is quite possibly the work of someone who does not wish you well, Miss Wyndham.'

'Or some kind of joke, Mr Holmes,' said she. 'Yes, a joke. That is what I think.'

'Who would be your choice for such a remarkable piece of hilarity?' persisted Holmes.

Miss Wyndham laughed, but it was a nervous laugh.

'Anyone,' she said. 'Any of my suitors, I suppose. My mother is bereft, or so she appears to you. But that weak little bird enjoys receiving sympathy and is probably playing up her despair to the hilt. Tell me, has she taken to bed? Oh, I am sure that she has.' The girl smiled, none too kindly.

'And your sister?'

'We are not friends. I stole her beau. Well, not really her

beau, he never fancied her. Her dream. Could be Atalanta.'

'Yes, the archer,' said Holmes.

'Perhaps it is someone who is "desperate" to have me found? Well, let's see. I suppose that might be my father.' That thought pleased her. 'Oh, the *scandal*.'

'What of your two young men? Do they know you are staying here?'

'*Three* young men. Two of them know. One does not. Freddie and Leo know.'

'And Freddie is Frederick, Lord Eden-Summers – your sister's dream?'

She shrugged and leaned forward to retie the laces of one of her tennis shoes.

'And Leo?'

'Ha! My parents know nothing of him! Leo Vitale. Studying physics. St Cedd's. Frighteningly intelligent. A bit unschooled with women, but he has potential.'

'And who is the third? Deacon Buttons?'

'Perry! Well, yes, but he is hardly in the running. He is besotted, a puppy. You ask too many questions.' She turned her attention to the other shoe.

'Please, Miss Wyndham. How do you suppose the culprit acquired your doll? I noted a large tree at the back of the house whose branches reach right up to the window of your bedroom. Which of your young gentlemen is in the habit of accessing your room via this route?'

She looked up in surprise. 'How do you know this?' she exclaimed before she could think to deny the fact entirely.

'It is my profession.'

'Well, it is none of your business.'

'There were several sets of footprints in the soft earth beneath the tree, in addition to your own. I suggest that one of these young men retrieved your doll and threw it in the lock. I also suggest that it would be to your advantage to know which. I don't like it. And neither should you.'

'I have no idea. Leo or Freddie have visited. But I can't imagine them doing this.'

'And the deacon has seen your room?'

'Yes, I suppose.'

I must have smiled as I pictured all of this. She turned to glare at me. 'Ah, Doctor! You seem amused. Have you never been young and in love?'

'Me? Oh, well—!' I exclaimed. Holmes shot me a bemused look. 'We were all young once,' I said.

'None of this matters. Who would have suspected anyone would summon Sherlock Holmes, all the way from London? My father must be desperate! His reputation above all.' She smiled to herself, pleased at the thought of giving her father discomfort.

Holmes stood up. 'Miss Wyndham, I will not give away your hiding place. But I will convey the news to your family that you are safe and well and will return to them when ready. I will also suggest to them that they open up a conversation by writing to you care of my address in London, where you can mail your responses.' He took out a calling card and jotted down our address on the back with a small silver pencil. He handed it to her.

'I shall leave it to you to sort out your grievances and your options in this case. If you find that this game – no, don't take offence, it clearly *is* a game – becomes cumbersome, I suggest you fashion a more open approach to declaring your well-deserved independence.'

'I don't—'

'If you do not achieve your desired results, but instead anger someone to the point where you feel endangered, you may feel free to call on me.'

She stared at him in surprise.

'I can be here in a matter of hours. It is my belief that you do not fully understand the effect you are having on those who have feelings for you. Also, I think you have more options than you currently see.'

'Oh, you men! You think you understand!' And yet I could read in her face that she had been affected by his words.

'In the meantime, please be careful, young lady. Not every man you toy with and mistreat will feel or act as I do. Keep your windows and door locked.'

Holmes picked up his hat and was out of the door before I could rise to my feet.

'Good day, Miss Wyndham,' I said, struggling with the uncharitable thought that I did not really wish her one. 'Be assured, Mr Holmes is a man of his word.'

She looked up at me from her sofa. I thought I saw tears glistening in her eyes. Then I, too, made my escape.

PART FOUR

STRANGE MAGIC

'Bid Suspicion double lock the door.'
—William Shakespeare
Venus and Adonis

CHAPTER 17

Smell the Roses

e left the young lady and were once again traipsing through the hot and dusty streets of Cambridge. 'Home, then, Holmes? The next train to King's Cross is in thirty minutes.' I said, having glanced at my *Bradshaw*.

'Not yet, Watson. Until I know who put that doll in the lock, I will not feel comfortable leaving that rather irritating young lady on her own. That doll's missing arm – my mind is not at ease.'

'You think she is inciting danger, Holmes, by running off alone and unchaperoned?'

'It is not her independence that concerns me, but her hostility. I wonder that she does not fathom the full effect.'

I thought (but did not voice) that Holmes, so terribly observant of minutiae, and so keenly aware of motives and emotional undercurrents, could still at times be completely oblivious to the effect *he* had on others.

Holmes was staring at me. 'I know, Watson, that obliviousness can serve in certain cases. My brother champions it when it suits. Miss Wyndham, however, is making things harder for herself.'

'I agree, Holmes. But who would have thrown that doll in the lock?'

'As her sister says, there is a long list. I have a few questions for our distressed deacon. The church next, Watson.' He made a right turn. 'This way.'

A few minutes later, we arrived at the Church of Our Lady of the Roses. It was an ancient stone church tucked behind newer college buildings, near to the river and the Jesus Lock. Next to it was an overgrown graveyard and, by contrast, a small, extremely well-kept garden of forty or so rosebushes. They were still in full bloom on this humid September day, and glowed in diffuse pinks, reds and corals in the unfiltered sunlight which beat down on the crowded space with relentless intensity. I wondered how long a rose garden had existed here and if the flowers came before or after the name of the church.

A light tenor voice trilled out a charming melody behind a dense row of red and white roses. Holmes indicated with a finger to the lips that I should make no sound and began to sing out a melody which seemed to echo and answer the singing gardener most prettily.

A heavyset priest of about fifty, wearing a wide-brimmed hat against the sun, popped his head up behind the roses.

He continued to sing, Holmes right with him. They came to a rousing cadence. '*Ta da!*'

The man laughed, rosy cheeks and bright blue eyes giving him a cheery countenance. 'Pachelbel's canon!' he exclaimed. 'Another baroque music aficionado! Lovely contrapuntal lines! Do you play an instrument, sir?'

'I do,' said Holmes pleasantly. 'The violin.'

'Wonderful. I am an organist, myself.' The man came around from behind the rosebushes. He was a large fellow, but soft, well-fed, with the build and easy movement of a man who had been athletic not so long ago.

A monocle dangled down his chest, its chain entwined with that of a large cross. The secular and the religious, I thought, tangled together. I had always been wary of men of the cloth. Where others found many of them to be avuncular and receptive, I frequently felt patronized and, well, judged. But perhaps that was my upbringing. The clergy of my parents' church had indeed been rather unpleasant.

The man's piercing, merry eyes were nearly lost in the folds of his pale, chubby face. At this moment they conveyed an amused welcome.

'Father Lamb, I presume,' said Holmes.

'Atticus Lamb, at your service, sir. And you are—?'

'Sherlock Holmes. This is Dr Watson. We are up from London on some business here in the town. May we steal a moment of your time from this beautiful day?'

In a few minutes we were seated in an anteroom off a transept of the church, with hot tea in hand. Even in this common area, the ancient stone walls gave off the chill of antiquity. A velvet silence surrounded us, the mild hubbub of Cambridge completely obstructed inside the building. I wondered aloud when it had been built.

'Fifteen hundred, or thereabouts,' said the priest.

'Father Lamb, I have come to you about a young man of your church: Deacon Buttons,' said Holmes.

Lamb laughed. 'Well, he is the *only* young man of my church, sir. We are a small operation here. Lamb and Buttons. The source of much merriment, you can be sure.'

The names were odd. But it was the phrase 'small operation' which caught my attention.

'I see,' said Holmes. 'You have not been long in this location.'

'No. Six months only. This church had been abandoned and stood mostly empty for some eight years. A shame really.'

'And your congregation? I suppose a few hovered about, awaiting a . . . resurrection, so to speak?'

Here the man's face clouded slightly. He seemed to share with me the characteristic of having a face which reflected every thought, like a glassy pond with clouds floating overhead.

'Well, a few have returned to the flock, although frankly we are having to start, more or less, from scratch.'

'I imagine there is competition here, though mostly Anglican,' said Holmes.

'Well, competition is perhaps not the right word. But we do hope to find our people. Rome will only support us insofar as we gain a following. I am optimistic, however. Why do you ask?'

It was not the first time that I considered that running a church was not unlike running a business. I became aware of a pounding sound that started up from somewhere beneath us.

'Deacon Buttons seems like a promising young man to have with you, then,' remarked Holmes. 'Charming fellow.'

'He is, indeed. He is set to be ordained soon, and he already gives a stirring sermon. I am counting on him to bring more young people into the fold. Our lifeblood, so to speak. Please forgive the noise, we are having some construction work below.'

The muffled banging continued under our conversation.

'How is it that you know young Buttons?' asked Father Lamb. 'And what did you wish to discuss?'

'He came to us in London in the matter of a young lady who had gone missing. A Miss Dillie Wyndham.'

'Came to *you*, sir?'

'Mr Holmes is a consulting detective,' I offered. 'He has a considerable reputation in London for his work in locating missing persons and solving crimes.'

Lamb's regard clouded, then he turned his gaze on me. 'And you, sir?'

'This is Dr John Watson, an army surgeon and my colleague in work,' said Holmes.

Lamb took me in, then turned abruptly back to Holmes.

'London, you say? A consulting detective who plays the violin? Well, you certainly must be unique. How is it that I can help you, sir?'

'Is Deacon Buttons here at present?' asked Holmes.

'No. He is with the Carews, a family struck by illness. Terribly sad, the mother will expire soon.'

'May we wait for him?'

'I suppose so. Though it is not clear how long he may be.' The priest smiled politely. 'You are a detective. Has a crime been committed?'

Holmes glanced around him. Through an open doorway we could see the altar and the pulpit. A small vase of roses sat next to the pulpit, clearly cut from the garden outside. Lacking all the gilded paraphernalia, the embroidered draping, the accoutrements of the popular and well-funded Catholic Church, these were a modest though charming offering.

'Perhaps, Father. Deacon Buttons mentioned that a Miss Odelia Wyndham is a congregant here?' said Holmes.

'She is.'

'Is her family Catholic?'

'The mother, perhaps. Lapsed.'

'But the young lady? How long has she been attending church here?'

'For some months now. Shortly after we began here.'

'Interesting. You are aware that the family has reported Miss Wyndham missing?'

The priest paused, feeling the weight of Holmes's gaze settle upon him. He shifted uncomfortably. 'Young Buttons mentioned it, yes.'

'And that her doll was found floating in the Jesus Lock?'

'What? A doll? No. But she is a mature young lady—'

'Her childhood doll. A favourite, apparently. And found by the deacon in the lock.'

The priest looked puzzled. 'I see. How can I help you?'

Holmes had stood up and was now moving about the room. As it was bare stone with only the benches on which we sat, I wondered what he would be looking for.

Holmes's movements made the priest uneasy. My friend looked down at the stone floor with interest and brushed his foot across two of the stones. A few pebbles scraped underneath his boot.

Lamb stared at Holmes. 'Did her parents call you in?'

Holmes smiled at him but said nothing.

'We have had some repair work done. Ongoing. Some loose stones replaced,' the priest said.

'Ah! Was anyone buried here?' drawled Holmes. 'I know that in many churches it is the custom to bury past clergy or notable congregants directly under the church flooring. Although usually there is a plaque memorializing them.'

'I am afraid that information has been lost to time,' said Lamb. 'Those records have not come down to us. The church has had a number of lives. It was a kind of sanctuary for the vagrants of Cambridge until recently. And, I believe, someone attempted to open a restaurant here before that. But back to the young lady . . .'

'Ah, too bad. The stories these stones could tell!' murmured Holmes. A sound from the nave had us all turn to see three men in dusty overalls, carrying some tools, passing through. One of them saluted the father.

Lamb waved them away.

'I am sorry. Workmen. Quite a few repairs to be made.'

'Repairs or construction?' asked Holmes.

'Both, actually. The restaurant, when it was here, had a wine cellar in the crypt below. I am having it expanded.'

At Holmes's raised eyebrow, the priest continued. 'The crypt is the perfect temperature for wine storage. We will be renting out space to several local restaurants to store their bottles there.'

'Ah, a welcome bit of income, then!' said Holmes cheerfully.

'One must be resourceful,' said the priest. 'But again, sir, I don't wish to be rude. What is your business with the deacon?'

'I understand there have been some problems with this church. I read about a flood some years ago.'

The priest frowned. 'But what has that to do—?'

'Church histories are a special hobby of mine,' offered Holmes. 'They reflect so much about the changing populations and customs of our towns. And this one is particularly colourful.'

His thoroughness never failed to impress me.

'Yes, there was a flood,' said Father Lamb. 'But we have taken precautions. There is a drainage system in the crypt, somewhat complex. The workmen are attending to that.'

Holmes turned to me with a smile. 'Watson, the Cam regularly runs over her banks during a heavy rainfall. You have noticed the broad fields which line the river, where cattle and sheep graze? They are floodplains, and that is where the water spreads harmlessly. Most buildings are set back from the river for this reason. But not this church.'

I wondered at this seemingly irrelevant disclosure.

'Yes, flooding has been a problem,' the priest replied.

'Hmm,' said Holmes. 'Some records survived, then?'

'The floods are a matter of town history.'

'You should be secure then, I suppose, though not from human disaster. I believe I read that this church has been touched by scandal. Just after the flood, was it?'

Lamb smiled thinly. 'You are well informed, Mr Holmes. But I still wonder why you are here.'

'Something about the previous priest,' Holmes continued. 'What was his name, Watson?'

I said nothing but Holmes turned to me as though I had. 'It's true – a terrible scandal! It reached all the way to London, Father Lamb, did you know?'

The priest's face slowly coloured, and he stiffened. 'Yes, of course I am aware. That, however, had nothing to do with us.'

'Dr Watson and I were just discussing this on the way here. What a scandal indeed! No one would have expected Father – what was his name? – well, he was quite the roué, I understand. Before the – before the terrible event.'

We had discussed no such thing. However, I nodded my head and made a mental note to ask him to catch me up a bit more in advance of these meetings.

Holmes regarded Father Lamb, who sat unmoving, his face now a mask of guarded but extreme displeasure. I became aware of a dripping sound. It seemed to come from underneath us.

Lamb cleared his throat and forced a smile back upon his face.

'We are trying to put that all behind us, sir. Father Menenius was ill; he contracted brain fever, during the flood you mentioned . . . and it affected his thinking. He had many, many years of devoted service to the Church with no hint of misbehaviour. But then suddenly—'

'A sad tale. The girl was found drowned in the crypt, Watson! After she had been horribly – well, never mind. Has there been more flooding since?'

'No. Mr Holmes, we are taking contributions to the reparations fund, if you would consider a small donation?' The man's face, previously so benign had now shut as tight as a pub at breakfast time.

'Certainly! Watson? Have you any cash on hand?'

I dug into my pockets, although resentfully. I had a couple of five-pound notes, as I usually set out with Holmes well prepared for possible needs. Holmes snatched the one I retrieved and gave it to Father Lamb.

'No use dwelling on the negative, then, Father,' Holmes said cheerfully.

'We begin anew. It is up to me – and to Deacon Buttons – to rebuild trust, to re-establish our glorious church in this small corner of the world.'

'And Rome? They support you?'

'We are at present . . . on our own. But not for long, I expect. We will be brought back into the fold, I am sure.'

'Your young deacon is charming,' said Holmes. 'But with apologies, Father, I need to confirm that it was not Deacon Buttons who placed Odelia Wyndham's doll in the Jesus Lock, thus terrifying her family, alarming her friends, and causing me to come all this way to investigate her disappearance.' He paused. 'Which is what he wanted me to do a day or so ago.'

'For Mr Holmes to come, that is,' I said, feeling the need to clarify.

Father Lamb stood firm. 'Has the young lady been harmed in any way?'

'No. But that is not to say she is out of danger.'

The priest stared at Holmes. 'But why is your attention turned to young Buttons? I cannot imagine he would be so devious. He is simply looking after a troubled young person.'

'He is barely older than she, Father,' said Holmes.

'You begin to disturb me with your questions, sir.'

From inside the nave, I could see a workman conferring with others and gesticulating urgently to Lamb. But the priest's back was to them and they evidently did not want to interrupt.

'You say there has been no murder, no abduction. What are you inferring? A relationship of any type at all outside of confessor and advisor would – well, I would not believe it of him. Deacon Buttons is a paragon of virtue.'

'So that my time in Cambridge is not wasted, may I please inspect Deacon Buttons' rooms? I would like to content myself with what I know we all believe to be true – that this exemplary young man had nothing to do with the doll found in the lock.'

Pastor Lamb smiled thinly and acceded. 'If it will put an end to this, then certainly,' he said.

CHAPTER 18

Buttons Unbuttoned

e were led to the rectory, an adjoining small building, more recent in construction, which held a meeting room and the private sleeping quarters of both churchmen. Buttons' small room was spartan in the extreme, with few places to hide anything. Lamb left us there on our own.

Holmes's initial examination was rapidly done. A narrow single bed, a desk and a plain armoire crowded into a small space gave the room the look of a gaol cell. A window draped by a single panel of stained linen opened out to an unused part of the garden, and beyond that, the river. The barren, tight quarters were not dissimilar to Holmes's own ascetic bedroom in Baker Street, minus the smoking paraphernalia, the maps and the portraits of various criminals, and with the addition here of a crucifix hanging on the wall. Against another wall, the small pine armoire contained nothing but two changes of cleric's vestments, two pairs of boots and a rather flamboyant set of silk pyjamas.

But upon the second pass, Holmes discovered, somewhat to his dismay, what he was looking for. It was on the young deacon's small, rough-hewn desk that Holmes found traces of ink.

'Look, Watson!'

As I looked closely at the minuscule ink stains, Holmes felt all around the desk. With a cry of triumph, he discovered a small leather bag, hidden and hanging by a peg behind the desk. He removed it to reveal a nearly full bottle of ink and a dip pen. The ink was an unusual purplish-blue colour, and it unmistakably matched the blurred writing on the doll.

Hearing a slight sound, I turned to see Father Lamb standing in the doorway. Not having heard the entire story of the waterlogged writing on the doll, it seemed he may not have caught the inference.

Suddenly young Deacon Buttons appeared just behind him in the hallway. He called out 'Hello, Father!' to Lamb, but upon spotting me in his room, a look of panic washed over him.

'Dr Watson!' he blurted. 'What brings you to my—' But at that moment Lamb stepped to the side, and the young man got a clear view of Holmes at the desk with the ink bottle. The words died in his throat. He knew in an instant the game was up.

'Mr H-Holmes,' he stammered.

Holmes held up the bottle of distinctly coloured ink.

'Deacon Buttons,' he said, 'why would you use such a unique colour of ink? A more common colour would have made it much more difficult to trace.' Holmes glanced at Lamb and explained, 'A note was written on the doll in this ink.'

The young man looked between his accuser and his mentor, in the manner of a rabbit that has been cornered by two foxes. 'I found it – discarded in a bin,' he mumbled.

'Explain yourself,' said Holmes.

'I can . . . I . . .'

'Do so,' said Holmes. 'I am eager to hear it.'

The young man looked up at his superior and dropped his eyes in shame. He seemed more afraid of the kindly father than my clearly antagonized friend.

'Dillie . . . er . . . I think she may be in danger. I felt it was important to have Mr Holmes come out,' he addressed the father. 'I did not think he would come unless . . . unless . . .'

Father Lamb sighed. 'My son, you should have come to me with this.'

'What kind of danger?' asked Holmes.

'She has received letters. Or at least one threatening letter. I don't think she has shown it to her family.'

Lamb sighed. 'Young man. Many a time an intrigue such as this can be cleared up with the help of a friendly clergyman. Miss Wyndham is known to be highly strung. Is it not possible that she is playing on your sympathies for attention?'

'But a threatening letter you say, Mr Buttons?' demanded Holmes. 'That would have sufficed. You did not mention this.'

The young man coloured. 'I—'

'Has there been more than one?' persisted my friend.

'I am not sure. I think so.'

'What was the nature of the threat?'

'I do not know exactly. She . . . read a part of one aloud.'

'What did it say?' Holmes impatiently waved him to continue.

'I don't remember the exact words. But it warned her to stop playing games and to choose among her suitors or to suffer dire consequences. She made light of it.'

'The letter did not specify this consequence?'

'No.'

Holmes set down the bottle of ink on the desk. He took a deep breath, willing control. I could sense his mounting anger.

'Why did you not mention this to us earlier?'

'It was told to me in confession.'

Holmes glanced at me then turned back to the young man. 'She mentioned nothing of this to us! Did she suspect anyone in particular to have written this letter?'

'Mention, sir? Then you have seen her?' asked Buttons, flushing with excitement.

'We have just come from her, Mr Buttons. You may rest assured she is safe.'

'Thank the heavens!' the young man exclaimed. 'But where is she?'

'To the point, did Miss Wyndham venture a theory about the writer of this letter?'

'No. But it must be one of her young men!'

'Your delay in telling me of the letter is inexcusable,' exclaimed Holmes. 'It changes everything.'

'My son—' began Lamb.

'Her fears were expressed in confidence, Father. During confession,' cried Buttons. He turned to Holmes. 'My vows do not permit . . .'

Holmes exhaled in impatience. He stood up. 'Mr Buttons, if a life is at stake, surely the most pious member of the Church would use common sense to take action.' He turned to face the older man. 'Isn't that right, Father Lamb?'

The priest's face betrayed sadness and a certain resignation. 'It is a loaded question, Mr Holmes, and one that has been debated over the years,' said he. 'Largely, the sanctity of the confession is one to which we cleave quite literally and in all instances.' He turned to the younger man. 'My son, we will discuss this at length later today.'

'Shall we?' continued the priest, indicating the door. 'Mr Holmes, Dr Watson,' he continued, 'it appears that you have been summoned to Cambridge under false pretences. And that the family of this young lady, a not unimportant one in the hierarchy of the University, I might add, have been unduly alarmed, all in the service of reassuring Deacon Buttons that an excitable member of his flock is unharmed.'

'At least at present she is unharmed,' said Holmes.

'Where is she, sir?' blurted the young cleric. 'Please!'

Holmes gave Buttons a sharp look. 'I wondered if she

might have thrown the doll herself, but she had not,' said
he. 'My suspicion naturally then fell to you. Is there anything
else you have managed to leave out? How did the arm part
company with the body of the doll?'

Buttons looked uncertainly at his mentor. 'I, er, don't
know about that,' he said. 'I left the doll on the Jesus Lock
bridge, hoping she would see it. The next I saw it, it was
in the lock with the arm missing.'

Holmes glowered at the boy. 'Is this precisely true?'

'Yes, sir. She did offer me one thing, Father. May I share
this with Mr Holmes?' begged the deacon. 'I fear for the
young lady, I really do.'

Lamb sighed. 'Use your judgement, my son. She has been
found safe, remember?'

'Share, young man, and be quick about it,' said Holmes.
'You have wasted my time enormously.'

Peregrine Buttons continued to struggle. The moral
dilemma of this young clergyman seemed the height of
hypocrisy even to me. He had lied to Holmes and gone to
great trouble to create a false alarm that caused anguish
to at least the girl's mother, even as it set Holmes on the
case. Surely that in itself was some kind of sin.

'She said she was feeling a great deal of pressure to
become engaged. That the pressure had put her near
breaking point.'

'It appears you know this young lady quite well, Mr
Buttons,' said my friend. 'Then you must also know how
she may strike out when she feels cornered. You worry
about her, don't you?'

Buttons was silent. He looked down at his feet. I noticed that Father Lamb was staring at his young disciple unhappily.

Holmes turned to go, then suddenly turned back.

'What did the writing on the doll say?'

The boy looked embarrassed. 'I don't know it by heart. But . . .' He reached into a pocket and removed a small folded paper 'It was a stanza by someone or other. Something about a lock."

He handed it to Holmes, who glanced at it, 'The Rape of the Lock. Pope.' Holmes snorted. 'Pope's poem is a parody. A classicist would recognize it. The lock. Your humour eludes me. What of this missing arm?'

'I did not pull off the arm. Or throw the doll into the lock. I just sat her there on the footbridge. Dillie walks there most mornings. But I did not throw it in.'

'Peregrine, my boy,' said Father Lamb, 'perhaps Dillie herself threw it in, rejecting the message upon it. Consider that, my son.'

And even though the girl hadn't mentioned such an act, it seemed to fit.

Holmes's eyes bored into the young man. 'Deacon Buttons, I think it is time for you to think carefully about your commitments, your promises, and perhaps your own sense of what is right and proper. This is certainly a question for each man to ask himself. Gentlemen, you have your work cut out for you. Good day.'

Holmes exited the room. Father Lamb followed us out. At the gate leading from the rose garden to the street,

Holmes paused and faced the priest. 'Good luck with the re-establishment of your church, Father Lamb,' he said.

Without further comment, he strode out into the lane and down the road. As I followed, I glanced back at Father Lamb, standing forlornly at the entrance to the garden.

While not a religious man myself, I nevertheless felt a pang of sympathy for him. And I rather liked Buttons, for reasons I could not explain. Despite the younger man's subterfuge, I wished them both well.

CHAPTER 19

Those Men! Those Women!

I convinced Holmes shortly after to stop at a café for a sandwich and lemonade. The temperature remained oppressive, but the bright sun was now occluded by dark thunderclouds. I was sweating even in my linen suit. We sat at an outdoor table amongst a small crowd of animated students, who were arguing philosophical problems which were so much gibberish to me. I ordered a ham sandwich and lemonade, but Holmes abstained. He sat reading the paper from Buttons, then handed it to me. I read:

> Say what strange motive, Goddess! could compel
> A well-bred Lord t' assault a gentle Belle?
> O say what stranger cause, yet unexplor' d,
> Could make a gentle Belle reject a Lord?

In tasks so bold, can little men engage,
And in soft bosoms dwells such mighty Rage?

I gave him back the page. '"A gentle Belle reject a Lord."
What does this mean, Holmes?'

'A general warning, no doubt. Note the reference to rage,'
said he. 'But the deacon penned this note, and he has a
vested interest in warning Dillie off her two rival beaus.
My worry is about those threatening letters one of them
might have sent.'

'*Might* have sent?'

'The deacon has lied to us before. And who tore off the
arm? Someone in a rage or wishing to threaten. My instincts
tell me that the deacon was telling the truth, at least about
that.'

'What about this line here, Holmes: "A well-bred Lord
t' assault a gentle Belle"? Isn't one of her beaus in line for
a dukedom?'

Holmes nodded. 'Yes. I am not yet ready to leave that
irritating young lady on her own. Watson, we must visit
the two young suitors so that I may take the measure of
each. Finish your sandwich.'

The aristocrat Freddie Eden-Summers was to be first. His
Great Court lodging at Trinity was the perfect picture-postcard
subject of romantic Cambridge. Three storeys high, with
ancient stone arches, gargoyles and mullioned windows with
leaded glass, the student lodgings were designed to face a
spacious green of great beauty. After a brief chat with the
porter, in which Holmes mentioned the revered Professor

Wyndham's name, implying that we were in service of that august person, the porter informed us that Freddie Eden-Summers was playing tennis at that moment with friends some ten minutes' walk away.

We came upon the courts, and were pointed to a tall, pink-cheeked lad with a luxurious mop of golden-brown curls, who was in the midst of smoothly annihilating his opponent. His movements were elegant and graceful, his expensive sports clothes, teasing manner and natural charm giving the impression of a privileged and self-confident young gentleman of leisure.

The game finished a minute or two later, and Holmes seized the moment to approach the boy.

'Mr Frederick Eden-Summers,' he called out cheerfully. 'May I have a word, please? My name is Sherlock Holmes, and I am up from London on behalf of the Wyndhams. I am a renowned planner of weddings.'

'Weddings?'

'Miss Odelia Wyndham has requested me to organize her upcoming wedding and asked me to consult with you.'

My jaw must have dropped, for Holmes quickly clenched my arm, saying, 'And this is my partner, the celebrated London florist, John Watson. You are thinking lilies and roses are you not, John?'

'I, uh . . .'

'And clematis?'

'Certainly, clematis. Orange blossoms,' I added, 'but only a few. They overpower.'

162

Eden-Summers laughed. He had perfect white teeth, long blond eyelashes and was a young Greek god in every aspect. I could see why Dillie's older sister Atalanta would describe him in such glowing terms – and why any young girl would consider him a prize.

'Wedding? To Dillie! Why, that cheeky young thing! I have not even proposed yet! Silly girl. A bit presumptuous, wouldn't you say?'

'Not proposed? Why, er, then there must be some mistake,' Holmes blustered.

'Well, I am close to it, to be sure. Ah, those Wyndham women! Her sister, Atalanta, she is something. Watch out for that one! A narrow escape on my part!'

'But Miss Odelia? Dillie? She has not accepted you yet?'

'I tell you I have not proposed. But I don't see why she should refuse.' He shrugged, smiling. 'She's certainly been welcoming to my, er, attentions. Hmm . . . I say, old man, you are getting a bit personal! You are here to plan her wedding? This must be her idea of a joke!'

Holmes as the 'wedding planner' looked suitably contrite. 'I am quite embarrassed, sir, and beg your pardon. It seems Mr Watson and I are here in error. Good day.'

'Oh, don't go away all sorry like that. Here's something for your pains.' He reached into his pocket and pulled out a crumpled five-pound note, and offered it to Holmes, who looked at it like it might be a snake. I took it and doffed my hat. As a florist might, I supposed.

'Do not worry, gentlemen. We'll hire you for the wedding if we do decide to tie the knot. That Dillie! Quite a sense of humour she has!' His lighthearted guffawing followed us off the court.

'Not our man, then, Holmes?' I said when we were out of earshot.

'He would not be an obvious choice. If there were a threat, he is low on the list of suspects, though I'd like to know more of his temper. Let us pay a quick visit to Dillie's other suitor, Mr Vitale.'

'May he be her *only* other suitor,' said I.

Holmes laughed.

We reached St Cedd's College, but Vitale was not in his rooms either, and we were directed to the Cavendish Laboratory. We headed south and upon arriving at the imposing stone building on Free School Lane, Holmes paused a moment, staring up at the dramatic, Gothic arched entrance.

'I wanted to attend this University, study here,' he remarked. 'At the Cavendish.' It was an uncharacteristic personal admission, and I looked at him in surprise.

'Why did you not, Holmes?'

'Did you know that James Clerk Maxwell's personal library has just been donated by his widow? I would love to spend some time with that collection.'

'You have not answered my question.'

'Perhaps another time, Watson.'

After wandering the halls briefly, we were directed to the physics lab. There we found ourselves in a long, narrow room facing an array of strange glass tubes, electrical equipment, wires, and beakers of chemicals. A much larger version of the strange device in our sitting-room that Holmes had called a 'Ruhmkorff Coil' stood on a table near the door. Long stone counters ran the length of the room.

A lone young man sat at the far end of the room, poring over a single sheet of paper, his head in his hands, concentrating in a manner that looked as if he could burn a hole in the page. He was so thin and pale that he made Holmes look positively blooming in comparison. Dark reddish-brown hair, worn unfashionably long, flopped over his forehead.

'Mr Vitale?' said Holmes as we approached him.

The boy looked up as though surprised by a human presence. Perhaps twenty or twenty-two, Leo Vitale had a handsome but serious young face, with high cheekbones and piercing green eyes, magnified slightly by a pair of round silver spectacles. A 'surprised baby owl', Atalanta Wyndham had called him.

He was rather a good-looking fellow but appeared to have a mind in the clouds.

'Why is the sky blue?' he asked, dreamily.

'What? Why is the rain wet?' I exclaimed, already annoyed at this second overprivileged youth. What would England come to with these debauched characters cluttering up our finest institutions?

The boy looked at me blankly.

'It is a physics problem, Watson.' Holmes turned to the boy. 'Rayleigh scattering,' he said. 'The sunlight bouncing off the molecules of the atmosphere.'

The young man blinked and seemed to arrive back on

earth. A shy smile, followed by 'Yes, you have it, sir. But Mr Fortuny will be in later. I am busy now.' He turned away from us and picked up a long, delicate glass tube in the shape of a corkscrew.

'Ah, Cosimo Fortuny, I know of him!' said Holmes. 'And I would love to chat with him about artificial lightning. A storm in a glass tube. But we are here to see *you*, Mr Vitale.'

No reaction. Vitale continued to busy himself with the glass tubing before him.

'Young man, I am here in regard to Miss Odelia Wyndham.'

The fellow started, dropping the glass tube which shattered on the counter.

'Careful, I would imagine those Geissler tubes are not easy to come by.'

'Who are you?' asked the boy, his voice barely a whisper.

'I am Sherlock Holmes, and this is Dr John Watson.'

I was tempted to add 'florist' but restrained the impulse.

Leo Vitale regarded us with a remarkably flat, contained expression. I wondered if he masked himself in this manner consciously or truly was feeling next to nothing.

'Mr Vitale, if we could go somewhere to discuss—?' began Holmes.

'Excuse me, gentlemen,' said a voice behind us. We turned to see a charismatic and darkly handsome young man in his late twenties, with a swath of thick, black hair and the chiselled features of a theatre performer. 'I am Cosimo Fortuny. We do not allow visitors in this laboratory, for the very reason you have just witnessed. Who are you and what is your business here?' He had a mellifluous, cultured voice.

'Ah, Mr Fortuny!' exclaimed Holmes. 'I have read of your work on the effects of rapidly alternating currents on various gases! A pleasure to meet you. I see you are trying Geissler tubes of various shapes and diameters. Why, I wonder?'

If Fortuny was impressed, it was not apparent. 'What is your business, sir?' he asked coldly.

Holmes gave our names again. 'We are up from London on personal business that concerns Mr Vitale. Nothing to do with your research.'

'Then how do you know of it?'

'Mr Holmes follows such things,' I said. 'Much as other men follow football. Those Hiburnians, quite something, eh?'

Fortuny laughed. 'Ah, all right! An amateur scientist. I know your kind. You doubtless have some arcane specimens of something in a glass case. Perhaps even a small Bunsen burner in your sitting-room. Go ahead, Leo. Remove yourselves to the hall, please.'

I sensed Holmes about to make a stinging retort and pulled him through the door.

In a moment, we stood facing Leo Vitale in the hallway. There was something awkward about the thin young man, something not at ease. It was as if he had only newly inhabited this body and still didn't know how it worked. His gestures were stilted, self-conscious. But when he smiled, which was rare, this awkwardness melted away and the fellow did, I suppose, have a certain uncultivated charm.

'How can I be of help, Mr Holmes?' he asked.

'Mr Vitale, I have been called in by Miss Wyndham's family,' said Holmes. 'They are worried about her disappearance. May I see the bottom of your left shoe?'

I looked down at Vitale's shoes. They were of good quality but worn. What on earth was Holmes on about?

The fellow hesitated, then raised and twisted his foot to display the sole, on which a large patch was evident. Holmes smiled at this.

Vitale frowned, then understanding dawned. 'My footprint?' he mused. 'You are a detective. But where . . . ?' His eyes flicked back and forth, and he put a hand to his forehead. 'Oh, the tree! Her house!' He coloured violently. 'How careless of me,' he mumbled. 'But she hasn't truly disappeared.'

Holmes smiled at the boy's quickness. 'I am aware. We have just come from her. I am not here to censure, Mr Vitale. Rather to understand who might have sent a threatening letter to Miss Wyndham.'

'What? Someone has threatened Dillie? Sir, I must know more!' He brushed the hair out of his eyes nervously. 'What is the nature of these threats? Enough to call in a man from London? Who called you, sir? And why have you come to me?'

'Are you not seeing the young lady? I believe you have also visited Miss Dillie at her hideaway?'

'Er . . .'

'No use prevaricating. She said so herself.'

'If *you* know of this place, and *I* know that she hasn't disappeared, then you know that I have been there.'

'Did you threaten Miss Wyndham?'

'No, sir! You confound me!'

'Do you know the Jesus Lock footbridge? Do you go there often?' Holmes studied the young man closely for a reaction.

'Yes, I know it, and no, not often. What is this about?'

'Did you find Miss Odelia's doll there, the one that looks like her, and throw it in the river after tearing off its arm?' Holmes did not take his eyes off the boy's face.

The young man went white, and he tried to speak but couldn't. 'Has that happened?' he finally asked.

Holmes said nothing but kept his eyes on the boy.

'By God – if there were a God, I'd ask Him to protect her,' said Vitale. 'We must go to the police!'

'The police know of it. It is why I have been called in.'

'But why you are questioning me? You cannot think I would threaten Miss Odelia Wyndham? I . . . I have feelings for her.' He followed this with a nervous glance back at the laboratory door. 'Sir, I hope to make her my wife. Now you know, and I hope that you will retain this confidence. My position here is hard won. Science requires a devotion that, well—'

'Devotion to science can be all-consuming, Mr Vitale,' said my friend.

'With all respect, sir, how would you possibly know about that?'

169

'Because Mr Holmes has made a science of his own work,' said I.

Vitale shrugged dismissively. 'You can know nothing of real science, sir. Nor of my feelings!'

Holmes paused, evaluating. 'Watson, come. I am satisfied.' He turned on his heel and marched away in his precipitous manner, leaving me to face the young scientist.

Vitale called out, 'But Mr Holmes, what of this threat?'

Holmes was already halfway down the hall.

'Don't worry, Mr Vitale,' I said. 'Miss Wyndham is in good hands. Sherlock Holmes will ensure it.'

In retrospect, I wish with all my heart that I had not said those words.

CHAPTER 20

The Mind Reader

n hour later, our train steamed south towards London. Outside, a white haze of rain softened our view of the green fields, hedges and trees speeding by. We were alone in our first-class compartment. Holmes tried several times to read a newspaper, but finally flung it down in frustration and stared out of the window at the passing scenery.

'That arm,' he said at last. 'I don't like the dismembered doll. I do not like it at all, Watson.'

'Any further thoughts on the perpetrator?'

'That is what troubles me. It could be either of her obvious suitors, one arrogant and entitled, the other strange and secretive. Or it could be our mendacious deacon, who has his own agenda. I suppose it could also be someone unknown to us at present. Dillie is both an attractive and a highly inflammatory young person. She is the flame to which many moths are drawn, to be sure.'

'Perhaps we should not have left her on her own,' I said. 'With all those "moths".'

'And what do you suggest? That we camp out in her hideaway? It is clear she will be neither advised nor controlled.'

I could not argue with him. We sat in silence as the green countryside passed by.

'That makes two rather formidable ladies, Holmes, in the course of only two days. Madame Borelli seems to be similarly, shall we say, independent.'

'Yes. Both of these women strike me as—'

'Well, they did both *strike* you, Holmes. And you were not even being half as rude as I've had occasion to see you be.'

He laughed. 'Yes, I suppose they did, didn't they?'

'Perhaps we would be as quick to anger were we in the same position as either of them.'

Holmes grimaced. 'Empathy comes naturally to you, Doctor. No wonder the ladies love you so.'

'Well, they are only human, Holmes,' I said. 'To whom are you more sympathetic, Miss Wyndham or Madame Borelli?'

'Neither. I look only to see if I can be of use. Women think differently than we do. It seems that everything is far more personal, more charged.'

'Except, Holmes, as you have often said, it is a capital error to generalize.'

'True enough. In Odelia Wyndham's case, her disdain and casual cruelty puts her in jeopardy, I fear.'

Holmes sighed, then tilted his straw fedora over his brow and leaned back in his seat to nap. I attempted to admire the scenery, but the green fields held no particular attraction. High in the sky and off in the distance were the gathering thunderclouds I had noted in Cambridge.

As our train steamed on, I supposed that being slapped twice in twenty-four hours might set a man off in a negative direction. I have never been struck by a woman in my life. I could not imagine that would ever happen to me, save perhaps by some gross misunderstanding.

No, not even then, I mused. Shortly after, I put my newspaper down and must have dozed.

Strangely, the sweet face of my long-dead mother appeared in a dream. She was frowning and waved an index finger at me. In the moment, I was much shorter than she, a small boy. She was admonishing me, but I could not hear the words, try as I might to understand her. This image faded, blurred and reappeared. Now my mother was slightly older, but her face looked wavy, eerily tinged with blue green as if underwater, and her eyes were bulging.

I awoke with a start as our train was pulling into King's Cross. My mother's image stayed with me, and I was left with a feeling of dread. When I was eleven my mother had drowned, and the circumstances of her death were cloudy. I never could believe suicide. The tragedy had scarred our family, and my elder brother Harry had never recovered.

The brakes of the train squealed loudly as we slowed

into the station, and I turned sharply away from these thoughts. I had rarely been troubled by nightmares.

In minutes we were back at Baker Street. Holmes sent a cable to the Wyndhams, explaining that Odelia was safe, and they could communicate to her via our address. I retired to my room and checked that my silver box was safe in my desk drawer.

As I closed and locked the drawer, I suddenly saw my mother's drowned face again. I shuddered and blinked it away, feeling the full effect of two tumultuous days and the blinding heat. I was exhausted. Tomorrow, I would take my box to someone Holmes recommended.

The next morning, I awoke to find Holmes had already breakfasted and was out on an unknown errand. It had rained overnight but the oppressive heat had turned the summer showers into a steamy downpour. I sat over coffee, contemplating the small silver box which I had freed from my desk drawer. I toyed with the slender metal bands that braided decoratively around it, culminating in that mysterious lock. Would moving them trigger the lock in some way?

I heard Holmes arrive downstairs and tucked the bonny thing into my dressing-gown pocket.

He joined me at the breakfast table. His eyes raked over me in that disconcerting fashion. 'There is Chubb's over near St Paul's. They were tasked with locking up the Koh-i-Noor Diamond during the exhibition. You could try there,' he said.

'What?'

'Most famous locksmith in London. If he cannot help you, then Boobbyer, 14 Stanhope Street, the Strand, might.'

'Boobbyer? Odd name!'

He smiled. 'Probably an attempt at anglicization of a French word. Bobbière, or something.'

'Holmes, how on earth do you know of—'

'Simple research, Watson!'

'No! You are not a mind reader! How did you know that I was thinking of the box?'

'Bulge in your dressing-gown pocket. Cigar-cutter on the table. You don't smoke cigars in the morning.'

'But I might.'

'But you do not. You have been attempting to open that box. Fruitlessly, I might add.'

He picked up a large envelope which had arrived for him, opened it and gave a shout of delight. 'Ah! Files on the Cavendish Laboratory. I have an inside track there, Watson. I have learned a bit more of Cosimo Fortuny's work. Fascinating!' He eagerly removed a stack of files, tossing the envelope onto the floor.

Mrs Hudson brought more coffee. She skulked out with a glance at the littered floor, clearly irritated at Holmes's continual additions to the disarray.

'Holmes, I'm going to try that second locksmith you named – Boobbyer?'

'Do go, dear fellow, I must read these files. You'll be back in an hour, I warrant. Then we are off to visit Santo Colangelo. I have gone to the address Madame Borelli gave for her former flame while you lingered abed this morning. It seems he has moved on to cheaper lodgings. I sent him a note, and he has agreed to see us. Go, Watson, have your consultation with Boobbyer!'

My visit to the second locksmith was a disappointment. Mr Boobbyer, a kindly old man with an eyepatch and a pendulous lower lip, attempted for fifteen minutes to assail my mysterious box. He then handed it back, unopened.

'Trick lock,' he said. 'Specialty item. No one can open this. You'll need the key, and instructions.'

'What do you mean a trick lock?' I demanded.

'I mean it's tricked. Picking won't work. It will either take more than one key or something like a key partially inserted, turned, then inserted further and turned another way two times, followed by pressure on this little lever – some odd combination like that. Unless you know how to open this lock, you won't be able to.'

'I thought all locks were assailable in some fashion,' I said.

'No, they are not. Would you like me to try drilling it open?'

I hesitated. Not knowing the contents, or their placement in the box, I was leery to progress to this. 'Let me consider it,' I said, and pocketed the box.

I arrived back at Baker Street in a surly mood, aggravated by Holmes's irritation at having been made to wait. We then set out at once for Colangelo's new address.

The rain had done nothing to dispel the tropical heat which suffocated London. As we rattled towards the Strand past limp plane trees and drooping pedestrians, Holmes exuded a jittery energy I had seen often enough when he had not enough to occupy that great, churning mind.

Borelli's fate was of marginal interest to him, of that I was sure. Holmes was convinced the fellow could look after himself and was perhaps even guilty of rigging his own accident. Nevertheless, he had promised Ilaria Borelli to investigate her former lover, magician Santo Colangelo, to determine conclusively his involvement with last night's near fiasco.

Santo Colangelo's lodgings were in The Blackbird Arms, on a dingy side street off the Strand. As we stood outside the door to his rooms, the strong smell of onion soup filled the shabby, dimly lit hallway. Holmes admonished me to say little. I wondered what story he had concocted for the man to receive us.

Santo Colangelo opened the door and I was struck by his strong resemblance to the Great Borelli. Tall, dark-complexioned, and with some heaviness about the middle, he sported the same pointed beard and moustache, making him appear like an older, less athletic brother of the more famous man. There was something softer about him, rounder, less aggressive, but still quite handsome. Like Borelli, he had a thatch of thick, shiny black hair, worn long, but groomed back from his face.

Madame must have a particular kind of man who attracted her, I thought. I wondered if her new love, the professor, also fit the mould.

Colangelo was dressed in threadbare street clothes, over

which he had thrown a once expensive but equally worn Chinese silk dressing gown. In the room behind him, I could make out a massive clutter of books, papers and magic paraphernalia. A crystal ball glinted in the sun from an open window, and decks of cards spilled onto the floor. Various other items which I did not recognize, decorated imaginatively with glittering stars and symbols, were strewn about the room. No fewer than four cats were draped on the backs of chairs, the sofa and a table. They appeared to be asleep and I hoped they remained so. I disliked cats for their sudden surprises.

The man fingered a coin in his left hand which he made dance between his fingers, right to left, then left to right. I noticed his right hand stayed in the pocket of his dressing gown.

'Sherlock Holmes and Dr Watson,' said Colangelo, greeting us with a certain chilly reserve. 'Ilaria sent word you were coming. I would otherwise have turned down your request, Mr Holmes. If you will forgive me, I no longer shake hands. Enter.'

Something strange glinted in his mouth as he spoke.

We stepped into a large room which served as both a sitting-room and bedroom in this hotel. A small double bed was tucked into a corner and two large armoires were cracked slightly open, revealing a jumble of items and what I presumed was the man's entire wardrobe, including some rather garish velvet jackets. Several tables were about, including one containing foodstuffs and a heating device not unlike Holmes's Bunsen burner, and another that served as a dressing table. A sink sat in one corner; piled in it were several cheap dishes encrusted with food. A makeshift living arrangement, I thought, poor, yet infinitely better than those of the many vagrants who littered the parks and alleyways of London.

We were invited to sit on a lumpy velvet sofa which faced the windows, and Colangelo took a seat on a high-backed wooden chair, sharply silhouetted. It put us, or at least me, at a distinct disadvantage, for the man's features were hard to make out.

Holmes hesitated to join me and moved instead to the windows, where he pulled back the curtain and glanced out at the street.

Colangelo regarded him strangely.

'Do sit, Mr Holmes,' he said.

Holmes scanned the room once more, then joined me on the sofa and proceeded to waste no time.

'Mr Colangelo, you know that I am here on behalf of Madame Ilaria Borelli. She is concerned about the incident in which you lost a finger from a small device provided to you by the Borellis. She believes that you blame her husband for this accident. Do you, in fact, believe he tampered with the device in order to cause you injury?'

The magician shrugged. The coin continued to dance across the fingers of his left hand.

'She fears retribution,' continued Holmes. 'We all are wondering if perhaps you were behind the accident which befell Mr Borelli the night before last. You know of it?'

'Of course. The police questioned me.' His English had only the slightest trace of an Italian accent.

'And—?'

The man snorted. 'If I were guilty, I would hardly say so.'

'Where were you throughout that day?'

'Here. Practising.'

'Alone?'

The man nodded. But his sideways glance gave evidence, even to me, that he was lying.

'Then you have no alibi?' persisted Holmes.

'The police did not ask for one.'

'But I do.'

'I . . . Yes, all right then. I do have an alibi. She will prove I was here. A young lady. She was with me all day.'

'Will she vouch for you?' said the detective.

'Her reputation—'

'Will she vouch privately for you, to me?'

A pause. 'Yes.'

'Her name?'

'Eloise Marchand.' Colangelo continued to weave the coin through the fingers of his left hand. I noticed he did so without looking.

'Summon her,' said Holmes.

'I cannot, she works in the daytime at a milliner's.'

'And the day before yesterday—?'

'Her day off. Easy to confirm. I tell you, she was with me all day. And late, past ten.' He smiled. The mysterious glint was revealed as a small diamond embedded in one of his canines. A theatrical touch!

'And the name of the shop where she works?'

'Capital Toppers. In Soho.'

'I will check,' said Holmes. 'But back to the sad accident causing damage to your finger. Do you blame Borelli for the incident?'

Colangelo's smile dropped. 'No! That idiot. Borelli could not have done so. He is an ignoramus.' He pronounced it 'ig-nor-a-*moose*'. 'I thought Ilaria sent you to find who actually did tamper with the device.'

'So then Madame Borelli has no reason to worry that you intend her husband harm?'

'Ilaria? She wishes to cause me trouble, perhaps? She is angry with me because I left her.'

'She states otherwise, Mr Colangelo. She says that she left you for Borelli. She told me this accident ruined your act, and for that you blame Borelli.'

'Why would that fool do me harm? If she left me for Borelli, truly, then he has "won the prize", as you say. Ilaria is his.'

'Then Madame Borelli did leave you?'

Colangelo was silent for a moment. Then, finally, 'Well, yes. We had a . . . a falling out.'

Just then the coin slipped from his left hand where it had continued its dance. It hit the floor and rolled over to me, stopping when it struck my foot. I leaned down to retrieve it and handed it to Colangelo.

'Mr Colangelo, we could save valuable time if you would only begin with the truth instead of arriving at it by circuitous means. Is Madame Borelli accurate in saying that locks are not your forté?'

The man shrugged. He placed the coin on the table, stood up, and approached me, standing close. Uncomfortably close. I remained seated but felt uneasy.

'How adept *are* you at dealing with mechanical contraptions, Mr Colangelo?' persisted Holmes.

'I am not so good with the locks. I am what's called the "sleight of hand".' He gently waved his empty left hand in the air. With a sudden lunge, and before I could react, Colangelo struck me a sharp blow on the side of the head.

CHAPTER 21

The Tables Turned

'*uch!*' It happened so fast that I had no time to duck.

A coin appeared in Colangelo's left hand, as though he'd removed it from my hair.

'Sleight of hand will be learned by the left hand! Progress, you see!' he exclaimed triumphantly, holding up this second coin.

He sat back down in the chair facing us and placed this coin next to the first on the table. A third appeared as if by magic in his left hand, and he resumed threading it back and forth through his fingers. 'Though now I am mostly a mind reader.'

'A mind reader, yes, of course,' said Holmes, archly. 'Madame Borelli so informed us. Perhaps a more difficult trick.'

'It is no trick,' said Colangelo. 'Mind-reading, this is the *real* magic.'

Holmes shook his head.

'I see that you doubt me, Mr Holmes. Then tell me this: how do I know that you drink your coffee black? That you eat very little? That you play a stringed instrument? That you care very much for the man sitting beside you? Too much, perhaps. It may be the death of you.'

There was a pause. I glanced at Holmes, realizing at once that my reaction to this could easily give something away. I turned back to Colangelo, attempting to keep my face neutral.

To my surprise, Holmes laughed.

'Not bad,' said he. 'Three of four are correct. But a trifle obvious.'

'How so?' asked Colangelo, his irritation evident.

'The cuff of my left sleeve has the slightest coffee stain, but dark, with no milk. You are lucky in that one. I did not notice this, or I would have changed shirts before coming.'

'It is surprising, as I see from the rest of your clothes that you are very – what is the word? – fastidious.'

'I was in a hurry. I am thin, although this could be from illness—'

'There is no sign of ill health.'

'Therefore, I am a light eater. Obvious. And I have calluses on the fingers of my left hand, but not the right, from which you infer a stringed instrument. That, at least, indicates keen observation. They are not terribly noticeable, but you are looking for such clues.'

Colangelo smiled broadly and shook his head. 'No. It is all magic.'

'I do not believe in magic.'

'You are one of few. So you think number four is wrong? That you do not care—'

'There is no magic, Mr Colangelo. But how, then, do I know that you are a hypochondriac, have recently gained weight, hide sweets in your humidor, and are currently seeing not one but two young ladies?'

Colangelo froze. His jaw twitched.

Holmes waved his arms in a flourish. 'Magic!'

'You have been spying on me!'

'No. We met for the first time just now.'

Colangelo's eyes darted around the room. 'You are guessing!'

'Not at all. You look perfectly healthy, if perhaps overfed, but you have more medicines than six consumptives, and these are visible in the small cabinet above your sink with the door slightly ajar. That, coupled with your copy of Gunn's *Home Book of Health* marked with dozens of bookmarks by your bed over there, reveal without a doubt your hypochondria.'

'Sir!'

'There is more. Your humidor is nowhere near your smoking paraphernalia – but instead sits next to your collection of biscuits and teas. And wrappings from several horehound candies I recognize by their distinctive red stripes are visible in this small bin nearby, and two more under the bed, there. Also, there is no indication of any cigar smoking nor odour of it, either. Why, then, a humidor? Your consumption of sweets explains the minute holes in the waist of the trousers you are wearing, which indicates they have been let out, and very recently, as several threads are still hanging from the last hole.'

'That is simple observation, not mind-reading!'

'This can hardly surprise you.'

'But what of the two young ladies, Holmes?' I asked. 'If I may be so indiscreet?'

Holmes turned to me with a smile. 'There is a dressing gown, I have noted: pink, in Mr Colangelo's closet there, Watson. And it is of petite proportions – you really should be careful to close your cabinet doors, Mr Colangelo. I also note a hairbrush, over here, which I suppose could be yours, except for the long blonde hair entangled in it.'

'I have already told you I am seeing a young lady!'

'But two?' I persisted.

'Well, Watson, at this very moment, a tall *brunette* young lady is pacing across the street, staring at these windows in considerable pique.'

Colangelo ran to the window and peered carefully through the narrowest of openings in the sheer curtains. 'Clara!' he cried. 'Damnation!'

'So, two young ladies, then,' said Holmes.

Colangelo turned from the window, quivering with rage. 'Get out!'

'Mr Colangelo, I have no doubt that your new trade is not really so very different from my own. Fear not, I have no intention of revealing your secrets. Before we go, let me simply examine the device which caused your accident.'

'No!'

'You still have it, I presume. Is that it on the table over there?' At the magician's hesitation, Holmes continued. 'Do you not want to get to the bottom of this mystery? Surely you wish to know how this harm befell you?'

Holmes stood, retrieved the device, and sat back down, examining it.

'Careful, Holmes,' I said.

Colangelo hesitated, his face working to disguise his fury, and something else. Guilt, I thought.

'Or perhaps you already know how it happened?' said Holmes.

The magician looked down at his feet, ashamed.

Holmes said nothing, staring at the man. 'You did it yourself.'

Colangelo looked around him as if imploring help from unseen beings. His eyes glistened. 'I am not sure,' he said. 'I thought to improve the trick. Make faster. Make a loud sound. More dramatic. I try to adjust the mechanism.'

'And Madame Borelli?' prompted Holmes. 'You accused her husband—'

A tear coursed down the man's cheek which he wiped away quickly with his right hand. I got a glimpse of the ruined index finger, mangled and missing its tip. He thrust his hand into his pocket. 'Honestly I do not know. Dario Borelli visited me the day before my accident. He picked up the guillotine. I think maybe he did something. Or maybe it was me. But if Madame thinks it was him, she might—'

'—feel guilty and return to you? You love her still,' said Holmes. 'Understandable. She is a magnificent woman.' He peered into the small device. 'I take it you are unskilled with mechanical things.'

'Yes. I have help when I can afford it. And Ilaria, she is very, very good.'

'I believe you were not the person behind Borelli's accident. But carry on, sir, I am sure you will profit by your "mind-reading".'

Holmes set down the little guillotine, rose, and with a polite goodbye exited the room. I took my leave and followed, Colangelo right behind me. I caught a brief glimpse of the morose magician just before he closed the door with a click.

Out in the hallway I said, 'Holmes, there is something I do not understand. Why on earth did he draw that silly conclusion about—?'

The door flew open and Colangelo peered out at me. 'Ah, Dr Watson! That fourth observation? Correct, as were the others. You did not see the expression on Mr Holmes's face when I struck you on the side of the head.'

He slammed the door shut.

Presumptuous fellow, I thought. Utterly ridiculous.

I turned to say something to Holmes, but he was already at the end of the hall, disappearing down the stairwell.

'Holmes!' I called and dashed after him.

CHAPTER 22

Danger in the Doldrums

pon returning to Baker Street, Holmes informed Madame Borelli via a brief letter that Santo Colangelo may have mangled his own finger accidentally, although Dario Borelli was not entirely in the clear. Colangelo had not engineered her husband's near drowning, however, neither was he jealous (having two paramours himself) nor handy enough. Holmes suggested the culprit in Borelli's accident was closer to home, naming both Falco Fricano, the stage-hand, and Borelli himself as the likely culprits. In this missive, he offered to continue along those paths in the investigation, should she wish.

By return post, and within the hour, Madame curtly dismissed both the theory and Holmes from the case. The letter enclosed a cheque for a modest sum.

'And that is the end of that saga,' he remarked wryly. 'I think it most likely to be her husband, and by now she has figured it out.'

'Well, that is her problem then, isn't it?' I was secretly sorry, as the arcane elements and the colourful client herself were at least a welcome distraction.

Holmes retired to his bedroom with a book about physics, closed the door and did not emerge for supper.

Three days passed. We heard nothing from Cambridge, and neither Dillie nor her parents communicated with Holmes. Holmes cabled once or twice to Inspector Hadley, but, receiving no response there, was forced to let that case moulder as well.

Two fascinating cases, at least to my mind, had stagnated. What I did not realize at the time was that both were sleeping monsters. But of course I was keenly aware that another danger lurked in our very rooms. Torpor bred peril of its own kind for my friend.

While London continued to suffer under relentless, oppressive heat, no fresh cases presented themselves. For days he never once left our rooms, nor did he dress, but spent hour after hour sprawled on our sofa in his white cotton nightclothes. The blue dressing gown he often wore had been discarded in the heat, and it was like having some great white ghost lying in sullen stillness in the centre of our sitting-room.

From time to time Holmes arose, sawed tunelessly on the violin, then sank back down again. He would not eat and refused the cooling beverages Mrs Hudson offered to him.

These were the precise conditions under which my friend was most likely to turn towards artificial stimulants. While I longed to escape, or to pursue my mysterious silver box with another try at a locksmith, I resolutely remained with him, and vigilant. I busied myself with notes on old cases, a couple of cheap yellow-backed novels, and the newspapers. As the days passed, even the mystery of my silver box seemed to fade in the atmosphere of indolence and malaise that had settled into 221B.

It was upon the fifth day of this self-imposed confinement that I chanced upon a notice in *The Times* that Professor Richard Wyndham of Cambridge had announced the engagement of his daughter Miss Odelia Wyndham to Mr Frederick Eden-Summers, eldest son of the Duke of Harbingden. An unsmiling portrait of the young lady appeared next to the notice. Holmes's response was a dismissive wave of the hand and silence. Nothing I could say would entice him to dress or to leave our rooms and go for a walk or any other activity.

By the next day, Thursday, I could stand internment with my morose companion no longer and ventured out into the sweltering city with my mysterious silver box to Chubb's Lock Company, the second of the locksmiths that he had recommended.

Two hours later I returned, after having received the identical response I had gotten earlier from Mr Boobbyear and having been charged an exorbitant price for this useless information. The infernal box was secured with a trick lock and apparently was impregnable, except by destroying it.

As I entered into the foyer, Mrs Hudson greeted me with a worried look. 'What is it?' I asked.

'Listen.'

I could hear the strains of Holmes's violin playing a racing, frenetic melody.

'Well, better that than his recent tuneless atrocities,' I remarked.

'But it has been going on since you left. Some two and a half hours, Doctor. With no pause. None at all!'

That set me back. 'Since *immediately* after I left?'

'No, about ten minutes after.'

That could mean only one thing. I raced up the stairs.

Holmes was standing silhouetted in the window, his nightshirt billowing in the faint breeze, playing in a frenzy of excitement.

'Holmes!' I cried.

He did not hear me but continued playing. The piece reached a crescendo and ended. He put down the violin with a flourish and waved his bow in the air.

'I have done it!' he shouted.

'What?'

'I have memorized all six of Bach's Sonatas and Partitas! Without a flaw! I recreated them in my mind, retrieving it page by page. I could *see* it!'

His eyes were feverishly bright. His face was damp with perspiration, and his whole body vibrated with excitement.

'In two hours? How do you know it was perfect?'

'Memorization! I review it once! I have it here,' he cried, tapping his forehead with his bow.

'Sit down, Holmes. You are in a kind of mania!'

'No, I am inspired!' But he did set down his bow. 'What, no luck with your box again?'

'How did you—?'

'Never mind. Just listen! I will play them for you!' He reached for his violin again, but I snatched it up and placed it in a far corner of the room. I moved over to his desk and tried to pull open the top drawer. It was locked. I turned to face him.

'What have you taken?'

He shrugged.

'Tell me now. Or I shall leave you in this mess, go to an hotel and send for my things. I mean it, Holmes.'

'Just the usual, Watson. A seven per cent solu—'

'Cocaine! The moment I leave. And something else. What else? Open this drawer. It is locked again.'

He waved and turned away. 'That is my business.'

'I would like my chequebook!'

'I would like an end to starvation and the discovery of the missing seventh Bach Partita.'

Madness! I picked up the fireplace poker, inserted the sharp edge into the drawer and with a loud crack, broke it open.

I yanked out the drawer. There, at the front, was the small morocco case with his hypodermic. Near to it was a half-empty bottle of cocaine solution, and further back in the drawer several small blue bottles. I pulled one out. Upon a flowery pink and blue label were the words 'Phillips Blissful Baby Soother'. It was a sleeping medicine for infants containing laudanum.

My God, he'd combined laudanum with cocaine! The combination could be lethal.

I glanced down at the small waste receptacle under the desk. Papers were piled to the top. I pushed them aside. At least twelve empty bottles of the Baby Soother were at the bottom. He must have been drugging himself with laudanum for days as I sat in the same room.

I looked up to see his look of guilt and alarm.

'It was only a mild soother, Watson, no harm done. I would have driven you mad without it. You would have run shouting into the streets, demanding roast beef and chorus girls.'

'No, you are the one on the edge of madness. Surely you know that laudanum is highly addictive and—?'

'Not in this small amount.'

'Holmes, I despair!' I cried. 'You are wrong and will turn that God-given intelligence to porridge. And combining it with cocaine? What on earth were you thinking?'

I snatched up the hypodermic, threw it to the floor, and crushed it under my boot, grinding it onto the wood at the edge of the carpet.

'Watson!' came an anguished cry.

I took up the small brush by the fireplace, swept the shards into a dustpan, and dumped them into that same waste receptacle. I then marched upstairs with the four bottles and flushed the remaining liquid down the toilet.

When I returned to the sitting-room, Holmes sat defeated on the sofa. He looked like a small child who had been deprived of his favourite toy. My patience was at an end. I flung a stack of unread newspapers at him.

'Good God, man!' I cried. 'Go through these newspapers. Surely there will be something to inspire you there. See who has been murdered. Check the agony columns. I guarantee you that something will engage that great heaving brain of yours.'

He looked up at me with sad, resigned eyes. 'It is unlikely, Watson. We have hit the bottom of the barrel. Our last two cases have gone nowhere but into the dung heap of sordid love affairs.'

'Self-pity does not become you, Holmes. It's the drugs. Pull yourself together.' I snatched one of the news-papers off the top of the pile and took it to my usual chair. 'I will find something if you will not!'

'What did Chubb's say about your box?'

'The same as Mr Boobbyer.'

'As I expected.'

'Then why did you suggest them?'

'A vain wish. I had hoped to avoid the one man I fear that you do, in fact, need.'

'What do you mean? What man? Give me the name.'

'You cannot visit him alone.'

'Oh, for God's sake, give me his name. You are going nowhere in this state.'

'He is . . . a somewhat shifty and malevolent character. In a rather forbidding area of town. No, Watson, out of the question.'

'Now you have piqued my curiosity. What is he – some kind of criminal?'

Holmes sat up on the settee. A change came over his

face as he savoured the idea. It took on the mien of an eager fox. 'He is a dangerous man with peculiar habits. But if anyone can open your lock, it is he.'

'Peculiar habits, you say? Pot, kettle, black!'

'Pot, kettle, black?'

'An expression from my childhood. You are the pot calling the kettle black. My mother read it somewhere and she used to . . . never mind.' But the idea was a good one. Getting him outside and moving could not hurt. 'Get dressed, Holmes. I want to go there now.'

Just then Mrs Hudson entered with a sandwich and a lemonade for Holmes. She set it down before him. 'Gentlemen, you will get out of this house or I will have you out on your ears. Mr Holmes, you will eat this first. And drink this. I have run you a bath. And then you will go out with the good doctor while I tidy this rubbish. And I will brook no objections. Get going, young man. Now.'

Mrs Hudson and I stood side by side, staring at the present shipwreck of a human being who never ceased to surprise me with his infinite and extreme variation. To my surprise, Holmes stood up, and without a word did exactly what our landlady had commanded.

And indeed it was just as well that I did not go to see Mr Knut Lossop alone.

PART FIVE

THE TUMBLERS

'From the point of view of the physicist, a theory of matter. . . ought to furnish a compass which, if followed will lead the observer further and further into previously unexplored regions.'

—J. J. Thomson

PART ONE

FINAL REMARKS

CHAPTER 23

The Story Collector

n just under an hour, Holmes – refreshed, perfectly groomed and impressive in his summer city suit of impeccable linen – emerged from Baker Street, looking as though he could easily stop en route to our next destination to take tea with the Queen or confront an errant MP in Whitehall. In fact, when not lounging about Baker Street in his dressing gown, this sober, conservative elegance was his natural presentation. The transformation was both rapid and profound, but I had to remind myself that I had seen it before, and regression could be swift. With my precious box stowed in a small satchel, I hailed a cab and we made our way to Hackney.

The address was hard to find even for Holmes, who had as clear an image of the London map in his head as I had of the human skeleton. At last we narrowed it down to one building. It was missing a number on the door, and there were no signs outside.

However, it was there, on the ground floor of an ancient Tudor construction of plaster and timber, on Durham Grove near a paint factory, that locksmith Knut Lossop ran his business. We entered the shop and squinted in the dim light. The windows were small, and a few candelabra provided the only illumination.

We had stepped back in time.

The proprietor emerged from the murk and in a moment we stood before the strange, gnome-like man. Lossop faced us in the flickering light over a long counter, on which were displayed a number of locks of varying sizes, shapes and levels of complexity. He was wizened, somewhere between forty and sixty years old, but lined and greasy, with long, thin blond hair plastered to his skull and draping limply down the back of his neck. An equally desultory moustache hung down by either side of moist pink lips, but in contrast to this lacklustre presentation, a pair of rheumy, pale blue eyes focused with pinpoint intensity on whatever they found.

At this particular moment, those eyes were riveted on Sherlock Holmes, who had just said something to him in a language I could not make out.

Lossop stood very still and chewed on one side of his moustache.

'Have I got that right, Mr Lossop?' asked Holmes.

'Speak only English here,' growled this pestiferous individual.

Holmes smiled. 'I gather, then, that your name is your own choice. Knut is common enough – it means "lock" in Norwegian, Watson – but Lossop? That sounds like an anglicization of *"låse opp"* – which means "unlocked". Therefore, a kind of self-advertisement in your choice of a pseudonym.'

'No pseudonym. Is my real name,' said the locksmith.

'Holmes, you speak Norwegian?' I asked.

Holmes frowned at me and nodded curtly. 'As you wish, Mr Lossop. I am sure there is an interesting reason for your choice to remain anonymous. Though one might easily trace you by your speciality. In any case, we bring before you a unique challenge. I am Sherlock Holmes. Ah, I see that you have heard my name before. This is my friend and colleague, Dr Watson. He received a package in the mail, containing a highly decorative silver box with an unusual lock. Both the good doctor and I have attempted to open this box—'

Lossop held out his hand, palm up, to receive the object. I noted thin, spidery fingers and long nails.

'Give,' he said.

'But let me complete the thought. Watson here brought it to – who was it, Watson?'

'Boobbyer on the Strand, and Chubb's.'

The locksmith snorted in derision.

'—with no luck. I have done my research. Your name, hard to come by, Mr Lossop, was at last given to me. You are in a class by yourself, apparently.' Holmes smiled solicitously.

'The box, please. I shall have a look.'

I took the scented soap container from my satchel, extracted the mysterious and beautiful silver box, and placed it on the counter between us.

Lossop crossed his arms in front of him and leaned towards it. He stared at the box for a full minute without touching it. Thoughts flickered across his sharp features, and a slow smile lit his pale face.

Holmes and I waited patiently. The locksmith then picked up the box, placed a jeweller's loupe over his spectacles and examined it minutely. He hummed tunelessly, and brought a candelabrum closer, holding the box to the flickering light to scrutinize something that evidently interested him.

He put the box down with a smile.

'Well, can you open it?' I asked.

'It is most probable. But not quickly.'

'If you cannot, can you break it open?'

'Yes, but that may well destroy the contents.'

This confirmed my fear.

He held up the box and pointed to a place on the side. I saw nothing but the swirling Celtic tracery. 'Look closer,' he commanded, and handed me the loupe.

I did, but could see nothing. The fine workings on the box were complicated, with lines of different depths, small pinpoint dots, and—

Holmes took the box and the loupe from my hand and, holding it up to the light, examined the area the locksmith had indicated. He handed both back to Lossop. 'I see,' he said.

'Well, *I* don't,' I said with some irritation.

'Someone tried to drill into this box, revealing that it is lined with something. I presume this material is much harder than silver, and blocked the drilling,' said Holmes.

'Exactly,' said Lossop.

'Like what?' I asked.

'A steel alloy, perhaps, even with tungsten?'

'Ha!' cried Lossop. 'Tool steel! Nothing harder. Except diamond.'

'Exactly,' continued Holmes. 'And that would explain why the box is so heavy for its size. One cannot drill into it to unlock it, Watson. Not easily, and perhaps not at all. I wonder where your family might have come upon such a box?'

'It was commissioned,' said Lossop. 'I recognize the workmanship, and I know the maker. Or I think I do.'

'Perhaps this person could help us?' asked Holmes.

'No. He is dead some five years. I have seen his work once before. My mentor, Andelan Schutz, showed one of his creations to me. He could not unlock it, but I did. It took me a month, however.'

'A month!' I exclaimed.

'Excellent that you exceeded your mentor,' said Holmes.

'Is that not the purpose of having a mentor?' murmured the man, taking the box back into his hands. Holmes's compliment had landed well. 'I relish the challenge.'

'Then you will open it for us?' I asked.

He set down the box abruptly. 'Perhaps. If you can meet my price.'

'We are not wealthy men,' said Holmes.

'I know that. You, at least, dress well, if conservatively, but you have a hungry look. You—' he turned to me, 'are more in fashion, but lack great means.'

Holmes had removed his chequebook.

'Put that away,' said the locksmith sharply.

'Yes, do. I will pay for this,' I said, reaching for my own, but then remembered that Holmes had locked it back in a drawer, having moved it from the one I had smashed open. That he thought to bring his own but not give me back mine gave me a moment of pique.

The locksmith held up a hand. 'I have not yet named my price. And I doubt *you* will have what I require, Doctor.'

Before I could rise to the insult, Holmes replied, 'What *is* your price, Mr Lossop?' His tone made me uneasy.

Lossop smiled and stepped back from the counter. Turning to the wall behind him, on which were shelves and shelves of locks, bolts, keys, tools and parts, he pulled a key which he wore on a chain around his neck and leaned towards a keyhole under a small handle at the back, dead centre of these shelves. There was the sound of a click, and to my surprise the shelves split and rolled apart to reveal a secret wall behind them.

On this wall were hung a series of locked metal boxes of various sizes. Each had a tag hanging from it, but the tags faced the wall, and I could see from my angle that something had been written on them, but what?

'I require a personal commitment from you. And a personal token. Something which you have in the past taken great care not to lose. Something that is very dear to you.'

Holmes was stone faced. Had he known? I, on the other hand, was puzzled in the extreme.

'I will lock it for you in a special box which I construct for the purpose,' Lossop continued, 'hang it on this wall, and I guarantee there is no locksmith alive who can open it but me.'

'But . . . why?' I asked, frankly amazed. 'And more to the point, how can you afford to live, paid in such a manner?'

'Banks, Watson,' said Holmes. 'The banks pay him handsomely for custom, unassailable locks. And there are other clients, not all of whom are legitimate businesses. Am I not right, Mr Lossop?'

Lossop's answer was the briefest smile. I shook my head, unconvinced.

'But why—?' I began.

'These are trophies, Watson.'

'What do you do with these things? Extort people?' I could not stop myself.

'No,' said Lossop. 'I . . . treasure them. I take them out upon occasion and ruminate on their value to the depositor. I revel in the human story. You see, I have few stories of my own. You might say I live vicariously. Oh, I see you don't understand. They offer a kind of sustenance.' He laughed, an unhealthy, percussive sound like a dry cough. 'Does that make it any clearer?'

I suddenly saw this strange, oleaginous little man as a kind of enchanted toad, hiding under a rock and picking over sparkling valuables stolen from people who had wandered too near – feeding on them. I was revolted.

But I looked down at the box in my hands. I had to discover what was inside it. *I had to know what my mother had left for me.* I did not trust Lossop but felt I had no choice.

'I . . . I don't know what I have to give you that would serve,' I said. 'Something I have kept and treasure? I don't know. Perhaps the charm off my brother's watch? No? The watch itself?'

Lossop shook his head.

'I believe I have . . . my childhood wooden soldiers, one or two . . . somewhere – er, a little clock, ticket stubs to the circus in 1860; my first stethoscope?' I had a vague recollection of something like these in a trunk in the attic at 221B. Lossop stared at me. 'I have a favourite hat?'

That laugh again. 'Dear Doctor, you are infinitely – what is the word – *ordinary.*' Lossop turned to stare at Holmes, who remained silent. 'But *you* have something. I know a man with secrets when I see one. What will you give me?'

Holmes, without taking his eyes off the man, reached into the inside pocket of his coat and removed a small brown envelope.

'You came prepared, Mr Sherlock Holmes,' said Lossop.

'I did indeed. I had heard of your collection.'

'Then why ask my price?'

'I was hoping money would suffice.'

Lossop stared at the envelope. He licked his lips.

'But clearly not,' said Holmes. 'Here is . . . here is a photograph.'

Lossop took the envelope and opened it. It was the

photograph of a beautiful young woman, a photograph that Holmes had taken in payment on a case which I had not yet published at that time. Remarkably, as it had seemed at the time so out of character, Holmes once said of the lady, 'She had a face a man might die for.' His feelings for this woman remained a mystery, as did much about my friend.

'And who is this?' asked Lossop, savouring the image like a gourmand contemplating a mound of expensive pâté.

'An opera singer,' said Holmes simply. 'I am a music lover. I would like it back when you are finished with it.'

'Music lover, eh? You know I do not give these things back.'

'Ah, but you will to me. You will require my services one day, Mr Lossop, and perhaps soon. There are certain people in Norway, and one in London, who wish to see you dead.'

Lossop backed away from Holmes in surprise. He attempted to hide his reaction, but his face had gone white with fear.

'I alone will be able to help you,' Holmes continued. 'You can confirm this, I think. And when you do ask me for this help, the return of this photograph will be my payment.'

Lossop swallowed. He reached into a drawer and pulled out a Webley, not unlike my own gun. He placed the gun on the counter, between us.

'I can protect myself quite well, Mr Holmes,' said he.

'Against most, I do not doubt it,' said Holmes. 'But the

man in London is far more than your match. I think you have already begun to realize that. He has employed you twice. Now, will you help my friend Dr Watson and unlock the box for him?'

Lossop put the gun down and looked at the box resting on the counter. He took up Holmes's small, precious envelope and placed it in his own pocket, patting it gently. 'I will. And I will look after this lady, do not fear.' His broad smile revealed two or three teeth missing.

'221B Baker Street. When you are successful, let us know,' said Holmes.

But Lossop had picked up the box and was already engaged in the task, breathing heavily, and turning the mysterious object over and over in his skeletal hands.

As we exited into the summer sunlight, I breathed a sigh of relief in leaving this dark and decidedly strange place. I wondered who the man in London might be, who had struck such terror into the locksmith, and from whom my friend offered protection.

But that fearsome identity would remain only as a flickering shadow until several years later.

CHAPTER 24

Two for One

pon leaving the locksmith, I managed to sidetrack Holmes to a favourite Italian restaurant in Dorset Street, not far from 221B. The heat had inspired the proprietors to set several tables out on the pavement, and there we enjoyed a leisurely al fresco meal, along with a bottle of good Chianti. We returned to Baker Street around eight in the evening. I was pleased to have enabled some small transformation in my friend, but I knew that unless a new case arrived on our doorstep to occupy his feverish mind, danger would persist.

I had not long to worry, for upon our arrival we discovered a visitor, seated in a hall chair near our front door awaiting our return. It was Polly, the maid who served Odelia and Atalanta Wyndham. The poor girl was trembling, and her reddened eyes and pale face spoke volumes.

'Mr Holmes, Dr Watson, I was hoping you'd return sooner,' said Mrs Hudson. 'Miss Polly here has been waiting for you for over an hour. She has some urgent business, it seems.'

We brought the girl upstairs and sat her in a comfortable chair. I noticed with relief that Mrs Hudson had once again restored order to our sitting-room.

The girl perched on the edge of the chair, stifling sobs.

'Polly,' said Holmes kindly, 'please gather yourself together. You are among friends. What has happened to bring you here?'

'My . . . my first time in London, sir,' she said.

'Well, that is enough to unsettle anyone,' I said with a smile. 'Are you all right? May I offer you a refreshment?'

'Mrs Hudson gave me tea and a sandwich, thank you.'

'Nothing untoward has happened to you?' asked Holmes, sitting himself across from her.

'No. No! I, er . . . it's her. She . . . she's fixin' to leave.'

'Miss Dillie, you mean?' asked Holmes gently.

'Yes.'

'Leave her parents? I thought she just announced her engagement to Mr Eden-Summers?'

'She don't mean to go through with that, I don't think. She ran away from home again. Went to the secret place. The place you know . . .'

'This place is still a secret from her parents?'

'I think so. But Atalanta . . .'

'Polly, what has you so upset? Perhaps she just changed her mind, needs time to think.'

'No. She . . . asked me to bring more things from home.'

'I see. What things?'

'Miss Atalanta saw me leave with a carpet-bag and I had to lie, I said my mother was sick. I can't go back. But . . . Dillie, she don't . . .' A tear ran down her face and she wiped it away.

'She doesn't what, Polly?'

'She don't want me with her. She sent me away.'

'What things did she ask you to bring her?'

'Everything she cares about. Photographs. A bracelet. Some money she hid.'

Holmes stood up and began to pace. 'What of her engagement ring?' he asked.

'She has them already.'

'Well, of course she would take her engagement ring,' I said. 'Although—'

Holmes paused, alert. 'Hold on, Watson.' He turned back to the girl. 'Them? Plural? More than one ring?'

'Yes. Rings from both her fellas.'

There was a silence as Holmes took this in.

'Polly, we read of the engagement to Freddie Eden-Summers. Do you mean she accepted tokens from more than one young gentleman? She was betrothed to more than one man?'

'Yes. Two of them.'

'Who was the second?'

'Leo Vitale.'

'The physics student? That tall, rather pale fellow in the Cavendish Laboratory?' I said incredulously.

'Yes, that's him,' said the girl. 'Her folks don't know about that one.'

Holmes smiled. 'Ah. Now that is something! I smell a plan of sorts. A rather daring one. Did you happen to see both rings, Polly?'

'I did.'

'Can you describe them?'

'Holmes, what on earth? The girl is surely more important than the rings?'

'Polly?'

'Both of 'em were old. I think the mother's or the grandmother's. Freddie's ring, it was huge. The diamonds, well, they were large and several of 'em. Some emeralds on it, too. He had it cleaned afore he give it her, and it was sparkling something fierce. A beauty.'

'And the other?'

''Tweren't quite so dear, maybe, but very nice. Smaller, but very pretty, with sapphires and two little diamonds.'

'Costly rings, then?'

'Far as I know, sir. Looked like it to me. She were right pleased with them.'

'The rings, I presume, rather than the young gentlemen?'

Polly ventured a tiny smile. 'The rings. She don't talk to me so much about the gentlemen.'

Holmes leaned closer to the lady's maid.

'Polly, is it possible that your mistress decided to run away? I mean, permanently? Perhaps to start a new life away from her family. Because the rings might . . . buy her passage, so to speak.'

Polly's eyes filled with tears.

'Do you understand what I am asking?'

The girl nodded.

'But . . . ?' Holmes prompted.

'But she . . . she would take me with her. She promised to take me.'

'She is good to you, then, Polly?'

The girl nodded. 'Yes, sir. She's a good lady, Miss Odelia. When she gets her way.'

Just then the doorbell sounded, followed by a frantic knocking. There were thunderous footsteps on the stairs and in rushed young Hamilton, a newly minted police detective and Lestrade's favourite, whom we had met on the Portsmouth strangler case the year before. The tall, gangly fellow stood before us, pale and sweating, with a look of horror on his face. 'Come quick, Mr Holmes. There's been a terrible death. A man burnt alive!'

'Who?'

'The Great Borelli!' he cried. 'At Wilton's. Oh, my God—'

Holmes looked up in surprise. 'Borelli? But he is laid up with a broken ankle.'

'He went onstage anyway. He was roasted alive in a copper cauldron set over flames. The audience could hear the screams. They—'

'How long ago?'

'Less than an hour, sir.'

'And Madame Borelli?'

'That's just it, Mr Holmes. She's gone. Done a runner.

213

Mr Lestrade thinks she's the killer. Can you come, sir? Time is of the essence!'

Holmes turned to Polly, who was frozen in horror. 'Polly, you must stay here for the night. Providing I can take care of pressing business here, either Watson or we both will return to Cambridge with you in the morning.' He ran to the landing. 'Mrs Hudson!' he shouted. 'We will have a guest.'

CHAPTER 25

The Cauldron of Death

e arrived at Wilton's Music Hall to find the auditorium had been emptied except for one slender young lady sobbing in a corner, attended by a matronly figure I recognized as the ticket taker.

'Annie! Oh, Annie!' wailed the young woman.

At the end of the hall, a small crowd of police clustered onstage next to a large, strange copper vessel suspended by a thick chain and floating three feet above the raised floor of the stage. The thing, perhaps five feet in diameter, looked oddly like an ornate bathysphere, ready to transport an intrepid traveller to the dark ocean depths. It was only missing a porthole. A decorative stage sign prophetically named it 'The Cauldron of Death'.

As we approached, I became aware of the terrible odour

of burned flesh. There was another smell mixed along with it, some kind of chemical.

We mounted five steps to the stage and approached the vessel. It was decoratively covered in rivets and piping, with the occasional large crystal, making it look for all the world like a fanciful creation of Jules Verne. A three-foot square hatch opened to the front and was ajar, but only a crack. Another smaller hatch on top was wide open.

Dangling from both of these openings were a variety of ornate padlocks, all hanging open. A grate underneath the cauldron revealed still smouldering coals in a pit below the stage. A ladder with a platform on top stood next to the thing.

And next to this ladder was the first horror of the evening.

Lying on the stage was the body of a slender woman in a sparkling red dress. A cloth had been laid over her face and upper torso. I gasped.

I started towards the body, but a young policeman put a hand on my shoulder. He shook his head sadly. 'Dead,' he said.

If Madame Borelli was a suspect on the run, who was in her costume? 'Who is it?' I asked.

'Name's Annie Durgen. A girl they just hired today.'

'Watson, examine the girl's body, please,' said Holmes, approaching the front hatch of the giant cauldron. He peeked inside and grimaced. I noticed his extreme reaction and he waved a finger at me, coughing at the fumes.

Without preamble, he launched into an inspection of the outside of the cauldron by running his hand over its surface.

His face was grim, but I sensed the humming excitement beneath. Near to him stood the stolid figure of Falco Fricano, Borelli's brother-in-law.

I turned my attention to the corpse, and a stagehand quickly informed me of the means of death. The poor young woman had been up on the ladder and leaning over the cauldron, conversing through the top opening with Borelli, supposedly trapped inside – all part of the planned act.

But an unexpected explosion blew up in her face, and she fell backwards off the ladder to the stage below. My examination confirmed third-degree burns on her face and hands. However, the broken neck from her fall was the apparent cause of death.

I looked up to see Holmes in conversation with Falco Fricano just a few feet away. The muscular Italian stood woodenly, his face pinched in what might be grief, a reaction to the gruesome events. His fists were clenched, and he leaned strangely backwards on his heels, which rather than making him look frightened gave the impression that he was gathering himself to launch at Holmes or to flee. He struck me as someone holding himself back at great cost.

'Mr Fricano, you hired Miss Durgen just today to go on in place of Madame Borelli?' asked Holmes.

'Yes.'

'And why is that?'

'Madame refused to perform.'

'Did she give her reason?'

'The Great Borelli and she had a big argument, I do not know about what. The hotel said there was much shouting.'

217

'Where is Madame now?' asked Holmes, looking about the stage.

'No one knows. Mr Borelli told me they were finished.'

'Mr Lestrade is at their hotel room now,' said Hamilton as I approached.

I glanced over at the front hatch of the cauldron. I knew I should lean in and take a look, but I hesitated. In due time, I would. I joined Holmes and Hamilton.

'I see,' continued Holmes. 'Describe this act in detail. I need to know precisely what happened. Tell me exactly what the audience saw, and how it works.'

Fricano cleared his throat. He began with great effort. 'First, the Great Borelli, he comes onstage.'

'In a wheelchair tonight, I presume. Watson set his broken ankle recently.'

'No. With a walking stick only. The Great Borelli, he is very strong. He removes the cape. Then the young lady, she spins cauldron to show no door in back.'

'Like this?' asked Holmes. He placed one hand on the cauldron and gave it a shove. The thing was set to rotate on the chain hanging from the rafters above the stage, twirling easily so that now the back faced us. Holmes stopped its movement with a hand. 'Except for this well-disguised hatch, here?'

'Yes.'

Initially I saw nothing, but I leaned in closer . . . and could just perceive the outline of another large hatch on the opposite side of the sphere from the front opening. It was well-hidden among the rivets and piping.

'Go on,' said Holmes.

'Then Dario, he gets in from the front and the girl locks it very good, many locks in front here.' Fricano spun the cauldron, so the front now faced us again. That opening remained ajar and I got another strong whiff of that awful smell. I sneezed. Fricano closed the front hatch.

'Hmm,' said Holmes. 'I suppose Borelli normally slips out the back hatch and makes his exit through the split in the curtain behind this contraption?' Holmes spun the sphere again, so the back faced him. He opened the secret hatch an inch or so, then closed it. He ran his hand along the edges.

'Yes. Normally he is out in five seconds through the back.'

Fricano attempted to spin the thing again facing front, but Holmes stopped it from moving.

'But not this time?' he said.

'No.'

'Why did he not come out?' asked Holmes.

'I do not know. Maybe he fainted.'

'There are fumes, Holmes,' I offered. 'Shall I take a closer look now?'

'It's bad, doctor,' said Hamilton, who had shadowed me and now stood behind Fricano.

'In a moment, Watson. Stay with me. Mr Fricano, do continue. Were you not waiting to help him out?'

'No, at this part, I am under the stage, tending to the fire. Another man, Paolo, is in back. The girl pretends to light the fire onstage, which I help from below. When Borelli did not come out, Paolo ran to get me.'

'What then?'

'Paolo yells at me that Dario is still inside the cauldron. Since I cannot stop the fire, I ran up from backstage and put my hands though the curtain, trying to open. But the hatch will not open.'

Holmes unlatched the secret back hatch easily, opened it and closed it again.

'Hmm. It seems to work fine now. Ah, but what is *this* small bolt?'

'What bolt?' Fricano's eyes widened.

Holmes leaned in, pulled out his magnifying glass and said, 'This bolt here that – yes, if I slide it like so – would secure the hatch shut. Seems to have been attached recently. Look, the soldering or brazing is pewter-coloured. The rest here is brass or copper.' Holmes handed me his glass. 'With this shut, the person inside could not open this door.'

'Oh God, we tried to pull it open but did not see,' said Fricano.

With magnification, the bolt indeed looked different from the nearby pipes and ornamentation. I would never have noticed, either. It was a subtle piece of work. I handed the glass back, nodding.

'Yes,' said Holmes. 'Nicely hidden. What happened next? In the act, that is. The audience sees Borelli get inside. The front hatch is apparently secured. What does the girl do?'

Fricano took a deep breath. 'The girl lights fire under the cauldron. Then she climbs up this ladder and stands up high next to top of the cauldron. She touches the surface and pretends it is very hot. *Ssss!* Of course, it is too soon and not really hot yet. It makes drama. The whole act designed to make big drama.'

'You have succeeded, I would say.' Holmes's humour could suffer in the timing, I noted.

'Then the girl opens the top latch and calls down to Borelli, pretending to hear his answer. She smiles at the audience, then picks up the bottle of whisky.'

'Whisky? That bottle over there? All part of the act?' Holmes pointed to a bottle lying on the stage near the girl's body.

'Yes, and she pours it down in on him. That gets a big laugh from the audience.'

'Big laugh. Right. Meanwhile you are still trying to open the back?'

'Yes!'

I pictured the frantic efforts. I glanced again at the newly added back latch, which was nearly impossible to see. But of course, Holmes had the eyes of a bird of prey.

'Go on.'

'Then the girl leans down on top and looks in, but she pretends she cannot see.'

'Still part of the act?'

'Yes.'

Holmes glanced over at me. 'Watson, could you retrieve that bottle and smell it, please?'

I complied. Given the overwhelming odour of burnt flesh in the room itself, smelling anything else would be difficult, but I inhaled deeply. 'Nothing,' I reported.

'What was in that bottle, Mr Fricano?' asked Holmes.

'Just coloured water. Is all a trick.'

Holmes hesitated, and I could tell he had some doubts. 'Yes, go on,' he said.

'After she pours it in, she calls down but gets no answer.'

'Part of the act as well?'

'Yes, yes! Normally no one is inside by this time. So then she lights a match and holds it at entrance as if to look, and then pretends to drop match in by accident. Audience cry "Oh no!" because they think it will ignite the alcohol. Big excitement.'

'Again. Still part of the act?' prompted Holmes.

'Yes.'

'But this time . . . ?'

'This time . . . oh . . .' Fricano put a hand to cover his face a moment, then recovering, he continued, 'She drops the match in, and a big flame comes out top. And there is a big sound. Like . . . *FOOOF!* We hear screaming from inside cauldron. And the girl . . . her face . . . oh, horrible! She is burned! She falls back off the ladder. The audience screaming . . . it was terrible.'

'What did you do then, Mr Fricano?'

'I am on stage, trying to help the girl. But it is too late, she is dead. Then I unlock the cauldron's front hatch. I burn my hand, you see!' He held up his hands.

Holmes took them in his two hands, and jerking Fricano forward examined them closely. The man winced in pain. 'Ah! Yes, burns!' said Holmes. He dropped Fricano's hands. The man backed away, affronted.

'And then?' Holmes prompted.

'I find . . . I find . . . Oh, God,' moaned Fricano. He covered his face with his injured hands. 'I find Dario.'

'Doctor? The body, now, inside the cauldron, if you please? Take a very close look.'

I moved a few feet around the sphere and spun it so that the front opening faced me and was well lit from one of the stage lights. Hamilton appeared behind me, a pocket lantern in his hand to help illuminate the interior.

While my wartime experiences had somewhat inured me to the sight of grievous injury and death, what I encountered here sickened even me. I opened the front hatch and the stench of burned flesh gagged me, but there was another smell as well, a metallic odour – not exactly paraffin, not exactly petroleum, but similar. I quickly placed my hand-kerchief over my nose and mouth.

Inside was an image that will forever be seared into my mind.

It was the figure of a large man, contorted into a kind of foetal position, arms raised in what is known by coroners as the pugilistic pose. The clothes, the shoes and most of his skin was burned away, leaving a shiny black coating overall. The face was unrecognizable.

I was filled with revulsion, but I had a job to do.

Gingerly, I leaned in through the opening and touched the corpse's shoulder. A large flake of cinder fell off, leaving what looked like raw meat below. I have seen many a gruesome death, but this was a horror. I backed out to catch my breath.

'Dear God, Holmes. The man was incinerated under

some extreme and sudden heat. All the clothes and skin are gone,' I said. I leaned in and continued my examination.

After few terrible minutes, my investigation was done. I stood next to Holmes, wiping my hands as best I could on my handkerchief. Hamilton, much affected by the sight, had followed and stood behind me.

'An accelerant, then, Watson?' said Holmes.

'Definitely,' I replied. 'It was a kind of flash burn. Uniformly across the entire body. No one's skin and clothes would ignite in such a way without some kind of chemical present.'

'A petrochemical from the smell, wouldn't you say?'

'Perhaps. I don't recognize the odour.'

'Could it have been poured in from that bottle by the young lady?'

'I would say not.'

'Why?'

'To get this result, you would need much, much more. And uniformly covering the body. Perhaps in some kind of gel or powder.'

'The entire body?' asked Holmes. 'Prepared, then?'

'It would appear so. That body was . . . soaked with it. Or painted.'

'Death would have been instantaneous, then,' remarked the detective.

'We heard screams,' said Fricano.

'Well, very quickly then,' said Holmes.

I shuddered. 'Yes.'

Fricano looked aghast at the thought. It seemed the man might pass out. I felt in my pocket for my smelling salts.

'Excuse me, sir. I must sit down a moment,' murmured Fricano, seemingly overcome with the emotion of the events. He moved away, offstage.

Holmes turned to the young policeman. 'Hamilton, stay with Mr Fricano, would you?' Hamilton, relieved to have something to do, nodded.

At precisely this moment, Lestrade entered at the other end of the hall with two of his men.

'Lestrade!' cried Holmes. 'Have you found Madame?'

Lestrade approached, coughing at the terrible odour. 'Madame Borelli has fled! Flown the coop. All her things – her clothes, her personal items – packed up and gone.' He waved a slip of paper in triumph. 'I found this receipt for a train to Palermo. The Borellis had a huge row earlier today.'

He arrived on the stage to stand near us and gestured towards the cauldron. 'It is clear that the lady engineered this terrible thing. I'm sure you concur!'

'Madame is now en route to Italy, then?' asked Holmes.

'Ha! I have men on their way to the station and have cabled ahead,' Lestrade crowed. 'We will catch this murderous witch!'

'What of Mr Borelli's things? Are they still in the hotel room?'

'Well, they were all still there, of course.'

'Everything?'

'So far as we could tell. He expected to return, but obviously she killed him here and escaped.'

'So it appears,' murmured Holmes. 'Were his things of

an elegant or expensive nature? A silver hairbrush, jewelled cufflinks, a silver-tipped walking stick – anything like that?'

'Mr Borelli's? Why?'

'Please, just answer the question.'

Lestrade bristled. 'I can't say they were. Just . . . regular, rather ordinary ones.'

'New or used?'

What was Holmes on about, I wondered.

'I did not notice,' the inspector snapped. 'Well, newish, perhaps. But everything was still there. I don't think he was a wealthy man.'

'Perhaps. But Mr Borelli had a taste for fine things,' remarked Holmes.

'You digress, Mr Holmes, at a terrible moment!'

I will admit that thought was mine as well. Just then a cry was heard from behind a makeshift wing at stage left. I dashed towards the sound and found Fricano crouched over the floor, looking behind a stack of bulky, fake boulders. Hamilton stood next to him.

Fricano arose with a shout! 'Come quick! Come quick! It is Madame Borelli!'

And then I recognized the lady's red scarf. It snaked out across the floor, seeming to ooze from behind the boulders like a bloodstain.

CHAPTER 26

The How and the Why

olmes and I knelt beside the prostrate form of Madame Borelli. I felt for a pulse. 'Alive, Holmes!' I said. He exhaled in relief.

One of her arms cradled an empty bottle of gin, the other was splayed out along the dusty floor. Her flamboyant clothes in her signature red and black were awry and spread out around her. She reeked of alcohol. Holmes leaned in to sniff her lips then backed away.

I patted her cheek gently and applied smelling salts. She snorted and opened her eyes.

'Madame Borelli?' I whispered, leaning in.

She belched and struggled to consciousness. I could smell cheap gin.

'Where am I?' she slurred. 'And what is that smell?'

'Your own breath,' snapped Lestrade. 'Get up.'

'You are backstage at Wilton's,' I said.

She blinked and stared up at Sherlock Holmes.

'What has happened? How did I get here?' She sniffed the air. 'What burned?'

She struggled to sit up, discovered the bottle of gin in her hands, looked at it in surprise, and pushed it away.

'What is the last thing you remember, Madame Borelli?' asked Holmes.

'Let us not waste time, Holmes,' barked Lestrade. 'Madame Borelli, I am arresting—'

'One moment, Lestrade, please!' said Holmes. 'Madame?'

'Our room at the hotel. I entered and I . . . someone came from behind and—' She paused, struggling for clarity.

'. . . and did what? Were you drugged?' asked my friend.

'Stop this, Holmes. You give her ideas!' cried Lestrade.

'Someone hit me in the back of my head,' murmured the lady. 'Suddenly I was choking. A cloth . . . I don't remember what . . .' She blinked and shook her head. 'And now I am here.' The poor woman remained on the floor.

I felt her pulse. It was racing. 'Gentlemen, where is your sympathy? Help me lift her to a chair,' I said. Soon, Madame Borelli was seated, with all of us clustered around her.

'Take slow, deep breaths, Madame,' I said.

'Where had you been,' asked Holmes, 'just before this happened?'

'How is this our concern?' cried Lestrade. 'This is clearly a ruse!' The policeman leaned past Holmes and placed his face inches from Madame Borelli's. 'I am not interested in your made-up stories, Madame! It is all too clear what happened here.' He stood back and gestured for his second man to approach. 'Madame Ilaria Borelli, I am arresting you on the charge of the wilful and sadistic murder of your husband, Dario Borelli. Boys, take her away.'

'Murder? Dario?' Her face went white. 'Dario? *Dario Mio* is dead?'

Hamilton and a constable each took Madame under an arm and dragged her roughly to her feet. She moaned as they held her facing Lestrade.

'Careful there!' I said. 'This lady is in shock.'

'Your husband is dead, and you know it,' said Lestrade. 'He was burned to a crisp tonight in that infernal prop over there, which I understand you designed.'

Madame Borelli gagged. She wrenched one arm free and covered her mouth. 'No!' she sobbed.

Lestrade leaned in close to Madame, sniffing her breath, then with a pointed look at Holmes, picked up one of her hands and smelled it. He smiled proudly. 'You have gin on your breath, some kind of chemical on your hands – and your husband was soaked in it. A receipt for a one-way ticket through to Palermo was found in your hotel room, and . . . here . . .' Lestrade leaned into her and plucked out a small white token which protruded from the pocket of her skirt. 'Aha! Yes, just as I thought! Here is a token for a locker at Victoria. Will we find your packed valise in there, Madame?'

She stared at him in apparent confusion.

'I wager we will,' said Lestrade. He turned to Holmes triumphantly. 'Two can play at your game, Mr Holmes. Sometimes, you see, things are best left to the professionals.'

'Bravo, Lestrade. A remarkable chain of inferences, all based on solid evidence,' said Holmes quietly. Lestrade beamed and nodded to his two men.

'Except that you are entirely wrong,' added my friend.

The room went silent. I became aware of the soft sobbing of Annie Duggan's friend near the entrance.

'Do you think so, Holmes? Let us see you prove it,' said Lestrade, folding his arms across his chest.

'This lady is in distress. Allow her to sit,' I demanded.

Lestrade waved at his men to comply. Madame was returned to the chair. I moved to the lady's side and patted her shoulder.

'Try if you must,' said Lestrade, 'but you know you are beaten this time, Holmes.'

Holmes knelt down before the lady, taking both her hands in his. 'Madame,' he said gently, 'what was your errand when you left the hotel?'

'Dario sent me to pick up a velvet jacket he had made on Jermyn Street.'

'Expensive tastes, as I said, Lestrade. What then, Madame Borelli?'

'I returned to our hotel room. I stepped inside and it looked like a tornado had passed through. Then from behind someone put a cloth on my face, pressing, pressing. I could not breathe . . . a terrible smell—'

'You smelled the petrochemical and the gin, but missed the third odour which lingers under the gin, Lestrade. The lady was chloroformed. The gin was applied to her lips later.' He gestured politely towards the woman's face.

Lestrade hesitated, then leaned in for a sniff.

'Ah, well, possibly. But to what purpose?' sneered Lestrade.

'Obvious. She is being framed for a murder,' said Holmes.

'By whom? Who would want Borelli dead and his wife in gaol?'

'Well, that's the other little problem with your theory.'

Holmes strode over to the cauldron and opened the front hatch wide, so we all had a clear view of the blackened remains inside.

'This body is not Dario Borelli,' said Holmes.

Even I was surprised at this revelation.

Oblivious to the lady's extreme distress, the two detectives faced each other. But Madame Borelli was transfixed on the body. I stepped in front of her to block the grisly sight.

But Lestrade was not swayed. 'Of course it is Borelli, Holmes,' said he. 'Smith, bring out what you found.'

A young policeman with thinning blond hair and drooping eyes came forward with something wrapped in a handkerchief. He drew back the covering to reveal a ring and two shiny buckles, married by ash.

'Recognize these, Madame Borelli?' asked Lestrade.

She turned away, repelled, and did not answer.

'Of course you do. Your husband's ring, and the buckles from your husband's shoes. All part of his stage costume, confirmed by his crew. And removed from the corpse earlier by Smith here.'

I glanced at Hamilton, who shrugged.

'You withheld evidence from me, Lestrade. Hardly

sporting.' Holmes smiled ruefully. 'I will admit Borelli wore both the ring and buckles in the show I saw.'

'Exactly! And there is more,' crowed Lestrade. 'Two hundred people witnessed Borelli climb into the cauldron. Normally, he would simply escape through the secret hatch in the back right away, according to Mr Fricano, the stage manager. But he did not come out . . . because he could not! Take a look, Mr Holmes.'

Lestrade shut the front hatch on the corpse and spun the cauldron on its chain to the back. He pointed to the tiny, hidden latch.

'A new latch. Recently welded on, look at the solder here – pewter-coloured, when everything else is copper and brass,' said the policeman.

'Very observant, Lestrade. You improve.'

'I found it because I was looking for it,' announced Lestrade, 'as you like to say. Trapped in his own trick. As he nearly was last week.'

'Dario!' wailed Madame. I patted her shoulder.

Holmes simply smiled at Lestrade. 'There is a similar new one on the front, as well.'

Lestrade shrugged this off. 'And so there was no escape! Few people in the world are familiar enough with this stage contraption to hide a little latch like this—'

'Two latches.'

'Fine. Madame was familiar with both,' said Lestrade. 'And she had motive. They had been heard arguing. Mr Fricano himself said he felt that the couple was on the verge of separating.'

'Yes, where is Mr Fricano now?' asked Holmes innocently. Next to me, Hamilton started, remembering that Holmes had asked him to keep an eye on the fellow. 'He might be able to shed some light.'

'He is a witness, to be sure,' said Lestrade. 'Hamilton, find the fellow, would you?' Hamilton moved off, rounding up two more policemen.

'Madame Borelli, is it true that you fought with your husband earlier today?' asked Holmes.

'Yes,' said the lady, 'but I welded no latch.' She rose shakily to her feet. 'I must see inside,' she said, nodding towards the cauldron.

'Madame, perhaps not,' I suggested. 'It is a pitiable sight.'

But Lestrade nodded to his remaining man, who took the lady's arm and conveyed her to the front of the cauldron.

Madame Borelli looked inside, went white and turned away. She steeled herself and looked again.

'That is not Dario.'

'As I said,' remarked Holmes.

'Of course it is,' sneered Lestrade. 'The man is burnt to a crisp.'

'No,' said she, wiping her tears.

'Why do you think not, Madame?' asked Holmes.

She shrugged. 'Too fat maybe. But it is not him.'

Holmes stepped up and took one of her hands and led her back to the chair.

'Madame, I believe you are correct. But if your husband went to such trouble to frame you, where would he be now?'

She hesitated and looked stricken. Tears coursed down her face. She said something in a voice so low I could not catch the words.

'Speak up,' said Lestrade.

'He would be on a train.'

'To where? asked Holmes.

'To Berlin.'

No one said anything, but she was not forthcoming.

'Madame?' prompted Holmes.

The woman took a deep breath and sat very straight. 'Gertrude Aufenbach,' said she.

'The German soprano?' said Holmes, evidently surprised. She nodded.

'Ah, yes!' Holmes enthused. 'A beautiful woman. And that voice—'

'Holmes loves the opera,' I interjected, attempting to cover this insensitivity.

Catching himself, Holmes turned to the police detective. 'But never mind. I suggest you send your men to the station after all, Lestrade.'

'On the trail of a dead man! Now why should I do that? Borelli's clothes are still in his hotel room.'

'Expensive tastes, remember? Look for that velvet jacket. It will be gone, I wager. In his room you will only find cheap replacements bought for the illusion. And it is indeed an illusion, worthy of a conjuring star. I can prove the body in the cauldron is not Dario Borelli.'

Lestrade snorted. '"Data, data," as you like to say. The buckles?'

'Certainly. Borelli broke his ankle last week, Dr Watson here set it, and the man could not have been wearing two shoes when he entered the cauldron. He could not get a shoe on over that splint. Ask your audience that. Some will remember.'

Lestrade blinked. 'No one could pull that off: get in, and then leap out and put another person in! His own stage manager said he did not emerge.'

'Yes, have you found Falco Fricano yet?'

Hamilton appeared behind Lestrade. 'No Fricano,' he said.

'I expect he was Borelli's accomplice. There was much to arrange, and in a short time. Madame Borelli is no easy mark. Lestrade, I suggest you put more men on it. Fricano cannot have gone far.'

Lestrade paused, then to his credit, agreed. He turned to Hamilton and a young constable. 'Find the stage manager! *Now!*' Realizing this left the lady unguarded, he quickly handcuffed her to the chair.

'Mr Lestrade!' I exclaimed, finding this remarkably insensitive.

He stepped away, presumably to request reinforcements. Holmes flashed me a small smile.

Lestrade returned, and Holmes continued. 'Consider these facts. Someone went to a great deal of trouble to disguise the identity of the body. That man was soaked, painted perhaps in some kind of highly flammable liquid or gel. All identifiers including clothes and facial features would be destroyed. Of course, they wanted everyone to think it was

Borelli, and so they selected someone of a similar stature. Planted the buckles and the ring.'

'But,' said Lestrade, rubbing his chin, 'how did they get this "other person" into the cauldron? And who is he?'

'Borelli entered the cauldron and then immediately exited the back, as usual. Fricano, who was complicit, lied about that. I believe you will discover the corpse is that of a man named Santo Colangelo. Presumably he was drugged and covered in this chemical, then loaded in. The back hatch, which usually opened easily, was then secured with the newly added latch. The front as well.'

'Then he was unconscious, or he would have struggled. But screams were heard.'

'Colangelo must have come to at some point. Oh, and some kind of kindling substance, highly flammable, was added. That caused the "*foof*" described to us. And, sadly, the demise of the poor young lady.' He squinted. 'Powdered magnesium and potassium chlorate would be my guess.'

'What is that?'

'Quite a new thing. "*Blitzlicht*" it is called. It is used by photographers. You have, no doubt, been blinded temporarily when you were captured by a camera in service of the newspaper men?'

Madame Borelli moaned slightly at the thought.

Lestrade was still not convinced. 'Who added the latch – er, the latches – then, if not this clever woman?'

'Fricano, or Borelli himself. Both have the skills. And while Madame was on her errand earlier today, he worked very quickly to pack the bare minimum of his own things

– his favourites, no doubt – and replace them with cheap substitutes to make you think he had never left. He and his accomplice, for it must have taken at least two to manage all of this, drugged the lady and set her here in the manner you found her.'

'Yes, and I do not even drink the gin,' offered Madame.

'Applied to your lips, Madame Borelli,' said Holmes.

'Then what, Holmes?' said Lestrade.

'The act proceeded as normal, with the newly trained assistant, poor Miss Durgen, none the wiser. She lit the match and dropped it in, sealing both Colangelo's fate and her own. Perhaps more flash powder than was needed had been introduced and that killed her. I doubt that she was an intended victim.'

Lestrade hesitated. No one likes to be topped, even by Sherlock Holmes. 'Plausible, Mr Holmes, but I am not convinced the corpse is not Borelli's,' said he. 'The body is the same size; it has been confirmed.'

'Check his teeth. They will have survived. The man I mentioned, Santo Colangelo is a rival conjurer. He has a small diamond embedded in his left canine.'

Lestrade nodded at the young officer guarding the cauldron. 'Look at his tooth.'

With a shudder, the fellow leaned into the deadly sphere. A retching noise echoed within it, and he backed out quickly. 'Ugh. It's there, sir.'

'Dario Borelli is responsible for tonight's drama. I suggest you wire Berlin,' said Holmes.

Lestrade sighed. To his credit, he knew when he was

beaten. 'All right, Mr Holmes. But you must give me this. I do know when to call you in.'

Holmes smiled, a little too self-satisfied, I thought, in the face of all this tragedy.

'Please unlock Madame Borelli. She has suffered enough today,' I admonished. The poor woman was pale with emotion, her eyes closed. She opened them suddenly and handed Lestrade his handcuffs, having freed herself while we had been looking elsewhere.

'What?' exclaimed Lestrade.

Holmes shrugged and smiled insouciantly. 'Child's play, Mr Lestrade. I warrant your gaol could not have held her. Good evening.'

I turned to Madame. 'Do you have somewhere to go, Madame, to take comfort?'

She waved me off. 'I will be fine,' said she. 'I have friends here in London.'

CHAPTER 27

Vanished

nce again back at Baker Street, now near midnight, we were surprised to find Mrs Hudson still awake. 'That young lady, Mr Holmes. She would not stay. Insisted on returning to Cambridge, even at such a late hour. I tried to convince her.'

Holmes shook his head ruefully. 'What folly! She endangers herself needlessly.'

'Polly seems like a resourceful young lady,' I offered.

'You forget, Watson, the Spinning House. Cambridge at night is not safe for young women like Polly!'

'Ah, yes, Holmes.'

Holmes had the *Bradshaw* in his hands. 'We have missed the last train again! Oh, what a shame. Watson, to bed, quickly! We must be on the earliest train to Cambridge.'

*

As dawn broke the following morning Holmes and I found ourselves on a train bound for Cambridge with only a few hours' sleep. We were both attired in our linen summer suits and the day promised no break in the weather. Cambridge, I knew, would be hotter even than London.

To Holmes's extreme frustration, our train was delayed for nearly two hours due to an accident on the tracks and it was after ten when we arrived at our destination. We headed first to Dillie's bolt-hole, hoping to find both girls there. No one answered the door. Once again, Holmes used his kit to open the lock and was dismayed to find the room had been emptied. There was nothing left of Dillie Wyndham's that I could see.

But who had done this?

I have never known Holmes to curse but he came close to it that day, surveying the empty room. All of Dillie's clothes had been removed from the closet, all the personal belongings packed up and taken away, with drawers left open, two clothes hangers on the floor, and a bedside table upended.

Holmes made a careful inspection, even as his fury was evident. I knew well enough to leave him to his work and not to interrupt him with questions. It was afterwards, in a carriage en route to the Wyndhams' that he opened up to me.

'Watson,' said he, 'I am not, as you know, a great believer in hunches. I prefer data – real, tangible data. That room provided very little. And yet I have a very bad feeling.'

'Holmes, I know you. Surely there was something – a

tiny clue, perhaps not even registered consciously that has given rise to this "feeling"?'

'You may be right, but it is presently abstruse, Watson. And yet . . . I cannot shake my fear for Miss Wyndham at this moment.'

We pulled up to the front of the Wyndhams' house. At eleven in the morning, the heat was already oppressive. I could feel the sweat running down my back.

'Now,' said Holmes as we dismounted the cab, 'if only we would find Dillie here, healthy, spirited—'

'—and slightly pugilistic,' I inserted.

'Ha! Yes, even that. But I fear we will not.'

Five minutes later we were seated in the parlour of the Wyndham family home awaiting the appearance of the professor and his wife. Into the room swept the ethereal Atalanta, looking even paler than before, but with a strangely triumphant smirk on her elfin face. A bright rose dress accentuated her pallor, giving her skin an almost greenish cast.

'Well, the gentlemen from London,' she drawled, posing in the doorway like a Greek statue. 'You are days late for the engagement celebration. There might be the dregs of some champagne in the kitchen. It will have gone flat by now, but shall I ring for some anyway? You look parched.'

'Miss Atalanta,' said Holmes, 'I take it Miss Odelia is not here. Have you seen her?'

Atalanta smiled and shook her head.

'Is your maid Polly about?'

'No. She went to see her mother. Or so she said.' There

241

was mockery in her tone. A nasty smile darkened her features.

'When is she due back?'

'Who knows?'

Holmes and I exchanged a glance. He did not like that news and neither did I.

'Where does Polly's mother live?'

'Ask in the kitchen. I neither know nor care.'

'Do you know where your sister is?'

'Now, that is the question of the hour, isn't it?' said the irritating young woman. 'I neither know—'

'—nor care. Yes, indeed, Miss Atalanta you have made yourself abundantly clear on that point,' said Holmes. 'But the young lady seems to have disappeared.'

'I found her hiding place, you know,' said Atalanta. 'After the engagement, she began to show the signs. Her "tell", Freddie calls it. Something the card players like to say. I knew she was about to run and kept a careful eye, and when she made her break, I followed her there.'

'I see. Did you confront her?'

'To what end? No, I told our father. But by the time he . . .' Her face darkened. 'Well, by the time he *believed me* and we went there, Dillie was gone.'

'You went there with your father this morning, then?'

'Why? How do you know this?'

'It is too bad your father did not listen to you earlier,' said Holmes.

Atalanta shrugged, but I could sense the damaged girl under her practised coolness.

'Where do you think she is now?' asked Holmes.

'I told you. I simply don't care. My father has disowned her—'

At that moment Richard Wyndham strode into the room. It was as though there was a tide of invisible energy emanating from him, like the wake of a fast-moving ship, and his daughter backed away as if frightened of its impact.

'Atalanta, leave us!' he commanded, and the older daughter vanished. 'What do you want?' he asked Holmes.

'I am concerned about your daughter, Odelia.'

Wyndham gave Holmes a peculiar, threatening look.

Holmes waited.

'Yes, yes. She ran off. Again. Atalanta showed me where she had been hiding. But the damned little hussy has left there and . . . by God, if I get hold of her, she—' His breath caught, and he looked up. 'But what is this to you? And what brought you here?'

'I will get to that. Who cleaned out her rooms there?' asked Holmes, meeting the man's fury with his own cold anger.

'I and my man did. How do you know they were cleaned out? We only did so a couple of hours ago. How did you get in?'

Holmes did not answer the question. 'May I see her things?'

'No.'

'Professor Wyndham, your daughter may be in danger.'

'Of her own making, then. If Odelia returns here, she will find no refuge. Duplicitous little wench! Philip!' A footman scurried in. 'You have sent my request?' barked Wyndham.

'Yes, sir. Ten minutes ago, now, sir. With all haste.'

Wyndham waved the young man away. He took a deep breath, then turned back to us. 'Sit down. Over there.' He pointed to a sofa, facing away from the door. It was an order, not an invitation.

Perhaps it would calm him, I thought, and took a seat as directed. Holmes remained standing. His eyes bored into our host's.

'You seem to be more angry than concerned about your daughter's disappearance, Mr Wyndham.'

'Oh, please. The sun rises, the sun sets.'

'You are not worried, then?'

'No.'

'What about her fiancé, the young Lord Eden-Summers?'

'I doubt he knows where she is, either.'

'You've been in touch, then?'

'Well, when Dillie left our house yet again, he and I spoke. He suggested leaving Dillie to her plans.'

'Perhaps they have since eloped?'

'No. I checked this morning and know he is still in his rooms.' Wyndham snorted like an angry bull. 'If she breaks this engagement, the girl will be dead to me. She knows that.'

'Professor Wyndham, I found Dillie once before. And I advised you to do nothing but wait, to communicate through me, and to rest assured that I would endeavour to patch things up between you.'

'Yes, and look how well that has gone,' snapped the don.

'I am concerned for her safety,' said my friend.

'Based on what? Who told you she was missing this time?'

'A person with her well-being in mind.'

From behind us, I heard someone at the front door. I stood up. Holmes and I glanced at each other. My friend was on edge.

Wyndham moved to a small table opposite the door and poured himself a whisky. It was not even noon! We turned to face him. He did not offer us a drink.

'I have had it with your prevarication, Holmes. You knew where my daughter had gone to hide and yet you chose to conceal her location from me. Now look what has happened. For a so-called detective, you bring more mystery to the situation than you solve.' His voice grew louder.

He took his whisky and stood in front of the window. Wyndham took a sip, turned to his right and favoured us with a dramatic view of his profile, the mane of white hair in a sweeping wing. It was a studied pose. 'She saw the light of reason, returned home, and announced her engagement,' he continued. 'Who knows what you may then have advised her? Now she has gone off alone—'

'How do you know she is alone?' asked Holmes.

'Well, I don't.'

'Professor Wyndham, if anyone is responsible for your daughter's desire to flee, it would most certainly be you,' said Holmes. 'She was remarkably unhappy here. I can't imagine you are unaware of that fact.'

The man gave us a scornful smile. 'When she vanished again, I prevailed upon my household to find her,' said he. 'They canvassed the town. Began to go door to door. Polly flew from the premises on the flimsiest of excuses. But thank heavens for Atalanta. Not only did she find Dillie's hideaway, but she also followed Polly and saw her board a train for London. Visiting her mother, indeed!' His face darkened. 'She came to see you.'

Holmes and I exchanged a look. There was no use denying it.

'She did,' said Holmes. 'At considerable risk to herself. Where is Polly now? She returned by a late train last night.'

'Holmes!' I cried, thinking it dangerous for him to have given Polly away.

'We need to find her, Watson, if she did not return here.'

'Here? No. That maid was a thief. As was my daughter! I found one of Odelia's earrings in the back of a drawer in her hideaway, one that she swore was missing from the house a year ago. Come to think of it, several pieces of my mother's jewellery have gone missing from my wife's room over the last year. It got so that Ianthia would not mention this to me for fear of . . . but dear Atalanta noticed and kept me informed. I suspected my wife's carelessness . . . but now I think it was Odelia and Polly, stealing things and perhaps pawning them to fund Odelia's adventures. When I get my hands on either of them—'

A slight movement in the periphery drew my eye to a side door, near the fireplace. There, positioned behind her father, Atalanta was visible watching the proceedings. Her face was a blank and yet everything about her projected eager concentration. I got the distinct impression of a mongoose watching a snake.

Holmes regarded the father with disdain equivalent to the don's. 'Sir, your irresponsible actions have driven your daughter from you and have made it impossible for me to do my job.'

'What job? No one has hired you.'

'Rest assured I will find out what happened to your daughter, and if she is hurt, and you were involved, Wyndham, you will be sorry that—'

'You dare to threaten me! I hold *you* responsible for what has happened! Officers!'

A small sound behind us caused me to turn. Detective Inspector Hadley and the unpleasant Sergeant Pickering had arrived without our seeing, thanks to the don's careful choreography. They now stood on the threshold. A third policeman, a tall, muscular lad of twenty, with a black handlebar moustache, glowered behind them.

'Mr Hadley, did you hear what this upstart detective Mr Holmes just said?' bellowed Wyndham. 'He threatened me!'

'I did indeed, Professor,' said Hadley, in his reasonable manner. 'Mr Holmes, will you come with me to the station, please? I don't wish to cuff you but will if you resist.'

Sergeant Pickering removed shiny silver handcuffs and held them up. I had the sudden image of him polishing them, alone, each evening.

'You are arresting me, Inspector Hadley? On what charge?' asked Holmes.

'Trespassing,' said Hadley. 'We are told you forced your way in here.'

'I did nothing of the sort.'

'The footman and the butler will swear to the contrary,' said the don with a small smile.

Holmes turned incredulously to the man.

'Sir?' I said, equally outraged.

'Yes indeed! Trespassing!' Wyndham went on. 'And lying by omission to me about my dear daughter Odelia. Officer, I hold this man responsible for her disappearance, if not complicit!'

'What?' I cried. 'That is a ludicrous accusation, sir!'

'Mr Hadley! You saw it yourself with me this morning. My daughter had been living there on and off for some time,' said Wyndham. 'This man Holmes knew where she was, and few others did.'

'By the way, sir, we have new information,' offered Hadley. 'A man by the name of "Leo" was heard just outside the Cross and Anchor at two in the morning last night, having a violent argument with your daughter. Something about wanting the return of his ring. The neighbour said the man skulked about for a bit after.'

Wyndham looked aghast.

'That would be Leo Vitale,' came a voice over my left shoulder. Atalanta Wyndham was more than happy to add to the scene. 'St Cedd's. Cambridge Laboratory. Besotted with her. Gave her a ring as well.'

'A ring? Why did you not say this sooner?' bellowed Wyndham to his daughter.

'She threatened me,' said Atalanta in her best approximation of a wounded deer.

Holmes tore his eyes away from this treacherous sister.

'Inspector Hadley, you saw the room, then, before Mr Wyndham emptied it?' asked Holmes. 'Did you note any signs of a struggle?'

'A struggle? No, not exactly.' The man caught himself. 'But I will not discuss this with you. Come along, now, Mr Holmes.'

Holmes did not move. 'Sir, I expect better of you. Why would I harm that young lady? What would be my motive?'

'Why, to get yourself hired to find her, of course,' snarled Pickering.

'I believe you know better, Inspector,' said Holmes, addressing the older man. 'And you may easily ascertain that I have been in London the last three days.'

'We will be checking on that, Mr Holmes,' said Hadley. 'But for now, you'll need to come with me, sir. You too, Dr Watson.'

'Surely you don't think Watson—'

'Just a formality. He is coming for questioning, that is all.'

Pickering moved towards Holmes with his handcuffs at the ready.

'No need for those,' said Holmes, calmly. 'I will not resist.'

But Pickering could not. He fastened Holmes's hands behind his back and pushed him roughly out the door.

Hadley shook his head at this action but did not stop him. 'Come along, Doctor.'

'Good riddance,' I heard Wyndham say as we exited the room. Atalanta giggled.

PART SIX

THE SETUP

An object is frequently not seen, from
not knowing how to see it,
rather than from any defect of the
organ of vision.
                                    —Charles Babbage

CHAPTER 28

The Spinning House

nce at the local police station on St Andrews Street, we were questioned at length. I was released, but Holmes was taken to a cell, alone. As we parted, he called out to me, 'Find Polly, Watson! I shall be out shortly.'

Pickering laughed. 'We will see about that.'

I stood in front of the police station, at a loss. It was midday, and the sun was high in the sky, the heat shimmering through the air causing the edges of the building to waver in front of the eyes. Or perhaps it wasn't the heat . . .

I mopped my forehead with my handkerchief. I felt faint. I had eaten nothing since dinner yesterday. I didn't know how Holmes managed to go without food. It was as though a fever of energy overtook him while on a case.

But what to do? My friend was more confident of his release from gaol than I was. At a nearby post office, I wired Mycroft Holmes, informing him in the briefest terms of his brother's circumstance. What happened next, while deeply disturbing, nevertheless proved to be providential in this case, in which so much went so terribly wrong.

I decided to return to Dillie's hiding place in the diminishing hope that at least Polly might have returned there in our absence.

I walked down St Andrews Street and came upon a forlorn two-storey brick building with bars along the upper windows. As I passed, I heard a female scream emanate from a window above me. '*Noooo!*' came the anguished cry, followed by a shriek of pain.

I hesitated. The cry came again and turned into a wail. Someone was suffering agony in that building. Without a pause, I raced through the front door. It was some sort of public place, and a sharp-faced man sat at a reception desk and looked up at me with a face compressed into a permanent scowl. 'What do you want?' he said.

'I – I heard a cry!' I said. 'A woman. It sounded like she was in pain.'

'Sir, you have no business here.'

'I am a doctor. If someone is in such pain, perhaps I can be of help.'

'Be gone! It is not your affair.'

'What is this place?'

'It is the Spinning House.'

The Spinning House! This was the place Holmes had mentioned where women were held without trial by the special University police – outside the regular law.

'But what is happening upstairs?'

Abruptly the wiry gatekeeper stood, picked up a walking stick and came round from his desk. He held the stick in a way that said he might make creative use of it. 'Now, be gone!' he growled.

'As a member of the public, I demand to know what is going on here,' said I, placing my own stick in front of me. I would not be intimidated by this toad.

'Don't you know what this place is?'

'Yes! I have heard that you people arrest women who seem to be consorting with students and hold them here without trial.'

'Trial!' he spat.

'Do you torture them as well? I will call the *real* police if you do not explain to me what I just heard.'

'The University has sovereignty here, in case you were not aware.'

The shriek came again, followed by a sob.

'Dear God, man, have you no empathy? What is happening to that poor woman?'

'Nothing untoward, you nosy know-nothing. We are protecting the students of the University – from illness, madness, and death! Many whores prowl the town and prey on these innocent young men.'

'Innocent young men? I'm told that girls are taken in for merely speaking to a student after curfew.'

'Well, then,' he sneered, 'what are the little trollops doing out at those hours?'

I suddenly realized the extent of the danger to Polly when she ran off from Baker Street last night. My chest went tight. 'How are they released? Is there a bail system?'

'Not officially. Why?'

'Well, surely their parents come for them. Or their husbands, brothers, employers? You can't tell me that none of them are released?'

'Well, eventually, of course. Under certain circumstances they are released early.'

'What circumstances?

'There is a—' he lowered his voice to a whisper '—a private bail system. It is not cheap.'

'I have means.'

The man paused, then lowered his stick. He moved back behind his desk and sat down, staring up at me thoughtfully.

'Whom have you come to release? Or did you want to meet a few? Take your pick.' He smiled. My stomach turned. 'Want to set one free, then?' He continued. 'We do process them for illness, so you'll be getting a clean one. Tell me you're her brother, perhaps. Father, maybe even, if she's a young 'un.'

'You *process them for illness*?'

'Examine every one of 'em. And treat 'em if necessary.'

As a doctor, I did not need to hear more. I knew this was done in London on a regular basis. But here, outside of municipal law? 'Do you have a young lady named Polly, red hair, about sixteen, brought in last night?'

'Surname?'

'I don't know.'

'You fellows never do.' The man hesitated. 'I will have to check.' He went to a cabinet and ruffled through some files. He pulled out a sheet of paper and turned to me. 'We have a Polly. She's a dangerous one. Feisty. Caused some damage, I think. Bail is set at five pounds.'

I paused. There was the chance I would need to bail out Holmes. I had brought a sizeable amount of money with me, as I had learned to do on such adventures. Who knew what Holmes's bail might be? But this situation demanded action now.

I reached into my pocket to discover the crumpled five-pound note from Freddie Eden-Summers. What better use for it? In five minutes, a dishevelled Polly was freed and stood with me in front of that awful place, pale, and with her hair escaping her braids in copper-coloured strands. A hot breeze blew old newspapers and chip wrappings down the street but did nothing to cool the air.

'Dear God, Polly,' said I. 'You should have stayed at Baker Street last night. Cambridge is no place for you alone after dark.'

'I know about it, sir. I have managed before.'

'Are you all right, my poor girl? Not hurt in any way?'

She held up her right hand. Her knuckles were bruised. 'I am less hurt than some chap named Pete in there.' She smiled.

'Mr Holmes is incarcerated as well,' I said.

'Don't worry, Doctor Watson. He's in regular gaol, right?'

'Yes.'

'They play fair over there. Not all of 'em. But mostly.'

'How do you know that?'

'My sister. She is a bit of a thief. Nice girl, though. And she don't work at night – for the reason you just saw.'

'Where is your sister now?'

'At work. Well, her lawful-like work. She has a room nearby,' said Polly, indicating with a thumb in an easterly direction.

'Write down the address on this slip of paper. Can you take refuge there 'til we come for you? Wyndham will have you arrested. He thinks you stole from him. Will you be safe?'

She nodded, and I watched her, relieved, as she vanished up the street. She nearly ran into two boys of about the same age who galloped towards me down the street, ringing a bell. 'A dead body! A dead body! A ha'penny for the news,' they cried.

My stomach lurched. I grabbed one by the arm as he brushed by me. 'What news? What body?'

The boy held his hand out and I slammed a coin into it. 'Dead girl. In the Jesus Lock. Drownded!' he rasped.

'Girl? How old?'

The boy shrugged. 'Dunno. Grown up, maybe?'

'A love affair gone wrong, methinks,' intoned the other with a knowing look and his hand out for another coin. But I was off and running for the police station.

CHAPTER 29

The Lady in the Lock

he place was a madhouse. Evidently news of the body had arrived at the station only minutes before, and the officers were assembling in the reception area, with Hadley barking orders. Before I could approach him, he spotted me and gestured me over brusquely.

'Dr Watson,' he said, 'a body was spotted in the Jesus Lock some hours ago. A young woman, drowned. Long blonde hair. Age twenty or thereabouts. It is looking like a murder. We've just managed to get her out of the water.'

My stomach sank. Dillie.

'Can you accompany me, please? I know you have experience with . . . such things,' Hadley said.

Pickering materialized behind him with a length of cloth,

his face like an eager wolf. 'We have it in hand, sir. No need to bring the Londoner in.'

Hadley turned sharply to his subordinate. 'Attend to the men, Pickering. I'll bring whom I like.' Pickering gave me a sour look and melted away.

'Sir,' I said, 'if it is Miss Wyndham and there is foul play, Mr Sherlock Holmes can prove invaluable. Might you not free him to join us?'

'No, Dr Watson. Follow me.'

I would have to stand in for my friend. As we hurried to the river, I could not help but wonder how the body could have been spotted but not removed until recently. I was soon to learn the awful reason why.

The Jesus Lock was surrounded by some twenty or thirty eager townspeople who crowded the banks, craning necks and whispering in excitement. On the bank of the lock, near the eastern end, lay what looked like a mound of clothing on the grassy slope.

As we drew closer, I could see it was a body, the head protruding. The face had been covered by two white hand-kerchiefs which clung to the damp features, creating a ghostly visage. The rest of the corpse was concealed by layers of summer jackets and shawls. Two delicate white feet extended out the other end of this motley pile.

Her shoes must have come off in the lock.

Five or six policemen attempted to discourage the crowd, waving hands and admonishing the gawkers. The public's response to horrible deaths never failed to disturb me. Two constables stood directly over the corpse, attempting to act as human screens.

'Pickering! The cloth!' barked Hadley and indicated that the younger man should hold up the fabric to keep the crowd from seeing the body. Even as he did so, I could see running towards us a newsman and his assistant carrying photographic equipment. Pickering held up his fabric shield just in time.

Hadley and I kneeled by the body. He nodded to me, and I peeled back the handkerchiefs.

'Dear God,' I said. The face was indeed Dillie Wyndham's, her blue eyes half-lidded and lips parted. She looked peaceful, but I could tell in an instant that her end had been anything but calm. A bruise above her left eye was telling. One hand was visible at the edge of the coverings, and I looked closely at it.

'Blood under her fingernails,' I said. 'Clearly not a suicide.'

'Not with that bruise,' agreed Hadley.

I started to pull back one of the coats covering the body but Hadley stopped me with a hand on the arm. 'Not here.' He looked up at one of his men. 'A full post-mortem. Inform the coroner.'

Pickering, who had the knack of insinuating himself into every discussion, had handed off the fabric screen, and was now kneeling beside us. 'But sir, perhaps the family would prefer—' he began.

'No. This is my responsibility,' said the senior man, gruffly. 'Summon Dr Caswell. And cover the face. Now.'

Pickering hesitated.

'Do it!'

The mortuary was in the basement of a building some five minutes from the river. As Hadley filled in paperwork upstairs, I descended the iron steps to the examination room where Odelia Wyndham's body had been brought. The temperature had dropped a good twenty degrees, as it always did in such places.

Dr Caswell, a rotund, porcine man with a grey brush cut, was laying out his instruments. My nostrils were assailed by the familiar yet always disturbing odours of carbolic acid, ammonia and death. I shivered in my linen suit at the sudden chill, contrasting so sharply with the damp heat of the day.

Caswell looked up and nodded. A combination of gas and electric light gave the place a strange brilliance. On the table, covered by a white sheet, lay the body of poor Odelia Wyndham. An attendant pulled back the draping, and once again I stared down at the girl's dead face.

The young woman, of late so vibrant, volatile and lively – was now a marble carving, white and still. Her blonde hair, free from its constraints, billowed about her on the table, a wet and tangled mass of curls. Her beauty was transformed into an ethereal shell of young womanhood. Our first meeting had been troubled, but even so, in this quiet, cold room, I felt a sharp pang of grief. A wasted young life, tempestuous but nevertheless promising, that promise now never to be fulfilled.

Had Holmes been there, he would no doubt have chided me for the sentiment.

'May I begin?' I asked, and with Caswell's nod I withdrew the covering, took out my pocket lens, and began to examine the corpse in the manner I hoped was like my friend's.

Sherlock Holmes's protocol was unique, as he never took the means of death for granted. Although it would appear Miss Wyndham had drowned, I checked her nails, inside her mouth, her neck and head, and all the major and minor bones. The body had been in the water for several hours, and in that amount of time and with the heavy current in the lock, vital evidence could have been washed away.

Hadley joined us and stood silently against the wall to give us room to work.

'Serious bruising,' I said. 'Two fingers broken, and possibly two – no, three – ribs. She fought someone, and fought hard.'

Caswell followed behind me, confirming these larger injuries and undertaking his own business. He vouched that the young lady had not been molested. At least there was that.

Thirty minutes later, I had all the information that could be gleaned from Miss Wyndham's corpse. Her wrists bore the bruises of someone's strong grip. The broken fingers and more bruises along the side of her right hand and across the knuckles indicated she had struck something, more than once, with considerable force. I announced those findings to the others.

'I concur on all,' said Dr Caswell.

'If she struck the face of her murderer with the force this indicates, there would surely be a mark on him,' said Hadley, who had been watching with interest. 'Or *her*, if the murderer were female,' said I. 'But I rather think a larger person, so more likely a man. Her left fourth finger was bare, with an abrasion near the second joint. Had a ring been torn from her hand? And yet this wound looks slightly less fresh.'

'Ah,' said Caswell, 'I missed that.' He looked closer. 'As to the timing of this injury, the immersion makes this uncertain.'

'By the amount of liquid in the lungs, Miss Wyndham was alive and breathing when she hit the water,' I said. Her hair was tangled, more so than one might have predicted. A small patch of hair was torn free, the scalp had bled, but very little. Torn off in the lock, no doubt.

'Oh, to be trapped in the lock like that,' said Hadley, shaking his head. The senior man had more feeling than I had credited.

Unbidden, a sudden image washed across my mind, another woman, perhaps thirty, floating in water, tangled in some branches, the river rushing past her. A flash and then an image of a six-year-old girl, her body floating underwater and undulating with a strong current.

A wave of sadness flooded me. I closed my eyes for a moment, shaking my head to dispel the vivid thought.

I focused again on the body of Odelia Wyndham. Evidence of a severe blow to the forehead, and gentle palpating revealing a shattered skull, divulged the *coup de grace.* 'From this head injury, I believe she was knocked unconscious before hitting the water. She would have died soon after from bleeding in the brain, but it is likely that she did not suffer in the drowning.'

'A small blessing,' murmured Hadley.

Holmes would have the entire picture of the struggle in his head, no doubt, and minutes before our own conclusions.

I then asked to see the items of clothing in which she'd been found.

'There were none,' said Hadley.

'No clothing?' I cried, aghast that this fact had not been mentioned to me earlier. But of course, it was why they would not let me examine her *in situ* at the river. That Odelia Wyndham fell or was thrown naked into the lock put an entirely different light on events.

'We did not wish for this fact to receive public attention,' said Hadley, 'given the prominence of the family. My men have been sworn to secrecy.'

'Who found the body?'

'A baker en route to his shop at five in the morning.'

'But that was hours ago!'

'He was not immediately sure. He saw something white floating in the lock – he thought it was a lily. But it bothered him, and he came back some time later. It was still there. He went in for a closer look and discovered it was a foot. It apparently took him some time to get anyone to pay attention to his claim.'

The foot presenting on the surface was highly unusual, as it was the torso – lungs filled with air and abdomen with fat – that floated more readily. 'Then she must have been trapped underwater, submerged . . . face down. Perhaps her hair was tangled into something?' I said.

The policeman nodded. 'Yes. Exactly. The gates were opened and she was sucked into the sluice tunnel, her hair tangled into the gate mechanism.'

This image was horrifying, but she had been unconscious at the time, I reminded myself. Unaware. Thank the heavens for this, at least. 'Sir,' said I, 'Sherlock Holmes may have something useful to offer us. If you will permit?'

Minutes later, back at the station, we were both in for a surprise. Where Holmes had been locked in, Hadley and I now faced an empty cell, the door ajar, and handcuffs on the floor. In spite of it all, in spite of the horror of our discovery, I felt a small tingle of delight. Holmes had managed to free himself!

Hadley missed the humour. 'Now this is a real shame,' said he.

'Mr Holmes can help you solve this case,' I said. 'He has only to—'

'He has ruined his chances,' said Hadley. 'You must realize that his arrest was a courtesy to the don. I planned to hold him overnight only. He will now face serious charges.'

I inwardly cursed my friend's impatience, while admiring his skills. But where was he now?

CHAPTER 30

Freddie Eden-Summers

s Hadley began instructing his men to begin the investigation into Dillie's death, I made my way outside and walked down the sunbaked street, unsure of what to do next. I had no idea where Holmes might have gone, but I had not long to ponder this as a hiss drew my attention to a narrow alleyway. In the shadows, a head of tousled dark hair peeked from behind several stacks of rubbish. A skinny arm waved me over.

I glanced about me, then ducked into the alley. 'Holmes!' I whispered. 'You have made a mistake. Hadley was planning to release you tomorrow, and now—'

Holmes pulled me down next to him behind the heaping waste. 'Tomorrow will be too late, Watson!' He grasped both my arms, too hard, his face inches from mine. He was the picture of dismay. 'Dear God, I have failed that young woman!'

'No, Holmes. You gave her clear advice which she ignored.' He shook his head. 'You warned her that her provocations put her in danger.'

'Not her provocations. It was her casual cruelty that made me fear for her.'

'And you tried to tell her this, while still supporting her independence, Holmes. You did the right thing.'

'No young woman deserves such a fate!' he cried and released my arms. I almost fell backwards into the refuse.

'Careful, Holmes. We are out of our element here. And you do not have a client, remember.'

'Dillie. The late Odelia Wyndham is my client,' said he. 'And I will find her murderer.' We stood, but he yanked me back down when he spotted two policemen running in the direction of the river. After a minute, he peeked out. 'It's clear, Watson. We must do our work before the police. Tell me of the post-mortem along the way.'

I did so as Holmes and I hurried down side streets and ducked into alleys. Holmes's plan was to visit each of Dillie's beaus in turn, as quickly as possible. It would require a fair amount of luck, but there was no dissuading him. He knew the Cambridge police were not up to the case. I had to agree.

Our first stop was Trinity College, and the rooms of Freddie Eden-Summers. Perhaps the missing engagement ring meant Dillie had broken off her engagement with this young man. And Eden-Summers was fit and strong enough to overcome the girl. Perhaps he had torn his ring from her finger.

If luck was with us, we could question him and be gone before the police arrived to pursue the matter themselves.

Minutes later, we found ourselves facing his elegant student lodgings in one of the more beautiful courts in Cambridge. Upon entering the foyer, the heat faded instantly to a delicious coolness. The Wyndham name gave us immediate cachet, and a porter led us to Mr Eden-Summers' room without hesitation.

We followed him up a spiralling staircase to the third floor. As we passed each door in the stairwell, I took in muffled laughter, the sound of a tennis ball hitting the wall, and when both inner and outer doors were open, caught glimpses of young men lounging, studying, smoking. There was a distinct aura of sports, coffee, whisky, cigarette smoke and sweat, with an occasional waft of expensive cologne. It was the beginning of term, and studies not much in evidence, at least here.

I was struck intensely by the difference between this renowned institution and my own less prestigious alma mater. The outer door to Frederick Eden-Summers' room was open, indicating he was in. The porter gave a short knock on the inner door and called out, 'Mr Eden-Summers. You have visitors!' There was no reply. 'Be patient. He is there,' said the porter. 'I shall return with coffee.' He left us.

Coffee, rather than a key, I wondered. The urgency of our mission tightened my chest as several loud knocks on the door went unanswered.

Holmes withdrew his lockpick kit, and we were soon inside. The room was enormous for a student accommodation, larger than our sitting-room in Baker Street. It was nicely appointed with a wide bed, a number of quality bookcases and an intricately carved armoire. Linen curtains billowed in the hot afternoon breeze. The moth-eaten rug on the floor must once have cost a king's ransom. Hung on one wall was a magnificent longbow, the patina of its glorious wooden limbs gleaming in the morning sunlight. I remembered Atalanta mentioning 'Freddie's' passion for archery. And there, to the right, at one end of the spacious room, was a most curious sight.

It was an antique card table, littered with bottles of ale at each corner, around which were three empty chairs, two turned over on their sides, and numerous discarded bottles. Cards were spread across the table in a jumble, as were various coins and numerous crumpled white fivers. Everything spoke of casual wealth.

Two young men were still at the table, although this was not exactly accurate. The feet of one were up on the table, the rest of him lying down on the floor face up, dead to the world. And seated but draped across the table, head facing away from us, was Freddie Eden-Summers.

His tousled mop of golden-brown hair was instantly recognizable, with the familiar tennis sweater clothing his torso. But his lower half sported only undergarments, feet bare. Both arms were outstretched on the table, one hand on a stack of five-pound notes, the other grasping a bottle. Just as I had begun to worry that we'd come upon a second murder scene, a loud snore emanated from this partially clothed figure.

'Mr Eden-Summers,' said Holmes, the sharpness of his tone intending to cut through the torpor of the room's denizens. There was no response.

Holmes shook his head. He moved to the bed, pulled off one blanket from the jumble that was upon it, and placed it on the table next to the slumbering golden-haired boy. At the washbasin he filled a small drinking glass and then returned to the table, where he poured it over the head of Frederick Eden-Summers.

The young man sprang awake with a snort. 'Wha – wha—?' He coughed.

'Mr Eden-Summers!' Holmes said. The boy nodded, then in a series of moves worthy of a pantomime actor he stood, took us in, noticed his lack of trousers, looked about in confusion for something with which to cover himself, grabbed the blanket Holmes had placed next to him, and wrapped it around himself to cover everything from the waist down. He then turned to face us blearily, but with a certain pluck.

Holmes opened his mouth to speak but Eden-Summers held out one finger, signalling us to wait. He turned back to the table, noticed the feet resting on it, peered over at the figure on the floor. 'Laurence?' he mumbled, then grinned at us. Scanning the table, he seized a nearby bottle, took two long swigs, emitted a sonorous belch, and turned again to face us.

'All right, then. Gentlemen, to what do I owe this

pleasure?' he intoned with all the grace a half-clad, drunken man of twenty could manage. 'You look, er . . . familiar?'

'Mr, Eden-Summers, I am here on the matter of Miss Odelia Wyndham. Or Dillie, as you know her,' said Holmes.

'Have we met?' the boy slurred. 'Oh, yes. Wedding planner? I . . .'

'This is Mr Sherlock Holmes, a consulting detective. I am his friend, Dr John Watson,' said I. 'We are here—'

'A detective? What? Oh, Dillie, my God, what has she done now?'

'You are engaged to the young lady, are you not?' asked Holmes, sternly.

'Why, yes. She has the ring. It was in the newspaper . . . erm . . .' The youth peered at Holmes with bloodshot eyes. 'Tell me, old man, why is a consulting detective and his . . . whoever you are . . . barging into my room at this hour of the morning?'

'It is after three p.m.' I said.

'I'll need you to account for the last eighteen hours,' said Holmes.

Just then the young man on the floor stirred. His feet fell with a thump onto the threadbare oriental carpet, where he lay sprawled.

'Where are my manners?' said Eden-Summers. 'Let me introduce Laurence Manon Le Cru – my friend and fellow Dallier. That's our club. He was with me.' Eden-Summers waved grandly at this figure, then peered over the table at him. 'Larry, where are the others?'

'Gone,' moaned Le Cru from the floor. 'You cleaned them out.'

'I say!' Eden-Summers turned to us with an unsteady smile. 'After I lost my shirt, or rather my trousers, I suppose I had something of a comeback. Yes, I remember it now.'

'To the point, young man!' said Holmes sternly.

'All right. What was the question?' The fellow blinked, swayed, then closed his eyes in an effort at cogitation. 'But wait, just a moment! How did you get in here?'

'Down through the chimney, Mr Eden-Summers. Put on your clothes, send your friend away, and call up for coffee at once, if you know what is good for you,' barked Holmes.

'Oh, I seldom know what is good for me,' slurred Eden-Summers.

'And when he does . . .' came an even blurrier voice from the floor.

'It matters not a whit!' said both in unison, then laughed.

'Mr Eden-Summers, pull yourself together. You may talk to me or to the police.'

'My word!'

Holmes nodded to me, indicating 'Larry'. I helped the boy up with a touch more force than he clearly was used to, and handing him his shoes, ejected him into the hall. As I returned, Frederick Eden-Summers was just fastening his trousers.

'Sit down, young man,' said Holmes sternly. 'Where were you last night between suppertime and this morning at six?'

The boy flopped into a chair and looked about for his

shoes. 'I do not like the sound of this. What has Dillie done exactly?'

Holmes was silent.

The boy's face went grave. He stood up. 'Something is wrong, isn't it?'

'Again, I ask, where were you?'

'Right here. The Dalliers. Our bi-weekly game.'

'Tell me about the Dalliers,' said Holmes.

'A club I started. We . . . er . . . we gamble, dine, drink and generally carouse. It's a small group. We are dedicated to bringing a special touch of levity to our otherwise quite dreary studies. We study the law. Before the wig, before the bar, we . . . drink. And gamble.' He smiled charmingly. I could see the appeal he would have had for a young woman. Rakish, and rich beyond compare. Even his dishevelled clothing probably cost more than my entire wardrobe.

'Will anyone vouch for you besides your inebriated friend?' Holmes asked.

'Several. Although I think they wandered off at various times. Must have been this morning, though. I recall losing big at five-thirty.' He nodded to one wall, where a grand-father clock, another unusual component of student lodging, stood bedecked with a variety of coloured socks. It did, however, read the correct time, three-thirty p.m.

The porter knocked and entered with coffee. He brought only one cup, handed it to young Eden-Summers, who leaped up and, as a parched desert traveller might grab a drink, took the cup and gulped it down. The porter retreated.

The young man shook his head, then met our eyes. 'Sir, I see you are here on serious business. What?'

'Sit down again, Mr Eden-Summers, and put that cup on the table.'

'I prefer to stand.'

'Very well. Miss Odelia Wyndham was found drowned some four hours ago.'

The boy dropped the cup with a clatter. His face went white.

'Dillie! But . . . but I was with her just yesterday. She . . .' His voice trailed off as he focused on an image which seemed in the far distance. His face clouded, and he closed his eyes. He took a deep breath and gave a long, shuddering sigh.

Holmes glanced at me in frustration. After a moment, Eden-Summers opened his eyes and stared at Holmes, all traces of the night's debauchery gone. 'Has her body been . . . er . . . are they sure that it is her?' he asked in a new, serious voice.

'Yes,' said Holmes.

'Found by whom?'

'A baker passing the location.'

'Where?'

'You tell me.'

'What? You think that I—? Why would—?' Eden-Summers scowled. 'My father will have something to say about this!'

'Threats will get you nowhere, Mr Eden-Summers. The police are soon to arrive and will take you in for questioning. They'll be considerably less patient than I.'

'How do they know this drowned . . . person . . . is Dillie?'

'Watson attended the post-mortem and confirmed the identity,' said Holmes.

'It was she,' I said.

Eden-Summers nodded. 'My God. That is a shame. A shame and a loss. She was—' Here he paused. 'She was . . . a fine girl. A very fine girl indeed.' I saw no trace of tears. And an odd turn of phrase for one's fiancée, I thought.

Holmes smiled. 'I will need the names of your "Dalliers". Everyone who was here and could vouch for you. I will, of course, have to confirm your presence here during the time of her death.'

'Then you believe it was murder!'

Holmes said nothing.

'You must believe so, else why be here? What makes you think it was a murder and not some kind of terrible accident? You said "drowned". Where? Might she have fallen into—'

'Fallen in? No.'

'Dillie was an adventurous girl.'

'There were marks. She struggled with someone.'

The boy shook his head. 'But Dillie was a formidable young lady. Strong. Unafraid. I cannot imagine her being easily overcome.'

'She was not easily overcome.'

These words hit their target. 'Oh, my God! Dillie! I must wire my father. He – he – he will be . . .' The boy paused. 'But my mother will be relieved, I suppose.'

'Relieved that your fiancée was murdered?' I could not hold back this exclamation.

'Then it *was* a murder! No, of course not relieved about that. But relieved that the wedding is off. She did not like Odelia. Our marriage was my father's idea.' He paused, his eyes going glassy once more. 'Although no one would have wished . . . Dillie,' he said softly. 'Oh, Dillie.' He looked up sharply. 'And the scandal. What of the ring? The ring I gave her?'

'There was no ring on the body,' I said.

'No ring! Perhaps in her rooms?'

'No. What did it look like?' asked Holmes.

'A . . . an enormous diamond. Several smaller ones, and two serious emeralds. My aunt's ring. Family heirloom. My father will have my head.'

'Why your aunt's ring, and not your mother's?'

Eden-Summers shook his head, attempting to clear it. He looked up suddenly at his interlocutor with a new resolve. 'Because she is still wearing it, old boy. What of my other ring? Gold. No jewels but a simple golden arrow? I gave it to her a month ago. Though she never wore it.'

'No ring of any sort was found.'

The boy's face fell, and his eyes filled with tears. 'Dillie.'

Holmes stared at him a moment, then said to my surprise, 'I believe you are innocent, Mr Eden-Summers. Let us help to prove it. Dr Watson can examine you in private and confirm there are no signs of a struggle.'

Freddie Eden-Summers frowned, and I sensed a certain belligerence.

'Whoever killed Dillie will bear marks of the fight,' said Holmes. 'This can be done here, or more publicly at the police station, if you so choose.'

Eden-Summers' jaw clenched, but he acquiesced and collapsed onto a worn velvet chair near the window, where I made quick work of the examination. In rapid succession I searched his hands, arms and torso thoroughly for signs of bruises, scratches, blood, or any indications that he had fought physically with the victim.

To my considerable surprise he did indeed bear the marks of a fight. He had a deep bruise under the left ribs, as though from a hard right punch, and, perhaps more telling, his own right knuckles were bruised and abraded, which I pointed out to Holmes. The young man angrily pulled down his tennis sweater and said, 'I punched a fellow in the stairwell last night. A bit drunk, he wanted to barge into our private party.' Holmes looked at him askance, and the boy added, chin jutting in anger, 'This was seen by several of my Dalliers. They will vouch for me.'

'What is this man's name?'

Eden-Summers hesitated just a moment too long. He shrugged. 'He had never been seen here before.'

Holmes and I exchanged a look. Undoubtedly prevarication. But before we could pursue this line of inquiry, the porter knocked crisply and opened the door without waiting.

'Mr Eden-Summers,' he said formally. 'The police are downstairs. They wish to have a word.'

In a moment, Holmes and I had escaped down a back

staircase and were outside in the late afternoon heat, keeping to alleys and vigilant for the police.

'Your thoughts, Holmes?' I asked.

'Inconclusive. Those knuckles. And the odd story of the second ring. I wonder where it went?'

'In the lock perhaps,' I offered.

'Even if his fisticuffs are verified, Eden-Summers has the financial means to have hired Dillie's killer, if that were his intention. And his reaction was most odd.'

'You told Eden-Summers you thought he was innocent,' I said.

Holmes shook his head. 'To put him at ease so that you could examine him. He is enormously entitled.'

'That is putting it mildly, Holmes. Where next?'

'We must see Leo Vitale before the police get to him.'

CHAPTER 31

Leo Vitale

itale was lodged in the second court at St Cedd's not far from the Cavendish Laboratory. At the entrance to this large court, in which several buildings faced a plain green, we were confronted by a porter. A small, grizzled man, his upturned nose and large teeth putting me in mind of a hungry squirrel, he sat in a cubbyhole off the arched stone entrance. The porter set down the *Illustrated Police News* to demand our business. Intuiting instantly that the Wyndham name would not impress this man, Holmes mentioned that he was investigating an exciting murder, and time was of the essence! He explained that a young woman had been killed, implying that he was an official on the case, and that he needed to speak to Leo Vitale urgently.

'Murder, you say! Well, that is fascinating. Leo Vitale!

Now there's a strange fellow. Well, these scientists are a queer lot. They are all clustered in staircase K and L, across the green there. Do you suspect him?'

'No, but he may be a witness. Our business is urgent, sir! His room, please?' said Holmes.

'Odd, folks, these science fellows, I tell you. Strange smells. They set their rooms afire – exploding things. And always wanting coffee, coffee, coffee.'

'His *room*, please?' I said, before Holmes lost his temper.

'Room Five. Top of staircase K. You'll tell me what you find, then? So's I can be prepared?'

'Certainly,' lied Holmes.

We found K and were up the stairs in a trice. By contrast to those of Eden-Summers' lodgings, this staircase was dark and shabby, the wooden treads deeply scuffed, and the outer doors to all the rooms were all pockmarked and firmly closed. As we ascended, the heat grew oppressive.

The outer door to Room Five was ajar. We were in luck – Vitale, too, was in. Holmes knocked and opened the inner door to discover a single room, low ceilinged and dark.

Leo Vitale was seated at a desk, sweltering under the eaves, once again poring over a single sheet of paper, his head in his hands. He did not look up. Stacks of books, papers, and the odd bit of laboratory paraphernalia were piled high on every available surface. Two valises with a jumble of clothing and linens poked out from under the narrow bed, and the young man's student gown, jacket and hat were hung from pegs all over the room. Even within the hallowed halls of Cambridge, our British class system made itself precisely known. Vitale looked up at us, his face devoid of expression. I noted dark circles under his eyes and a kind of sadness reflected there.

'Mr Vitale,' said Holmes. 'Forgive the interruption. We are here on a matter of utmost urgency.'

The young scientist inhaled and sat up straight. 'You again. What is this about now?'

'A crime has been committed against a certain young lady. The police will be arriving shortly to question you,' said Holmes.

'What young lady? What crime?'

'You are a suspect, Mr Vitale,' said Holmes. 'Now listen carefully. I am a scientist like yourself, and inclined to trust what you say. The police will look at you as an exotic bird, believe me, I know about this. There is evidence against you, and they will arrest you without hesitation.'

'Be clear, sir! Arrest me for what?'

'You were seen and heard outside the Cross and Anchor, having a shouting argument with Miss Dillie Wyndham at about two o'clock this morning.'

Two spots of colour appeared on the young man's white cheeks.

'How is that anyone's business? What crime? Is Dillie all right?'

'I need to know the subject of that argument.'

Vitale stared at Holmes. 'Miss Wyndham has taken flight again? Is that it?'

'Mr Vitale, tell me now, and I may be able to help you. What was the subject of your argument?'

I volunteered, 'Mr Holmes is trying to help you, young man.'

Vitale blinked, thinking quickly. 'I asked Dillie for my ring back. She refused.'

'A ring you gave to her? What kind of ring?'

'My mother's ring: a small sapphire with two diamonds. A family heirloom. Please tell me what has happened.'

'I see. You proposed marriage, then? She accepted you?'

The young man nodded.

'But then you saw that Miss Wyndham's engagement to Freddie Eden-Summers was announced in the papers,' said Holmes.

Vitale stiffened. 'Eden-Summers is a damned fool. That foppish idiot could never make her happy! And she had already . . .' His eyes glazed over, and he blinked rapidly.

'She had accepted you?' Holmes murmured.

Leo Vitale nodded, back in control.

'But last night, when Miss Wyndham refused to give you back the ring, you lost your temper. Shouts were heard. What happened after your argument?'

'I left. I walked the streets for a while,' said Vitale.

'You did not go up to her room?'

'No.'

'Not to retrieve your mother's ring?'

'No.'

'Why not?'

'I was more upset about the . . . about *her* . . . not the ring.'

'Even so, why did you not go up and see her?' persisted Holmes.

'Have you met Dillie?'

'Yes, I see. Did you encounter anyone while walking in the streets? Anyone who might remember you?'

The young man leaped to his feet. 'Tell me what has happened. Why are the police involved? Is Dillie all right?'

Holmes was silent. Vitale looked from one of us to the other.

'She is dead, isn't she? Dillie Wyndham. Is she dead?'

Holmes nodded.

Vitale inhaled sharply as though someone had punched him in the stomach, but only a flicker of emotion reached his face. There was much of Sherlock Holmes in this boy.

Just then I heard a noise in the hallway. 'Police!' we heard a gruff voice bellow nearby. This was followed by a furious knocking on a nearby door.

Holmes glanced at the window. 'The fire escape. Now!' he barked.

The young man hesitated.

'We are trying to help you,' said Holmes. 'Act quickly!'

'I'll go first,' said Leo Vitale, opening the window and stepping through it onto something. 'There is a trick to it. You must be careful.'

We followed the young man and clambered out of the window and onto a rickety iron construction. I wondered what had occasioned Vitale to exit this way before.

The spidery, long-limbed student and the always spry Holmes had no trouble navigating the rickety ladders heading to the ground, despite a railing that had come loose and two missing steps. I struggled but managed to follow.

We found ourselves in an alley behind St Cedd's court, safe but only for the moment. The oppressive heat seemed to settle into the grime and rubbish around us and be reflected back from it.

'I am going to the laboratory,' said Vitale.

'They will soon look for you there,' said Holmes. 'Is there no other place we can take refuge?'

Vitale shook his head. 'If I am to be arrested, I must secure my papers, first. Do what you like, but that is where I am going.'

After a quick and frantic run through Cambridge's back alleys, we arrived, drenched in perspiration, at a back door of the Cavendish Laboratory. Once inside, we raced down a cool hallway and into the large room where we had first encountered Vitale. The windows of this laboratory were now strangely blacked out with thick fabric. Vitale threw a switch and electric light flooded the room.

Holmes looked around. 'No way out. I don't like it. Is there another egress, Vitale?'

The boy did not answer but focused on his business. He opened a desk drawer, reached deeply in it to the back and removed a stack of papers. He hesitated, looking around the room, evidently for a place to hide them.

'There.' Holmes pointed to a ventilator grate high on a wall near the sink.

Vitale nodded, clambered onto the stone counter nearby and stuffed them inside the vent, where they could not be seen.

As he did so, I noticed that in addition to the covered

windows, something else had changed in the laboratory since our last visit. Rows of glass tubes shaped like long, thin sausages now crisscrossed along the walls, all dangling by wires and making long patterns of what looked like random, gigantic ant trails.

'Aha' said Holmes regarding this same display. 'This is interesting.'

'*Pah!*' said Vitale. 'This is Cosimo's work. My senior lab partner has lost the story!'

What, I wondered, did that mean?

Satisfied that he had secured his research notes, Vitale leaped nimbly down from the counter and approached us.

'And now, Mr Holmes,' he said. 'I . . . I will wait no longer. Tell me all, sir. What happened to Dillie? Please. How did she die?' He swallowed, his face hardened, and he placed a hand on the stone counter, bracing himself for the news.

'Watson attended the post-mortem. Explain, Doctor.'

I could only presume that he wanted to observe the boy's reactions. 'Her body was found trapped underwater in the Jesus Lock,' I said. 'Her hair was entangled in the mechanism.'

'Dillie drowned?'

'Officially, yes. But there was a concussion and it is likely that she was unconscious when she entered the water. Then she was sucked under.'

Vitale's eyes glistened though he remained stiff. I could see he was holding back. Was it possible that this young man had more feeling for the dead girl than her wealthy fiancé did?

'Other signs revealed that Miss Wyndham fought someone before entering the water,' I said.

'That does not surprise me. Dillie was . . . quick to anger,' said he, sadly. 'I worried about her. It took little to provoke her.'

'Indeed,' said Holmes. He prowled the laboratory, glancing up at the glass tubing. 'Interesting. These will light up, in sequence.' He pulled at the blackout curtains but they had been nailed in place. He looked about for an exit. 'Ah, a cupboard. Mr Vitale, if the police come I suggest you – we all – hide for the moment. He returned to face Vitale.

'I will not hide. I am innocent.'

'It looks bad for you, Mr Vitale. You would be wise to buy yourself some time.'

The young man looked stricken. 'I would never harm a hair . . . She . . . I wonder about the ring.'

Yet another young man worried more about his token?

'What about the ring?' asked Holmes, gently. He was, I thought, providing the boy rope with which to hang himself. Both of Miss Wyndham's betrothed were suspects, I decided. I was now beginning to sense something odd, held back, about Leo Vitale's manner.

'Why would she accept me, take my ring, and then accept another the next day? None of this makes sense. Oh, Dillie, I . . .' The boy's eyes moistened.

'I need two things from you, Mr Vitale,' said Holmes. 'First, your exact whereabouts, hour by hour, between your argument outside the Cross and Anchor and this morning at six a.m. And I need you to allow Dr Watson to examine you.'

'Examine me?'

'Whoever did this received a beating. She fought back.'

A wave of grief contorted his features and then in an instant was gone. 'Yes. She would, of course. But I . . . oh, no, this will only make it worse. I . . . well, you see . . .' He unbuttoned his shirt. Several bright bruises and abrasions were visible. Vitale brushed back a long lock of dark hair that hung down over his forehead and onto his cheek. There, next to the left eye, was another recent bruise and a small cut. I felt Holmes stiffen beside me. Neither of us had expected this.

'It is not what you think,' said Vitale. 'I got into a fight last night.'

'With whom?'

He did not want to say.

'With *whom*, Mr Vitale?' insisted Holmes.

'Freddie Eden-Summers.'

Holmes and I exchanged a look.

'Where did this take place?'

The boy looked embarrassed. 'In the stairway outside his room. Not very wise of me, in retrospect.'

'Which college was that?' asked Holmes casually, as if he could not remember.

'Trinity.'

'Had you been there before?' asked Holmes.

Vitale shook his head.

'How did you find his room, then?' I asked.

'I knew it was Trinity, Great Court. I arrived with a large box of cakes and biscuits. The porter was happy to direct me.'

'In the middle of the night?' asked Holmes. 'Where did you find those?'

'I stole them. A student on my floor is always well provisioned by his parents.'

'Then that student, at least, saw you?'

'No, he was asleep when I took them. He heard nothing.'

Holmes stared at Vitale for a long moment. 'You are holding something back, Mr Vitale. I might even say lying. May I suggest you be forthcoming?'

A noise behind us made all three of us turn to the door. Silhouetted in the doorway, the light behind him, was Cosimo Fortuny.

'Leo!' cried Fortuny. 'What are you doing here? I gave you calculations to run and a report to write up.' He glanced at Holmes and me. 'Not these two again! I told you – no visitors!'

I could see the form of a woman hidden behind Fortuny. It appeared that the handsome young scientist had other plans in the laboratory that night.

'Then who is with *you*, Cosimo?' said Leo Vitale angrily. 'There cannot be one rule for you and another for me!' He waved towards the dangling tubes. 'And what is all this nonsense?'

'This is not a visitor, this is a donor to our research,' said Fortuny irritably.

I grasped Holmes's arm. 'Holmes, shouldn't we be leaving?' I whispered.

But my friend's face was frozen in surprise. I followed his gaze to the door. Cosimo Fortuny had entered, leaving us a clear view of his guest. It was none other than the flamboyant Madame Ilaria Borelli.

'Madame!' I exclaimed, gaping in astonishment at what I perceived to be an incomprehensible coincidence.

I turned to Holmes.

He stared at her, fascinated. A slow smile of under-standing crossed his face. He nodded. 'Madame Borelli, the research. *Brava!*'

CHAPTER 32

Lucifer's Lights

t is Mr Holmes! And the doctor!' exclaimed Madame Borelli. 'What a pleasant surprise.' She turned to Fortuny. 'Cosimo, this man, Mr Holmes, he saved me when I was being accused of murder!' She gave Fortuny's arm a squeeze.

I could not fathom the nature of this coincidence. But my friend clearly did. He continued to nod in understanding.

'I am on the trail of a great new illusion,' she said, by way of explanation. 'You are a detective of murder, Mr Holmes. I am a detective of magic. And I perceive the next great stage effect will come from this laboratory. With this man, Cosimo Fortuny.'

'Cosimo!' exclaimed Vitale. 'A stage effect? Explain this to me!' He gestured at the hanging mass of tubing.

'All in good time, Leo,' said Fortuny.

291

'Ah yes,' said Holmes. 'I can see it.'

'Holmes, should we not all repair to some safer location?' I said. 'The police—'

'I will not hide from the police. I am innocent!' cried Vitale.

'Innocent of what, Leo?' asked Fortuny.

'How precisely did you arrive in the Cavendish Laboratory, Madame?' asked Holmes, his eyes fixed on the glamorous illusionist.

'You must remember, Mr Holmes, I mentioned to you my friendship with a professor. I was speaking then of Cosimo.' She took his arm. 'He came to see our act in Birmingham, two weeks before London. After, he invites me to dinner, and—' She smiled and took the handsome young scientist's arm in hers. Cosimo Fortuny seemed to grow taller before our eyes as he beamed with pleasure.

It became clearer. More than a friendship, then. Cosimo Fortuny was Madame's next 'project', as Holmes had predicted. Though perhaps here was the last place one would expect to find him. For a brief moment I will admit that this new mystery distracted me – distracted us all – from our dire circumstance.

'Dinner with Mr Fortuny in Birmingham? I take it your husband was otherwise occupied,' said Holmes.

'The soprano,' said Madame. 'Remember? Touring there as well.'

'I see.' Holmes turned to Fortuny with one eyebrow raised. 'Yet this is a rather fortuitious leap from your work, Mr Fortuny, to what I see here. Unless . . .' A look of further understanding passed over his sharp features, and he closed his eyes, threw his head back and laughed.

'Of course! Madame Borelli! The papers on my table at Baker Street. The ones you stole!' He turned to me. 'Sorry, Watson, I accused you of burning them.'

The lady smiled.

'What papers?' I asked. I had no idea about any of this.

She nodded. 'Always the good ideas, Mr Holmes. Good fortune for me, as it turns out.'

'Cosimo! What is happening here with these people? What of our work?' Vitale nearly shouted with frustration.

'Patience, Leo,' said Cosimo. 'I have loved stage magic since I was a small child. Many scientists do. I proposed to Madame and her husband that we use Geissler tubes in their act. But I was not sure how, precisely . . .'

'A magic act for the music halls!' cried Leo Vitale. 'You trivialize our work, Cosimo!'

Holmes turned to me. 'The monograph I was writing – remember Watson, I have recently become interested in stage illusions – explained it all. The Geissler tubes are filled with various gases. When an electrical current passes through them, they light up and glow in the most ethereal and glorious manner! Pass your hand near these and the lights will move! Over there, that Ruhmkorff coil—' he pointed to that strange black tube of about three feet long and one foot in diameter, set with a series of switches and wires '—it creates the spark and generates the current. A smaller one was at Baker Street, Watson. I jotted some notes on this!'

I nodded.

'I find it remarkable that I did not see you pocket those notes, Madame,' said Holmes.

She patted the front of her dress. 'To fool the fooler is an art you know well.' She smiled. 'Watson's keys?'

He laughed.

'I struggle for such an idea when I see Cosimo's work. But I see instantly that your ideas complete the circle,' said the lady. 'I call this 'Lucifer's Lights'.

To my view, this was all beside the point. I glanced over at Leo Vitale. He had gone white and was staring at the floor, supporting himself against one of the laboratory tables. The girl he loved had been murdered, and here was Holmes babbling about a magic act. I pulled out a wooden stool nearby and gently sat Vitale on it, fearing a collapse.

'Good thinking, Watson. I am sorry, Mr Vitale,' said Holmes.

'I was right about you, Mr Sherlock Holmes,' said Fortuny. 'The Bunsen burner in your sitting-room . . .' He laughed.

Leo Vitale groaned. I turned to attend him but even the younger scientist seemed now to have ventured down this rabbit hole. 'Oh, Cosimo!' he exclaimed. 'You debase, you subvert, you prostitute our efforts!'

'No, Leo. Madame Borelli donates to the Cavendish Laboratory,' said Fortuny. 'I do this for funding.'

Vitale looked from Fortuny to Madame and back again. 'No, Cosimo. You do this for a woman!'

Fortuny grinned at his younger associate. 'You are in love yourself, Leo. Did you think I did not notice?'

At this, Leo Vitale seemed to crumple, and he covered his face with his hands.

'Gentlemen, please,' I said. 'The lady in question has met a violent end. We are in the midst of investigating, and the police will surely come here. Holmes!'

I became aware of noises coming down the hall. As did my friend.

'They are here!' he cried. 'We have wasted valuable time. Fortuny, be quick. Fire those up and create a diversion! We must hide.'

Fortuny hesitated.

'Do it for your friend. I will explain later,' said Holmes, and he dashed to the cupboard door and opened it, but it was filled to bursting with glass retorts, tubing and other equipment. No room to hide!

'That one!' cried Fortuny, pointing to a second cupboard at the back of the lab near the sink. Holmes ran to it and threw open the door. There was room inside, in front of some crowded shelves.

At the same time, the senior scientist dashed to the end of the lab near the door, to fire up the Ruhmkorff coil.

'Down here!' I heard a familiar, gruff voice in the hall outside.

'Holmes! It is Pickering,' I whispered.

Holmes grabbed my arm, pulling me into the cupboard. 'Mr Vitale, you too – inside! Mr Fortuny, work your magic. Not a word, Madame! Hurry!'

But Leo Vitale pulled away.

'Vitale! Come!' Holmes grabbed Leo Vitale's cuff, but the young man yanked his arm free.

'No! I am innocent. I will face the police!' he cried.

'They will not believe you,' said Holmes. But the young man moved out of reach.

We heard noises at the door of the laboratory, and Holmes and I ducked back into the darkness, closing the cupboard door in front of us, leaving only a crack. We were concealed but could see what was going on in most of the room.

Fortuny, down at the end near the door, doused the lights. In the dimness I saw him pull a large-handled lever near the Ruhmkorff coil. There was a hum, then a sudden loud *crack* as a bolt of miniature lightning arced between two metal poles adjacent to the black tube. A sizzle sounded, then a hiss of gas as the tubes slowly swayed gently in their wire cradles fastened to the wall.

Fortuny threw another switch. All along the walls the small sausage-like tubes suddenly lit up in glowing, ethereal greens, reds and blues. He ran past us and took up a position with Leo Vitale behind us, at the darkest end of the room.

'Fantastic!' whispered Holmes. It was indeed a strange and marvellous effect.

Just then the door burst open and silhouetted against the light in the hall were Pickering and two constables. The flicker of the glowing coloured lights danced in patterns across their surprised faces.

'What the devil is all this?' boomed Pickering. 'Light the lights, someone!'

Madame Borelli now emerged into our view as she

walked past our hiding place and the glowing tubes, slowly towards the door where the police stood. Her arms were outstretched, as if in a trance. She spoke in a deep, other-worldly monotone.

'*Welcome to the humans. Beware, beware! I summon the spirits,*' she intoned. '*I call forth here, the powers of the dead – to come, to come . . . and to change the energy of this room . . .*'

Pickering and his two men backed up in alarm but held open the door. As Madame drew closer to them, she gently passed her hands near the largest of the tubes. As she did so, the glowing substance inside danced strangely in response! Off to one side, but still in near darkness, Fortuny worked some gas valves then retreated behind us again.

'*Come, spirits, come!*' The red, then the blue, then the green—all glowing substances—snaked and writhed with the touch of her fingers.

It was indeed unearthly, weird and beautiful – truly magical, as if Madame Borelli were a real-life sorceress. For a moment, I forgot where we were and what we were doing.

'Good God!' exclaimed Pickering. His two constables backed into the hall.

'Sir, can we go, please?' begged one.

'Ha ha, yes!' whispered Holmes.

Just on the other side of the cupboard door, I heard Leo Vitale's voice. 'Oh, Cosimo, I despair!'

'But isn't it magnificent?' returned Fortuny.

'Who's there?' shouted Pickering. 'Holmes? Vitale?' He turned to his men. 'Find the lights and turn them on!'

But his men hesitated. Neither dared enter the room.

Cosimo Fortuny stepped forward through the murk and into our view. The glowing lights cast coloured patterns on his face.

'It is I, Dr Fortuny. You interrupt my experiments. What do you want?'

'We are looking for Leo Vitale,' boomed the sergeant, squinting into the dark. 'This is his laboratory, isn't it? What is all this . . . this fairyland nonsense? Turn it off and light the lights. The normal lights.'

'This is Mr J.J. Thomson's laboratory. It is also *my* laboratory, and Leo Vitale is sometimes here,' said Fortuny.

'I am here now,' cried Leo in a shaking voice. 'I am here, and I am innocent.'

'The young fool!' Holmes hissed.

At this point, one of the policemen found a master switch. The electrified illumination came on brightly, and the glow of the tubes seemed suddenly pale and weak.

Vitale stepped forward, passing into our line of sight. 'I am the one you want,' he said. 'I am innocent, and I will prove it.' I wondered if the boy, in his frenzy of valour, would expose us as well.

Pickering grinned. 'Leo Vitale, I am arresting you for the murder of Miss Odelia Wyndham. You were heard arguing with her at two in the morning last night and she died not long after that. Come forward and make no sudden moves. Extend your hands before you.'

Fortuny gasped. 'What the devil?'

Vitale reached Pickering and held his hands out. Pickering

snapped the cuffs on him roughly. 'Take him in to the station,' he said.

'I had nothing to do with her death, sir,' said Vitale as he was hurried out the door. Pickering paused, scanning the room.

'Good day, Officer,' said Fortuny dismissively.

'I am not done,' snarled Pickering. 'I am looking for a Mr Sherlock Holmes and Dr John Watson. They were spotted not far from here. Holmes is a tall man, built like a lamp post, dark hair, full of himself. The other fellow is shorter, fair, moustache, heavier build. Quite ordinary.'

I did not wish this man well.

'And who might they be?' asked Fortuny.

'Wanted in connection with this same murder,' said Pickering. 'I'd like to have a look around.'

'No one else is here, Mr Pickering,' said Fortuny. 'But this equipment is very delicate. Displace one small thing and the entire apparatus could collapse. You and your police department would then be liable to the University for hundreds of pounds. Hundreds. But by all means, come in and have a look, if you must.'

'Never mind,' said the sergeant. 'But . . . who is that *woman* who playacts at magic like a loon?'

I heard what sounded like a growl from Madame.

'She was joking with you, Officer. Madame Borelli is a student of my work.' Fortuny approached the policeman and now stood by Madame.

Pickering stayed on the offensive. 'No student dresses like that!'

Indeed, Madame Borelli was perhaps a bit outstanding in her signature black and red.

Fortuny shrugged. 'Ask, if you do not believe me. It is true.'

'Yes? Well, I cannot imagine that *ladies* are allowed in these labs,' said Pickering. 'Perhaps I will report you.'

'Well, Mr – er, I am sorry, but you did not give me your name,' said Fortuny.

'Pickering.'

'Well, Mr Pickering, the late Mr James Clerk Maxwell – he is the founder of our laboratory, in case you did not know – was progressive in this matter. Ladies study and even work here.' He smiled. 'But strangers – that is another matter. Trespassing without invitation here is strictly regulated. Perhaps *I* will report *you*.'

Pickering hesitated only a moment, then grunted and departed.

Holmes and I exhaled in relief and exited the cupboard. Holmes quickly thanked Madame Borelli and Fortuny.

'Is it true, then, about Maxwell admitting ladies?' I asked.

'It is,' said Fortuny. 'What is going to happen to poor Leo?'

'Nothing, if he is innocent,' said Holmes. 'And Madame Borelli . . . you *do* land on your feet like a cat. Watson, come, we have two more places to search. The trail grows cold.'

Landing on her feet? Madame, I thought, had a way of landing dead centre in luck. I wondered when and where she might next appear.

PART SEVEN

ILLUSIONS

'Atoms can swerve so there's always the small
possibility even for air molecules of not being
forced to follow the determined laws.'
—James Clerk Maxwell

CHAPTER 33

A Palpable Hit

n moments, we were on the run through Cambridge once again. Ducking into alleys, turning to look in shop windows, we flitted anxiously through the ancient city like desperadoes. We were heading, per Holmes's direction, back to the Cross and Anchor and Dillie's abandoned bolt-hole. Holmes was certain that he had missed something in our earlier visit and was determined to take a closer look.

'But the place has been cleared,' I said as we raced up the stairs at the back of the Cross and Anchor.

'I did not spend the time I needed, Watson. There is something there that will help us, I feel sure of it.'

The waning sun slanted in through the sheer linen curtains, lighting up the room with a yellow glow. It was nearly seven, but the Indian summer hours were still long. The room, abandoned and stripped of possessions by her angry father and jealous sister, appeared just as it had that morning. It felt like a lifetime ago. The family had made quick work of removing all traces of Miss Odelia Wyndham.

The furniture and few remaining items were in disarray. Holmes began what he had hoped to do earlier, which was a detailed inspection of the empty closet, the empty drawers, the windowsill and the floor.

He turned to look at me where I was seated on the blue velvet sofa in front of the window. 'Up, Watson,' he directed. 'I need to look underneath.' Together, we pushed it aside.

There, back against the wall, something glinted in gold. Holmes seized it and examined it with his lens, then handed both to me. It was a simple gold ring, in the shape of an arrow, looped in on itself. 'It's a Woodman ring,' he said. 'Freddie's – the one he mentioned. I am surprised she left it when she fled.'

'Perhaps she didn't flee but was abducted from this room?' I offered. 'You did say earlier that something did not feel right here. Could there be something in plain sight, something we have missed?'

'I do not think she was abducted from here, Watson. Even the Cambridge police – or at the very least, her father – would have noticed obvious signs of a fight or a disturbance. I wager Wyndham found nothing telling. I believe she packed up her most treasured possessions and fled from this room of her own accord. Nevertheless, we do not have the whole story.'

Holmes stood in front of the window, scanning the room. He drew back the sheer linen curtains only a sliver and stared down into the street. 'It does not look like anyone could have climbed out this way. Not without a ladder or a convenient tree.' He let the curtains fall back across the window, and the evening sun glowed through them. Holmes moved to the centre of the room and turned slowly in place. 'But there is something here. I can feel it.'

'Wyndham must have been in a hurry. Everything has been moved,' I said.

'Or angry, yes.' He paused, then his face lit up. 'Everything except this.'

He pointed to an innocuous painting, an unimpressive seascape on the wall opposite the sofa, hanging next to the door. In contrast to the disarray of the rest of the room, it hung straight and undisturbed.

Holmes took down the painting and examined the back. 'Watson, we are in luck!' he cried.

He removed an envelope that was fastened to the frame. Eagerly he opened it. 'Pawnshop receipts!' he said, flipping through them. 'Her father was right! But she managed to keep it a secret from him, even after death. Watson, Dillie had been pawning off her mother's – or someone's – jewellery.' He paused and looked up. 'Saving, no doubt, for this moment.'

'To do what?'

'To buy her freedom. I would be willing to wager that Miss Wyndham pawned her two engagement rings just before she was killed. Or perhaps was on her way to do so. And this would explain why she accepted rings from both Eden-Summers and Leo Vitale.'

'Then she did not intend to marry either.'

'I would theorize not.'

'Could there have been a third person with whom she planned to leave? Like Madame Borelli and her scientist fellow?'

One of the low stools we had sat on near the door to put Dillie at her ease had been upended. Holmes turned it upright and sat down, the receipts in his hand. He closed his eyes. 'I need to think.'

The room was nearly dark. I found a sconce and lit it, and the room was immediately bathed in a warm light.

'What pawnshop?' I asked.

'Piotr Flan. Here is the address.' He handed me the receipts. As I moved towards the light to look at them, the door flew open and to our surprise in burst Freddie Eden-Summers. He took us both in and frowned in confusion.

'What are you two doing here?'

'My question for you, Mr Eden-Summers,' said Holmes, on his feet.

'This was Dillie's *private* room,' said Eden-Summers.

'Yes, but no longer. Have you come to retrieve something? A ring perhaps?' said Holmes.

The boy stammered, backed up. 'Well, I thought perhaps . . .'

I held up the golden circle ring and stepped forward. 'This one, by chance?'

Freddie Eden-Summers squinted at the ring from across the room. 'Oh, that one. I gave her that a month ago. My Woodman ring. I was hoping for the engagement ring. But give it to me—'

The young man stepped towards me into the glow of the lamplight near me on the wall. The next moment has been frozen in my memory, with the movements slowed, bathed in greenish-golden light, as though underwater.

The soft gaslight illuminated Eden-Summers' pale, handsome face, and I noticed the blond peach fuzz which covered his cheeks and the straw colour of his eyelashes. The ring in my hand gleamed.

To one side, Sherlock Holmes had his eyes pinned on Eden-Summers. That is the last thing that I remember, for at that moment there was the splinter of glass and the slight huff of tearing fabric, and I felt a searing white-hot blade pass into my right thigh.

I heard a cry of agony which must have been my own.

And then I was on the floor with Eden-Summers leaning over me. He was staring at my thigh.

'The little minx!' he exclaimed.

What was he talking about? The pain in my leg was excruciating. I groaned and tried to sit up to see what had happened.

Holmes elbowed the boy aside and peered down at me. 'Watson, be still. You have been shot! Eden-Summers, go for a doctor!'

I craned my neck to see the boy at the window, staring down at the courtyard. 'Better yet, I'll get a cab and take you there! I know just the man,' he cried, and ran from the room.

'Have a care!' cried Holmes.

'She will not try again,' said the young man, his voice disappearing down the hall.

Holmes leaned down to peer at me, a worried expression on his face. Pain made my eyes water and my head swim.

'Holmes . . .' I said. 'What . . . ?'

'You were shot with an arrow. No, keep your hand away.'

'What? Pull it out!' I cried, trying to reach it.

'No, Watson!' he said, stopping my hand with his own. 'Lie back. As a doctor, you know better. Pull it out and you could bleed to death!'

In retrospect, of course I did know this, but for the life of me I could not summon the reason at that moment.

I gritted my teeth. 'Who on earth would shoot me?'

'The target was more likely Mr Eden-Summers.'

'How? Who—'

'Come, Watson! Who is an archer with reason to wish harm to that young man? Think!'

I was spared coming up with a retort, for at that moment I passed out.

CHAPTER 34

Just a Bodkin

 came round blearily in what must have been a doctor's surgery. A small, serious man of about forty with bright red cheeks was bent over me, busily tugging at something. I do recall that my right leg was numbed and felt like a gigantic loaf of bread and nothing to do with me, although somehow attached. The smell of carbolic acid filled the room. He brought up a pair of forceps and leaned in. I felt a dull pulling and could hear him snipping at sutures.

'My . . . uh . . .' In a haze, I located in my mind the spot on my leg which was receiving the attention. 'The . . . the femoral artery?' I mumbled.

The diminutive surgeon looked down at me over a pair of silver reading glasses. His round face and sharp brown eyes brought to mind a small bear. I noted a carefully groomed and waxed moustache, with the ends precisely turned up in matching curls. Meticulous was precisely the trait one would wish for in a surgeon.

'Awake, are ye? You're a doctor, then, tae be askin' about that?' said the surgeon. A Highland accent. Scottish medical training, another good sign. 'Missed the artery. You were lucky.'

'Yes. Watson here was an army surgeon,' said Holmes. 'How soon can you have him on his feet, Doctor?'

'Macready is the name,' the surgeon said pleasantly to me. He then looked up at Holmes, who loomed nearby. He frowned. 'Stand back, sir, you are dreadfully underfoot.'

Holmes was taken aback at a phrase I'd heard him rudely bark at our own dear Mrs Hudson, but he complied, disappearing from my view.

'What is the extent of the wound, Doctor?' I asked.

'Mr Eden-Summers brought you to the right place. Arrow wounds are my speciality. Get little call for it, now. Arrow missed the femoral by less than an inch. As I said, you were very, very lucky.'

Holmes's voice floated over as he held up the bloody arrowhead so that I could see it. 'Hmm, bodkin point! Small favours, Watson.'

'Indeed. I used one of my smallest tubes to retract it with minimal damage,' said Macready. 'You'll appreciate that, Doctor Watson.'

'Not as bad as a broadhead, though. You are lucky, my friend,' continued Holmes. 'Bodkins have much smaller ears.' At my puzzled look, he added. 'Shoulders. Barbs. The parts that tear the flesh when pulled out.'

Macready looked up from his work. 'Get back from there!' Holmes disappeared again. 'You are an archer, then?'

'Formerly,' said Holmes.

'Hit the *adductor longus*?' I asked.

'Yes. It could have been much worse,' said Macready.

'Meaning what?' asked Holmes.

'It means he should pass on any Morris dancing for the immediate future,' said the surgeon. 'That muscle moves the leg from side to side.'

'How soon for normal walking, Doctor?' asked Holmes.

'And what is your hurry in that?' replied Dr Macready, coldly. 'Stand further back, over there, would you? What is your relationship to this man, might I ask?'

'I am Sherlock Holmes, consulting detective, here in Cambridge on a case. This is my friend and colleague Dr John Watson.'

'Yes, yes, army surgeon, you said. How does a medical colleague help a detective?' When neither of us answered, he looked down at me. 'Now . . . think of something else while I sew this up.'

'*Aaah!*' I distracted myself with Holmes's exploits. 'Eh . . . so . . . how did you get out of gaol, Holmes?'

The surgeon stopped what he was doing and reappraised my friend. 'Do I have a criminal in my midst? Put that down, I say, and go and sit over there by the door. You are a damnable distraction, man!'

I craned my neck to see Holmes wiping off the bloody

arrow tip with his handkerchief. He pulled off the tip from the arrow shaft and pocketed it.

'Evidence,' he said with a smile.

Macready shook his head.

'It is true. I do need to be back on my feet shortly,' I said. 'How much do I risk by activity, please?'

'Ach, you put me in mind of a college footballer whose lady love shot him in the leg accidentally. He was out dancing the following week, then took half a year to recover.'

'No dancing, I promise.'

'Well . . . I'll patch you up good. You'll be as well as you choose to treat yourself, Doctor. 'Twere me, I'd catch up on my reading and run about with this gaolbird much less than I'm guessing you might.'

'Can you give him something for the pain – something that will not fog his brain?' asked Holmes.

'You have need of my brain?' I almost laughed. '*Ow!* The anaesthetic is wearing off, Doctor.'

'I know. Almost finished. Who shot you, man?'

'I am not sure—'

'Oh, come, Watson, you know exactly who did this,' said my friend.

'Well, I hope he is brought to justice,' said the surgeon.

'She,' said Holmes. 'And I doubt it. Although Eden-Summers is reporting this to her father as we speak.'

She? I closed my eyes and lay back. *Of course.* 'Atalanta Wyndham,' I said.

'She shot you through the curtain, Watson. I believe she

mistook your silhouette for Freddie's. He was in the room with you, remember?'

'But I thought she had feelings for Freddie?'

'Watson, think! A few days ago he announced his engagement to her sister. Passion is like an alternating current. Love in one direction, and when reversed, equally strong hatred.'

'It sounds as though you were in the wrong place at the wrong time, Doctor,' said the surgeon.

A groan escaped me as the dull ache grew into something keener and more difficult to ignore. I felt a sharp prick and looked down to see the surgeon injecting something near the bandaged wound.

'I am giving you a little more local anaesthetic, Doctor. Short term, however.'

'Can you not give him something else for later? Something that will not dull his brain?' asked Holmes.

'You ask me again?' Macready looked up and stared hard at Holmes. 'Like a little cocaine, for instance? An injectible solution?'

'Yes.' Holmes said. 'For later?'

The surgeon smiled at him. 'May I have a look at your arm?'

'Mine? Certainly not!'

The doctor looked down at me. 'Dr Watson, I will leave this to you.'

I supposed Holmes's habit was evident to the astute medical man. 'Give me some now, but I'll do without later,' said I.

'All right then.'

He filled another syringe, tied off my arm and injected the liquid into a vein. 'This is a three per cent solution of cocaine. It will tide you past the local. But now you must be very careful. Cocaine makes some feel invincible.'

I was about to reply when a wave of warmth and good will swept over me. I suddenly knew that everything would be absolutely, perfectly, fantastically all right. I sat up eagerly.

Holmes gripped my shoulder. 'We have work to do, Watson. On your feet.'

'Work? It's nearly midnight! This man needs rest,' said Dr Macready.

I swung my legs off the table, eager to depart.

'Careful!' cried Dr Macready, stepping between us. 'Slow down!'

With the doctor's help, I gingerly set my feet on the floor.

Holmes was halfway out of the door and turned back impatiently. 'Come on, Watson!'

'Your observation powers fail you!' I found myself shouting. 'I'll need my trousers first!'

CHAPTER 35

The Pawnshop

ust outside the doctor's office, we looked about for a cab to convey us to Holmes's next destination: Piotr Flan's pawnshop, which was on the far outskirts of town. I must have been out for some time at Dr Macready's for it was indeed midnight, and at that moment I was feeling no pain. Darkness engulfed the city and it had begun to rain in great pelting drops. No cabs were to be found.

When I noticed that we were standing somewhat near the police station, I suggested to Holmes that we be less visible. He turned into an alleyway and in five minutes, we were lost.

'The map, Watson?'

I no longer had it with me. We would have to ask for help. The rain grew into a downpour, but luck was with us. Or in reality, luck had been following us. Upon exiting an alley near the Round Church, we came upon Polly. We had not seen her since Dillie's murder. She was breathless, pale and – as we were – dripping wet.

'Mr 'Olmes! Dr Watson! I been trying to flag you. I was outside the Cross and Anchor when you left with an arrow in Doctor Watson, and I tagged on back of that cab and waited for you outside the surgery. But you left so fast. I wants to help you, any way I can. For Miss Dillie. Please, can I help?'

'Do you know the way to Piotr Flan's pawnshop?'

'Yes, I knows it. Follow me. It's quite far.'

'Can you make it, Watson?'

I nodded. I was feeling no pain.

'Then you pawned items for Miss Wyndham?' asked Holmes as we hurried through the streets.

'No. I always waited outside. This way.'

We arrived at Piotr Flan's pawnshop at one in the morning. Thanks to Macready's cocaine, I felt nothing of my wound, but I knew this long walk would do me no good. Of course, the shop was closed and dark, but Holmes rang the bell repeatedly.

'Holmes, we will have to wait until morning!' I said, but he persisted.

'Chances are he lives upstairs,' said Holmes. 'If not . . .'

Polly eyed the large padlock on the grating that had been placed in front of the door and front window of the shop. She removed a lockpick from her sleeve. 'I could maybe unlock this,' she said.

Holmes and I turned to her in surprise. I wondered briefly if everyone but me had mastered this skill. But before she could begin, a small light appeared in the back of the shop. A grizzled old man approached, peering at us owl-like from the interior, directing his lantern to shine on our faces. He had a strange corona of corkscrew hair that stuck out in all directions from an ill-fitting nightcap and an expression of what I imagined was permanent distrust on his lined visage.

He did not look inclined to open up. Polly put her lock-pick away.

'Vat you vant?' he shouted, barely audible through the closed and locked door.

From his waistcoat, Holmes unclipped his gold watch, a high-quality timepiece which I had long admired, and held it up with what appeared to be a desperate and conciliatory smile.

Soon we faced Piotr Flan across a glass and mahogany counter filled with jewelled and gilded items. He had lit several lights and the small shop was now almost bright as daylight. His wife, in her nightdress and dressing gown, had come down to join him, apparently with the explicit purpose of keeping a sharp watch on Polly and me during the transaction. I felt a little like a rabbit in hawk territory. The woman was more than ready to pounce, and she carried a battered policeman's truncheon in stark contrast with her flowered nightclothes.

'All right then, you had better make this vorth my vile,' said the man, with an accent I could not identify.

Flan spread out a large velvet cloth and tapped it, inviting Holmes to lay out his treasure. Polly began to wander through the small shop and the pawnbroker's wife followed close on her heels. 'Touch nuffink,' the woman growled in a distinctly Cockney accent, 'if ye know what's good for yer.'

'Just looking,' said Polly. 'No trouble, ma'am.'

'Nuffink, hear me?' the woman repeated, slightly jiggling the stick at her side.

Holmes laid the watch out on the velvet cloth. The pawnbroker took out a loupe and leaned in to examine it.

'Got it! Both of 'em!' cried Polly from across the room.

Holmes looked up, scooped up his watch and crossed over to Polly. I followed. She pointed to a locked case in which were a wide variety of jewelled rings. 'Those two,' said she. 'The big diamond one, there, with the two emeralds – that's from Mr Eden-Summers. And the littler one with the sapphire is Mr Vitale's.'

'You're sure, Polly?' asked Holmes.

'As sure as this lady thinks we're about to steal 'em.'

Indeed, the woman now held her stick aloft and ready to strike, and her husband appeared behind her, now pointing a gun at the three of us.

'Hold your stick, please, madam. And sir, be assured,' said Holmes, 'we mean you no harm.' Holmes raised his hands and nodded to Polly and me. We followed suit. The woman lowered her stick, but her husband kept his gun trained on us, or rather on Holmes specifically.

'This is as I thought,' said my friend. 'Dillie had planned

this all along, to fund her escape. May I see these two rings please, sir?' asked Holmes. He began slowly to lower his hands.

The pawnbroker hesitated but did not lower his gun. 'You buying or you selling?'

'I am buying,' said Holmes, clipping his watch back onto its chain and replacing it in his pocket.

'Vat is this all about?'

'I would like to purchase information from you, sir. There is a young woman who I believe has been bringing in items, including these, to your shop. I would estimate she has been doing this over the last year.'

'Year and a half, more like,' said Polly.

'I wish you had mentioned this before,' said Holmes.

'She weren't dead before.'

'Dead?' exclaimed Mrs Flan. 'Piotr! This is a police matter!' She raised her stick menacingly. 'You three! Out!'

'Calm yourself, Luisa! People die. That's life.'

A philosopher! I suppressed a grin, catching Holmes's sidelong glance at me.

The man turned to Holmes. 'I don't gossip about my customers,' rasped the old man. 'Otherwise I vould have no customers.'

'Understood,' said Holmes. 'But I am prepared to buy this information from you. There is no threat implied, you obviously run an honest business. Here is a picture of the young lady.' From his pocket he removed a daguerreotype of Odelia Wyndham.

'Where did you get that?' I asked, surprised.

'Freddie was kind enough to lend it to me,' he said. 'Without his knowledge.' A little smile.

The old man eyed the picture. 'I am not sure. I may have seen her. May have not.'

There was a long pause.

Holmes took out two sovereigns and laid them on the counter. The man pushed them back towards Holmes.

'No. I am still not sure.'

Holmes frowned. 'Watson?'

I reached into my pocket. I found a five-pound note I was carrying and reluctantly added it to Holmes's coins on the counter. The man's face melted into what passed for a smile.

'I remember now! Yes, she has pawned six items here. Three have sold. I can show you the other three,' said Mr Flan. 'Luisa, the diamond earrings in case six.' He nodded towards his wife. 'And that gold bracelet vith a seahorse . . .'

'I am only interested in these two rings,' said Holmes, leading Flan to the case where Dillie's two engagement rings sat.

'Girl in the picture did not pawn those.'

'Are you quite sure?'

'Positive. They only just came in – last night, vasn't it, Luisa?'

'I don't trust these 'ere people,' said his wife, eyeing us malevolently.

She was right to be suspicious of us. Holmes was certainly lying by omission.

'Last night? Who brought them, then?' asked Holmes.

The man hesitated, and glanced from Holmes to me and back again, estimating his chances. He smiled. 'I am not sure.'

We exchanged a look. Then we both reached deep into our pockets, and between us found only a few additional coins. We laid them on the glass case containing the two engagement rings. The man paused, then shook his head.

'This is all I have. I am not a wealthy man,' said Holmes.

Flan waved his fingers at Holmes's gold chain and watch.

My friend sighed. 'All right. I will not give it, but will pawn it, and pay you from the fee. How much will you loan me for it?'

'Five.'

Holmes swallowed. 'It is worth much more. You make this difficult.'

The man shrugged.

'All right, then. You won't sell my watch, then?' said Holmes, anxiously. 'I will be back for it, you can be sure.'

The man shrugged. 'That is vat they all say.'

Holmes placed his watch on the velvet cloth. Flan took up the watch without even looking at it again and pocketed it with a small grin of satisfaction. He handed Holmes a five-pound note.

Holmes took it, sighed, then handed back the five-pound note he had just been given.

The pawnbroker pocketed that as well. This put the fellow twelve pounds *and* Holmes's good watch ahead. We had nothing more to offer, and I hoped he would cooperate.

'A young man. Came and pawned them in the middle of the night. Last night.'

'A young man?' I exclaimed.

'Can you describe him, please?' said Holmes.

'Twenties. Fair hair. All curly. Gold-rimmed spectacles. Nice ones.'

Deacon Buttons! It must have been! Even Holmes looked surprised. We exchanged a look.

Never one to assume, Holmes pressed on. 'Tall?'

'Fairly so.'

'Awkward looking, or a handsome man?'

'Both. A good-looking young man. But something about him. Shy, perhaps.'

'Small gold ring on the left fifth finger?' asked Holmes.

'Yes. He tried to pawn that, too, but vould not take my offer.'

It was definitely Deacon Buttons.

'Understandable. At what time was this?'

The man shrugged.

'Three-thirty in the mornin',' said his wife.

'Was he wearing a cleric's collar by chance?' asked Holmes.

'No.'

'I would have removed it as well. All right, thank you.' Holmes appeared to be disappointed. 'Sir, you have been a great help. Madam.' He turned to leave. 'Oh, before we go, may I have my watch back, please? Without it you are twelve pounds the richer, for naught but a few minutes of your time. Surely you have the advantage of me, even so.'

Flan shook his head, patting his pocket with the watch. 'We have made our deal,' said he. 'It will be fifteen if you get back before I sell it.'

'Well, then,' said Holmes, 'let me offer you this in exchange for the watch. That small diamond tiara over there? It was stolen from a minor royal with a country house nearby. Lady Debenby, you have heard of her? The thief killed a treasured servant in the taking, and the family are offering a hefty reward to identify the culprit. May I suggest you bring your information to the police?'

Flan looked askance at Holmes.

'I am a good friend of Detective Inspector Hadley,' remarked Holmes.

We left with the watch.

CHAPTER 36

A Holy Place

e ran – well, Holmes and Polly ran, and I limped – through the rain across town towards the Church of Our Lady of the Roses. My wound was now throbbing. I wish I had taken Dr Macready up on his offer of medication.

At last, the church was in sight. And there, thankfully, Holmes espied a constable on his rounds. Gripping my arm, he whispered, 'Ask him to see Polly home safely. Tell him to wake up Hadley and say that Sherlock Holmes has been seen at the church and to come at once.'

Holmes carried on and I did as he asked. Regretting the need for this, I vouched for Polly's honour with the young fellow and asked him to accompany the girl to her sister's, so as to avoid the horror of the Spinning House. He was more than happy to do so.

'I'm not so fond of those proctor's men, myself,' he said. 'Bulldogs, we call 'em. Come, little lady.' Polly rolled her eyes at 'little lady' but waved a thank-you to me.

'But before that, please! Tell Inspector Hadley that Sherlock Holmes has been seen at the Church of our Lady of the Roses. And to come at once,' I urged.

'I'll not be waking up the Inspector—'

'Sherlock Holmes . . . who escaped from gaol earlier today!'

'Oh, *that fellow*!' cried the man, not realizing it was Holmes who had just left us. 'By God, then, I'll do it! Come along, young lady!'

I caught up with Holmes just outside of the Church of Our Lady of the Roses. The rain continued to beat a tattoo on the stone pavers and the garden soil. A small lantern high on the stone church wall sent a faint glow out over the rose garden, where the delicate flowers danced and vibrated under the heavy downfall, some knocked from their fragile stems into the growing puddles of water.

As we passed the church en route to the outer building which housed the two clergymen, I could see glowing lights coming from the basement clerestory windows and heard the sounds of banging and a few shouts. Two men ran past us with ropes and buckets. A rubber hose extended out of one of the windows, spewing water into the already soaked and pooling flowerbeds.

'Where are Father Lamb and Deacon Buttons?' shouted Holmes to one of them.

'The father is down below, no idea about Buttons!' cried one.

I glanced at my watch. It was two-thirty in the morning.

'Picked a fine time to disappear!' shouted another. 'And with the father gone to London yesterday! We've a flood on our hands!'

'We'll send for help,' said Holmes. He grabbed my arm and whispered, 'Quick, to Buttons' room!'

Shortly we stood dripping at the entry to his small quarters. We knocked on the door and it swung open. Empty. I started to step inside, but Holmes blocked my entry.

'Wait, Watson. We must disturb nothing. Go and fetch some candles, please. A lantern. As much light as you can gather.'

I scavenged quickly, returning with several candles I discovered in Lamb's spartan room down the hall, and two more from a niche nearby. Holmes had lit the paraffin light on Buttons' desk, then quickly lit all the candles and placed them around the room. One near the window guttered and went out. I noticed the window was open a crack and the rising storm was seeping into the room.

'Holmes, shall I close the window?'

'No! And keep back – out of the room.' I paused at the threshold. Holmes ran to the window, and noting something on the sill, said, 'Stay there, in the hall, Watson.' He left the room and returned after five very long minutes. I waited nervously, hoping that Father Lamb would not appear to confront us.

Buttons' quarters, at first glance, were unremarkable. All

seemed to be in order. The bed had been made to near military perfection. Clothes hung neatly in the open armoire, shoes aligned below it. Holmes would learn nothing here, I feared.

My friend returned shortly, his knees muddied, boots caked with mud. 'Find anything?' I asked.

'Yes. Stay in the doorway. Touch nothing.'

He took off his boots and left them at the door, although his wet socks left prints behind on the stone floor. He began a process I had witnessed many times before. I thought of it as his strange dance of detection, in which he moved with great animation and a kind of electrified focus, examining minutely even the most prosaic and benign objects, and from them piecing together a complete and detailed sequence of events.

As usual, I was relegated to the position of observer – and in this case, lookout. If a crime had been committed here, I could as yet see nothing of it.

Holmes took out his lens and worked his way around the small, neat room.

From the doorway, the desk, like everything else, looked pristine. Holmes ran his finger across the top, sides and back, examined and smelled the inside of the drawer. He picked up the bottle of purple ink Buttons had used in the doll incident, now paired next to the original black bottle on the desk. 'Half empty,' he remarked. 'Cap is cracked.' He flipped through a Bible with numerous small bits of paper marking pages. Noting something on the wall, he scraped it with a fingernail. Then he picked up a candle which had been knocked from its holder and lay on the desk.

The deacon's small carpet-bag stood upright in the same corner. Empty.

Holmes spent a long time on the bed. Folding back the coverlet, he removed a small card from his pocket, gently brushed something into it, folded it, and replaced it in his pocket. He smelled the pillow, examined the coverlet in minute detail, removed it and examined between the sheets. He moved the bed away from the wall and carefully inspected the newly uncovered area.

At the washstand, he picked up a water-jug. 'Ah!' he said, then ran his hands along the back of the desk chair, the arms of the chair, the desk and its drawers. He dropped to the floor, crawled to the corners, looked under the bed and desk, and finally got up, dusting off his clothing.

The window remained open and a steady spray of small droplets pattered against it, some wetting the sill and the stone floor directly below. Holmes re-examined the sill, the lock, the edges of this window, nodding and murmuring something unintelligible as he did so.

It took no incisive deductions on my part to see that some invisible history was playing out vividly in his mind.

He turned to look at me and exclaimed in surprise. He dashed across the small room towards me and minutely examined an area of the wall abutting the doorframe. 'Your pocketknife, Watson,' he commanded. 'I have forgotten mine.'

I complied. He scraped something from the edge of the

doorframe. 'Aha!' The scrapings went into a second small card which he folded and placed in his pocket.

The armoire came last. Deacon Buttons' few clothes hung neatly. Three pairs of shoes were perfectly aligned along the bottom. Holmes picked up each in turn, exclaiming over the last, 'Hmm. This pair is damp, the others are dry.'

He frowned, perplexed, then moved to the centre of the room and remained there for some time, unmoving, with one finger to his lips.

It was coming on to four in the morning. My energy was flagging and the wound in my leg was now shouting for attention. 'Holmes?' I ventured. I would need to sit down soon.

He shook his head ruefully.

'It is a singular case, Watson. A kind of obsession. Miss Wyndham arrived with a plan, I would estimate. Either she asked Buttons to pawn the rings, or . . . he took them from her. Somehow things went terribly wrong.'

'I would never think Buttons capable of hurting the girl.'

Holmes shrugged. 'Great violence was done in this room.'

'I don't see it. But of course, I am standing out here.'

'Watson, it is obvious! Candle wax spattered on the wall. Broken glass in that corner over there, cleaned up but not fully. Dents on the arm of that chair. Picture it, Watson! I found evidence that the girl was in his bed. Her scent on the pillow. A hair. And that ironstone water-jug. Cracked along the edge with a smear of blood.'

'The head wound!'

'Precisely. And the ink bottle! The ink!'

'What of the ink?'

'The bottle was thrown – there – at the door about head height. The cap cracked, some ink spattered. The ink was then cleaned off the wall, leaving a small amount, here, in the moulding. Whoever cleaned up did so quickly, missing much. Even the police might deduce that a fight raged here.'

'Or I would, had I been allowed into the room!'

Holmes smiled up at me. 'Yes, even you, Watson. Dillie put up a tremendous fight. She was overcome, and the killer pushed her naked, unconscious body out of this window and into the garden just below.'

'The killer? You mean Deacon Buttons, then, do you not? Or do you mean Leo Vitale? Or Eden-Summers?'

'I do not know yet.'

'But how can you tell that she was put out through the window?'

'Because I was looking for it. Another hair, caught on the edge of the sill, just there. And a tiny smear of blood on the clasp. Outside I saw an indentation in the earth just below, where the body landed. This was under an eave, and so the rain had not entirely washed away the imprint. Although the footprints nearby are indicative but not conclusive. One appears to be Vitale's. But damn this rain! I cannot be sure.'

Vitale's!

Holmes continued to stare around the room, willing more information.

'I suppose the mud was washed off in the river as I saw none in the autopsy,' I said. 'But I don't understand *why* the killer would dump her body out of the window?'

'Simple. It was safer than carrying her through the corridor and risking running into someone. The window faces away from the church and towards the river. It would not be seen. Remember, this was between four and six a.m. There was no moon last night. It would have been quite dark. And raining. There are no buildings or roads with a nearby view of this place.'

I shook my head at the image. 'Appalling.'

Holmes said. 'It was as I feared. Poor Dillie underestimated whatever fury was unleashed here. She did not read the signs.'

'Perhaps there were no signs, Holmes.'

'She accepted rings from two suitors, Watson. Then asked a third young man to pawn them. Consider what she said or did to induce him to do this in the middle of the night?'

'But . . . Buttons, then? The deacon was so eager to have you on the case,' I continued.

'Well, he was eager to find her. And he lied to us – twice.' Holmes retrieved his boots from the hall and sat at Buttons' desk to put them on.

'But where is the fellow now?' I asked. 'And where is Hadley? I would have thought the police would be here by now.'

Holmes stiffened suddenly and looked up from his own boots. 'The shoes.' I followed his gaze to the armoire. 'Watson! The shoes!'

'What about them?'

'There are three pairs there! Three pairs are all he owns. I noticed on our last visit: two there, and one pair on his feet. Wherever Buttons is, he is barefoot. I fear for the young man. If he is not the killer, he is perhaps dead as well.' Holmes stood abruptly and continued to scan the room. 'Why? And where would he go without shoes . . . in this pouring rain?'

Thunder cracked and a flash of lightning flooded the room for a brief moment.

My eyes closed and a flash to my childhood trauma came unbidden. *A pair of ladies' shoes, lined neatly up by the river, under a tree. Green, with ribbons. My mother's shoes.*

'Swimming,' I said.

Holmes stopped moving and stood perfectly still.

'My God, Watson, sometimes you surprise me!' He ran to the window and looked out. 'Of course! Look!'

I joined him at the window. Through the sheets of silver rain, barely lit by the new moon, I looked across the field to the dark, rushing Cam. Silhouetted in front of it was a ghostly white shirt only dimly visible against the black of the glittering river, and seeming to float in the air was the figure of a man. He moved, and a halo of light, curly hair was caught in the glow of a streetlamp.

Deacon Buttons.

CHAPTER 37

The Sinner

e were out and rushing through the muddy fields in seconds. As we approached, we could see that it was indeed young Buttons, standing poised on the wooden footbridge over the Jesus Lock, staring down into swirling dark waters.

Was he Dillie's killer, returning in guilt and horror to the site of his transgression? Perhaps to the exact spot where he had dumped her, still alive but unconscious, and where she had met her watery end.

The rush of the river and the hiss of the late summer downpour masked our footsteps, and the boy heard nothing as we approached. We came within ten feet and Holmes put his hand on my arm to stop me. With a finger to his lips, he shook his head.

As we watched, Buttons leaned over the railing, mesmerized

by the churning current. Lightning flashed again and lit up the scene for a brief flickering second. A moment later came the boom of thunder.

We had not made a sound, but in that strange way that one feels the regard of another, the young man sensed our presence and turned. His face was ghastly pale, and his hair was dripping as it was the first time we had met him at Baker Street. He was not wearing his glasses, and his white face was drenched from the rain and, I could only assume, tears.

'Mr Buttons,' said Holmes calmly, 'please step away from the railing.'

'Dillie died here,' said Buttons in a strange, high-pitched voice. 'Last night.'

'Yes, we know,' said Holmes.

'The river . . . the river . . .' The boy turned and looked at the rushing waters. 'It washed away her sins,' he murmured.

'How did she get into the river?' asked Holmes.

The boy did not reply but kept his eyes on the water. Holmes slowly inched closer. I stayed back, fearing the boy would panic.

'I have just been in your room, Mr Buttons. It is clear to me that Dillie visited you there last night,' said Holmes.

Buttons looked up at my friend in alarm, then looked at me.

'The signs were unmistakable,' I said.

The boy looked from one of us to the other, and sensed he was lost, though not sure how. 'She came to get me.'

'Get you?' Holmes asked.

'It was such a surprise. I never thought. But she . . . but she . . .' He closed his eyes.

'Let us start at the beginning. What time was this?' said Holmes.

The boy spoke, his eyes remaining closed. 'Two o'clock or maybe three. She woke me. She had brought her valise, all her things. She asked for my help. I had promised to help her if she ever needed . . . she told me that she wanted to run away with me. Right then. *With me.*' He gestured vaguely. I noticed that his right hand was wrapped in something white, with a dark stain on it.

'Holmes, his hand!' I whispered.

Holmes nodded without taking his eyes off the boy. 'Run away with you, where?' he asked.

Peregrine Buttons looked at us and smiled. Mad, definitely mad, I thought. 'Scotland. Or maybe Paris.' His eyes glittered briefly at the image of this joyful thought.

'Did you believe her?' asked Holmes.

'Of course.'

'But she wanted something from you. She asked you to do something.'

'The rings . . .'

'Yes. You pawned Freddie Eden-Summers' and Leo Vitale's engagement rings for her with Piotr Flan across town at three a.m. He gave you twenty-five for the two,' said Holmes. 'But it wasn't enough.'

'Holmes,' I whispered, 'take this slowly.'

'You are a magician! How can you know this?' stammered Buttons, staring in horror at Holmes.

'Not a magician, more like a bloodhound. I just came from Flan's. What was this money to be used for?'

'Holmes. The situation is precarious,' I whispered.

'Our train tickets. And a new start.'

'But then?' Holmes inquired. 'Something went wrong.'

The young man wavered. He placed a foot on the railing.

'Take your foot off there,' cried Holmes.

The boy took his foot down and looked about dreamily. '"You belong with me, Perry," she said. That was what she called me.'

'That is very sweet,' I said, hoping to distract him. Holmes gave me a sharp look and turned back to the boy.

'Running away together – was this something you had planned?'

'No. We had joked about it. But I never . . . I only dreamed . . .' Buttons replaced his foot on the railing.

'Step back from the railing, please,' said Holmes sharply.

'No. Stay away from me!' The young man turned and looked down at the water.

Holmes moved to one side. I took that moment to look about to see if the police might be visible yet. I saw no one. Had the message gone astray? The rain hissed down around us.

'You returned with the money, and then what happened?'

Buttons suddenly doubled over the railing as if hit in the stomach. A sob escaped him. 'Oh God! Oh God!'

Holmes took the opportunity to draw closer.

'Pull yourself together, Mr Buttons,' I said, trying to distract him by moving away from Holmes.

He made an effort and straightened, then crumpled again. 'Oh, Dillie.'

'Let me help,' said Holmes. 'You returned and found Dillie in your bed.'

'By God, how do you know this?'

'Mr Buttons, you remember why you came to me in the first place?'

'Because you read of Mr Holmes's particular reputation as a detective,' I prompted.

Lightning flashed, lighting up the sky and the boy's confused face.

'You came back with the money,' Holmes pressed on. 'But something happened. Perhaps Dillie refused you. You quarrelled. You fought.'

'No! No! But . . . she said the money was not enough. We would need more.'

'For train tickets?'

'No. To start a new life. Then Dillie said she remembered a third ring. A little gold one, shape of an arrow. That would ensure . . . but she had misplaced it. She sent me to search for it. Across town.'

'To her room above the Cross and Anchor pub?'

'Yes. That is the place.'

'Did anyone see you there?'

The boy had shut his eyes again. 'I didn't find that ring. I looked and looked.'

'Mr Buttons. Again, did anyone see you at the Cross and Anchor?'

'No. No one was about.'

'So you returned empty-handed?'

There was a long silence.

It struck me then that all three young men who had loved Dillie had been in some altercation the night of her murder. Had this volatile girl been attracted to young men of similar temperament? Or did she drive them to it? Someone had beaten that girl in his room. I glanced again at Buttons' bandaged hand. 'This is our man, I think,' I whispered.

Holmes sighed.

'What happened to your hand, Mr Buttons?' asked Holmes.

The boy looked at it like he had forgotten its existence. 'I hit the wall with my fist.'

'Did you leave a dent?'

The boy looked confused. 'Yes. Why, yes, I did.'

'I saw no such mark in your room.'

'I didn't hit the wall of my room. I hit the wall just outside. To the left of my door.'

'Mr Buttons, I have just come from a thorough inspection of your room. In spite of its apparent normal state, it had been cleaned up hurriedly. I found clear evidence of a mighty battle. Drops of blood. A chip on your water-jug, and two dents in the furniture. Dillie put up a valiant fight. That was very like her.'

'No.' The boy was inching away from us. 'No.'

'Holmes,' I warned.

'A smear of blood on the windowsill showed where you pushed her body out before bringing it here, to the

338

river. But the girl received her fatal blow . . . in your room.'

'No!' said the boy, now ghostly pale, his eyes wild. A young madman?

Holmes stepped forward and held out his hand. 'You realize, of course, that I must present this evidence to the police. And that you will be arrested for murder. There may be a faint ray of hope for you. It is possible the Church will come to your defence. They have been known to rally mighty forces. And there could be mitigating factors. Did Dillie attack you? Were you hurt? Was anyone else present during this altercation?'

I knew better than to voice my thoughts, which were that it was damnably clear that the young man was Dillie's murderer and that no 'mitigating factors' or Church interference would save him. Dillie had been a provocative young woman and sometimes a cruel one. But no provocation justifies murder. Offering a lifeline to a killer was a tactic Holmes had used before to extract a confession.

'Come with me now, Mr Buttons. I will make sure that you are treated fairly,' said my friend, now only ten feet from the boy. He reached out his hand towards Buttons.

A wind had come up and the trees nearby moaned with the sudden gusts.

'No! Get back! I am a sinner! I have sinned! Only God can forgive me!' cried Buttons as he recoiled from Holmes's outstretched hand and backed further towards the centre of the bridge.

A bolt of lightning bleached the sky and a crack of

thunder sounded milliseconds later. And before we could stop him, Buttons catapulted over the railing, plunging into the black waters of the Jesus Lock.

We both ran to the edge. There was no trace of him. Only dull concentric ripples where his body had entered the water, broken by raindrops distorting the widening rings.

'Get help, Watson!' cried Holmes, tearing off his coat.

PART EIGHT

THE UNLOCKING

'Let him have the key of thy heart,
who hath the lock of his own.'
                                    —Sir Thomas Browne

CHAPTER 38

Rescue

y God!' I cried. 'Can he swim?' I struggled to remove my boots.

'Watson, no! Your leg!' shouted Holmes. 'Get help!'

He plunged into the water.

I stood frozen as I witnessed the boy surface with a strangled cry some distance away, then go under, and surface again. His arms flailed, he gasped for air. 'Help!' he cried and went under again. Holmes swam with strong strokes towards the drowning boy. But the boy's survival instinct and panic would endanger anyone trying to save him.

I could not leave them. I looked about for a pole, for a rope – something to toss to Holmes.

Lightning flashed again across the sky. It was five in the morning. Would anyone be near? It was then that I heard bells and a police whistle. I turned to see a police van pulled by four horses, lanterns blazing, racing towards us from some distance away down Chesterton Road.

Then I remembered that Holmes had asked the young officer with Polly to send men to the rectory! Limping from the bridge into the centre of the road, I waved my arms to stop them.

Turning back, I saw that Holmes and the boy had disappeared. The water near where the boy had surfaced was roiling and a pair of white hands emerged and then went under.

And then, on the other side of the river, I saw something that made me freeze in terror. A figure swathed in a dark, shapeless coat and hood ran across the lock gates to the lock controls, seizing the crank handle and opening the sluice gates.

Lightning flashed and the top half of the face was revealed, eyes fierce and mad, but the lower half of the face was covered by a heavy scarf, even in this steamy, hot night.

There was the sound of a loud groan of machinery, and I could see the wall of the lock lifting at the far end. This put anyone in the lock in mortal danger from the severe and sudden undertow that opening the sluice gates would cause. Holmes and Buttons would be sucked into the slacker tunnel just as Dillie had been!

Both heads surfaced. Buttons panicked, clutching at Holmes, his hands raking my friend's face, ripping at his hair.

'Holmes, the lock!' I shouted.

But Buttons continued thrashing about, his arms flailing,

striking Holmes and dragging his would-be rescuer under-water again in a desperate dance of survival.

Holmes surfaced. 'Wats—!' he shouted, but was cut off when Buttons pulled them both under again. Both heads surfaced, gasping, then there was a loud whooshing sound as the lock gates fully opened, and both of them were abruptly sucked under as the rushing waters pulled them towards the dangerous tunnels.

'Holmes!' I cried. I raced off the bridge and towards the eastern side of the lock. I could see nothing in the black waters.

The Jesus Lock was efficient, and the water level had begun to drop visibly. I started across the bridge towards the lock controls. The mysterious figure had vanished. I had to stop the flow!

I reached the controls, but just then Holmes surfaced, treading water with mighty strokes as he fought not to go under. He looked wildly about for me.

'Over here, Holmes! I'll stop it!'

'No, Watson! Hold off!' he shouted. 'Buttons is caught in the mechanism! I'm going down.'

Before I could respond, he disappeared below the surface. Closing the lock now could trap and crush the two men down there. I was unsure what to do.

A police van and a Black Maria pulled up to the side of the river. I ran to the edge, horrified. 'Holmes!' I cried. The water level in the lock had dropped precipitously. *A minute had passed since he went under.*

By now there were five or six policemen on the scene.

'Two men in there!' I shouted.

'Close down the lock! They'll be sucked under!' cried an officer.

'No! Don't touch it! One of them is already caught in the mechanism,' I yelled.

Two brave policemen tore off their boots and coats and dived in. 'Which side? There are two tunnels!'

I pointed to the one on the south side. But was I sure? *Two minutes. How long had Holmes been under there?*

Lightning flashed, and the thunder cracked again. The swimming policemen dived under and resurfaced once, then twice, each time empty handed. Was it the south tunnel? Or had I been mistaken . . .

Three minutes.

Then, suddenly, I saw them.

It was Holmes . . . with Buttons cradled in one arm. Struggling to keep the young man's head above water, he managed – just barely – to keep them afloat with his other arm. But he was losing the battle, and despite my friend's immense strength, they were slowly being drawn backward towards the drain.

But seeing the boy had been freed, I struggled with the lever to shut the lock. It was not designed to close midway and resisted. I looked up.

The two men in the water had joined Holmes, and all three now held the boy's head out of the water, and their combined forces were able to withstand the current. A fourth policeman joined me at the controls, and together the two of us managed to close down the drain.

I ran to the bank just as the swimmers reached it. The two policemen lifted Buttons, and I reached down to grasp my friend's arm as he approached the shore, pulling him to safety.

Holmes gasped and coughed up water. I sat him down on the rain-soaked grass, and kneeled next to him to assess his condition. The rain had stopped, and the eastern horizon was glimmering in light, slanting in through the clouds. The dim rays lit up his exhausted face. He gagged, then coughed up water, and I struck him twice on the back to help.

He held his hand up. 'I am fine,' he gasped. 'See to the boy. May have been too late—'

Deacon Buttons was laid out on his stomach on the grass nearby. Two policemen were administering artificial respiration, with Buttons' arms stretched above him. A bloodied wrist showed where he'd been caught in the lock mechanism.

I ran to help. It was light enough to see the deacon's drowned face, young and innocent-looking in repose. And yet he was a murderer, I thought. The cut on his wrist was not deep, but he was not breathing. I instructed the two officers to sit him up and we began the arm lifts that sometimes worked when the prone position did not.

Still no breath.

'On his stomach again,' I ordered. Holmes was now standing above me.

'Will he live?' he asked.

I heard a voice in the distance: 'Buttons! My God, Buttons!'

With the two policemen's help, once again we turned the

boy over, raised his arms and began another set of rhythmic manipulations hoping to restart his breathing. There was no response. And then, to my surprise, Buttons coughed once and vomited up water. We changed tactics and sat him up, leaning forward. He coughed, gagged, and inhaled at last.

Behind him, Father Lamb had arrived, his face contorted in grief and worry. He leaned in to take the young deacon's arm. 'Peregrine, my son, my son,' he moaned. 'Dear boy. My God, what has happened here?'

'Stand back, Father,' I said. 'He came near to drowning.'

Silence, then a wheeze followed by another sudden cough, and water poured from Buttons' lips. He choked and began to breathe. Father Lamb stepped forward and kneeled next to the boy, tears streaming down his face.

The young man at last began to breathe on his own, great rasping breaths.

'Thank the Lord,' said Lamb, cradling Peregrine Buttons as though he were his dearest child.

I wondered if forgiveness was in the priest's heart, for learning of the violence that had transpired in the young man's room would surely burn all the love away.

CHAPTER 39

Gaol

his tender moment was interrupted by Inspector Hadley. He appeared on the scene, apparently straight from his bed, his hair awry, coat buttoned wrongly and his normally calm visage creased with anger and concern. He approached me.

'The deacon! Dr Watson, will this man survive?'

'Probably,' I said.

'Can you confirm a suicide attempt, Doctor?'

'Yes, I witnessed it.'

'What were you and Holmes doing here?'

'Investigating Deacon Buttons. Mr Holmes has discovered a great deal in his room at the rectory. Miss Dillie Wyndham was abducted from there, and he has much to tell you.' I looked up to see Holmes now standing some ten feet away with the same two constables who had helped him rescue

Buttons. Now each gripped one of his arms. The three of them – soaked and with the morning rain further splattering upon them – were a sorry sight.

Hadley approached the group. 'Mr Holmes, you are under arrest for your previous escape. Disregard for the law will not be tolerated. Palmer and Wright, convey Mr Holmes and Deacon Buttons to the station – Buttons on the charges of suspected murder and attempted suicide. Then dry yourselves off.'

'Inspector Hadley,' I cried, 'Mr Holmes just rescued a man!'

'True enough, sir,' said the young constable on Holmes's right, with blond, brush-cut hair. 'We helped, but this gentleman saved the fellow, sir.'

Holmes turned to the young man. 'Thank you, Constable—?'

'Palmer,' said the fellow.

'Thank you, Palmer,' said Holmes. 'Now, Mr Hadley. Dr Watson and I have been at the rectory, and—'

'Dr Watson has told me. We will follow up, but you're going to the gaol now,' said Hadley. 'Is that boy safe for transport?' he asked me, nodding towards Buttons.

'He needs care. Shock can follow a near drowning,' I said.

'We'll take that risk. Ride with me, Doctor Watson.'

And so it happened that Buttons, weak and shivering, and Holmes, frustrated and angry, were both handcuffed and bundled, soaking wet, into the single Black Maria owned by the Cambridge police.

In Hadley's private carriage, I attempted to reason with

the man. 'Mr Hadley! I do not exaggerate the dangers of shock. Deacon Buttons came close to death back there. Please let me examine him when we arrive.'

'The question is, did he confess to killing Odelia Wyndham before jumping?' Hadley smoothed his rumpled hair self-consciously. I wondered how often the inspector was pulled from his bed in this sleepy town.

'Not exactly,' said I. 'But Deacon Buttons expressed some kind of guilt. I am sure Mr Holmes has more to tell you.'

'I will hear it at the station,' said Hadley, brusquely.

Once there, Holmes and Buttons were placed in separate cells, and I was not allowed to see either, at least not right away. The early morning temperature had dropped from the night storm, and in spite of the humidity, a fire had been lit in the reception area. I shivered in front of it. It was nearly six a.m. and I had not eaten in over twenty-four hours. Seeing my distress, the second young officer from the rescue team, a dark-haired, handsome man with a luxurious moustache, brought me a coffee and a sandwich, and attempted to make me comfortable.

'I'm Wright,' he said by way of introduction. 'Close call out there.'

'Is someone seeing to Mr Holmes?' I asked him, thinking that if anyone needed to eat, it was my friend.

Wright leaned in close as he placed my food on a nearby table. 'He is fine, sir. More angry than distressed.'

'He needs food. Coffee. Brandy perhaps.'

'I will get something to him.'

I waited, growing more impatient by the minute. I felt

strongly the need to check on Holmes, and also Buttons. Yet still I waited. The clock above the police intake desk struck seven. At last I was ushered into Hadley's office, annoyed to see the older man must have returned home to shave and freshen himself, despite the urgency and gravity of the case. In contrast to my own muddy disarray, his well-dressed hair gleamed and his shoes were shined to match.

At his questions, I related succinctly what Holmes had discovered at Piotr Flan's pawnshop, and what he had revealed to me about Buttons' room at the rectory. To his credit, Hadley listened carefully, and then called in young Wright, directing him to see to Holmes and get his notes, and then follow up with his own investigation.

After a few more minutes in which I repeated the story of what Holmes and I had done the night before, I was made to wait, and then finally released to see my friend. I was hot, exhausted, sticky, damp and irritable beyond reckoning. Sherlock Holmes must only have felt worse.

The station had long ago been converted from a warehouse with offices, and the prisoners' cells were in random locations throughout the facility. Holmes's current cell was off a main hall and through an anteroom. I entered to discover Holmes seated in a metal chair in the centre of this isolated cell. To my surprise, he was strangely encumbered in a straitjacket with a few chains round it, and his ankles were handcuffed to the legs of the chair. It brought to mind the provocative posters I had seen for the escapist thrills of the Great Borelli. In my exhaustion and surprise, a thoroughly inappropriate laugh escaped my lips.

Holmes looked up. He was white with fury, his jaws clenched, and he clearly did not share my humour at the situation.

Pickering stood over him, holding another chain and set of locks, apparently in the hope of figuring out where to add these to the pitiful mess before him. Constable Palmer entered with apparent reluctance, carrying a long white rag.

'Gag him,' said Pickering.

'Sir?' Palmer looked at the sergeant dubiously.

"I think not,' said Holmes sharply. 'Do you think I'm going to undo these locks with my teeth, Pickering?'

'Do it.'

Palmer hesitated.

'Mr Holmes just nearly drowned.' I said. 'He is still recovering.'

'I don't care,' said Pickering.

'It *is* highly unusual, Sergeant,' the younger fellow stammered, his decency getting the better of him.

Just then Hadley entered the anteroom. Pickering dropped an ounce or two of swagger at the sight of his superior.

Hadley took in the ridiculous sight and frowned. 'Pickering, what's the meaning of this?'

'Well, we don't want him escaping again, do we, sir? I assure you, he will not be picking any locks this time.'

'Where did you get that straitjacket?'

'From the sanatorium. When we delivered Miss Atalanta yesterday.'

Her family had had Atalanta committed to an institution! A sharp pain in my leg reminded me of the reason. Dr

Macready must have reported the incident, and perhaps Eden-Summers as well. But a sanatorium! I thought I must look into this later.

Hadley, too, had the decency to be outraged. 'You managed to *ask for an extra straitjacket*? Sergeant, what on earth were you thinking? This is a gaol, not an asylum.'

'I was thinking ahead, of exactly this situation, sir. We have occasional unruly prisoners. Remember Willoughby last month – Palmer's broken finger?' He nodded fiercely at Palmer, who reluctantly held up his little finger, which bent sideways at an odd angle.

Pickering glanced down at Holmes and smiled. This was not lost on Hadley.

'Outside, Pickering, now!' he ordered. 'Palmer, you too.'

Pickering and the younger man left, leaving only Hadley and myself with Holmes. Hadley closed the door of the anteroom, which led to the rest of the station, and sat in a chair facing the cell. He eyed my friend wearily and shook his head. 'What a morning! You have made this extremely difficult for me, Mr Holmes. Your escape last time was reported to the Wyndhams, and the University has become involved, naming you as a dangerous threat. A great deal of pressure is being brought to bear on the police regarding you.'

'Mr Hadley,' said Holmes reasonably, 'I know that it appears that Deacon Buttons murdered Miss Wyndham, but when you know all, you will agree that it is not quite sewn up. I believe I am very near to closing this case for you and need only a short time more to finish my investigation. I

354

have given some details to Constable Wright which I have asked him to check for me at the rectory just now, but it would be best if you allowed me to complete the investigation.'

'You are bound by law to report all your findings to me, Mr Holmes.'

'Bound by law is an understatement in this case,' said Holmes wryly. 'Release me, and I will deliver Miss Wyndham's murderer to you.'

'You have tied my own hands, Mr Holmes – to continue the metaphor,' said Hadley. 'But I don't mean to be flippant. We have the two main suspects in hand now. Both had reason to kill the girl. Good reason. With Buttons' attempted suicide, I am afraid he slants the case towards himself.'

'You mean *three* suspects? You also have Frederick Eden-Summers and Leo Vitale?' asked Holmes. 'Three men were in love with the girl.'

'We have eliminated Eden-Summers for the moment. I will admit his alibi is weak. Most of the card-playing fellows he named as witnesses were inebriated during the hours in question. However, the sheer number of them who came forward weights the case in favour of his innocence. We have remanded him to his parents' estate.'

'Surely Eden-Summers is the most motivated of the three!' Holmes said. 'Miss Wyndham publicly announced her engagement to him, then became engaged to a second young man, and pawned both rings.'

I was surprised at this. I thought that Buttons had been confirmed in Holmes's mind as the killer, or at least that

355

our recent discoveries had moved the deacon into first position among the suspects.

'And,' said Holmes, 'Mr Eden-Summers apparently found out about that second engagement the night of Dillie's murder. Leo Vitale paid him a visit at his lodgings. Don't you find that sufficient to keep him in the running?'

'You have spoken to Mr Eden-Summers, then?'

'I have spoken to all three of her young men,' said Holmes.

Hadley's eyebrows lifted, but to his credit he took this in his stride. 'My impression from Mr Eden-Summers was that this was a marriage more of convenience than of love. His family desired closer University ties for political reasons which elude me,' said Hadley.

This would explain Eden-Summers' slightly odd response to the news of Dillie's death, I thought.

'The pawning of the rings, however, casts a new light,' continued Hadley, thoughtfully.

'Of course, Miss Wyndham also accepted Leo Vitale's ring and proposal,' I offered. Holmes shot me a look of reproach. I wondered if he didn't harbour an unusual bias towards the young scientist.

'We know that, Dr Watson,' said Hadley, smoothing his reddish moustache. 'I arrested him on the basis of his shouted fight with the deceased on the night of her murder, apparently all about this ring. It was heard by several in the street near the Cross and Anchor – where, incidentally the girl had been hiding out.'

'Yes, yes, Vitale is not beyond suspicion,' agreed Holmes, 'but I would not have let Eden-Summers off so quickly.'

Hadley looked uneasy at the thought. It struck me how odd it was that the Cambridge policeman was allowing the case to be led by a prisoner in his own gaol.

'I feel certain that Eden-Summers will remain at his estate,' said Hadley. 'The Duke is incensed at the loss of the ring – apparently a family heirloom worth a small fortune.'

The pawnbroker Mr Flan must consider himself in luck, I thought. He knew all along the worth of Eden-Summers' rather ostentatious ring and had vastly underpaid.

'It may be found, along with Mr Vitale's ring, at Piotr Flan's pawnshop on the Cheltenham Road. Brought there by Deacon Peregrine Buttons.'

'Good Lord!' said Hadley, clearly surprised by this news.

'If you will set me free, I will show you what I found in Buttons' room. Miss Wyndham received her fatal blow there in a fierce battle. The signs are there to be read. But I had not finished my examination when Watson spotted Buttons on the Jesus Lock footbridge. You know the rest.'

'Wright is a good man. He will find anything that is in the room.'

Holmes grimaced, the picture of frustration. 'Nevertheless, doing so without me is a mistake.'

'Perhaps, Mr Holmes, but you dug your own pit by escaping from custody earlier. Buttons is the most obvious suspect. His attempted suicide shows he is clearly deranged and racked by guilt. By several accounts he was utterly obsessed with the girl.'

As much as I had liked Buttons, I was beginning to agree with Hadley on this matter.

'I understand from Professor Wyndham that it was young Buttons who brought you into the case,' Hadley continued.

'An argument *against* his guilt, would you not think?' said Holmes.

'No, I would *not* think. I have seen boastful criminals taunt the police in precisely this way. It is sheer arrogance,' said Hadley, smoothing his hair self-consciously.

Holmes had used this same argument regarding Madame Borelli, and it was true. We had encountered this before. The more I considered the matter, the stronger I leaned towards Buttons as the culprit. The constraints of his chosen profession had weighed heavily upon him. He was a highly emotional man.

'At this point,' said Hadley, 'my suspicions are divided, however. I have not eliminated the rather unusual Mr Vitale. Now that is a strange young man. A touch inhuman.'

Holmes shifted on his chair. He must be devilishly uncomfortable, I thought, soaking wet and having just undergone tremendous physical strain while rescuing a drowning man from a powerful current.

'Miss Wyndham was attacked and dealt the fatal blow in Deacon Buttons' room,' said he. 'Her body was dumped out of the window and from there conveyed to the river. But I found evidence that at some point during the night in question, others were in that room. Possibly two others. Whoever killed her attempted to straighten up the room and remove evidence, but did so in haste. There is something still to be learned. You must let me finish there!'

'I am sorry, but no.'

Just then Holmes was taken by a sudden coughing spell and appeared to cough up more water. He gasped. 'I am having difficulty breathing in this thing. Doctor . . .'

I took his meaning at once. 'Sir! This man nearly drowned. At least let me, a medical doctor, examine him. You don't want the famous London detective to suffocate while in your custody because your inept sergeant was too enthusiastic. Believe me, I will make sure the full force of the law comes down upon you if he is hurt here.'

'Oh, stop threatening me, Dr Watson. I don't want him in here at all,' said Hadley. 'But you see my position. Yes, by all means check. But nothing funny, Doctor, or I'll lock you up as well.'

CHAPTER 40

Church and State

adley unlocked the cell and I moved inside and knelt by Holmes, to check that his breathing was not constricted. Behind me, young Constable Palmer entered the small room outside Holmes's cell. 'I cannot induce Father Lamb to leave, sir. He is very concerned about the prisoner.'

'Tell him to wait,' Hadley answered.

As I leaned over Holmes to check his bonds, he whispered in my ear, 'Give me your pocketknife, Watson.'

This seemed like a terrible idea. I gave Holmes my best 'you are utterly mad' look while saying aloud, 'I will need to loosen this strap here.' As I went about my task, I nevertheless managed to slip him the knife, unseen, pressing it into his hand from the bottom of the straitjacket. 'Careful, Holmes,' I whispered.

Giving him the knife had been against my better judgement.

'Father Lamb is awfully impatient,' insisted Palmer.

'Palmer, you have your order!' said Hadley, and then turned to me. 'Doctor? All is well with Mr Holmes?'

'I need another moment,' I replied.

'All right. Then would you be good enough to check on Mr Buttons?' said Hadley.

He departed, and I finished and exited the cell. Palmer shut the barred door with a loud clang and locked it securely. A quick glance at my friend showed him already at work, squirming under the straitjacket.

I wondered what Holmes's plan could be. He might free himself, and then what? He would not get far. The station was full of men and bustling with activity.

Meanwhile, I had an urgent mission. Buttons could be suffering from shock. Another suicide attempt would not be unusual. I said as much to Palmer, who assured me the bedding had been removed from Buttons' cell to prevent him hanging himself.

'Yes, but shock is now the risk. Can you bring a blanket and something warm to drink?' I said.

He nodded. 'I'll be right with you. He's down that hallway there.' He pointed me in the direction of the cell.

Echoing from the distant end of the hall and around the corner, I heard the familiar voice of Father Lamb. 'Yes, sir, thank you, sir. I do, I fear for this young man's soul.' The strident voice grew fainter.

Thinking to follow, I hurried down the corridor but made

a wrong turn. I saw neither Father Lamb nor Buttons' cell. I did pass one larger cell which contained two drunken, somnolent men. What a labyrinthine place this was!

I asked directions and at last I arrived at Buttons' cell. I peeked in through the door's barred window. The young man lay on the hard cot, curled into a foetal position, shivering and moaning. Father Lamb was nowhere in sight. The bedding had been removed, but it left him soaking wet and chilled. He was ghastly white, shaking mightily, and I did not like the look of him. The delay in allowing me to check him was unconscionable.

I put my face near the small window into the cell. 'Buttons!'

He looked up, saw me, and moaned. 'Why did you save me? I want to die.'

'Here we are, Doctor!' It was Palmer, with blankets and a coffee.

'Hurry!' I said. 'He appears to be in shock. We need to get him warm.'

We entered and I covered the shivering young man. Palmer handed me the coffee.

'Try to drink some of this, Deacon Buttons,' said I. 'Father Lamb is on his way,' although it was clear to me that the boy needed medical attention more than spiritual.

He moaned. 'Father? No, no! He can't see me like this.'

'Easy now. He already saw you at the river. He was terrified for you. You were very nearly successful in killing yourself.'

Buttons sobbed, burying his face in his arms. 'If only . . .' he wailed.

362

'Find him dry clothes, and make sure he stays warm,' I said and left as the young policeman helped Buttons to drink. Perhaps Lamb could offer some comfort or even some insight. As I left the cell I glanced back at the young deacon. It struck me that saving a man for the second time in a day only to send him to the gallows was a questionable act of mercy.

Back in the hallway, a red-haired constable I had glimpsed at the riverside hurried by me in the hall.

'Excuse me, Constable!' I called out. 'Father Lamb, the Catholic priest who was at the reception desk? He was called to see this prisoner. Do you know where he is?'

The man shrugged. 'He wasn't called for Buttons. It was for that other young man from last night.'

'One of your drunks in there?'

'Oh, no. Tall, pale fellow. Vittle or something, I think. Odd character.'

'Leo Vitale?'

'That's the one. Wanted to make confession.'

How strange. But Leo Vitale was an Italian name – perhaps he was Catholic. Did asking to confess imply guilt? Holmes had said something about Vitale possibly being a third man in Buttons' room at the rectory the night of the murder. And now Vitale wanted to confess.

This was news Holmes needed to hear.

'Where is Vitale?' I asked.

'Out back, I think. We have an extra cell in what used to be the stables. Five prisoners last night. That's crowded for us,' he said with a laugh, then departed.

I ran back to Holmes's cell in the desperate hope that he was still in the building. I was in luck. He had escaped his bonds and the cell itself but was still in the small ante-room where, as yet, no one had spotted him. There he had lingered and was leaning, rather casually, I thought, against the wall.

He glanced up. 'Buttons is all right?' His voice was weak.

'Yes. Mild shock, but he is being treated. Give me my knife back,' I snapped. Holmes reached into his pocket shakily. His face was ghastly white. 'What is the matter with you?' And then I saw it. 'Holmes, your shoulder! You dislocated it again, you damned fool!'

'Pop it in for me, Watson, that's a good fellow,' he said, handing me back my knife.

I could not take my eyes off him and fumbled as I put the thing in my pocket.

'*Now*, if you don't mind,' he said.

He was right. I needed to work quickly before swelling made it impossible. There was no time to bring him to task for this foolish manoeuvre.

'Stand away from the wall,' I ordered. 'Hold onto these bars with your other hand, and brace against me.' I felt the injured shoulder. 'Dear God! Why didn't you wait? Hadley will release you eventually.'

'Watson. Do it now!'

'Steady, there.'

I took hold of his right wrist and pulled it gently and firmly straight out from the torso. Then yanked. There was a distinct pop and Holmes stifled his own cry into the crook of his other arm. He sank against the wall, breathing heavily. 'I think I might need to give up on this trick.'

'Your best idea of the day. Let us do this right, Holmes, and get you officially released. I will post bail.'

He did not move for a moment, his eyes closed in an effort to recover. 'I must get to the rectory before the police destroy the evidence. I am not at all sure Buttons is our man, after all. But I need to confirm two details. I hope Wright—'

'Holmes! Vitale just called for Father Lamb.'

'Vitale called for the priest? Why?'

'To hear his confession,' I said. 'I didn't realize Vitale was a religious man.'

'He isn't. Don't you remember "if there is a God"?'

'Then what would drive a man to—?'

'Stop!' Holmes held up a finger. 'Be quiet.' For five seconds he was a perfect statue. His face reflected something I had witnessed before. It was like the tumblers of a lock, clicking into place inside his mind.

Vitale killed Dillie. It had to be. The loss of a ring he could not afford to lose. The quiet, logical demeanour masking a roiling, tumultuous emotional life, a love he had never experienced, ripped from his grasping hands. By now I had become more adept at following my friend's logic. And now, consumed with guilt, needing to confess—

'Where is Leo Vitale being held?' Holmes asked quietly.

'I am not sure. I think they put him in some kind of overflow cell somewhere behind this building. In the stables.'

Holmes leaped to the door and peered into the hallway beyond. It was empty.

'Watson, there is no time. Listen to me carefully. Go and get Hadley. Bring him to Vitale's cell. And hurry! A man's life depends on it!' And he was up and running down the hall before I could stop him.

I hurried to the front of the station. 'Inspector Hadley?' I asked the man behind the desk.

'Just left,' said the fellow, nodding towards the entrance. I departed on a run.

CHAPTER 41

A Spot of Trouble

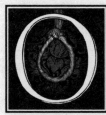utside, the rain had stopped, and it had washed the dense air clean. I saw Hadley down the street, walking quickly, the morning light highlighting his tan-coloured summer Mackintosh.

'Mr Hadley!' I shouted. My injured leg made running difficult.

He turned to see me limping after him.

'Mr Holmes has asked for you, sir! Can you please come back with me?'

'Dr Watson, I am sorely in need of a good breakfast. Perhaps you should join me. We can discuss bail for Mr Holmes.'

'Leo Vitale has asked Father Lamb to hear his confession!'

Hadley pulled up short at this. 'Well, that is interesting. Perhaps Vitale is ready to admit his guilt.'

'Possibly. But please come now! Holmes fears a man may die in your custody!'

And had Hadley not responded as he did, that man might well have been Sherlock Holmes.

We raced back to the station to find chaos there. Apparently Holmes's escape from his cell had just been noted, and Pickering was in a lather. Palmer and the red-haired young constable stood in the entry room. 'Find him! Find him!' Pickering shouted, strapping on his pistol.

If anyone could hide himself in this relatively small police station, it would be my friend.

The moment Pickering saw Hadley he rushed up to his superior. 'Holmes has broken out again. He must have had help.' He turned to me in a fury. 'You!' Pickering reached out and grabbed my wrist and was about to snap on handcuffs when Hadley stopped him.

'Step away, Mr Pickering. I have had enough of your temper,' said Hadley.

'Temper, sir?' cried Pickering. 'That Holmes has made a mockery—'

'Mr Pickering, you are on leave as of this moment. Finnegan and Palmer, follow me!'

I just caught a glimpse of Pickering's gaping response as the four of us headed down the hallway.

'Where is Leo Vitale being held?' asked Hadley of his young officer.

'We moved him to that cell out at the back when we took in the two drunks last night,' replied Palmer as we raced down the hallway and into a courtyard.

We dashed into a ramshackle back building. It was a former stable, now a storage area, containing a lone cell at the far end. The barred door to the cell was ajar. We heard a desperate cry. 'Help! Murder!'

It was Holmes's voice!

The scene that greeted us there was something I never expected. Two struggling figures blocked the entrance.

It was Holmes locked in mortal combat with Father Lamb!

The priest had his hands wrapped around Holmes's neck. The detective clawed at them, and then both lurched back from the doorway towards the centre of the cell, as Holmes managed to kick Lamb's feet out from under him.

They crashed to the floor, revealing behind them Leo Vitale, hanging by the neck from a noose created from the sheet of his cot!

The noose was tied to a pipe in the ceiling. Vitale's feet dangled and kicked six inches off the ground as he clawed desperately at it. He gagged and choked – the terrible sounds of a dying man.

'Take him!' Hadley directed his men to Holmes and Lamb. Palmer and Finnegan leaped into the fray as Hadley and I ran to the boy.

Hadley took Vitale's legs and hoisted him up, taking the pressure off while I removed my pocketknife and slashed through the fabric. In a moment, we had him down and onto the cot, where I tore off the noose. The thin young man was white and still. I gently felt his neck to determine if the windpipe had been crushed.

Suddenly Vitale gagged and choked. We had managed to cut him down just in time.

'We have him, sir,' said Palmer, and we turned to see Finnegan and Palmer holding Holmes between them.

Lamb was nowhere to be seen.

'Not him, you idiots, the priest!' shouted Hadley.

They hesitated. 'But—' cried Finnegan.

'After him, now!' ordered the Inspector.

They released Holmes, who would have collapsed had I not caught him. I did so and sat him on the edge of the cot. Holmes rubbed his own throat and glanced over at Vitale, whose hands were across his heart as he continued to inhale big gasping breaths.

'Vitale?' Holmes rasped.

'He will make it.' I said.

Leo Vitale's eyes opened part way and he took us in. 'Thank you . . .' he whispered, his voice ravaged.

'Lamb strung you up there?' Holmes asked.

'Yes,' murmured Vitale. 'He is stronger than he looks.'

He must have been strong to have nearly bested Holmes, I thought. 'Don't try to talk, Mr Vitale,' I said.

Holmes looked up at Hadley, who had been watching this exchange with deep interest.

The senior policeman, to his credit, did the decent thing and did it without hesitation. 'I apologize, Mr Holmes. We will catch Lamb. You have the lead, sir.'

'To your office, then,' said Holmes. 'I have a plan.'

'Have blankets and food brought for Mr Holmes,' I said.

Hadley spoke sharply to a deputy in the hall outside the room, and the fellow ran off to gather what was needed.

'But I need a moment first,' said Holmes. He reached over and pulled back the collar of the boy's shirt. I presumed he was looking at the wounds from the noose, but I gasped when I saw a purple ink stain on Vitale's neck.

'Mr Vitale. You were in Buttons' room the night of Dillie's murder. You lied to me about that,' said Holmes.

'Yes . . . yes, I was, but . . .' The boy's eyes filled with tears.

'Tell me what happened, and if you want to avoid the hangman, you will not lie to me again.'

'I . . . I . . .' the boy choked and coughed violently.

I took out my flask and poured brandy down his throat. 'He should not be speaking,' I said.

'Then I will speak,' said Holmes. 'Correct me if I am wrong, Mr Vitale. Fail to do so at your peril.' He glanced up at Hadley, who nodded in the affirmative. 'You were there because after arguing with Miss Wyndham outside the Cross and Anchor, you did not just 'walk the streets for awhile'. No! Instead you followed her to the rectory. You wanted your ring returned. You saw her enter the rectory, but you didn't go in right away. Instead, you stood outside her window, in the rain, watching.' The boy stared at Holmes in astonishment. I had seen that look many times before.

'I saw a partial footprint outside, but it was muddied from the rain and I was not sure until now. Through the window you saw Buttons with her, but soon after, he left. I warrant you did not want a fight. You only wanted your ring back from her.'

Leo Vitale continued to stare at Holmes, wide eyed. He nodded again.

'But your ring was not there. That is because Dillie had just sent Deacon Buttons to the pawnshop with it, and also with Freddie Eden-Summers' ring. But she did not tell you that.'

Vitale moaned. 'Dillie said her sister had stolen it.' His voice was barely above a whisper.

'Ha! Atalanta. A smart lie, and believable. Otherwise you would have followed Buttons and retrieved your ring. So you stayed.'

'And you attacked Miss Wyndham!' said Hadley, picking up Vitale's right hand. 'Look, gentlemen. His knuckles are abraded. You hit something with force. Odelia Wyndham was beaten before she died.' Vitale closed his eyes and shook his head weakly.

'Mr Hadley, please,' said Holmes. 'He fought with Eden-Summers later. That part is true, isn't that right Mr Vitale? We will get to that. No. You lingered in the doorway of Buttons' room instead of entering. A sense of propriety, perhaps?'

'Yes. She . . . she was . . .'

'Unclothed. Yes, I know.'

How did he know? I did not voice the question, Vitale did.

'How do you know this, sir? It is like you were there!'

'Traces in the deacon's bed. The girl got into his bed unclothed. But this was after you left. We will get to that, too. You remained in the doorway . . . and . . .' Holmes closed his eyes. I would swear that the scene was playing almost like a series of daguerreotypes, flipping in a carnival peepshow in his head.

'Yes, yes, I see it now,' he continued. 'That ink stain on your neck, Mr Vitale. The residue in the doorframe. Watson! The half empty bottle of purple ink with the dented cap! Do you remember?' Do you see?'

I remember him noting the ink bottle in Buttons' room. But . . . 'No, I don't see,' I said, frankly more puzzled than before.

Holmes stood up abruptly and looked down at Vitale.

'Miss Wyndham picked up that bottle of ink and flung it across the room at you. It hit the doorjamb, the cap cracked, and a few drops spattered on your neck, there. And on the moulding around the door, which I noted, even though it was cleaned up after you left.'

Leo Vitale was breathing in quick, shallow breaths.

'Slow, deep breaths, Mr Vitale,' I said.

'You might well have become enraged. You had been betrayed, stolen from, used – and attacked – and yet you left. You left the young lady unharmed.'

Vitale closed his eyes, nodding.

'But those torn knuckles!' insisted Hadley.

Holmes held up a hand. 'Tell us about the fight with Eden-Summers at Trinity. What happened there? Why did you go there?'

'I tried to tell him what Dillie . . . what I thought she . . .' He began to cough. 'Perhaps together we could . . . but he would not let me into the room, he would not listen.' Another coughing spell overtook him.

'Easy, Mr Vitale,' I said.

'He came into the hall. He told me he would have nothing to do with me. That Dillie would never do what I claimed. He was inebriated, belligerent. We fought . . .'

I remembered now that Eden-Summers claimed his injuries were from a fight with some stranger in the hall. He had obviously left out a key element of the story.

'But why did you go there?' asked Hadley. 'What did you expect?'

The boy was now coughing so hard he could not answer.

'He hoped that Eden-Summers would join him, and that the two of them together could perhaps recover their rings. Isn't that right, Mr Vitale?' said Holmes.

The boy nodded, recovering. 'I thought he might have more influence.'

'But as you said before, some combination of pride, ego and a great deal of alcohol prevented your rival from seeing the logic of your plan. You left Eden-Summers. What did you do next?' continued my friend.

'I went back to my room. I tried to sleep.' Tears ran down Vitale's face. 'I regret . . . I regret . . .'

'You are lying!' cried Hadley. 'What you regret is killing Odelia Wyndham!'

'No!' gasped Vitale. 'I regret *not* returning to her. Because I might have saved her.'

Holmes rose abruptly. 'May we finish this in your office, Mr Hadley?' said he.

Vitale closed his eyes and tears coursed down his cheeks. 'I might have saved . . . if only . . .'

Ten minutes later we faced Hadley in his spacious and well-lit office. The police inspector sat behind an imposing desk and leaned forward on it, attentive and fully ready to listen to Holmes. My friend and I were seated in chairs facing the desk. Holmes was wrapped in a blanket and holding coffee in his shivering hands, despite the rising warmth of the day. He had not eaten in a day and a half, and the rescue in the lock and contretemps in Vitale's cell would have laid low a lesser man.

'Mr Holmes, this remains a puzzle,' said Hadley. 'If you believe Mr Vitale, and it seems you do, then who killed Miss Wyndham, and why on earth would Father Lamb attempt to kill Leo Vitale just now?' asked Hadley. 'There are too many unanswered questions in the scenario you project.'

'I will answer these questions within the hour. I can tell you one thing, however. Miss Wyndham was killed for love. Has Constable Wright returned from inspecting Deacon Buttons' room?'

'Not yet. For love, you say? But here is another question. Who pulled the lever at the lock, nearly killing you and Buttons?' asked Hadley. 'Tell us again, Dr Watson, what you saw?'

The men turned to me. I shrugged. 'As I said, the figure was hooded and masked. I could make out nothing.'

'Height?'

'At least my height. Perhaps taller.'

At that moment, young Palmer burst into the room. 'They caught Father Lamb, Mr Hadley! He was running fast, but he claims Mr Holmes attacked him as he tried to rescue Vitale from a suicide attempt.'

Hadley stood up behind his desk. 'Is there any chance that you misunderstood the priest's actions, Mr Holmes?'

Holmes shook his head wearily.

'Mr Vitale told us that Father Lamb attempted to kill him,' I said.

'But Mr Vitale has lied before!' said Hadley. 'Holmes?'

'No. Father Lamb was yanking on Mr Vitale's legs to hasten his death.'

'But might you be mistaken? Couldn't he have been trying to hoist him and save the boy, as we did, just in time?'

We heard a commotion just outside the door and Father Lamb's strident voice: 'An outrage! Unhand me!'

'Shall I let them in, sir?' asked Palmer.

Holmes leaped to his feet, discarding his blanket. He was suddenly on fire. 'Wait!' He paused, finger to his lips. 'Mr Hadley, let me question the priest. What I say or do will seem strange. Give nothing away, please. All will become clear shortly. I will require Constable Palmer's help. Trust me. Mr Hadley, may I suggest that you do not indicate to the father that he is a suspect, rather that we made a mistake? Will you agree to all this?'

Hadley hesitated briefly, then nodded. 'In for a penny,' said he. 'Palmer, give Mr Holmes your full support.'

Holmes beckoned the young man over and whispered at some length to him. The fellow nodded. 'I understand you, sir.'

Palmer looked over at Hadley, who nodded approval. 'Do as he asks,' said the Inspector.

Palmer departed. Holmes turned to us both with a smile. 'As they call this in a conjuring show, gentlemen, you are about to witness . . . the Prestige.'

CHAPTER 42

The Prestige

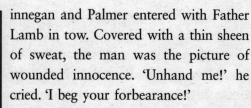innegan and Palmer entered with Father Lamb in tow. Covered with a thin sheen of sweat, the man was the picture of wounded innocence. 'Unhand me!' he cried. 'I beg your forbearance!'

'Men, you can let him go. Do be seated, Father Lamb,' said Hadley. The two policemen exited the room, leaving the four of us. 'Some brandy, sir? Or coffee?'

The priest shook his head but remained standing.

'We clearly owe you an apology. However, we have just a few questions for you. Why did you run from us?'

'I was trying to cut down poor Mr Vitale from hanging himself when this madman attacked me!' said the priest, gesturing to Holmes. 'I was so upset, all I could think of was to get away! I am afraid I panicked.' He glanced around the room taking in Hadley, Holmes and me. 'The young man? Did he survive?'

'No. I am sorry, Father,' said Holmes. 'You have my abject apology. Had I not mistakenly tried to stop you, Mr Vitale would be alive today.'

Hadley and I exchanged the smallest of glances.

The priest swallowed. 'Vitale is dead, then?'

'Alas, he is,' said Holmes, the picture of contrition. 'And may God forgive me. You were trying to save him. I made a dreadful mistake.'

'What a terrible shame indeed!' exclaimed Father Lamb, mopping his forehead with a handkerchief. 'You behaved precipitously, Mr – what was it? – Holmes?'

'Please be seated, Father,' said Holmes.

I was eager to see Holmes play this through. He continued the subterfuge. 'I suppose the only small recompense is that I saved the hangman's fee. That is, if Mr Vitale killed Miss Dillie Wyndham.'

The priest sighed and took a chair facing the three of us. 'Sadly, it is true. I do not reveal confessions normally, but in this case I must. I entered the room and Vitale was already standing on his cot, a sheet tied round his neck and ready to jump. "I confess, Father," he said, "I killed Odelia Wyndham. She betrayed me." And then before I could stop him . . .' Lamb shook his head ruefully. 'What a terrible, terrible end for what I hear was a promising lad.'

'Indeed,' said Holmes. 'Of course, it is true that Miss Wyndham had lied and cheated Mr Vitale. Can you shed any light on this for us?'

'Yes, we are all ears, Father,' said Hadley.

'Well, *now* you are,' said the priest righteously. 'Although if you had come to me in the first place—'

'What would you have told us?' asked Hadley.

'Mr Holmes knows all this, that Miss Dillie Wyndham came to Peregrine – to Deacon Buttons – for advice, for help. She was being hounded by two students and was afraid for her life.'

'For her life?' mused Holmes.

'Sir, you are being disingenuous,' replied Father Lamb testily. He turned to Hadley. 'I was present when Deacon Buttons told this man of threatening letters Dillie Wyndham had received. May I see Deacon Buttons, please?'

'Oh, yes, of course, I recall that now,' said Holmes, rubbing his forehead tiredly. 'It has been a fraught night and morning. Of course, no one has actually seen these letters. Unless perhaps your deacon. But was there a further threat, perhaps more specific, after this?'

'Yes, another letter from Leo Vitale.'

'I see. A letter from Vitale? What did it say?' asked Holmes. 'Do you have it now?'

Father Lamb shifted in his chair and turned to Inspector Hadley. 'Sir, why are you allowing this man to question me so?'

'Please consider him as an official representative of the police and answer him directly,' said Hadley.

The priest paused, fingered the cross hanging from a chain round his neck. 'Very well. In a letter Miss Wyndham had received, Vitale threatened to murder her. It seems the duplicitous girl had pledged herself to him, then became engaged to another.'

'Enough to enrage anyone, certainly. Where is Vitale's letter now?' asked Holmes. 'Or is this, too, conveniently missing?'

'The deacon destroyed the letter, of course, hoping to dissuade Vitale from murderous sin,' declared Father Lamb.

Convenient indeed, I thought. But what if there was such a letter? If this were true, it did indeed implicate the young scientist.

'Hmm. Are you sure it was not Miss Wyndham's other suitor, that terribly wealthy Freddie Eden-Summers, who threatened her?' asked Holmes. 'He, too, must have felt wronged.'

'I don't know. That fellow may have written also. Deacon Buttons knows the whole story. May I see him, please? Why are you holding him, Inspector Hadley?' asked Father Lamb.

'He attempted suicide,' said Hadley. 'That's against the law, and we are holding him for his own good.'

But Holmes was not finished with Father Lamb. 'It seems odd that Mr Vitale would murder Miss Wyndham in Deacon Buttons' room. Father, did he tell you why he did that?'

'No! My God!' Father Lamb shuddered at the thought. 'What on earth makes you think this happened under my own roof?' he cried.

'Both the police and I have confirmed it from the evidence,' said Holmes.

'How terrible. But *you* are the detective! Isn't it obvious why Vitale might have killed her there? To make it look like Peregrine did it! She had probably come to him for help. Vitale must have followed her!'

'He did indeed follow her, Father Lamb,' said Holmes. 'That, too, has been confirmed by the evidence.'

'Well then, there you have it,' said Lamb. He stood. 'I should like to see my boy now.'

'Sit down, please, Father,' said Hadley. The priest hesitated, but at Hadley's stern look did so, reluctantly.

'As I said, we know that Vitale did follow her there,' said Holmes.

And, of course, Vitale had just admitted it to us, I thought. Had he lied about the rest?

'It must have taken a great deal for you to hear him confess,' Holmes continued, 'learning that he was a murderer.'

'Even a murderer is God's creation,' said Father Lamb. 'I offer comfort where I can.'

Just then, Constable Wright burst through the door. 'Mr Holmes, Mr Hadley, I've completed my investigation of the deacon's room.'

Holmes smiled. 'Ah. The ink, then, Mr Wright? The dent?'

'Precisely where and how you described,' said Wright crisply.

'Excellent work,' said Holmes. 'Thank you. Stay now and enjoy the fruits of your labour. If he may, Mr Hadley?'

Hadley nodded, and Wright remained. The young officer stood in the corner, smoothing his black moustache and watching the proceedings with intense interest.

'Mr Wright's findings have just confirmed Peregrine Buttons' innocence. Dillie was beaten badly. All three young men had injuries to their hands: her two suitors and your young deacon, Father. Mr Buttons told me that his injury came from his punching the wall in frustration. When I examined the room, I saw no such dent, but it apparently was in the hallway just outside the door. Wright has confirmed the dent exactly as Buttons described. Ergo, Peregrine Buttons did not beat the girl.'

'Well, of course he would not!' cried Father Lamb. 'The boy is blameless!'

'Father,' said Holmes, 'it is such a puzzle. We all agree that Miss Wyndham went to the deacon for help. She received a fatal blow in his room some time later. I wonder, though, why she was naked in Deacon Buttons' bed at some time in the night.'

'What? She never; Peregrine would not have allowed such a thing!'

'I found unmistakable traces that Miss Wyndham was in the deacon's bed with little or no clothing.'

'You cannot prove this. And why would you want to? Are you so bent on ruining my young deacon's reputation?'

'No, in saving it. I have the proof right here. I collected traces from the bedding . . .' Holmes reached into his pocket for the small folded card into which he'd placed some evidence in the room, only to find it waterlogged and useless. 'Oh, no, well . . . washed away!' he fumbled. 'I, uh . . . you will have to take my word for it.' He seemed confused and dismayed.

383

'Some coffee, Holmes?' I said.

He waved me off. If this was an act, it was an effective one.

Lamb eyed him superciliously. 'You struggle, Mr Holmes. Naked in his bed? I tell you, no. Traces? What nonsense!'

'Well, to continue,' said Holmes. 'We all agree that Leo Vitale was in Deacon Buttons' rectory rooms. Then there is the matter of the bottle of ink.' It seemed that he was losing steam with his argument. I was worried about him.

Father Lamb looked confused.

'You remember the purple ink that Deacon Buttons used to write on Dillie's doll,' said Holmes, 'the reason I became involved in this case at the beginning?'

'What of it?'

'I wondered why Deacon Buttons kept the bottle. I noticed it was near full when I saw it earlier and half empty last night. And the top was cracked and leaking. Where had all the ink gone to in so short a span of time?' Holmes began coughing. He seemed to be struggling.

At a pause, the father interjected. 'What does it matter? Peregrine wrote with it, perhaps.'

'Half a bottle, so quickly? The notes in his Bible were all in black ink. So, I began to look. The ink had gone to several places, as it turns out. I discovered a small pool of purple ink had caught in the doorframe. It had dripped into the crack between the moulding and the wall, near eye level for a tall man. Then someone attempted to wipe it away. And tonight, I found a dot of it on Mr Vitale's neck.'

'Well there you have it!' said Lamb. 'As I have told you. Mr Vitale is the killer.'

'And Mr Wright reports a smear of ink . . .on the sheets on Deacon Buttons' bed. Someone got into that bed with ink on their hands.'

Father Lamb shrugged, dismissively.

'What does all this tell you, Mr Holmes?' asked Hadley.

'A great deal, actually. Thank you for that, Wright. Here, then, is what happened. Miss Wyndham went to see Deacon Buttons, and from the deacon's own testimony she sent him to pawn her two engagement rings so that they could run away together.'

'I doubt that,' sneered Father Lamb. 'Now you are simply concocting.'

'The rings have been found at the pawnshop, and Deacon Buttons has been identified as the one who pawned them,' said Hadley, coldly.

Holmes smiled. 'To continue, then. While Buttons was off pawning the rings, Miss Wyndham disrobed to enact the second part of her plans. Vitale had followed her from her hideaway at the Cross and Anchor to the rectory. There is evidence that he remained awhile under the window. Once Buttons had left, Vitale came to the room, lingered at the door and asked again for his ring back. Seeing her unclothed, he stayed at the door, whereupon Miss Wyndham threw a bottle of ink at him. The cap cracked as it hit the doorjamb, splattering there, and a small drop landed on his neck. Vitale left, went to Eden-Summers' rooms at Trinity College, where the two young men fought, both receiving damage to their hands and persons. Failing to convince his rival to join him in confronting Miss Wyndham, Vitale gave up, and returned to his dormitory to sleep.'

'What evidence do you have for this?' cried the priest. He turned to Hadley. 'Inspector Hadley, why have you turned over your investigation to this amateur? Leo Vitale confessed to me!'

Holmes continued, unperturbed. 'Meanwhile, Miss Wyndham cleared up the ink the best she could and awaited the deacon's return. My theory is that she got into bed so as to *appear* to provide a warm welcome. One can only presume she planned to offer herself to him. Hence the ink stain on the inside of the bed.' Holmes took a sip of water.

'Notice that I said "appear",' he continued. 'Because when Deacon Buttons returned, she told him that the money he received was not enough and she sent him next to retrieve a third ring, which she said was still back at the Cross and Anchor. It is my belief that she then got up, began to pack up her belongings, and was preparing to abscond with the pawnshop funds. Her plan all along.'

'You are conjuring,' said Lamb derisively. 'You will have better luck on stage as a novelty act!'

'I may consider it if work dries up,' said Holmes with a smile. 'In any case, Buttons returned to find that Miss Wyndham, the money and all her belongings were gone. He was staggered at this discovery. But he would have been even more so had he understood what had just transpired in that room. Because . . . while Deacon Buttons was at the Cross and Anchor, the killer came in and attacked Miss

Wyndham. They fought, and she received a fatal blow to the head, from the water-jug, most likely. The killer then quickly tried to erase all signs of the fight, even proceeding to dump Dillie's body in the convenient lock, pulling the lever so that the body would wash downstream, and then took her belongings somewhere we have yet to discover.'

'So . . . Vitale returned,' said Lamb.

'No, it was another.'

'You said Miss Wyndham was killed for love,' exclaimed Hadley. 'I don't understand which of the three young men, then, was her killer?'

'None of them. I have eliminated all three.'

Father Lamb looked at him in disdain. He turned to Inspector Hadley. 'Perhaps the great detective from London is a trifle overrated. Vitale has confessed! Dillie Wyndham's treachery destroyed him. Regret is the reason for his suicide. Let me collect Deacon Buttons, and we will be out of your hair.'

'I am not quite finished, Mr Lamb,' said Holmes. 'What has been missing in this investigation is a fourth suspect. There was a fourth person with a motive to kill Miss Wyndham. Perhaps a less obvious motive than the three men who loved her.'

'Atalanta Wyndham!' I exclaimed. Of course. 'She shot me. She was in love with Freddie Eden-Summers!'

The room sat silent. Everyone turned to look at me. Was it possible that for once, just for one time only, I was ahead of my friend in the matter? Perhaps I should not have blurted this out, but rather let him take the lead.

I faltered.

'I believe, Watson, that Atalanta Wyndham was incarcerated in an asylum at the time of her sister's murder,' said Holmes quietly.

Hadley cleared his throat. 'Er, no. She escaped almost immediately and returned home.'

Holmes stood still for a good five seconds. Once again, the tumblers were turning.

'Father Lamb, had Atalanta Wyndham approached Mr Buttons for counselling?' he asked.

'She had. But he discerned that she was merely spying on her sister. He was kind but gave her no information.'

Holmes laughed suddenly, with that strange enthusiasm which made him so odd at times like this. 'Yes! Of course! Thank you, Mr Hadley,' he shouted. 'Of course! Atalanta's escape clears up one final mystery. What a puzzle. What a glorious puzzle! Ha ha!'

Electrified by whatever this news meant to him, he strode to the door and knocked on it four times for emphasis as he said, 'One. Two. Three. Four. Atalanta! Peregrine! Leo! Freddie! So many tangled in this web. All with reasons to hate Miss Wyndham! And yet . . . still, I say, she was killed for love.'

His eyes shone and he looked, quite frankly, mad. I had noted these oddly theatrical performances on several occasions. He was truly pushing the boundaries with this one. 'Holmes—' I murmured.

'Love! When a murder is committed for love, it is the ultimate paradox! But what a capricious if not occasionally downright cruel young woman Miss Dillie Wyndham was!' he said.

'Well, the woman brought disaster upon herself,' said Father Lamb. 'It was as though she asked to be murdered.' He paused. 'God rest her soul,' he added.

Holmes made an immediate left turn. His manner abruptly turned sober; his voice became very quiet. 'Father, no one asks to be murdered. The poor girl was sorely used. Her private life was a misery.' He advanced on the priest and stood directly facing the seated man. 'Dillie confessed all of this to Peregrine Buttons. He offered her friendship. Kindness. Understanding. Her life at home was nothing short of a nightmare.'

'Oh, come now, Mr Holmes,' interrupted Inspector Hadley. 'Professor Wyndham is a respected man. He is known to be just . . . rather strict.'

'It is worse than that, Mr Hadley,' said Holmes. 'Wyndham is a cruel abuser, keeping the three women of his family in torment. Dillie responded by emulating him. And yet I had hope for her. Many children manage to recover from cruel treatment and turn the other way.'

This was not the first time that Holmes made me wonder about his own childhood.

'But Dillie did not get the chance,' he continued. 'Atalanta escaped, you say? It was she, then, at the Jesus Lock, opening the drain as we tried to save Buttons. Intending to kill Buttons, I suspect. My death would have merely been a bonus.'

The priest rose to his feet. 'If that is true, then you have your second villain. If you don't mind, Inspector Hadley, I would like to collect Mr Buttons and return to the church. You know Miss Wyndham's murderer is the late Mr Vitale. I shall leave you to deal with this attention-seeking actor.'

'Father Lamb, patience is not your greatest virtue,' said Holmes. 'If only you had had a shred more of it, two young people would still be alive today.'

'What?' exclaimed Lamb.

'Yes, do explain yourself, Holmes,' said Hadley.

Just then Palmer rushed in. 'Gentlemen! Sirs! Deacon Buttons has just breathed his last. He died from shock. We could not revive him.'

The news hit the room like a stroke of thunder. I felt sick.

Holmes was the first to break the silence. 'That makes three young people. Miss Wyndham. Mr Vitale. And now . . .'

A moan escaped the lips of Father Lamb. 'Peregrine?' he said. 'Not my boy. Not Peregrine?'

We all turned to look at the priest. He sank back onto his chair, ghostly white and unable to speak.

'You know, Father Lamb, it is a shame that you so badly mistook Dillie Wyndham's intentions that night,' Holmes remarked. 'I don't believe the young lady intended to seduce your Peregrine. It was merely a manipulation. Of course, we will never know for sure.'

The priest looked up, his eyes burning.

'Dillie Wyndham would be alive, in Paris perhaps. Vitale would be happily in his laboratory. And your young deacon would have been exactly where you want him.' Holmes turned to Hadley. 'I left something out earlier. While Peregrine Buttons was at the Cross and Anchor looking for the third ring, Father Lamb returned from London and went straight to his beloved young man's room. Yes, beloved. There he discovered Miss Wyndham, naked in Deacon Buttons' bed! What were your thoughts, Father Lamb?'

The man said nothing.

'You drew a wrong conclusion, that you had come across an affair – *in flagrante delicto* and instigated by a terrible Jezebel. You became enraged. Dillie had a formidable temper and met your fury with her own. A terrible battle ensued, the physical evidence, though mitigated, remained. Broken glass, a candle flung. It ended with you striking the fatal blow with the ironstone water-jug.'

The priest stared at Holmes with wolfish fury. I stood up, and noted Wright moving closer, protectively.

'If only you had just done nothing, Father Lamb! Dillie would have bolted, as she planned all along. Your young deacon, finding himself abandoned, would have been devastated. And you could have offered solace, comfort, a haven. Just as you had done when his father died. Peregrine Buttons, the boy you love so dearly, would be alive today. But instead, in a rage and assuming the worst, you killed Dillie Wyndham, pitched her body into the river, and then tried to erase the signs of your struggle.'

Father Lamb did not move.

Holmes turned to Hadley. 'So you see, it *was* done in the name of love.'

'This was not the kind of love I anticipated,' said Hadley with evident distaste. 'It would not be the first time, I suppose, among clergy.'

'That is unclear, and ultimately irrelevant. Love of any kind is not for us to judge,' said Holmes. 'What is critical is that Father Lamb's feelings became a kind of obsession. An obsession which propelled these horrible events. Confess, Lamb. Because there is nothing left for you, now, but to absolve your guilt in the manner of your Church.'

'You will never hear a confession from me,' said the father.

'But perhaps you will make one to me,' came a voice from the door. Peregrine Buttons stood there, weak but alive, and supported by Palmer.

My heart leapt.

The priest turned in his seat and staggered to his feet at the sight of his young disciple. 'Peregrine? Dear boy! You are alive!' He sobbed and started towards the boy, but Wright stepped forward and quietly slipped on handcuffs. The priest looked down at them in surprise. Then up at his young deacon.

'Peregrine! I did this to save you,' he cried.

'No, Father. You did it so as not to lose me,' said Peregrine Buttons. 'But I was already lost.'

CHAPTER 43

221B

t was on a Tuesday morning, five days after the events in Cambridge, that Holmes and I were ensconced at Baker Street, recovering from our adventure at the great university town. Holmes's mood had been morose. He would not speak of it, but I knew that despite solving Dillie's murder, his inability to prevent her death haunted him. I pointed out that without him on the case, Vitale might have hanged for the crime – in his cell or on the scaffold. The murderer would be free and young Deacon Buttons' fate uncertain. But my words did not appease him. Time, I suppose, might give him perspective.

Shortly after breakfast, I reclined on our settee, my injured leg elevated as I attempted to enjoy the last of my coffee and the relative calm of a sitting-room that had been neatened once again by Mrs Hudson. A note from Polly had been left on the table, presumably by Holmes, and I was amused to read in her untutored printing that Miss Atalanta Wyndham no longer lived with her parents, but had run off with the gardener. Holmes had correctly intuited that relationship, to the young lady's displeasure. And Polly herself had found a new position in Inspector Hadley's household.

With the Cambridge complexities mostly resolved, I suppose I should have been at peace. But I was not and was still awash in anxiety. I had heard nothing regarding my mysterious box. Two letters to the strange Mr Lossop had gone unanswered. Holmes had admonished me to wait, but I was gathering my nerves to travel to the man and confront him, alone if need be.

The clock struck eleven. It was unlike Holmes to sleep in this late.

To distract myself, I returned to the newspaper and came upon an article that thoroughly surprised me. I tore it out in anticipation of showing Holmes, whenever that layabout finally arose.

To my surprise, he entered from the hallway, fully dressed, and somewhat pale from exertion. A large bruise bloomed red and purple on his cheek, and a rim of caked blood was just visible in his left ear.

'Holmes! I thought you were still abed. Where have you been? And what has happened to you? You are a wreck.'

'Am I?' He moved into his bedchamber and I could see him examining himself in the mirror over his washbasin. He began to scrub at his ear.

'Would you like me to have a look?'

'No.' Holmes dried his face gingerly. He would tell me in his own time.

'Holmes! In the paper today – it seems Gertrude Aufenbach has married!'

'Who?'

'That German Soprano. Berlin. Remember, Dario Borelli's secret lover?'

He stood in the doorway, suddenly all attention. 'Married? Not to Borelli, then?'

'No! To some Russian count. Apparently, they had been engaged for two years.'

Holmes entered the room, drying his hands. 'Let me see.'

He flung the towel back in the general direction of his room, snatched the paper from my hands and spread it on our dining table. While reading, he rummaged absently for leftover toast, and finding nothing but my last crusts, popped them into his mouth.

'Shall I ring for some more breakfast, Holmes?'

He didn't answer but tore the article from the broadsheet and laid the clipping on the table. He threw the rest of the paper to the floor.

While staring transfixed at the six lines of text, he felt in his various pockets. From one he removed a small brown envelope, and from another a small package wrapped in dirty paper, both of which he flung on the table in annoyance.

As he did so, I noted his left sleeve and the entire back of his frock coat were streaked with dirt. Even someone of my limited observational abilities could deduce that his nighttime escapade had been tinged with the dramatic. 'Holmes have you been rolling in the London byways again?'

'Ah!' he said, discovering at last what he was seeking in his waistcoat pocket. It was another torn newspaper clipping. He smoothed it out on the table next to the one about Gertrude Auerbach. Trying for some coffee, he discovered the pot was empty and set it down with a clatter. He then stared at the two clippings for a long time.

I cleared my throat to remind him that another human being inhabited the room.

'Ah, yes, Watson, read,' he said. 'I was right! Ha ha!'

I came over to the table and stared down at the second clipping. It was dated a week ago, with the headline 'Body Fished from Thames'. It read:

'The body of a deceased male was removed from the Thames after being spotted by a Mr Camphor Rooney, a pilot with the J. Benson Ferry Co. Police despair of a positive identification due to the decomposition of the corpse, which is believed to have been in the water some two weeks or more. However, the police have revealed that the body was found unclothed and was male, between thirty to fifty years of age, strongly muscled and slender, indicating athleticism. Dark hair and dark black moustache. No other identifying features were noted. Anyone with any information . . .'

'Holmes! You don't think—'

He smiled at me, that impish smile of having known

something all along. 'Yes, Watson. Dario Borelli. Your clipping seems to confirm it.'

'Then he never ran off to Berlin with Gertrude Aufenbach?'

Holmes said nothing. Instead, he peeled off his frock coat with a wince of discomfort and reclined himself on the settee exactly where I had been sitting. He then picked up my coffee cup next to the settee and drained it.

'Madame Borelli! Do you think she . . . extracted revenge on her husband for his attempt to frame her?' I mused. 'Without your intervention, she could have very easily been convicted of frying him up in the Great Cauldron.'

'I suppose,' said Holmes.

'Or perhaps she still loved Colangelo. That is another explanation,' said I with enthusiasm.

'Possibly. But I favour a third.'

'What is that, Holmes?'

'That the Great Borelli remained in London after faking his death and threatened her later. Perhaps Madame Borelli killed her husband in an act of self-preservation.'

Upon reflection, that sounded more logical. 'What a dangerous woman!' I exclaimed.

'Was that ever in doubt, Watson?'

Another thought struck me. 'But what of her lovestruck professor, Cosimo Fortuny? Might he, and by association Leo Vitale, be in her clutches now?'

'They are not. Two days ago, an anonymous buyer in London purchased the rights to 'Lucifer's Lights', as Madame Borelli called the invention I helped to inspire. For a rather exorbitant price. Madame profited and was well pleased.

The two young men have returned to Cambridge considerably the richer, and in Mr Fortuny's case, his thirst for a life in theatre has been quite thoroughly quenched. I believe he gained some insight into Madame via a letter from a "concerned friend".'

I laughed. 'You? And were you the anonymous buyer, as well? With what funds?'

'My brother makes himself useful from time to time. In this case, in support of the Cavendish Laboratory. Not hard to convince him.' Holmes smiled enigmatically. 'Mycroft is sure, as I am, that great things are to come from that place.'

'But you will let Madame Borelli roam free to continue with her life?'

'For the present, yes.'

'But isn't she a dangerous madwoman? May not others be in danger?'

'I think the population at large have nothing to fear.'

'Then you condone her action! You condone revenge?'

'Revenge, no. Self-preservation is perhaps understandable.' At my silence, he continued, 'Watson, as I have said before, I do not exist to supply the deficiencies of the police.'

'Yes, you do.'

'In any case, I think I shall leave Madame to them.'

'Well, it is fortunate for Deacon Buttons that you did not do so in Cambridge. He might have hanged for a crime he did not commit. Or ended up in the clutches of Lamb.'

Holmes smiled and adjusted the cushions. He looked about to doze.

'Holmes, on another matter. I've brought this up twice

to no avail. I'm going to pay that Lossop a visit today. With or without you.'

His eyes opened sleepily. 'Oh, that won't be necessary, Watson,' he said. He closed his eyes. 'That package on the table there. I assisted Mr Lossop last night against a rather formidable threat. He is now safely en route to Peru. But your box . . . have a look.'

I was already at the table, tearing off the brown paper. Inside was the mysterious silver box! It gleamed attractively in the morning sunlight, its Celtic dragons looking nearly alive. The lock had been sprung and it was open a crack.

'You have not looked inside, Holmes?'

'Of course not.'

I paused, staring at the thing. Something kept me from lifting the lid. Something I didn't expect. A kind of dread.

'Watson, you hesitate. Perhaps you might consider holding off,' said Holmes quietly.

'Then you *have* seen what is in there!'

'No. But think of this. You have long since put to rest whatever family drama caused this extraordinary act on the part of your mother. It troubles you greatly. I might have ferreted it out, dear friend, but I have left you your privacy—'

'You had better!'

'Consider the difficulty for your mother to procure such a unique and unassailable item as this box. She must have given you or sent you the key.'

'How could she? She died two days after she gave this to Elspeth Carnachan!'

399

Bonnie MacBird

Holmes sat up, awake now, and looked around for his pipe.

I turned back to my box. Again, I hesitated.

'The design of this box, the letter to be held for later delivery, all this smacks of planning, detailed planning,' said he. 'All the more reason to think she gave you the key. How did she die, Watson? You have never said.'

I put my hands on the box, feeling its cool, smooth surface so lightly engraved.

'Watson?'

'Ah? Oh . . . my mother. She drowned. Oddly very near where Rose had drowned three years earlier.'

I felt his eyes upon me. 'Rose?'

'My twin. We were both six when Rose died.' I said. 'Drowned as well.' I felt suddenly naked, exposed. 'I think I shall ask for more coffee. Would you like some more coffee?'

'A twin sister!' He took some time lighting the pipe. 'Ah, I am sorry for this. But your mother's death, Watson – was it by her own hand, then?' he asked gently.

'We were never sure.' I felt sick thinking of it. I kept running my fingers over the engraving.

'Was she despondent? Hysterical? Grieving, perhaps.'

'No. This was several years after Rose. My mother was not subject to moods, Holmes.'

'Nor are you, most of the time.' He paused. 'This box may have been long in the planning. She must have given you the key. Think! Was there any unique, decorative, mysterious item of metal in anything she gave you before this?'

'I was only eleven when she died. She would not have entrusted a key to a small child!'

Open the box, a voice inside me shouted. No, don't open the box, came another. I closed my eyes. *My mother's face, smiling at me. Then my mother's face, still and white, eyes bulging.*

'Watson, I wager your sterling qualities were well evident to your mother, even during your early childhood. Do you still have that small box of mementos from your youth?

Ah, the one with the wooden soldiers that I had mentioned to Knut Lossop? But why was he asking now, I wondered?

'Is there nothing metal, oddly shaped, in that box? Nothing that could be a key?'

I snapped back to the present. 'Well, I – oh!' There *was* one thing. It was a small ornate clock puzzle that had never worked to keep time. I had forgotten it when prompted for a 'treasure' at Lossop's and was later glad of it. It was my dearest possession, my mother's last Christmas gift to me, eight months before her death. I said as much to Holmes.

I limped upstairs, retrieved the small cigar box of childhood treasures, and set the gilded clock puzzle on the table near the silver box. Holmes arose from the settee and faced me across the table, pipe in hand.

'Go on, Watson. The clock puzzle first.'

I sat down before the box, and because he was so insistent, reluctantly took up the little clock. It was ornate and odd, constructed of several pieces. It had never kept time and was decorative only. But it had pleased me inordinately. I unpacked its pieces. To my amazement, one of them was silver, and filigreed in a style just like the box. I held it up and it was the right size to match the small keyhole below the box's lock.

This was too damnably easy.

'I—my God, you may be right!' I said. I touched it to the edge of the keyhole. 'It looks like it fits!'

'Good,' said Holmes 'Then your mother planned this for you, as I thought.' In a sudden move, he snapped the lid of the silver box down, and the lock clicked shut once again.

'No!' I leapt to my feet with a shout.

'Turn it in the lock.'

I inserted the key. I jiggled it. Nothing. Twisted it again. The box opened with a snap. I had had the damned thing all along! I sank into the chair before the box, relieved.

Holmes yawned and ambled back to the settee, collapsing back onto it. 'I shall leave you to it, Watson. I am a bit tired. Now, off to slumberland.' He laid his pipe on an errant plate, stretched out, and closed his eyes.

I stared at the box.

What had my mother meant by this?

I opened it fully, not sure what to expect. A jewel? A keepsake? Another puzzle? But inside the box was nothing but two folded pieces of faded pink paper. I unfolded them and recognized my mother's precise and beautiful hand. I read:

August 11, 1863, on the occasion of your eleventh birthday, my dear, darling John—

With luck you are reading this on August 11, 1873, and you are now twenty-one years old and ten years past my death.

I pray that you will forgive me for all that I am about to tell you and will understand my delay in doing so.

You no doubt suspected, and I will confirm, that my death was at my own hand. Please be assured there was nothing you or anyone could have done to dissuade me. It was not despair. As I write this, I face a terrible and incurable cancer, which over the next six months will consume me and put not only myself, but all our family through needless torture. I decided to spare us all.

I have chosen to shed my earthly bonds, but I trust, dearest son, that I will rest in the hands of a forgiving God and am now looking down at you with love. At eleven you were not ready, but I believe that as a man of twenty-one you will understand.

The second fact you must know is this. You were *not* responsible for the death of your twin. I know that you and Rosie argued that day at our picnic on the river, and that you left her and walked home, thinking your brother had stayed to look after her.

But when you discovered Harry at home in the bath, you thought you had made a terrible error leaving Rosie alone at the river. You ran back, but the poor child was already dead, drowned in the rapids, and you blamed yourself.

403

I must set the record straight. Your brother admitted the following to me yesterday. Harry was in fact with Rose when you left, as you thought. But what you didn't know was that he saw her slip in the river and hit her head on a rock. He leaped in to save her, but the currents took her out of reach. Harry then saw her dashed against the rocks downstream and knew she was dead.

It happened so fast, he panicked and ran home taking a shorter route, and beat you to the house, where he jumped into the bath so that no one would see him wet from the river. That is where you found him.

Of course, his story later was that you had left Rose alone and that is why she drowned.

While her death was not your fault, neither was it his, but he allowed you, John, to take the blame. Harry is fourteen now, at the time of this writing, and yet I already see his future. There is a flaw in his character, dearest son, like a vein of poison that runs in my family, but which has not touched you. Even at fourteen, Harry is troubled with drink. He thinks me blind to this.

I made a difficult decision. Knowing that you could shoulder the guilt better than your weaker brother, I delayed imparting this story to you until now, when you could, as an adult, make a choice – to confront your errant but fragile sibling or, knowing the truth, to spare him the confrontation and to move on.

And so I decided on this box, and this secrecy. I pray that Elspeth remembers to give it to you, and the hint about 'your mother's clock'. In this way, I knew no one but you could ever open it.

And the final thing, John, is my wish for you. You have nerve and courage, dearest son, and are destined for great things.

I glanced over at my sleeping friend. He had not read this and yet he intuited this assessment by a woman he had never met. I turned back to the letter.

I know you will grow to be a man of honour and accomplishment. I pray that you find a quest worthy of your gifts, my son, and that you take comfort and pride in lending your courage to that cause, that ideal, or that person. Then, looking down, I shall be happy for you.

You have it in you to be a force for good, John. The world needs you.

Your loving mother,

Mairead

I held the pages in my hands as my vision blurred for a moment. Her words sadly presaged my brother Harry's alcoholism and early demise. And I thought it more likely that she had overstated her hopes for me, as parents do. Did the world really need John Watson?

I folded up my mother's letter and my heart swelled.

Had she really seen such promise in my young character? Perhaps any good deed I had done was in compensation for my regrets over Rose's death. Suffering needlessly, as it turned out. I looked over at my friend, pale with exhaustion and asleep on the settee. Was this not like Holmes, suffering over his inability to save Odelia Wyndham?

Only in the abstract. I did not fool myself. My friend was a tireless warrior for the wronged, possessing gifts in the realm of genius, and making contributions to justice far beyond anything I could imagine. His work was life changing, his intellect beyond compare.

The world was indeed a better place for the existence of Sherlock Holmes.

I smiled as I placed the letter in my breast pocket. A sense of peace, of purpose, washed over me. I knew exactly what I needed to do. I covered Holmes with the afghan and rang down for lunch. And then I picked up my pen to write.

My mother, I was sure, would be pleased.

For interesting facts and photos of people, places and things mentioned in this novel, see the online annotations here:
https://macbird.com/the-three-locks/notes

Acknowledgements

Thank you to my wonderful editor David Brawn and agent Linda Langton, and, to quote Dorothy Parker, my severest friends and dearest critics Harley Jane Kozak, Luke Kuhns, Miguel Perez, Robert Mammana, Alex Bennett, Patricia Smiley, Jonathan Beggs, Linda Burrows, Bob Shayne, Craig Faustus Buck, Matt Witten, Andrew Rubin, and Jamie Diamond. Also my very grateful thanks to the incisive Dana Isaacson, Lynn Hightower, and Dennis Palumbo. Hugs to a young woman who inspires me and to whom this book is dedicated: Miranda Andrews, a nurse on the front lines of the pandemic, working ER at Mass General and FEMA. And to Kirstin Kay, a deep Sherlockian and courageous spirit. Thanks to Jonathan and Elaine McCafferty, accomplished Sherlockians and Cantabrigians, and to Sherlockian experts and good friends Les Klinger and Catherine Cooke. Thanks also to the expertise and kind consultation of E.J.

Wagner and D.P. Lyle, forensics, Brian Morland, lock expert and curator of Master Locksmith's Association museum, Dr Christopher Stray on classics and Cambridge, and Tom Larnach, River Manager of the Cam, and Dr Tony Hughes for confirmation of medical details. A very special thanks to Dan Stashower, Victorian magic expert and deep Sherlockian. Thanks to Shakespeare experts and theatre makers Rob and Sarah Myles whose 'The Show Must Go Online' gave me such a boost, and to Richard Crabtree for spirit-lifting violin lessons and laughs. To dear friends Rob Arbogast and Paul Denniston, the Holmes and Watson of the cover art. And to actors Luke Barton and Joseph Derrington for some 'Holmes on Lockdown' fun which lightened a dark moment and Jonathan Le Billon for earlier Holmes fun.

Biggest thanks of all goes to my husband Alan Kay, my port in this battering storm of 2020, giver of hugs, cooker of omelettes, and Voice of Reason, who bought an actual Ruhmkorff coil and installed it in our London flat, just because.

About the Author

Bonnie MacBird, BSI (*Art in the Blood*) and ASH (*The Professional Enthusiast*), was born in San Francisco, educated at Stanford, and now lives in London and Los Angeles.

A fan of Sir Arthur Conan Doyle since age ten, she's active in the Sherlockian community in both the UK and the US, and lectures regularly on Sherlock Holmes, writing, and creativity. A longtime veteran of Hollywood, MacBird has been a screenwriter (original script for *TRON*), an Emmy-winning producer, a playwright, studio exec (Universal) and actor.

MacBird attributes her enjoyment in capturing 'voice' to both her acting and screenwriting experience and her music training as well. She teaches a popular screenwriting class at UCLA Extension, which approaches writing for film using techniques of other art forms.

In her Sherlock Holmes novels, she aims to accurately

portray the brilliant detective and his friend as closely as possible to Doyle, yet expanding the original shortform fiction to full-length novels. *Art in the Blood* features a child who has disappeared and a bloody art theft, and touches on the theme of the perils and blessings of the artistic temperament. *Unquiet Spirits* features a murdered girl, a threatened scientist and a haunted whisky estate, while considering the dangers of not dealing with the ghosts of one's past. *The Devil's Due* brings Holmes to the edge of evil in order to combat a devilish multiple murderer.

Visit her at www.macbird.com

Also available

Unquiet Spirits

BONNIE MacBIRD

*An attempted murder, a haunted castle,
a terrible discovery . . .*

Sherlock Holmes has found himself the target of a deadly vendetta in London, but is distracted when beautiful Scotswoman Isla MacLaren arrives at 221B with a tale of kidnapping, ghosts, and dynamite in her family's Highland estate. To Watson's surprise, however, he walks away in favour of a mission for Mycroft in the South of France.

On the Riviera, a horrific revelation draws Holmes and Watson up to the McLaren castle after all, and Holmes discovers that all three cases have blended into a single, deadly conundrum. To solve the mystery, the ultimate rational thinker must confront a ghost from his own past. But Sherlock Holmes does not believe in ghosts . . . or does he?

'*A rollicking tale worthy of Sir Arthur Conan Doyle himself.*'
HISTORICAL NOVELS SOCIETY

Also available

The Devil's Due

BONNIE MacBIRD

London, 1890. A freezing November . . .

As anarchists terrorize the city, a series of gruesome murders strikes deeper into its heart. Leading philanthropists are being slaughtered in alphabetical order, all members of a secret club, the Luminarians. And with each victim, a loved one mysteriously dies as well.

As the murders continue, the letter 'H' climbs closer to the top of the list – and then Mycroft Holmes disappears. Hampered by a new head of Scotland Yard, a vengeful journalist and a beautiful socialite with her own agenda, must Sherlock Holmes himself cross to the dark side to take down this devil? Even John Watson, the man who knows him best, can only watch and wonder . . .

'One of the best Sherlock Holmes novels of recent memory.'
MICHAEL DIRDA, *WASHINGTON POST*

Coming next

What Child is This?
A Sherlock Holmes Christmas Adventure and Other Stories

BONNIE MacBIRD

It's Christmastime in London, and Sherlock Holmes takes on two cases. The angelic three-year-old child of a wealthy couple is the target of a vicious kidnapper, and a country aristocrat worries that his handsome, favourite son has mysteriously vanished from his London pied à terre. Holmes and Watson, aided by the colourful Heffie O'Malley, slip slide in the ice to ensure a merry Christmas is had by *nearly* everybody . . .